THE LAND OF STORIES

THE ENCHANTRESS RETURNS

By Chris Colfer

The Land of Stories Series

The Wishing Spell

The Enchantress Returns

A Grimm Warning

Beyond the Kingdoms

An Author's Odyssey

Worlds Collide

The Ultimate Book Hugger's Guide

A Treasury of Classic Fairy Tales

The Mother Goose Diaries

Queen Red Riding Hood's Guide to Royalty

The Curvy Tree

Trollbella Throws a Party

Goldilocks: Wanted Dead or Alive

A Tale of Magic…Series

A Tale of Magic…

A Tale of Witchcraft…

A Tale of Sorcery…

THE LAND OF STORIES

THE ENCHANTRESS RETURNS

BY CHRIS COLFER

ILLUSTRATED BY BRANDON DORMAN

LITTLE, BROWN BOOKS FOR YOUNG READERS

To Hannah, for being the bravest, strongest, and most honest person I know, and for showing that it's impossible to be "cursed" when one has a heart as courageous as yours. Also, for giving me my first black eye—you were four, I was nine. It still hurts. Bubba loves you.

LITTLE, BROWN BOOKS FOR YOUNG READERS

First published in the United States in 2013 by Little, Brown and Company
First published in Great Britain in 2013 by Little, Brown Books for Young Readers
This paperback edition published in 2014 by Hodder and Stoughton

9

A CIP catalogue record for this book
is available from the British Library.

ISBN 978-1-510201-81-1

Printed and bound in Great Britain by
Clays Ltd, Elcograf S.p.A.

The paper and board used in this book are
made from wood from responsible sources.

Little, Brown Books for Young Readers
An imprint of
Hachette Children's Group
Part of Hodder and Stoughton
Carmelite House
50 Victoria Embankment
London EC4Y 0DZ

An Hachette UK Company
www.hachette.co.uk

www.hachettechildrens.co.uk

"THE WORLD WILL NOT BE DESTROYED
BY THOSE WHO DO EVIL, BUT BY THOSE WHO
WATCH THEM WITHOUT DOING ANYTHING."
—ALBERT EINSTEIN

THE RISE AND THE RETURN

The East was in a period of great celebration. Daily parades marched through the village streets, every home and shop was decorated in colorful banners and wreaths, and handfuls of flower petals were thrown and floated through the air. Each citizen smiled, proud of what they had recently accomplished.

It had taken over a decade for the Sleeping Kingdom to fully recover from the horrific sleeping curse of the past, but at last, it had restored itself to the prosperous nation it had been before. The people of the East charged into the future, reclaiming their home as the Eastern Kingdom.

A week's worth of celebrations concluded in the great hall of Queen Sleeping Beauty's castle. It was so crowded the entire kingdom seemed to be there; many had to stand or sit on windowsills. The queen herself; her husband, King Chase; and their royal advisor sat at a high table overlooking the festivities.

A small performance was taking place in the center of the hall. Thespians reenacted Sleeping Beauty's christening, portraying the fairies who had blessed her and the evil Enchantress who had cursed her to die after pricking her finger on the spindle of a spinning wheel. Luckily, another fairy reformed the curse, so when the princess eventually pricked her finger, she and the entire kingdom simply went to sleep. They slept for a hundred years and the performers took great delight in re-creating the moment King Chase kissed her and awoke them all.

"I think it's time we dispose of our little gifts from the queen," a woman shouted from the back of the hall. She stood up on a table and cheerfully gestured to her wrist.

Everyone in the kingdom wore flexible bands around their wrists made from tree sap. In the years prior, Queen Sleeping Beauty had instructed them to snap their wrists with them whenever they felt unnecessary fatigue. The bands helped the citizens stay awake, fighting off the lingering effects of the curse.

Fortunately, the bands weren't needed anymore. Everyone in the great hall ripped them off their wrists and threw them happily in the air.

"Your Majesty, won't you tell us again where you learned a trick like that?" a man asked the queen about the bands.

"You'll think strangely of me when I tell you," Sleeping Beauty said. "It was from a child. He and his sister were visiting the castle a year ago. He said he had used a band to keep himself awake in school and suggested the kingdom try it."

"Remarkable!" the man said and laughed with her.

"Fascinating, isn't it? I believe the most extraordinary ideas come from children," the queen said. "If only we all could be so perceptive, we would find the simplest solutions to the greatest problems are right under our noses."

Sleeping Beauty lightly tapped the side of her glass with a spoon. She stood and addressed the eager people.

"My friends," Sleeping Beauty said, raising her glass. "Today marks a very special day in our history and an even better day for our future. As of this morning, our kingdom's trading deals, crop production, and overall consciousness have not only been restored but *improved* since the sleeping curse was cast upon this land!"

Her people cheered so loudly the castle shook with joy. Sleeping Beauty looked to her side and shared a warm smile with her husband.

"We should not forget the horrible curse of the past, but when we look back upon the dark time, let us remember how we triumphed over it," Sleeping Beauty continued. Small tears formed in her eyes. "Let it be a warning to all who try to interfere with our prosperity: The Eastern Kingdom is here to stay and stands united against any force of evil that gets in our way!"

The approving roar was so loud it actually knocked a man off the windowsill he sat on.

"I have never been prouder to be among you than tonight! Here's to you!" the jubilant queen said, and the room joined her in sipping from their glasses.

"All hail Queen Beauty!" a man in the middle of the hall shouted.

"All hail the queen!" the rest cheered with him. "All hail the queen! All hail the queen!"

Sleeping Beauty waved at them graciously and took a seat. The festivities continued into the night, but just before midnight the queen was overcome by a strange sensation—a feeling she hadn't felt in years.

"Well, isn't that bizarre?" Sleeping Beauty said to herself, looking off into the distance with a smirk.

"Is there something wrong, my love?" King Chase asked.

Sleeping Beauty stood and headed toward the staircase behind them.

"You'll have to excuse me, dear," the queen said to her husband. "I'm rather *sleepy.*"

She was just as surprised to say it as he was to hear it, because Sleeping Beauty hadn't slept in years. The queen had made a promise to her people that she wouldn't rest until the kingdom was properly restored; now, looking around at all the joyous faces in the hall, both the king and the queen knew that the promise had been fulfilled.

"Good night, my love, sleep well," King Chase said and kissed her hand.

In her chambers, the queen changed into her favorite nightgown and slipped into her bed for the first time in over a decade. She felt as if she were being reunited with old friends. She had forgotten the feeling of the cool sheets against her legs and arms, the softness of her pillow, and the sinking sensation as she settled into the mattress.

The sounds of celebration could be heard in the queen's chambers, but she didn't mind: They were actually soothing to her. Sleeping Beauty took a deep breath and fell into a very deep sleep—almost as deep as the one during the one hundred years' curse, except she knew she could awaken anytime she wished.

When King Chase joined her later, he couldn't help but smile at the sight of his wife peacefully sleeping. He hadn't seen her look this way since the day he saw her for the first time.

In the great hall, the celebration finally concluded. The lamps and fireplaces were extinguished throughout the castle. The servants finished cleaning up and were dismissed to their quarters.

All was finally quiet in the castle. But a few hours before dawn, the silence was broken.

Sleeping Beauty and King Chase were awoken by a thunderous banging on their chamber door. The king and queen instantly sat up.

"Your Majesty!" a man shouted from the other side of the door. "Forgive me, but we must come inside!"

The door burst open and the royal advisor ran into the room, followed by a dozen suited guards. They surrounded the bed.

"What on earth is going on?!" King Chase yelled. "How dare you barge into our—"

"I'm so sorry, Your Highness, but we must get the queen to safety immediately," the advisor said.

"Safety?" Sleeping Beauty asked.

"We'll explain on the way there, Your Majesty," the advisor said. "But right now we must get you into the carriage as fast as possible—*only you*. Traveling alone will be much less conspicuous than a carriage transporting you and the king."

The advisor looked at her with frantic eyes, begging her to oblige. The queen froze.

"Chase?!" Sleeping Beauty said and looked to her husband—she wasn't sure what to do.

The king was at a loss for words. "If they say you need to go, you must go," was all he could muster.

"I cannot leave my people," Sleeping Beauty said.

"With all due respect, Your Majesty, you're no good to anyone dead," the advisor said.

Sleeping Beauty felt the pit of her stomach drop. What did he mean, *dead*?

Before Sleeping Beauty knew it, the guards had lifted her out of the bed and onto her feet. They quickly escorted her and the advisor to the door. She didn't even get to say good-bye.

They rushed down a spiral staircase to the lower levels of the castle. The stone steps were rough on the queen's bare feet.

"Someone please tell me what is happening!" Sleeping Beauty said.

"We must get you out of the kingdom as quickly as possible," the advisor said.

"Why?" she asked, starting to fight off the guards escorting her. No one replied, so she stopped in the middle of the stairs, solid as a rock. "I won't move another step until someone informs me! I am the queen! I have the right to know!"

The advisor's face went pale.

"I don't mean to alarm you any more, Your Majesty," he said, his jaw quivering. "But shortly after midnight, after all the guests had gone home, two soldiers on duty near the front of the castle witnessed a bright flash of light, and a *spinning wheel* appeared out of thin air."

Sleeping Beauty's eyes grew wide and the color faded from her face.

"They didn't think it was anything serious—a foolish prank to spoil our party this evening, perhaps," he continued. "The soldiers went to inspect the spinning wheel and it burst into flames. As soon as it did, something else happened."

"And what was that?" she said.

"The vines and thornbushes that covered the castle during the sleeping curse—the plants that were cleared out and dumped in the Thornbush Pit—are *growing back*," he told her. "I've never seen anything grow so fast; nearly half the castle is covered already. The plants are consuming the entire kingdom."

"Are you telling me that the curse in the Thornbush Pit has spread throughout the kingdom?" Sleeping Beauty asked.

"No, Your Majesty," the advisor said with a heavy gulp. "That was just an old witch's curse. This is dark magic—*very powerful dark magic*! The kind our kingdom has only been exposed to once before."

"*No.*" Sleeping Beauty gasped and covered her mouth. "You don't mean—"

"Yes, I'm afraid so," the advisor said. "Now please cooperate with us—we must get you out of the kingdom as quickly as possible."

The guards grabbed hold of the queen again and they traveled deeper into the castle; this time she did not fight them. They ran down the stairs until there were no more stairs to descend. They shot through a pair of wooden doors and Sleeping Beauty found herself in the castle stables.

There were four carriages in front of her. Each was circled by a dozen soldiers on horses and ready to depart at any second. Three of the carriages were bright and golden, of the queen's personal collection, but she was escorted to the fourth, a small, dull, and unassuming one. The soldiers surrounding this carriage weren't dressed in armor like the others but were disguised as farmers and townspeople.

The guards lifted the queen inside it. There was barely enough room inside for her to sit.

"And my husband?" Sleeping Beauty asked as she put a hand out to prevent them from shutting the door behind her.

"He'll be all right, ma'am," the advisor said. "The king and I will be traveling as soon as we send out the decoy carriages. We've had this planned in the event the castle should ever be under attack. Trust me; it's the safest way."

"I never authorized such plans!" Sleeping Beauty said.

"No, it was your parents' order," the advisor said. "It was one of the last things they instructed before they died."

This news made the queen's heart pound even harder. Her parents had spent the majority of their lives trying to protect her, and even in death, they were still trying.

"Where am I going?" she asked.

"The Fairy Kingdom for now," the advisor said. "You'll be safest with the Fairy Council. The decoy carriages will be sent in other directions as a distraction. Now, you must hurry."

He gently pushed her the rest of the way inside and shut the carriage door firmly behind her. Even the dozen guards surrounding her small carriage did little to comfort her. She knew the situation was beyond their ability to protect her.

The advisor nodded to the decoy carriages and they set off. A few moments later he nodded to her driver and, like a cannonball, the queen's carriage shot off into the night, the horses galloping at full speed.

Through her carriage's tiny windows, Sleeping Beauty saw the horrors that the advisor had described to her.

Scattered all across the castle grounds she saw soldiers and servants fighting off the rogue thornbushes and vines growing around them. The plants grew straight out of the ground and attacked them, like serpents wrapping around their prey. The vines crept up the sides of the castle, breaking through the windows and pulling people out, dangling them hundreds of feet in the air.

Thorns and vines shot out of the ground toward Sleeping Beauty's carriage, but the soldiers were quick to slice them with their swords.

Queen Sleeping Beauty had never felt so helpless in her life. She saw villagers—some within reach of her carriage—fall victim to the leafy monsters. There was nothing she could do to help them. All she could do was watch and hope she could find help once she reached the Fairy Kingdom. The guilt of leaving her husband and kingdom behind weighed heavily on her, but the advisor was right: She'd be no good to anyone dead.

The castle grew smaller and smaller behind her as the carriage traveled away from the devastation. Soon they were passing through a forest and all the queen could see outside were dark trees around them for miles.

Even after an hour of traveling, Sleeping Beauty was as scared as ever. She kept whispering to herself under her breath, *"We're almost there. . . . We're almost there . . ."* though she had no idea how close they were.

Suddenly, a high-pitched *whoosh*ing sound came from the trees. Sleeping Beauty looked out the window just in time to see a soldier and his horse thrown high into the forest beside the path. Another *whoosh*ing sound swooped toward them, and another soldier and his horse were thrown into the trees on the other side of the path. *They had been found.*

Every other second was filled with the terrified cries of the soldiers and horses as they were flung into the forest. Whatever was out there, it was picking them off one by one.

Sleeping Beauty crouched down, trembling, on the floorboard of the carriage. She knew it was only a matter of time before all the soldiers were gone.

One final swoop took the remaining horses and soldiers with it; their cries echoed in the night. The carriage crashed to the ground, falling on its side and skidding across the ground until coming to a stop. Everything was quiet in the forest now. There wasn't a sound of wounded soldiers or horses to be heard. The queen was all alone.

Sleeping Beauty crawled through the carriage door and carefully made her way down to the ground. She was limping and clutched her left wrist but was so frightened she barely felt her injuries.

Was the attack over? Could she safely call for help or search for survivors? Surely, if whatever was out there wanted her dead, she would have been killed by now.

Sleeping Beauty was just about to call for help when a blinding flash of violet light filled the forest. The queen screamed and fell to the ground, covering her face—but the flash lasted only a second. She smelled smoke and got to her feet and looked around. The entire forest was ablaze and every tree had been turned into a *spinning wheel*.

There was no denying it now; the kingdom's greatest fear had come true.

"The Enchantress," Sleeping Beauty whispered to herself. *"She's back."*

CHAPTER ONE

A TRAIN OF THOUGHTS

The subtle jerks of the train rocked Alex Bailey awake. She looked at the empty seats around her while she remembered where she was. A long sigh came out of the thirteen-year-old girl and she neatly fixed a strand of strawberry-blonde hair that had escaped her headband.

"Not again," she whispered to herself.

Alex hated dozing off in public places. She was a very smart and serious young woman and never wanted to give the wrong impression. Luckily for her, she was one of only a few people on the five o'clock train back into town, so her secret was safe.

Alex was an exceptionally bright student and always had

been. In fact, she was so advanced she was part of an honors program that allowed her to take an additional class at the community college in the next town.

Since she was too young to drive and her mother worked the majority of the day at a children's hospital, every Thursday after school Alex would ride her bike to the train station and travel the short distance into the next town for her classes.

It was a questionable trip for a young girl to make by herself, and her mother had had reservations at first, but she knew Alex could handle it. This short journey was nothing compared to the things Alex had handled in the past.

Alex loved being a part of the honors program. For the first time, she was able to learn about art and history and other languages in an environment where everyone *wanted* to be there. When her professors asked questions, Alex was one of many people to raise her hand with the answer.

Another perk of the train ride was the downtime Alex got to herself. She would gaze out the window and let her thoughts wander while the train traveled. It was the most relaxing part of her day, and many times she'd find herself drifting off to sleep, but only on rare occasions like today would she accidentally drift off completely.

Normally, she would wake feeling embarrassed, but this time Alex's embarrassment was laced with annoyance. She had just been having a disheartening dream: a dream she had had many times in the last year.

She dreamed she was running barefoot in a beautiful forest with her twin brother, Conner.

"I'll race you to the cottage!" Conner said with a huge smile. He shared his sister's looks but, thanks to a recent growth spurt, was now a few inches taller than her.

"You're on!" Alex said with a laugh, and the race began.

They chased each other through trees and over grassy fields without a care in the world. There were no trolls or wolves or evil queens for them to worry about, because, wherever Alex and Conner were, they knew they were safe.

Eventually a small cottage came into view. The twins bolted toward it, putting all their energy into one final sprint.

"I win!" Alex declared when both of her open palms touched the front door a millisecond before her brother's.

"Not fair!" Conner said. "My feet are flatter than yours!"

Alex giggled and tried opening the door, but it was locked. She knocked, but no one answered.

"That's funny," Alex said. "Grandma knew we were coming to visit; I wonder why she locked the door."

She and her brother peered into the window. They could see their grandmother inside, sitting in a rocking chair near the fireplace. She seemed sad, and slowly rocked back and forth.

"Grandma, we're here!" Alex said and cheerfully tapped on the window. "Open the door!"

Her grandmother didn't move.

"Grandma?" Alex asked, tapping on the window harder. "Grandma, it's us! We want to visit you!"

Her grandma raised her head slightly and looked up at them through the window but remained seated.

"Let us in!" Alex said, tapping on the glass even harder.

Conner shook his head. "It's no use, Alex. We can't go in." He turned away and headed back in the direction they came from.

"Conner, don't walk away!" Alex said.

"Why bother?" he said, looking back at her. "Clearly she doesn't want us in there."

Alex began banging on the window as hard as possible without breaking it. "Grandma, please let us in! We want to come inside! *Please!*"

Grandma looked up at her with a blank stare.

"Grandma, I don't know what I did wrong, but whatever it is, I'm sorry! Please let me come back inside!" Alex said as tears began to spill down her face. *"I want to come in! I want to come in!"*

Grandma's plain expression turned into a frown and she shook her head. Alex realized she wasn't going to be let in, and every time she came to this realization in the dream, she would wake up.

It might not have been a pleasant dream, but it had felt so good to be back in a forest and to see her grandmother's face again.... It was obvious to her what the dream represented, and had been since the first time she had dreamed it.

However, Alex felt something different when she awoke this time. She couldn't help but feel as if someone had been watching her while she was asleep.

When she had first awoken, although she hadn't paid much attention to it at first, she could have sworn she saw her grandmother sitting across from her on the train.

Was this an actual sighting or just her imagination getting the best of her? Alex couldn't deny the possibility that it had been real. Her grandmother was capable of many things....

It had been over a year since Alex and Conner Bailey had discovered their family's biggest secret. When they were given an old storybook from their grandmother, they'd never expected it would magically transport them into the fairy-tale world, and never in their wildest dreams had they expected that their grandmother and late father were *from* this world.

Traveling from kingdom to kingdom and befriending the characters they grew up reading about had been the adventure of their lives. But the biggest surprise of all was when the twins learned their own grandmother was Cinderella's Fairy Godmother.

Their grandmother eventually found them and took them back home to their anxious mother.

"I had to tell the school you both had chicken pox," Charlotte, the twins' mother, said. "I had to come up with a good excuse for why you had been gone for two weeks and thought 'traveling in another dimension' would probably raise a few eyebrows."

"Chicken pox?" Conner said. "Mom, you couldn't come up with anything *cooler*? Like a spider bite or food poisoning?"

"Did you know where we were the whole time?" Alex asked.

"It wasn't difficult to figure out," Charlotte said. "When I got home from work I went into your room and found the *Land of Stories* book on the floor. It was still glowing."

She looked over at the large emerald storybook held tightly in Grandma's hands.

"Were you worried?" Conner asked.

"Of course," Charlotte said. "Not necessarily for your safety, but for your sanity. I was worried the experience would overwhelm and frighten you, so I called your grandmother immediately. Luckily, she was still in this world, traveling with her friends. But after the second week of not knowing where you were...well, let's just say I pray I never have to experience that again."

"So you knew about *everything*?" Alex asked.

"Yes," Charlotte said. "Your dad was going to tell you eventually; he just never got the chance."

"How did you find out?" Conner asked. "When did Dad tell you? Did you even believe him at first?"

Charlotte smiled at the memory. "From the minute I saw your father, I knew there was something different about him," she said. "I had just started my first week of nursing at the children's hospital when I saw your grandmother and her group of friends come to read stories to the patients. But I was completely smitten by the handsome man who was with them. He was so peculiar; he stared around in amazement at everything. I thought he was going to faint when he saw the television."

"It was John's first trip to this world," Grandma said with a smile.

"He asked me to give him a tour of the hospital, and I did," Charlotte continued. "He was so fascinated to learn about it: the surgeries we performed, the medicines we used, the patients we treated. He asked if we could meet again later after I was done working so I could tell him more. We ended up dating for two months and fell in love. But then, strangely, he disappeared without warning and I didn't see him again for three whole years."

The twins looked to their grandmother, knowing a bit of the story already.

"I made him go back to the fairy-tale world with me, and forbid him to return," Grandma said and slumped a tad. "I had my reasons, as you know, but I was very wrong."

"And that's when he discovered the Wishing Spell and started to collect the items like us, so he could find a way back to you," Alex said excitedly.

"And it really didn't take him that long; it just seemed like it because we hadn't been born yet, and there was still a time difference between the worlds," Conner added.

Charlotte and Grandma both nodded.

"I eventually saw him again at the hospital," Charlotte said. "He looked so frail and dirty, like he had been to war and back. He looked at me and said, *'You have no idea what I went through to get back to you.'* We were married a month later and became parents a year after that. So to answer your question, no, it wasn't hard to accept that your dad was from another world, because somehow I had known all along."

Alex reached into her bag and pulled out the journal their

father had kept while he was collecting the Wishing Spell items, the same journal they had followed while collecting the items themselves.

"Here, Mom," Alex said. "Now you can know exactly how much Dad loved you."

Charlotte looked down at the journal, almost afraid to take it. She flipped it open and her eyes watered as she saw her late husband's handwriting.

"Thank you, sweetheart," she said.

"Just to let you know," Conner said, "me and Alex did all the same stuff. We're pretty great ourselves. Just keep that in mind if you ever feel inspired to give us an allowance in the future."

Charlotte playfully glared at her son; they knew she couldn't afford to give them allowances. Since their dad died, she'd had a hard time supporting the family and paying off debts from his funeral. But that got Alex thinking: With all the connections their family had in the fairy-tale world, why exactly had their lives been so tough the last year?

"Mom," Alex said, "why have we been struggling so much when all this time Grandma could have just waved her wand and made everything better for us?"

Conner looked up at his mother, thinking the same question. Their grandmother went quiet; it wasn't her place to say.

"Because your father didn't want that," Charlotte said. "Your father loved this world so much; it's where we met, it's where we had you two, and it's where he wanted to raise you. He had come from a world of kings and queens and magic, a world of entitlement and undeserved luxury that he thought ruined people's character. He wanted you guys to grow up in a place you could get anything you wanted if you worked hard enough for it, and although there have been times a little magic would have gone a long way, I've tried to respect that."

Alex and Conner looked at each other; maybe their dad was right. Could they have managed what they had done in the last weeks if they hadn't been raised that way? Could they have collected all the Wishing Spell items or stood up to the Evil Queen if he hadn't taught them how to believe in themselves?

"So what happens now?" Conner asked.

"What do you mean, Conner?" Grandma said.

"Well, clearly our lives are going to be totally different now, right?" he said with a twinkle in his eye. "I mean, after two weeks of barely surviving encounters with trolls, wolves, goblins, witches, and evil queens, we can't be expected to go to school again. We're too mentally distraught, right, Alex?"

Charlotte and Grandma looked at each other and burst out laughing.

"So I'm guessing that means we still have to go to school?" Conner asked. The twinkle in his eye faded away.

"Nice try," Charlotte said. "Every family has its issues, but that doesn't mean you get to drop out of school because of it."

"Thank goodness," Alex said with a sigh. "I was afraid he was on to something for a minute."

Grandma looked up at the clock. "It's almost sunrise," she said. "We've been talking all night. I better get going now."

"When will we see you again?" Alex asked. "When can we go back to the Land of Stories?" Alex had wanted to ask that question since the moment they left. Grandma looked down at her feet and thought for a moment before responding.

"You've had an awfully big adventure, even by grown-up standards," Grandma said. "Right now you need to focus on being twelve-year-olds in this world. Be kids while you still can, children. But I'll take you back one day, I promise."

It wasn't the answer she wanted, but Alex nodded. There was one more question she had been meaning to ask all night.

"Will you ever teach us magic, Grandma?" Alex asked with wide eyes. "I mean, since Conner and I are part fairy, it would be nice to know a thing or two."

"I completely forgot about that!" Conner said, slapping an open palm to his forehead. "Please leave me out of this. *I don't want to be a fairy*—can't stress that enough."

Grandma went silent. She looked to Charlotte, who only shrugged.

"When the time is right, sweetheart, I would love nothing more," Grandma said. "But right now the Fairy Council and I are working some things out, things that are pretty time-consuming but that you don't need to worry yourselves about. As soon as we move past it, I would love to teach you magic."

Grandma hugged her grandchildren and kissed the tops of their heads.

"I think it might be best if I take this with me," Grandma said, referring to the *Land of Stories* book. "We don't want history repeating itself."

She headed toward the front door, but just as she reached for the doorknob, she stopped and looked back at them.

"I forgot, I didn't drive here," Grandma said with a smirk. "Looks like I'll have to leave the *old-fashioned fairy way*. Good-bye, children, I love you with all my heart."

And slowly, Grandma began to disappear, fading into soft, sparkling clouds.

"Okay, now *that* is something I'd like to learn how to do," Conner said. He waved his hands through the sparkles in the air. "Sign me up for *that* lesson."

Alex yawned contagiously and her brother followed.

"You kids must be exhausted," Charlotte said. "Why don't you go to bed? I'm taking tomorrow off so I can be here with you guys, in case you have any more questions. And because I've just missed you."

"In that case, I've got an important question," Conner said. "What's for breakfast? I'm starving."

Alex's train finally reached her station. She retrieved her bike from the bike rack and pedaled home, still thinking about her grandmother.

Alex had expected to live a dual-worldly life after discovering the fairy-tale world. She imagined spending summers and holidays with her brother in the Fairy Kingdom or Cinderella's Palace with their grandmother. She imagined a brand-new life of magic and adventure would begin immediately. Sadly, Alex's expectations weren't met.

More than a year had gone by since the night their grand-mother disappeared. They hadn't received a single letter or phone call explaining why she had been gone. She missed every holiday and their birthday—days she *never* missed. And to make matters worse, the twins hadn't been back to the Land of Stories, either.

The twins couldn't help but be angry with their grand-mother. How could she just disappear and never make con-tact again? How could she take them to a place they had been dreaming about since they were kids and then never let them return?

Their grandmother herself had even said it; a part of the Land of Stories lived inside them—so who was she to keep it from them?

"Your grandmother is a very busy woman," Charlotte would tell Alex whenever the subject came up. "She loves you very much. She probably just has her hands full at the moment. We'll hear from her soon enough."

This wasn't enough to put Alex at ease. As more time went by, she began worrying whether her grandmother was all right—sometimes wondering if she was even *alive*. Alex hoped nothing had happened to her and that she was okay. She missed her hugs more than anything.

Life without their dad had been the most difficult thing the twins had ever experienced. But life without their dad *and* grandmother was nearly impossible.

"What do you think is going on?" Alex asked Conner on one occasion.

"I don't know," Conner said with a heavy sigh. "The last thing she said to us was that she and the other fairies were working something out. Maybe it's just taking longer than they expected?"

"Maybe," Alex said. "But I have a feeling that whatever it was, it's much worse than she was letting on. What else would be keeping her away from us for so long?"

Conner just shrugged. "I don't think Grandma would ever intentionally avoid us or exclude us from anything," he said.

"I'm just worried about her," Alex said.

"Alex," Conner said with a raised eyebrow, "the woman is magic and has lived for hundreds of years. What is there to worry about?"

Alex sighed. "I suppose you're right. She better have a great excuse next time we see her."

Unfortunately, "next time" didn't seem like it was happening anytime soon.

It was unsurprising that the situation had started affecting her dreams, but more than that, Alex was *depressed*. Ever since she had returned from the Land of Stories, she'd felt like a part of her was missing. The magical dimension had filled the emptiness she'd felt after losing her dad, and the emptiness grew every day she couldn't go back.

The weekly trips to the college were always a major trigger for feeling this way. College was a place that represented the future, and even though Alex was years away from actually going to college, she didn't like planning any future that didn't involve the Land of Stories. How could she live a normal life when she had proof that she was not normal?

Alex fantasized about moving to the Land of Stories one day. Could her grandmother teach her enough magic for Alex to become an official fairy? Could Alex become a member of the Fairy Council or, better yet, the Happily Ever After Assembly?

Alex tried doing magic on her own, but it never worked. The only time she had done something magical was when she accidentally set off her grandmother's storybook that transported her and Conner into the Land of Stories. But since it was her *grandmother's book*, she wondered if she was capable of doing anything alone.

Sometimes, when Alex was feeling particularly desperate, she would go into the school library and find a random fairy-tale treasury. She would hold it against her chest and think of how much she wanted to see the fairy-tale world, just like she did the night of her twelfth birthday. But it never did anything but attract unwanted attention from other students.

"Why is she hugging a book?" a popular girl said to her snooty pack on one occasion.

"Maybe she's taking it to homecoming!" another girl said, and they all laughed at Alex's expense.

Alex was tempted to yell, "Hey! My grandmother is Cinderella's fairy godmother, and as soon as she teaches me magic I'm gonna turn you into the lip gloss you wear too much of!" But she kept these thoughts to herself.

As Alex rode her bike the rest of the way home from the train station, she closed her eyes for a minute and pretended she was riding along Thumbelina Stream in the Fairy Kingdom—a herd of unicorns was to her left and a hovering flock of fairies was to her right—and she was meeting her grandmother for a magic lesson on how to transform rags into a beautiful ball gown.

Paradise, she thought to herself.

Alex opened her eyes a second before crashing hard into a set of trash cans. Thankfully, the only witness was a garden gnome across the street, but even it seemed to judge her.

She got up and brushed herself off, deciding to walk her bike the rest of the way home. It had been a brutal reality check.

The Baileys still lived in the same rental house with a flat roof and few windows, but things were looking up for them. Their mother had finally caught up on a lot of their financial troubles and wasn't working nearly as much as she used to. However, something else had been occupying Charlotte Bailey's time recently, and it wasn't nursing.

Alex parked her bike on the porch. The front door flew open just as Alex was about to walk through it. Conner was standing on the other side. He seemed upset and very concerned about something.

"What's your problem?" Alex asked.

"Sorry, I thought you were Mom," Conner said.

"Do you need her for something?" Alex said.

"No," Conner said. "Mom is just usually home by six o'clock every night."

"It's six o'clock right now," Alex said, looking at him like he was a crazy person.

"It's six-*fifteen*, Alex," Conner said, raising his eyebrows.

"So?"

"Well, where is she, then? Do you see her? Is there a car parked in the driveway?" Conner asked.

"Maybe there's traffic," Alex said.

"Or something *else*," he said. "Like something *keeping* her at work."

"Is there a point to all of this?" Alex asked, becoming annoyed.

"I need to show you something," Conner finally admitted. "But let me warn you, you aren't going to like it."

"Um . . . okay," Alex said and followed her brother in.

A series of barks and whimpers came from inside the house as Alex stepped through the front door.

"*Buster!* Down, boy! It's just Alex!" Conner shouted. "Why does this stupid dog act like everyone who comes inside this house is carrying explosives? We live here, too!"

"Are you going to tell me what's going on, Conner?" Alex asked, running out of patience.

"I'll show you. It's in the kitchen," he said. "There's been a *development*."

CHAPTER TWO

IT STARTED WITH A DOG

A few months ago, Buster the Border collie was rescued from the local animal shelter and given to the Bailey family. He was a gift from Dr. Robert Gordon, whom Charlotte worked with at the hospital and who had become a close family friend.

"Dr. Bob," as the twins called him when he occasionally came over for dinner, was a kind man whose face settled into a natural smile. He was balding and not very tall but had big, caring eyes that made him an instant friend to anyone he met.

"Oh, Bob! You shouldn't have!" Charlotte said as soon as he surprised them with the canine.

"What's up with the pooch?" Conner said when he came to see what the ruckus was about.

"He's all yours!" Bob said. "Your mom is always talking about the Border collie she had when she was a little girl and said she's always secretly wanted another one. I was volunteering at the animal shelter and as soon as I saw him I knew I had to adopt him for you guys."

"We have a dog?!" Conner exclaimed. Although the words came out of his mouth, he hadn't fully grasped the reality of it.

"I suppose we do," Charlotte said.

Conner immediately fell to the floor and started rolling around with his new pet. *"We have a dog! We have a dog!"* he exclaimed. "Finally, our suburban lives are complete! Thank you, Dr. Bob!"

"You're very welcome!" Bob said.

"What's your name, boy?" Conner asked.

"Buster," Bob told him. "At least, that's what they called him at the shelter."

The black-and-white dog was obnoxiously happy and had bright green eyes, one of which was larger than the other. Bob had placed a red bandana around Buster's collar.

Conner hugged him and almost cried tears of joy. "I know we've just met, Buster, but I feel like I've loved you my entire life!" he said.

"Who's this?" Alex asked when she came to see what was causing all the excitement.

"This is my dog, Buster!" Conner said. He took off one of his socks and he and Buster played tug-of-war with it.

"He's for *all* of you," Bob corrected him.

"Conner, don't use good socks!" Charlotte said.

Alex unintentionally let out a high-pitched squeal and her mouth dropped open. "We have a dog?!" she asked and jumped up and down. Something about Buster made the twins act like they were ten again.

"Yes, we have a dog," Charlotte said, and shared her smile.

"Don't be disappointed if he likes me more, Alex," Conner said matter-of-factly. "Dogs tend to bond with boys more. It's proven science, I think."

"Buster, come here!" Alex called. Buster ran straight to Alex's side and happily whimpered up at her.

"Never mind," Conner said, a little disappointed.

The twins were so excited to get a dog they never questioned the gift for a second. They were so distracted playing with the new addition to their family that they didn't see Charlotte give Bob a long, thankful hug, an embrace that lasted too long to just be a *friendly* gesture.

But as time went on, and the twins saw more of Bob, they were forced to notice the signs that their mother and the doctor were more than just friends....

Conner sat Alex down at the kitchen table as soon as she walked through the door. Although he saw them every day, Buster couldn't contain his excitement for the twins both being home. He jumped up and down and spun in circles around the kitchen.

"Buster, calm down!" Conner ordered. "I swear, that dog needs to be on medication."

"What's going on, Conner?" Alex asked. "You love that dog as much as he loves you."

"That was before I discovered Buster was a *bribe*!" Conner animatedly declared. "Take a look at this!"

Conner retrieved a beautiful bouquet of a dozen long-stemmed red roses from the kitchen counter. He placed them on the table directly in front of Alex.

"Those are beautiful! Where are they from?" Alex asked.

"They were delivered when I got home from school," Conner said. "They're for Mom . . . from *Bob*!"

Alex's eyes widened. "Oh dear," she said and gulped. "Well, that's very *sweet* of him."

"*Sweet?!*" Conner said loudly. "This isn't sweet, Alex! It's downright *romantic*!"

"Conner, you don't know he meant it in that way," Alex said. "People send other people flowers all the time."

Conner searched through the bouquet. "Daisies are friendly, sunflowers are friendly, a Venus flytrap is friendly—but *red roses mean romance*!" he said. "And he sent a card. It's in here somewhere—I read it like a hundred times before I threw it back in—here it is. Read it."

He passed a small card to his sister, and to her horror it was heart-shaped. She looked down at it like it had the results to an exam she knew she had flunked.

"I don't want to read it," Alex said. "I don't want to invade Mom's privacy."

"Then I'll read it to you," Conner said and tried snatching the card out of her hands.

"Fine, I'll read it!" Alex said and reluctantly opened the card.

Charlotte,
Happy six months!
Xoxo—Bob

Alex quickly closed the card as if trying to stop the truth from escaping it. Conner leaned close to his sister and studied her face, waiting for a reaction to surface.

"Weeeeeell?" Conner said.

"Well," Alex said as she ran through a dozen unlikely theories, "we don't know that this means they're in a *relationship*."

Conner threw his hands into the air and paced around the kitchen. "Alex, don't do that!" he said, pointing his finger at her.

"Don't do what?" she asked.

"That thing you do when you try to ignore a situation by making light of it!" he said.

"Conner, I think you're overreacting—"

"Face it, Alex, we were blinded by a Border collie!" Conner exclaimed loud enough for the neighbors to hear him. "Mom has a *boyfriend*!"

Hearing *Mom* and *boyfriend* made Alex squirm. In her opinion, the two words didn't belong in the same dictionary, let alone the same sentence.

"I'm not going to get too worked up about something until I hear it from Mom herself," Alex said.

"What more proof do you need?" Conner said. "Mom got a dozen red roses delivered with a heart-shaped card specifying an amount of time! What do you think 'six months' means? Do you think Mom and Bob joined a bowling league and didn't tell us?"

Both of their heads abruptly turned in the same direction when they heard the garage door open. Charlotte was finally home from work.

"Ask her," Alex mouthed at her brother.

"*You* ask her," Conner mouthed back at her.

Charlotte stepped inside a few moments later. She was still dressed in her blue scrubs from the hospital and carried a bag of groceries. She walked right by the flowers on the table without noticing them.

"Hey, guys, sorry I'm late," Charlotte said. "I stopped by the store on the way home to pick up something for dinner. I'm starving! I was thinking of making a chicken-and-rice something or other; sound good? Are you two hungry?"

Charlotte looked up when the twins stayed silent.

"What's wrong?" she asked. "Are you okay—*wait*, where did those flowers come from?"

"They're from your *boyfriend*," Conner said.

In the thirteen years of being her children, Alex and Conner could count on one hand how many times they had seen their mother become speechless. This was one of those times.

"Oh . . ." Charlotte looked like a deer in headlights.

"You have a lot of explaining to do!" Conner said and crossed his arms. "You should probably have a seat."

"I'm sorry, did someone promote you to parent?" Charlotte said and glared at her son.

"Sorry," Conner said and lowered his head. "I just think we need to talk about this."

"Is it true?" Alex asked with a half-concerned, half-horrified expression.

"Yes," Charlotte said with difficulty. "Bob and I have been seeing each other."

Conner slid into a seat next to his sister. Alex's forehead hit the table.

"I was going to tell you," Charlotte said. "I was just waiting—"

"Let me guess, until we were older?" Conner asked. "If only I had a nickel for every time we heard that. Alex, watch out—we may be two-thirds of a set of triplets but won't know until we're thirty."

Charlotte closed her eyes tightly and let out a deep breath. "Actually, I was waiting until I could figure out *how* to tell you," she said softly. "You guys have been so worried about not seeing your grandmother. I didn't want to add anything to your plate."

She took a seat and let the news sink in for a moment.

"I know this is hard to swallow," Charlotte said.

"Hard to swallow? We need an emotional Heimlich, Mom," Conner said.

"I actually think finding out our grandmother is a fairy in

another dimension was easier to process than this is," Alex added.

Charlotte's eyes fell sadly to her hands. The twins didn't mean to make her feel bad, but they were feeling so many things, they were forgetting to be considerate.

"Bob and I have known each other for a very long time," Charlotte said. "When your dad died, he became a very good friend. He was one of the few people I could talk to about everything that I was going through. Did you know Bob's wife died just a year before your dad?"

Both of the twins shook their heads.

"You could have talked to *us*," Conner said.

"No, I couldn't," Charlotte said. "I needed another adult to confide in. You'll understand one day when you have kids. Bob and I each knew what the other was going through. We talked every day at work and became very close, and recently, that friendship has grown."

The twins couldn't decide if what she was saying was helping or making it all worse. The more she explained, the more real it became.

"What about Dad?" Alex said. "Your and Dad's story was literally a fairy tale, Mom. He traveled from a different world to be with you. Don't you still love *him*?"

The question was heartbreaking for all of them, especially Charlotte.

"Your father was the love of my life, and always will be," Charlotte said. "And these years without him have been the hardest of my entire life. We were married for twelve years, and in that time we talked about a lot of things, a lot of *possibilities*. I know for a fact that if I spent another year missing your father, he would be so disappointed in me. He would want me to move on as much as I would want him to move on if the roles were reversed. It was a promise we made to each other."

Charlotte went silent for a moment before continuing. "The first year after he died, I thought I never would be able to move on," she said. "I thought part of me died with him and I would never be able to love anyone again. But then Bob told me he and his wife had made the same promises to each other just before she passed away, and he felt the same way. For some reason, just knowing someone else was in the same boat as me made everything feel so much better."

The twins shared a hopeless glance, knowing there was nothing they could do to ease their mother's heartache. "I know this is difficult for you two," Charlotte said. "I'm not saying you need to be okay with it. You can feel however you want, and rightfully so. Just know that Bob makes me really happy, and it's been a long time since I've felt this way."

Conner unsuccessfully tried keeping a question that popped up in his mind to himself.

"Conner, what's your question?" Charlotte asked and dabbed the corners of her eyes with the edge of her sleeve.

"I don't have a question," Conner said and shook his head unconvincingly.

"Yes you do," Charlotte said, knowing her son better than he knew himself. "You always purse your lips like that when you have something to ask."

Conner immediately repositioned his mouth.

"It's okay, honey, you can ask anything," she said.

"It's really childish and lame," Conner warned. "I guess it's something I've always wondered about people who lose their husbands or wives. But one day, if we're all in … well, *heaven*, I guess, isn't it going to be a little awkward with Bob and Dad there?"

Alex was about to let out a disapproving sigh but held it in. Even she had to admit it was a decent question. Although she felt horrible for feeling it, a part of her felt like her mom was being unfaithful to her dad.

A smile came to Charlotte's face and she let out a soft laugh. "Oh, honey, if there's ever a time or a place when we're all together again, I imagine we'd be too happy to let things be awkward."

Alex and Conner looked at each other and knew they were both thinking the same thing. The thought of their family being together again made them both smile.

Charlotte placed her hands on the tops of theirs on the table. "Nothing any of us do will ever bring your dad back," she said. "And nothing we do will ever push him further away, either. He'll always be with us in our hearts, no matter what."

"I guess putting it that way makes me feel better," Conner said.

"Me too," Alex said.

"I'm glad to hear it," Charlotte said and smiled at them. She got up from the table and grabbed her car keys. "I don't feel like cooking anymore. Let's go get pizza instead. It's good to eat something heavy after a heavy conversation."

CHAPTER THREE

LUNCH IN THE LIBRARY

The next day at school Alex was still having a hard time digesting the conversation (and the pizza) from the night before. The news of her mother's new relationship was a heavy thing to process and did nothing to help the gloomy state she was already in.

She felt like she was slowly losing control over everything in her life, and she hated it.

Alex desperately needed someone to talk to, someone who wasn't her mom or her brother, but an outside source who could hug her and tell her everything was going to be all right—she needed her *grandmother*. She would have given anything just to see her face again. However, since that was impossible at the moment, Alex settled on seeing a *form* of her grandmother instead.

At lunch she went to one of her favorite places in her world: the school library.

"Hi, Alex," the librarian said as Alex passed her desk. "You'll be happy to know I just ordered a new set of encyclopedias!"

"Really?" Alex said. "That's wonderful!"

She smiled for the first time all day. It faded a second later after she realized "new encyclopedias" was the most exciting news she had had in weeks.

"Thank you for your enthusiasm," the librarian said. "Earlier today I told another student I was getting new encyclopedias—he asked me how long I'd be in the hospital! Can you believe that? Times are definitely changing."

"They sure are," Alex said under her breath.

Alex went to the very last aisle of books, where the children's literature was kept. Students weren't allowed to check out these books, as they were mostly used as reference for the English classes. From the top shelf, Alex pulled down an old book that was several hundred pages thick. It was exactly where she had left it on her last visit to the library.

A Treasury of Classic Fairy Tales was written across its brown cover. It wasn't much to look at and didn't have nearly as much majestic charm as her grandmother's *Land of Stories* book, but it had become Alex's favorite book to visit in the library.

She looked around to make sure no one was watching her. Besides the librarian, who was busy at her computer, she had the library to herself.

Alex opened the book and flipped through the pages. She skimmed through the illustrations of Sleeping Beauty and Snow White, of Rapunzel and Red Riding Hood, and of Goldilocks and Jack and the beanstalk. Surprisingly, they were accurate depictions of the people she had met a year ago in the fairy-tale world.

Alex finally found "Cinderella" and came across the picture she wanted to see most: an illustration of the Fairy Godmother.

Alex couldn't help but chuckle under her breath every time she saw it. The artist's version of the Fairy Godmother couldn't have been further from what her grandmother looked like. In this book, she was a tall and voluptuous woman with big lips, wings, long blonde hair, and a large golden crown.

However inaccurate it was, it was technically still her grandmother, and that was all Alex needed to see.

"Hi, Grandma," Alex said quietly to the book. "You look great. I like your crown and your wings. It's funny how different you look in every book I read. Are they just dramatic interpretations, or has your style changed over the years?"

The Fairy Godmother was just a young fairy living in the fairy-tale world when she discovered there was another world. She was the first and only person in the history of both worlds capable of traveling between the two at will. She never understood why she was given such a gift, but magic had always had a mind of its own.

The world was in a very dark place during her first visits. It was the beginning of the Middle Ages, and war and plague were everywhere she looked. The Fairy Godmother told stories of her world to the children she met to brighten their spirits. The tales gave them such hope and joy that she decided to make it her life's work to spread the history of her world in theirs.

The Fairy Godmother eventually enlisted other fairies, including Mother Goose and members of the Fairy Council, to travel secretly with her and help spread the stories (hence the name "fairy tales"), giving a bit of magic to a world that had little of its own. Over time, the fairies recruited other people, such as the Brothers Grimm and Hans Christian Andersen, to help keep their stories alive.

The two dimensions operated on different time schedules; the fairy-tale world moved at a much slower pace compared to the other world. The fairies tried to visit the other world as much as possible, but though only months would pass between visits in the fairy-tale world, decades would have passed in the other world. It wasn't until Alex and Conner, the first children belonging to both worlds, were born that the dimensions began moving at the same pace.

Alex and Conner were the links that held the two worlds together. And as Alex held the *Treasury of Classic Fairy Tales* in her hands, she could almost feel that power running through her veins. It was no wonder they had loved fairy tales their whole lives.

Alex wondered if her grandmother had devoted the last

year solely to spreading fairy tales around the world. Or had something bad happened in the fairy-tale world?

"Grandma, I don't know what's going on, but I could really use you right now," Alex said to the book. "Everything is changing; everything is moving in directions I don't like. This whole growing-up thing is a lot harder than I ever thought it would be. And not getting to see you makes it unbearable."

Alex took another look around the library to make sure she was still alone. She hugged the book as tightly as she could without damaging it and whispered into the top of its spine.

"Please let me come back to the Land of Stories," she said. *"Let me join you and the other fairies. If something has happened, let me help you. I know I can. Please just send me a sign, let me know that you're okay."*

Alex held the book for a few moments more, hoping that maybe today would be the day she would be magically transported back into the world she loved so much. But to her disappointment, she stayed put in the library.

Her whispers didn't go entirely unnoticed, however.

"If hugging that one doesn't work, try one of these," said a voice from nearby.

Startled, Alex dropped the treasury. Down the aisle, seated on the floor with a few stacks of books piled around him, was Conner. Alex had completely missed him.

"You scared me," Alex said. She was embarrassed, not knowing what he had and hadn't heard her saying to the inanimate object.

"You're lucky I know you; otherwise I probably would have

reported you to the school psychologist," Conner said with a mocking but loving smirk.

"What are you doing here?" Alex asked him. She walked down the aisle closer to her brother and saw that the majority of the books around him were also different storybooks and fairy tales.

"Same thing as you, apparently," Conner said and then snickered to himself. "Although I didn't try getting to first base with any of them or anything."

"Very funny," Alex said and took a seat next to him. "Is this your first time ever being in the library?"

Conner sighed and shrugged his shoulders. "I've been in a bit of a funk today. I thought if I came in here and flipped through a couple of these I would feel better," he explained.

"Did it work?" Alex asked.

"For the most part, I'd say," Conner said. "Why do you think that is?"

"Well," Alex said, straightening her headband, "I read in a zoology book once that certain species of birds and insects that live in trees will climb down and hide in the roots if they ever feel like their home is being threatened."

Conner looked at her like she was speaking in tongues. "And *how* is that relevant to this topic?"

"Because," Alex explained, "our home is being threatened; things are changing. So here we are, in a library, reading old fairy tales. We returned to *our* roots."

"Sure," Conner said, only half understanding her comparison. "How can you remember *that* but you can never remember the names of singers on the radio?"

"My point is," Alex continued, "sometimes all we need to see are a few familiar faces to make us feel comfortable again."

Conner nodded. "Well, I wouldn't say I saw any *familiar* faces," he said.

He searched through his pile of books and pulled out a couple to show her.

"In *this*, the Egyptian version of 'Cinderella,' Grandma is a *hawk*!" he told her excitedly. "And in *this* one, Grandma's not even in it. Cinderella gets her gown and shoes from a tree! Can you believe that? Like a *tree* could give her a new dress. *Please*. A complete stranger with a wand is much more believable."

"We should write letters of complaint," Alex said. "Should we sign it as the grandchildren of the Fairy Godmother? Do you think they'll take it more seriously if we do?" They both laughed.

"Definitely!" Conner said. "Or personal acquaintances of the long-lost Charming prince! I bet no one has ever heard that one before."

Both the twins went silent for a moment and their amusement faded into despair. "I miss Froggy," Conner said. "I miss *saying* 'Froggy.'"

"There's not much we can do about it," Alex said. "If Grandma wanted us to come back, she would tell us what was going on. Until then, I guess we'll have to keep hugging books."

"Great," Conner said sarcastically. "I wonder what Dad would tell us if he were alive. I don't think there's a story even in *his* catalog that could help us get through everything we're going through now."

Alex had to think about it. Most of her dad's stories had

been perfect for their elementary-school dilemmas, but what advice would he give them now?

"I bet he would say that anyone can have a once-upon-a-time or a happily-ever-after, but it's the journey between that makes the story worth telling," Alex said. "And how characters face the challenges at hand is what makes them heroes."

"Yeah..." Conner said. "Something like that.... You're good at this."

A high-pitched beep sounded as an announcement was made over the loudspeaker.

"Conner Bailey, please report to the principal's office. Conner Bailey, please report to the principal's office."

Both of the twins looked up toward the speaker and then at each other.

"What did you do?" Alex asked.

"I don't know," Conner said with a gulp. He mentally rewound through the past four weeks of his life, thinking of anything he had done that could warrant a trip to the principal's office, but found nothing. "At least, I don't *think* I did anything."

Conner collected his things and put the library books back on the shelves.

"Well, wish me luck," he said to his sister. "See you after school...*I hope*."

Alex stayed seated on the floor, discouraging thoughts filling her head. What would happen if she never saw her grandmother again? Would she become a weird, book-hugging lady who traveled from one library to the next? Would her future children believe her when she told them about her connections to the fairy-tale world?

The bell eventually rang and Alex got to her feet. She picked up the *Treasury of Classic Fairy Tales* from where she had dropped it on the floor and decided to take one last look at the illustration before heading to class.

Alex turned to the same page she had been talking to before, and to her amazement, the illustration was completely different. Instead of the voluptuous woman with the wings and crown, the picture showed a petite woman with a kind smile in a sky-blue sparkly robe. *It was her grandmother.*

Alex looked around the library in shock as a smile grew on her face. Her grandmother had just sent her a postcard.

CHAPTER FOUR

THE PRINCIPAL'S OFFICE

Conner had only been sitting outside the principal's office for ten minutes, but it felt like two hours. The mystery of why he was there was picking at his psyche like a pair of hungry buzzards.

He had been a surprisingly good student this year—not as great as his sister, perhaps, but good nevertheless. Conner's grades were decent, although he probably could have done better in science and math, as he imagined most students could. Besides occasionally forgetting which revolution happened where, he was doing fairly well in his history class, too. And for the first time in his life, he was actually enjoying assignments in his English class.

He was confident he hadn't done anything wrong. So why was he there? He grew paranoid someone had possibly framed him. Was he being held responsible for the graffiti on the lockers or the goldfish put in the faculty toilets? Sure, Conner thought those pranks were hilarious, but he hadn't *done* them. If they didn't think he was guilty, did they think he knew who was and want him to testify? Could he plead the Fifth in school? Did he have the right to a lawyer or a phone call?

The door to the principal's office opened and a girl ran out in tears. Conner instantly tensed.

"Mr. Bailey?" Mrs. Peters called from inside her office.

Conner gulped. Hearing her call out his name was just as terrifying today as it had been when she taught him in the sixth grade....

A huge promotion was the last thing she had expected, but Mrs. Peters had recently come up in the world.

After twenty-five long years of teaching, Mrs. Peters had made the tough decision to retire. The subject had been on the veteran educator's mind for quite some time. Unbeknownst to her students, Mrs. Peters kept a calendar at her desk for years and marked down the days until she was eligible.

She often daydreamed about her life after teaching. She planned all the exotic vacations she wanted to take. She made a list of all the small fixes around her condo she'd finally have the time to make. She assembled everything she needed to start a vegetable garden in her small yard. In other words, she was more than ready.

But in the final weeks leading up to the conclusion of her teaching career, Mrs. Peters received the offer to become a *principal*. As appealing as a life of gardening and relaxation was, a life as principal gave her the essence of what she loved the most about being a teacher: *authority over impressionable youngsters*.

Needless to say, she didn't hesitate to take the job. She thrived in the powerful position of administering punishment, and occasionally something would come up that allowed her to do what she loved more than anything, which was why she called Conner Bailey into her office.

"Have a seat," Mrs. Peters ordered.

Conner sat across from her so obediently he reminded himself of Buster, but didn't expect to be rewarded with a biscuit. His eyes wandered around the room; he noticed Mrs. Peters decorated her office in the same patterns and floral prints as the dresses she wore.

"Do you know why I've called you in here today?" Mrs. Peters asked. She wasn't even looking at him. Her eyes were busy scanning through a stack of papers in her hands.

"Not a clue," Conner said. He could almost see what the papers were in the reflection of her glasses.

"I wanted to talk to you about the writing you've been doing in your English class," she said, finally making eye contact.

Conner realized the papers she was going through were in his handwriting. He panicked.

"Is this about my essay on *To Kill a Mockingbird*?" he asked. "I know I wrote, 'One of the saddest parts about this book is that a girl is named Scout,' but I talked to Ms. York about my approach and understand why it could have been better."

Mrs. Peters's eyes squinted and her brow flexed in a judgmental manner; this was bound to happen at least once when she was in the same room as Conner.

"Or maybe this is about my report on *Animal Farm*?" Conner said. "I know I said, 'I wish George Orwell had used something to represent politics that didn't give me a major craving for a bacon cheeseburger,' but that's really how I felt; I wasn't trying to be funny."

"No, Mr. Bailey," Mrs. Peters said. "I called you to my office to talk about the *creative writing* you've been working on in Ms. York's class."

"Oh?" Conner asked. Creative writing was actually his favorite part of the class. "How am I screwing *that* up?"

"You're not," Mrs. Peters said. "It's *fantastic*."

Conner's head jerked in disbelief.

"Did you just say what I think you just said?" Conner asked.

"I believe so," Mrs. Peters said, almost as surprised as he was. "Ms. York was afraid your stories might have been plagiarized, so she sent them to me to look over, but they're unlike anything I've ever read. I assured her they appeared very original to me."

Conner was having difficulty processing it all; Mrs. Peters of all people was complimenting *and* defending him.

"So I'm in here for a *good thing*?" Conner asked.

"A very good thing," Mrs. Peters said. "Your stories and

perspectives on fairy-tale characters are wonderful! I loved your stories about the Charming Dynasty searching for the long-lost Charming brother and the Evil Queen's long-lost lover being trapped in her Magic Mirror. And Trix the misbehaving fairy and Trollbella the homely troll princess are such imaginative new characters. It's very impressive!"

"Thank you?" Conner said.

"Can I ask you what inspired these stories?" Mrs. Peters said.

Conner gulped. He didn't know how to answer. Technically he had used the class to write about *his experiences*, so the stories weren't necessarily "creative writing." Was it considered lying even if he *couldn't* tell the truth?

"They just came to me," Conner said with a shrug. "I can't really explain it."

Mrs. Peters did something Conner had never seen her do before: *She smiled at him.*

"I was hoping you would say that," Mrs. Peters said. She retrieved a folder from the inside of her desk. "I took the liberty of looking at the student profile you filled out at the beginning of the school year. I found it interesting that under 'future career aspirations,' you simply wrote 'something cool.'"

Conner nodded. "I stand by that," he said.

"Well, unless you have the goal of becoming a professional snowman, is it safe to presume you're open to suggestions?" Mrs. Peters asked.

"Sure," Conner said. He still hadn't thought of any jobs that fit the description.

"Mr. Bailey, have you ever considered becoming a *writer*?" Mrs. Peters said. "If these stories are any indication, with time and practice, I think you may have what it takes."

Although they were the only people in the room, Conner had to remind himself she was talking to him.

"A writer?" Conner asked. *"Me?"* The thought had never crossed his mind. His head instantly filled with doubts regarding the prospect, like white blood cells attacking a virus.

"Yes, *you*," Mrs. Peters said and pointed at him for further distinction.

"But aren't writers supposed to be super smart?" Conner asked. "Don't they say things like, *'I concur'* and *'I don't identify with the likes of this'*? Those kinds of people are writers, not me. They'd laugh at me if I tried being one of them."

Mrs. Peters exhaled a small gust of air through her nose, which Conner remembered was her version of a laugh.

"Intelligence is not a competition," she said. "There is plenty to go around, and there are many ways it can be demonstrated."

"But anyone can write, right?" Conner asked. "I mean, that's why authors get judged so harshly, isn't it? Because technically everyone could do it if they wanted to."

"Just because anyone can do something doesn't mean everyone should," Mrs. Peters said. "Besides, anyone with an Internet connection feels they have the credentials to critique or belittle anything these days."

"I suppose," Conner said, but his defeated look said otherwise. "What makes you think I'll be a good writer? My stories are so simple compared to other ones out there. And I don't have a very good vocabulary—and I'm worthless without spell-check."

Mrs. Peters took off her glasses and massaged her eyes. Conner was still a challenging student to get through to.

"Having something worth telling and a passion to tell it are what make you a good writer," Mrs. Peters said. "I can't tell you how many times I've read novels or articles that used complicated words and witty wordplay to cover up the fact that they had absolutely no story to tell. A good story should be enjoyed; sometimes simplicity can go a long way."

Conner still wasn't sold on the idea. "I just don't know if it's for me."

"You don't have to decide right now," Mrs. Peters said. "I'm only asking you to think about it. I would hate it if somebody with your imagination graduated and didn't do 'something cool' with it."

She locked eyes with him and another rare, small smile appeared on her face.

"I have two loves in my career: reprimanding and encouraging," Mrs. Peters went on. "Thank you for letting me encourage today. I don't get many opportunities."

"No problem," Conner said. "It's nice to be in the other category for a change."

Mrs. Peters put her glasses back on and handed Conner his stack of papers. He figured their meeting was over now and headed to the door, relieved not to be in tears like his principal's prior guest.

"I am so proud of you, Conner," Mrs. Peters said just as he reached for the door handle. "You've come a long way from napping in my class."

All Conner could do was smirk sweetly at her. If you had told him a year and a half ago that one day Mrs. Peters would become one of his greatest supporters (or refer to him by his first name), he would have never believed it.

Conner mulled things over as he walked home. His thoughts soared into the realm of possibilities and sank into the realm of uncertainty. Had Mrs. Peters gone mad or was he, *Conner Bailey*, actually capable of becoming a writer one day? Could he actually make a career out of writing about the experiences he and his sister had had in the fairy-tale world?

Would anyone want to read his stories about Trollbella and Trix, or the Evil Queen and the Big Bad Wolf Pack, or Jack and Goldilocks? Would *those people* mind if he wrote about them? If he ever saw her again, would Goldilocks beat the living daylights out of him for writing about the love triangle between her, Jack, and Red Riding Hood?

Conner figured people had been writing the same stories about them for centuries; surely they wouldn't mind if he gave the world little updates here and there.

But what about Alex? She had as much ownership over their experiences as he did; would it bother her if he started sharing them with the world?

Alex had always been the one with a future, not him. Planning had always been *her* specialty; Conner always expected she would grow up to be a doctor, or a lawyer, or president.

Unfortunately, he hadn't given his own future very much thought, so any prospect seemed like a stretch.

Conner realized he wanted to get Alex's input on all of this. But as he reached their house, he came to a halt. There was something there he didn't expect to see.

"What's Bob doing here?" Conner asked himself, recognizing the car parked outside their home.

The front door flew open before Conner could open it himself. Alex was standing on the other side, wide-eyed and white-faced.

"Finally!" she said in relief.

"What's going on?" Conner asked. "Why is Bob here?"

"He wanted to talk to us before Mom got home," Alex said. "He knows that we know and said he wanted to ask us something. I'm pretty sure I know what it is."

"What?" Conner asked, completely oblivious.

"Just get inside," Alex told him. "I think there's about to be a *major* development."

CHAPTER FIVE

THE PROPOSAL

Alex and Conner hadn't looked like identical twins since they were four years old. It was around that age when Charlotte stopped dressing them in the same outfits every day and they started growing into their own unique features. But as they sat on the couch both staring daggers at Bob with their arms crossed, it was once again hard to tell them apart.

"So..." Bob said and shifted uncomfortably in a chair across from them. "Your mom said she finally spilled the beans about us."

It was brave of him to take the situation by the horns.

"She sure did," Conner said.

Bob nodded pleasantly, like it was good news. The twins didn't even blink—they were an intimidating pair.

"I apologize that those flowers came to the house. They were supposed to have gone to the hospital," Bob said.

"Yes, they should have," Alex said. Bob had done thousands of difficult surgeries over the course of his career, but he found being stared down by the children of the woman he was dating to be the most stressful experience of his life.

"I understand why this is difficult information to process," Bob said. "But it's still *me*, guys. I'm still the same Dr. Bob who you've had dinner with a dozen times. I'm the same guy who takes you to see the movies your mom doesn't want to see. I'm still the same guy who brought you Buster. I just happen to be—"

"Dating our mother?" Conner asked. "Nice try, but everything you listed makes the situation worse. We *thought* we knew you."

"Are you admitting that Buster was some sort of dowry, Bob?" Alex asked.

"Alex, what's a dowry?" Conner said out of the side of his mouth, not breaking his stare at Bob.

"It's a settlement of sorts," Alex said. "Like, in ancient times, a man would be promised a dozen camels or something in exchange for his daughter's hand in marriage."

"Gotcha," Conner said, diverting his full attention back to Bob. "You don't think our mother is worth a dozen camels, Bob? One dog and you think the deal is sealed?"

"I definitely don't think the deal is sealed," Bob said. "Yet."

Alex and Conner narrowed their eyes in perfect unison. Bob reached inside his pocket and pulled out a small velvet box. The twins wondered what it was for a second, but only a second. Once they realized it was too small to hold anything but a *ring*, it dawned on them what it meant.

"Oh my God," Alex said.

"No way," Conner said.

Bob looked down at the box with a smile. "You know, when my wife died four years ago, I never thought I would be happy again," he said. "I save lives every day, but for a long time I thought it would be impossible to save mine. And then along came your mom, and I learned I had been wrong."

Alex and Conner looked at each other out of the corners of their eyes. They had never seen Bob get so sappy, but still they appreciated how honest he was being with them.

"I know you've been seeing each other for a while, but this all seems so sudden," Alex said.

"We only found out last night," Conner said. "In our minds you guys have only been dating for one day. Are you sure you aren't rushing things?"

The way he looked down at the ring, with loving eyes and a heartfelt smile, made it obvious that Bob had never been so sure about something in his life.

"I've been around for a while, guys. And I've learned that things like this don't come around very often," Bob said. "*Not* taking this opportunity to ask your mother to be with me for the rest of my life would make me the biggest fool in the world."

Bob opened the box and showed the twins the ring. Alex gasped. It was the most beautiful ring they had ever seen. It had a silver band with two large diamonds, one blue and the other pink. They could have sworn they heard music playing while it twinkled in the light, but it was just in their heads.

"It took me a month to find the perfect one," Bob said. "I knew this was right as soon as I saw it. I thought the diamonds would remind her of you two; they're different shades of the same cut."

Alex's eyes immediately watered after hearing this. Conner folded his arms a little tighter.

"That's the most touching thing I've ever heard," Alex said between sniffles.

"Stop making me like you again," Conner said, brow furrowed.

Bob sat up straighter, happy their meeting was moving in a better direction. "I'm not trying to replace your dad and I'm not asking to be your new one," he said. "But I *am* asking for your permission to ask your mother to marry me. I don't want to do this without your blessing."

The twins couldn't believe it. They both felt like they were passengers on this ship, and now he was letting them be its captains?

"We need a minute to think it over," Conner answered quickly.

Before Alex knew it, her brother was dragging her into the kitchen. They stood there for a few moments in total silence, just staring at each other.

"What are you thinking?" Alex asked.

"I'm thinking this is uncomfortable," Conner said. "This is more uncomfortable than the time I walked in on you and Mom talking about training bras."

Alex rolled her eyes and peeked into the other room at Bob, making sure he couldn't hear them. "Honestly, Conner, I don't think we have any power over this. It was really nice of Bob to act like we're a part of the decision, but you just heard what he had to say and you heard what Mom said last night. I don't think anything is going to stop them from being together."

Conner sighed and ran his fingers through his hair.

"You're right," Conner said. "But who knows if Mom is even going to say yes? Maybe she'll have reservations about it?"

"Reservations about what?" Alex asked. "She loves him and he loves her. What's going to stop her?"

Conner looked away from her, not wanting to say what he was thinking, but they were both thinking it.

"Dad's dead, Conner," Alex said. "He's not coming back no matter how much we want him to."

It was hard for Alex to be so frank. Usually she let the adults in her life dish out the tough love, but since they were slowly disappearing, she had no choice but to serve it up herself.

Conner knew she was speaking to herself as much as she was speaking to him. Alex had a talent for saying everything he didn't want to think.

"I suppose Mom has given us so much over the years, our blessing is the very least we could give her," Conner said.

"Yeah, it is," Alex said and nodded. "This is another big one."

"Another big what?" Conner asked.

"A big moment," Alex said and sighed. "We've had a lot of them."

"Yeah, we have," he said. "You'd think we'd be immune to it by now."

"Immune to *life*?" Alex asked. "Is anyone ever that lucky?"

Conner grunted and put his hands on his hips. "Fine," he said. "He can marry Mom, but I'm still calling him Dr. Bob."

The twins returned to the other room. Bob anxiously stood and faced them.

"Well?" he asked with bated breath.

"The jury has spoken," Conner said. "Alex and I have decided you may ask our mom to marry you."

Bob joyfully clapped his hands together and tears came to his eyes. "Guys, you've made me the happiest man alive!" Bob said. "Thank you! I promise to take care of her for the rest of her life!"

Buster barked and jumped up and down, joining in on the celebration.

"Where are you going to do it?" Alex asked him.

"How about here, over dinner maybe?" Bob said. "I'll order food from her favorite restaurant and surprise her when she gets off work."

"When?" Conner asked.

"The sooner the better," Bob said. "I'm free next Thursday night. How about then?"

"I have class in the afternoon but I'll be home by six," Alex said.

"Great, then it's settled!" Bob said. "I'll propose next week on Thursday night at six o'clock! I'll ask a few of the nurses to keep your mom busy so she doesn't get home early and ruin the surprise. This is going to be terrific!"

The twins were looking forward to it. Not the event itself, but a chance to see their mom happy again.

"Hey, Bob," Conner said, "are you going to move in with us? Usually married people like to live with each other—for the first couple months at least."

"That's a good question," Alex said. "Where are we going to live?"

"My house?" Bob said and shrugged his shoulders. "Before she died, my wife and I bought a big house not too far from here, thinking we were going to raise a family. It'd be nice to finally fill all those rooms up."

The twins looked around their small rental house. The thought of leaving it made them feel sad; it had unexpectedly become home over the years.

"It'll be weird to move again," Alex said. "But easy since we never actually finished unpacking last time."

"I've got a swimming pool," Bob said, trying to cheer up the twins.

Conner's eyes grew big. "Whoa, whoa, whoa," he said. "Bob, you could have saved yourself an entire afternoon if you had just started with 'swimming pool.'"

Alex rolled her eyes. Bob let out a soft chuckle.

"Now Mom better say yes or *I'm* going to be so disappointed," Conner said.

It was hard for the twins to focus on anything the following week. The looming Thursday stood out like a bookmarked page in their future. The closer it got, the more anxious they became.

Alex and Conner didn't know why they were so nervous; after all, *they* weren't asking anyone to marry them. But in a strange way, Bob was marrying them, too. And as apprehensive about it as they were, the twins started to feel excited about Bob joining their family.

Conner was really looking forward to having another man around the house. As much as he loved his mom and sister, he missed having someone else there who appreciated the comedy in a bodily function.

He wrote a short story in his English class that week about a family of trolls whose mother was engaged to an ogre. It wasn't the most flattering depiction of any of them, but it was quite therapeutic for him. He drew little sketches in the margins of his paper; the troll children looked very much like him and his sister. The one based on Alex even had a headband in front of her horns.

Alex found Conner working on the story one afternoon after school. She had never seen him look so devoted to something before.

"What's this?" Alex asked him.

"Oh, it's nothing," Conner said, a little embarrassed. He still hadn't talked to her about his meeting with Mrs. Peters. "It's just some creative writing for English."

"That's nice—*wait*, is that supposed to be me?" Alex said and pointed to his sketch.

"Not at all," Conner said. "What would make you think that?"

"Because it says 'supposed to be Alex' underneath it!" she said, annoyed and offended. "That's so rude, Conner. How old are you?"

Conner guiltily looked up at his sister. "There's something I forgot to tell you," he said. "I've sort of been writing about the two of us a lot in my English class."

"What do you mean?" Alex asked.

"About our adventures in the fairy-tale world," he said. "They've made for some great stories—that's why Mrs. Peters called me into her office the other day. She really liked them and wanted me to consider being a writer. She said I may have what it takes, whatever that is." He paused. "Thoughts or concerns?"

Alex blinked twice. "I think that's a wonderful idea!" she said, and Conner sighed with relief. "Why didn't you tell me sooner?"

"I was worried you wouldn't want me spreading our business around," Conner said. "You're kind of the co-owner of our experiences."

"On the contrary," she said. "I think they *should* be told.

We saw so many things and met so many people it would be a waste to keep them to ourselves. Dad would be so proud of you."

Conner smiled to himself. He hadn't thought about that.

"Really?" he asked. "You think so?"

"Absolutely," Alex said. "He'd be so happy the storyteller gene went to one of us. I've always tried telling and retelling stories, but you're so much better at it than me. You're funny; people like listening to you."

Conner shrugged. "Aw, shucks," he said. "But I'm not going to argue." He pulled out the stack of his stories to share with her. "*This* one is about Trix's trial and this one is about Trollbella giving freedom in exchange for a kiss—wish I could forget about that. *This* was my first one, about the Curvy Tree, but I was super paranoid people would find out it was true so I changed it to the Curvy Giraffe. It doesn't make as much sense, but oh well, I'm learning."

"This is great, Conner," Alex said. "*Really* great."

Conner grinned from ear to ear. He believed her much more than he believed Mrs. Peters. Her approval gave him the validation he needed to believe in himself.

Alex flipped through her brother's stories. She smiled and laughed as she scanned through them, remembering the events they were based on.

"Oh dear," Alex said, looking up from the papers, a fresh thought behind her eyes. "*Bob.* Are we going to tell him? Are we going to tell him who Grandma and Dad really are?"

Conner couldn't answer. The thought hadn't crossed either

of their minds until now. How were they going to share their family's biggest secret with him?

"*Should* we tell him?" Conner asked.

"We probably should in case Grandma ever shows up with an elf or a fairy on our doorstep," Alex said.

Conner looked off into the distance. "Gosh, *who are we*?" he said. "What other family has a problem like this? Most skeletons in the closet don't have wings."

"I imagine he'll have a lot of questions either way," Alex said. She let out a long sigh. "But it's not like it's really relevant anymore. It may be pointless to tell him we have ties to another dimension if we don't get to interact with it ever again."

"Guess we'll just have to play it by ear," Conner said. "It may be a good excuse to have in our back pocket for when we get older. We could tell Bob we're going to the fairy-tale world and then go to a party instead."

Alex tilted her head and looked at him curiously. "Why would we ever choose a party over the fairy-tale world?"

Conner shook his head. Just for once he wished his sister would think like a normal teenager. "I keep forgetting you're an eighty-year-old trapped in a thirteen-year-old body," he said. "Never mind."

The end of the week slowly arrived and the twins woke up to a beautiful Thursday morning. They gave their mom extra-long hugs just before they left the house, causing her to raise a suspicious eyebrow at them as they headed to school. Alex and Conner felt like the day passed by extra slowly. They glanced up at the clock every five minutes only to be disappointed it hadn't changed much. As soon as school ended, Conner ran home and met Bob at the house to help prepare for the night. He cut corners over his neighbors' lawns and was so careless he nearly tripped over a lawn gnome.

Alex was too antsy to enjoy her honors course or be sleepy on the train ride back. She just wanted the night to be perfect for her mom. And from the looks of things when Alex finally got home, it was going to be pretty close.

The kitchen table had been covered with a silk cloth and there were candles placed in the center. A bottle of champagne and a bottle of cider were on the table as well, begging to be opened for a celebration. The whole house smelled delicious, as Bob had picked up food from Charlotte's favorite Italian restaurant.

He was dressed in a nice suit and tie and held the box tightly in his hand, afraid to let it go. Even Conner had dressed up, putting on his best button-down shirt.

Alex tried putting a bow on Buster's collar, but he wouldn't let her. The dog had been acting strange for a couple days. He stayed seated by the front door and growled at it occasionally. The twins figured a new cat must have moved into the neighborhood, or maybe their jitters were rubbing off on him.

But aside from the dog, everything seemed to be going according to plan.

Alex ran up to her bedroom and dressed in a skirt and her nicest headband. She came downstairs at half past six and joined Bob and Conner at the table.

"Mom should be here any minute!" Conner said. "Let's make this proposal quick, Bob, I'm starving!"

"I'll do my best," Bob said. He kept looking down at the ring. As excited as the twins were, they knew it was nothing compared to what Bob was feeling.

They couldn't wait for her to walk through the door and see them waiting for her. Alex hoped her mom wouldn't cry too much, because then *she* might start crying. Conner hoped Alex wouldn't start crying because then *he* might start crying and there was no dust to blame it on.

Unfortunately, Charlotte was running late, so the three of them were forced to wait. They waited...and waited...and waited some more. More than an hour had passed after the time she was supposed to be home.

"Should we call her?" Conner asked. "Maybe we should give her a *ring* to see where she is? Get it? Get it?"

"No, don't," Alex said. "She can't suspect a thing!"

After another hour the twins' anticipation turned to anxiety. Bob decided to put the food away so it wouldn't go bad.

"I guess Nurse Nancy is being very thorough," Bob chuckled. "She's probably making sure your mom doesn't get here too early."

But the twins weren't laughing. The last time they'd waited this long for a parent, they'd lost one.

"I'm going to give Nancy a call," Bob said after even more time had passed, and he dialed his colleague at the children's hospital. "Hello, Nancy? Hi, it's Bob. I'm here with the kids; has Charlotte left yet?"

Alex and Conner leaned toward him. They could barely make out what Nancy was saying on the other line. From what they could hear, she sounded surprised.

"She left two hours ago?" Bob said into the phone. "Are you sure? We haven't heard anything from her."

Alex and Conner exchanged fearful looks.

"Something's wrong," Alex said. "I can feel it. Something's happened."

"Mom is never late like this," Conner said, shaking his head.

"Okay, thank you, Nancy, I'll try calling her," Bob said and hung up the phone.

He quickly dialed Charlotte's number next. He didn't make eye contact with the twins, not wanting to add to their concern with his. Bob tried calling several times with no luck.

"She's not answering, guys," Bob said. "Do you think she spontaneously decided to run any errands tonight?"

Alex, worried sick, burst into tears. "We need to call the police!" she said.

"The police wouldn't do anything unless she's been gone for forty-eight hours," Bob said. "Let's not panic just yet."

Conner jumped up from the table and paced around the room. "There's got to be something we can do," he said.

"I'm going to get on my bike and go looking for her," Alex said.

"I'll go with you!" Conner announced.

"Nobody's going anywhere," Bob said calmly, although the twins knew he was just as stressed out as they were. "We've tried calling the hospital and her phone. Let's wait for a few more minutes in case she tries to call us back." Alex's tears began to flow faster the more she worried, and it was impossible not to. The twins feared that history, *their* history, was repeating itself.

Buster suddenly started a barking frenzy. He was staring intently at the front door, jumping up and scratching it, growling as loudly as he possibly could. The twins had never seen him like this before.

"Buster, what is it, boy?" Bob said. "Is someone at the—?"

The doorbell rang. All of them, including the dog, completely froze. It rang twice before any of them moved.

"Who could that be at this hour?" Bob asked and went to answer the door. The twins followed him into the doorway. They almost wished he wouldn't answer it. Whatever or whoever it was, it was too late to be anything good.

Buster began another barking and jumping fit. "Buster, get down, boy," Bob told him.

The dog backed away from the door and stood directly in front of the twins, protective of them. He was ready to pounce on something in an instant if he didn't like the looks of it. Was he sensing something they couldn't?

Bob looked back at the distressed twins. "It's going to be all right, kids," he said calmly. "Whatever happens, just know it's all going to be okay."

Bob slowly opened the front door and peeked out onto the porch. It seemed empty.

"Hello?" he said.

Still, there was nothing and nobody to be found.

"Hello?" Bob tried again. "Is anyone out there—?"

"Seize him!"

In a split second, a dozen soldiers dressed in silver armor barged through the door. One slammed Bob hard against the wall. Alex screamed. Conner grabbed her arm and they tried to run to the other side of the house, but the soldiers formed a tight circle around them and Buster.

Their swords were drawn and they held heavy shields with small glass slippers displayed on the outside crest. The twins recognized the soldiers immediately—they were from the Charming Kingdom—but what in the world were they doing here?

"Get your hands off of me this instant!" Bob yelled, struggling under the soldier's restraint. "Get away from those kids! Who are you people?!"

"We've securely surrounded the twins," the soldier closest to Alex called to the open front door. "Bring in the Fairy Godmother."

Alex and Conner looked to each other so fast they could have hurt their necks. *"Fairy Godmother?"* they said in unison.

Two other soldiers quickly charged into the house, led by none other than their grandmother.

"Grandma!?" the twins gasped together. They almost didn't believe their eyes.

She looked exactly the same as she did the last time they saw her. She was dressed in her long sky-blue robe that sparkled like the night sky. Her hair was styled up, with beautiful white flowers in it. She raised her crystal wand authoritatively as she walked into the house; the twins had never seen her look so worried.

"Oh, thank heavens," Grandma said.

The soldiers parted their circle for her and she threw her arms around Alex and Conner.

"You have no idea how happy I am to see you," Grandma said, hugging them so tight they felt like they'd pop.

The twins didn't hug her back. They couldn't believe they were seeing her in real life. Their heads were spinning with so many questions, but they only managed to spit out the basics.

"Grandma?" Alex said. *"Is it actually you?"*

"Where have you been?" Conner said.

Their grandmother gently placed a hand on each of their faces. "I'm sorry I've been gone for so long," she said sorrowfully. "I promise to explain everything later."

She took a moment just to look at them through teary eyes. They knew she had missed them as much as they had missed her. "Just look at you two—you've both grown a foot since the last time I saw you," Grandma said.

Just then, a familiar man walked through the front door. He had a distinguished jawline and wore a bright yellow suit. To Bob's amazement, the man's shoulders and his hair were actually on fire. The twins recognized him instantly; it was Xanthous, the only male fairy on the Fairy Council.

"I checked around the property," Xanthous said. "It's clear."

"Xanthous?!" Alex said. "What's he doing here?"

Bob fought restlessly under the soldier pinning him to the wall. *"What is going on?!"* he yelled. *"Who are you people?"*

Grandma raised her wand in his direction. Xanthous

pointed a few fingers at him and his whole hand suddenly lit on fire. Both were ready to fight if necessary.

"Do you know this man?" Xanthous asked the twins.

"Yeah, that's Dr. Bob," Conner said. "Don't set him on fire! That's our mom's boyfriend!"

"Boyfriend?" Grandma said and lowered her wand. "Well, I must have been gone for longer than I thought!"

"Release him," Xanthous ordered and lowered his hand. The soldier immediately dropped his hold on Bob.

"This woman is your grandmother?" Bob asked the twins. "Is she a part of the circus or something? What's with all the tricks and costumes?"

"What on earth is a *circus*?" Xanthous said, unsure whether he should take offense.

Alex and Conner didn't know where to begin.

"Bob, it's a long story," Alex said.

"In a nutshell, our grandmother is Cinderella's Fairy God-mother from the fairy-tale world," Conner said. "I know it's a lot to process, so take your time—but we promise that's the only baggage our family has got."

Bob's eyes grew bigger and he glanced at the soldiers, at their grandma, and at Xanthous.

"Uh-huh," Bob grunted, not convinced.

Their grandmother looked around the living room, gravely concerned. "Where's your mother?" she asked.

"We don't know," Conner said.

"She was supposed to be home a few hours ago," Alex said.

"Grandma, what's wrong?" Conner asked. "Do you know where Mom is?"

Their grandmother didn't answer, staying deep in thought.

"Grandma, what's happening?" Alex demanded. "We haven't seen you in over a year—why have you suddenly shown up out of the blue? You have to tell us what's going on. Where's our mom?"

Their grandma looked back and forth between them. "Children, what I'm about to tell you is going to seem very frightening," she said. "But I need you to be strong and trust that many qualified people are handling the situation."

The twins nodded impatiently. Any news was better than no news.

"I believe your mother has been kidnapped," their grandmother informed them.

They were wrong; having *no news* was much better than knowing this.

CHAPTER SIX

POSITIONING THE GNOMES

Alex and Conner stopped breathing. They felt like their hearts had fallen out of their bodies.

"What?" Alex asked.

"Kidnapped?" Conner gasped. "What do you mean, 'kidnapped'?! *By who*?"

Alex covered her mouth in horror. Conner frantically shook his head from side to side, not wanting to believe it.

Who would want to kidnap a nurse who worked at a children's hospital? How much danger was she in? The situation must be bad if soldiers and fairies from another world were standing in their house.

Their grandmother closed her eyes tightly. "I don't have time to explain," she said softly.

Conner turned bright red. "What do you mean you don't have time to explain?!" he shouted. "You give us *that* information and expect us not to have questions?"

Their grandmother looked down at them sternly. "I'm expecting you to trust that I am handling it to the best of my ability," she said.

"We're not children anymore, Grandma! You have to tell us what's going on!" Conner said. He had never had a reason to raise his voice to her before in his life.

"I know that, and that's why I'm being honest with you— you deserve to know the truth. There is much to discuss later, but right now, the less you know, the better. Is that understood?" Grandma said.

They didn't respond, because they *didn't* understand or agree one bit.

Buster barked up at the Fairy Godmother. Oddly, he hadn't been fazed by the newcomers in their home.

"Grandma, please, we need to know what's going on—" Alex managed to say through her tears.

"It'll have to wait. Right now I need to speak with Sir Lampton," Grandma said.

"What does he have to do with anything?" Conner asked, remembering the friendly head of Cinderella's Royal Guard he and his sister had met in the fairy-tale world.

Grandma bent down and looked into Buster's uneven eyes, and the dog sat straight up. The twins had never seen him look so obedient.

"Sir Lampton, have you seen anything strange or out of the ordinary?" Grandma asked.

Conner glanced over at Alex. Had their grandmother lost her mind? Did she forget dogs couldn't talk in their world? And why on earth was she calling him Sir Lampton?

Buster barked a single bark at her and nodded, as if he had understood perfectly.

"Oh, forgive me," Grandma said apologetically and waved her wand toward the dog. *"Speak."*

A flash of light traveled from the tip of her wand and into the dog's mouth. Buster began barking, but the sound slowly morphed into the sound of coughing—*human coughing.*

"Pardon me," the dog said. "My word, it's been a long time since I've had to pronounce anything."

Both of the twins gasped. They weren't strangers to talking animals, but hearing their own dog suddenly speak left them completely flabbergasted.

"Nothing out of the ordinary at all," the dog said. "Charlotte left for work this morning and hasn't been home since."

"Sir Lampton?" Alex peeped through the hands covering her mouth. *"Is that you?"*

"You're our *dog*?" Conner said.

"Indeed, children," the dog confessed and lowered his head. "I'm sorry I couldn't reveal my identity to you. Your grandmother wanted someone looking after you but thought having a soldier living in your house would cause you to worry, so she turned me into a dog."

Conner turned to his sister, reddening by the second. "We can't even have a *dog* without it being a magical conspiracy!"

"It's been very challenging," Sir Lampton said. "Dog food and cleaning oneself are some things I don't think I will ever get used to. And the urges to taste and smell *absolutely everything* are quite bothersome. But for you two, I would walk to the ends of the earth."

It was a sweet sentiment from their late father's old friend, but the twins didn't have any room for gratitude in their heads.

"Did you know about this, Bob?" Alex asked.

Bob had been so still the twins had almost forgotten he was there. He had turned a pale shade of green and was holding his stomach. It was clear by the horrified look on his face he had nothing to do with it. This was the first talking animal he had ever seen.

"I hope you can forgive me for casting a little spell on you at the shelter, but I had to make sure you chose Sir Lampton to bring home," Grandma said. "I thought you were just a friend of Charlotte's; I had no idea you were so . . . *involved*."

"I . . . I . . . I . . ." Bob muttered. *"I think I'm going to be sick!"* He ran straight for the bathroom on the other side of the house. Obviously, Bob had reached his surprise limit for the night.

"So this whole time we thought we had a dog when really we had a babysitter?" Alex asked, trying to wrap her head around it.

"A protector, not a babysitter," Grandma said.

"A protector from what?" Conner asked.

Their grandmother and Sir Lampton looked at each other. The twins knew they were set on keeping as much information from them as possible without being dishonest.

"I promise to share with you the appropriate information

as I learn it," Grandma said. "It's a concerning time in the fairy-tale world and it's kept me very occupied. The situation recently reached a peak and I was worried it would affect you, so I made the proper arrangements to make sure you were protected. Unfortunately, it seems your mother has fallen victim to it."

"Speaking of precautions, Fairy Godmother," Xanthous interrupted, "we should position the gnomes while the neighborhood is empty."

"Gnomes?" Conner mouthed to Alex.

"Very well," Grandma said and looked to the other guards she had entered the house with. "I'd like you to take the first shift watching the inside of the house. The rest of you, please follow me outside so I may place you."

Grandma and Xanthous quickly led the soldiers outside to the front lawn. The twins followed closely behind them, with Sir Lampton at their feet, and watched from the porch. Even though they knew she was a veteran leader of the fairy-tale world's Happily Ever After Assembly it was still strange watching their small grandmother give orders to the large soldiers.

"Take your places," Grandma instructed.

The soldiers positioned themselves on the perimeter of the Baileys' front yard. Their house looked like a miniature Buckingham Palace. The Fairy Godmother waved her crystal wand and one by one turned each soldier into a lawn gnome with a bright flash. They all had pointed red hats and white beards.

"They look just like the gnomes in our neighbor's yard," Conner said. "I almost tripped over one today."

"That was a soldier, actually," Sir Lampton said down by

his knee. "He's been watching the outside of the house for a couple of months."

"Creepy," Conner said.

"What's going on out here?" said a sweaty and green-faced Bob, stepping out of the house. "Where'd all the soldiers go—and where'd all those gnomes come from?"

"You just answered your own question, I'm afraid," Alex said.

Bob's eyes darted around the front lawn as he understood. The twins felt sorry for him; in less than an hour he had discovered his girlfriend had been kidnapped and had ties to the fairy-tale world. But overall, they thought he was handling it well.

"After the fourth time I vomited, I realized I wasn't dreaming," Bob said. "I have no history of mental illness in my family, so my best self-diagnosis is that *it's just one of those nights.*"

"Don't worry, Bob, the shock wears off eventually," Conner said to him. "I think—Alex and I have only known for a year and we're still waiting."

Grandma walked back to the porch with Xanthous, giving him careful instructions as they went.

"The soldiers may be an eyesore for the neighbors, but at least they're disguised," she said. "I want you to stay here and watch over the twins. No one is to enter or leave this house without my permission."

Alex and Conner only heard the tail end of their conversation but it was enough to infuriate them.

"What do you mean no one can come or go?" Conner said. "We're going to be stuck in our own home?"

"Until it's safe," Grandma said.

"But I have to work," Bob said. "I have patients and surgeries to attend to. People need me."

Grandma thought on this for a few moments. "You may come and go as you wish," she said. "With all due respect, it's my grandchildren I'm worried about."

"What about school?" Alex asked.

"You can go back as soon as everything has settled down and we figure out where your mother is, but for right now we can't risk it," Grandma said. "The less contact with the outside world, the better off you'll be. I'll write to the school and tell them you've both fallen terribly ill."

"You can't lock us up!" Conner yelled—loud enough for the whole street to hear.

"We haven't done anything wrong!" Alex shouted. *"Why are you punishing us like this—"*

Their grandmother waved her wand at each of them and they went silent. They tried speaking but no sound came out; she had magically muted them.

"Please obey my instructions," Grandma said. "Even with several soldiers, Xanthous, and Sir Lampton watching over you, I'll be worried sick."

Grandma looked down at Sir Lampton.

"I'd like for you to stay a dog for the time being," she said. "The gnomes will attract enough unwanted attention as it is."

"Yes, ma'am," Sir Lampton said with reluctance—he had been quietly hoping his dog days were over.

"Now, I must be going," Grandma said. She waved her wand and the voices of her silenced grandchildren returned.

"So that's it, then?" Conner said. "For a year we hear nothing from you and now suddenly it's, 'Hey, kids, your mom's been kidnapped and, oh yeah, I'm putting you both on house arrest'?"

"I never thought you could do something like this to us, Grandma," Alex said and looked at her grandmother as if she was a stranger.

Their grandma took these comments to heart. She didn't like disappointing them, but unfortunately she had no choice—she could only do what she thought was best and hope they'd forgive her one day.

"I know you dislike me a great deal at the moment," their grandmother said. "But you're the only family I have left. You mean more to me than anything else in the world. One day when you have families of your own, you'll learn that there is no length you wouldn't go to to ensure their safety, even if they end up hating you for it."

She left them on the porch, in the hands of the others, and walked off into the night, slowly disappearing into soft, sparkly clouds.

"I love you both," she said sadly, and a second later, she was gone.

"We should get inside before anyone sees us lingering on the porch," Xanthous said.

He and Lampton escorted Bob and the twins inside. Whether the lockdown would last days, weeks, months, or years wasn't certain. But for the time being, the Bailey twins were prisoners in their own home.

The first few days of captivity went by very slowly for the twins. They couldn't eat or sleep; all they could do was worry about their mother. The question that haunted them the most, however, was *why* had she been taken?

How could their mother, a simple nurse at a children's hospital, have gotten involved in all of this? Why had their grandmother been taking such measures to protect her grandchildren in another dimension? Was their mother even in this world, or had she somehow been taken into the fairy-tale world?

Xanthous and Lampton were tight-lipped about the whole thing. Despite the daily pleas from the twins to tell them something—*anything*—they insisted no news was the best news.

Unfortunately, the twins' imaginations did little to soothe their distress. Were the Troll King and Goblin King seeking revenge on the twins for stealing their crown a year ago? Had the Big Bad Wolf Pack somehow resurfaced? Did it have something to do with the Evil Queen and her Magic Mirror?

The twins didn't have any answers and it was driving them mad.

Also testing their sanity was how crowded their home had become. Their rental house felt small with just three people and a dog, but now a dozen grown men had been added to the mix. The guest room had been filled with cots, and most of the downstairs looked like an army camp, with swords and shields and pieces of armor everywhere you looked.

Xanthous ran a tight ship while he looked after the Bailey home. He was very strict about the soldiers' shifts, making sure they rotated being gnomes and being in the house evenly. Meals were always served at precisely the same times every day. The twins were only allowed outside once a day, in their backyard, and only if Lampton was watching them.

Xanthous was very devoted to his duties, too. He spent every day glued to the window facing the front yard, and the twins never saw him sitting down for more than a few seconds.

Bob had been very kind and checked up on the twins every morning on his way to work. His stories of the sick children he was taking care of at the hospital were the only contact they had with the world outside, so they looked forward to it every morning.

The bags under his eyes were a clear indicator that he felt as helpless as the twins did. He also unsuccessfully tried getting information out of Xanthous and Lampton. At one point he tried bribing Lampton with a bright bouncy ball in exchange for Charlotte's supposed whereabouts, but it just offended him.

The twins tried making small talk with the soldiers they were practically living with, but it was apparent that they knew as little as the twins.

"Do you enjoy your time as a gnome every day?" Conner asked a soldier.

"It isn't altogether unpleasant," the soldier said with a shrug. "It gives me a lot of time to think."

"Speak for yourself," the other soldier said. "I had a pigeon sit on my head for four hours yesterday, and he left a present on me, if you catch my drift."

"Gross," Conner said.

"Can't you just turn back into a man and shoo it away?" Alex asked.

"I wish," the soldier explained. "We can only transform back if there's danger. Otherwise we'd all be shooing off pigeons and blowing our cover."

Alex and Conner made a mental note of this.

Later that night, the twins had just finished dinner when a bright flash came out of nowhere. The twins looked up, and floating down from the ceiling was a sky-blue envelope.

"It's from the Fairy Godmother," Xanthous said and flew up into the air to retrieve it—apparently a fairy didn't need wings to fly. He hovered in the air a few feet above the ground while he read it, keeping it out of the twins' sight.

Alex and Conner stood below him. Xanthous's eyes grew large as he read the note from their grandmother. "I see," he said when he was finished reading. He floated down and faced the twins.

"Your grandmother would like me to pass along some information to you," Xanthous said.

"Yes?" Alex asked. They were practically vibrating with anticipation.

"We believe your mother is in our world," Xanthous said. "That is all." He placed the envelope on his shoulder and the flames devoured it.

"Is that a good thing or a bad thing?" Conner asked, unsatisfied with the update.

"Neither, it's just information she'd like you to have at this time," Xanthous said.

The twins let out exasperated sighs. Knowing more almost made it worse.

Later that night, Alex pulled Conner into her bedroom to

speak with him privately. She turned up her radio so Lampton's canine hearing couldn't pick up what they were saying.

"Mom's in the fairy-tale world," she said to him. "You know what that means?"

"What?" Conner asked.

"It means I think Grandma may have lied to us," Alex said. "How else could Mom have gotten there without her knowing about it? Maybe she isn't the only fairy who's capable of traveling between worlds."

Conner nodded.

"I don't think Grandma lied to us," Conner said. "I think we're just mad at her right now so now we're trying to blame her for anything we can."

Alex rubbed her tired eyes. She knew he wasn't altogether wrong.

"Just a few days ago I was worried about Grandma and angry with Mom, and now I'm worried sick about Mom and furious with Grandma," Alex said. "It's crazy how fast things can change."

"Yeah, it is," Conner said with a sigh.

"How do you think Mom got there, then?" Alex asked him.

Conner thought on it for a good moment. "I wonder if there's more than one way to get into the Land of Stories," he said.

Alex's head jerked back up at him. She had spent so much time hugging books and trying to re-create their last portal, she'd never thought about other options.

"Like what?" Alex asked.

"I don't know," Conner said. "But if Grandma's storybook had the capability, I'm sure she would have created other ways over the years, right?"

"It would only make sense that she would have created other ways to come and go," Alex said, thinking out loud. "Not for her, necessarily, but for the other fairies she recruited to help spread the stories around our world—right?"

Conner's eyes widened and he pursed his lips.

"What's your question?" Alex asked him.

"I hate that you guys know when I have a question!" Conner said and then asked, "Are you sure there's no way you could make a portal on your own?"

Alex would have loved to believe that she was capable, too, but knew in her heart that if she was, she would have surely found a way by now.

"No, it was Grandma's magic," Alex said. "I just...I just..."

"Turned it on?" Conner asked.

"Right," Alex said.

"Then I wonder if Grandma has anything else we could turn on," Conner said.

Another thought dawned on Alex as soon as he said this. "And maybe that's why she didn't know where Mom was," she said, nodding to herself. "Maybe someone had gotten hold of something, like her storybook, and used it to get to Mom."

They looked to each other and small smiles appeared on their faces. They weren't smiles of happiness, but smiles of achievement. They knew they were on to something—they could feel it.

"But *who*?" Conner asked.

CHAPTER SEVEN

LOOSEY GOOSEY

The next evening the twins sat in the living room and watched the news with Lampton. He sat with his nose just a few inches away from the screen, completely mesmerized by it. His head was tilted and a single ear was raised.

"I must say, of all the technologies in this world I've been introduced to, this is by far my favorite!" Lampton said with a wagging tail. "The television is remarkable!"

"I've seen Magic Mirrors do much more impressive things," said Xanthous, perched by the window, devotedly watching the neighborhood. "Although one thing I think I definitely could do without is the *fire alarm*. If I set it off one more time, I swear I'm going to yank it off the wall and smash it into pieces."

"Well, with all due respect, being on fire in this world is never a good thing," Conner said.

Xanthous raised an eyebrow judgmentally and turned back to his window. The flames on his shoulders rose in spite.

A bright flash suddenly filled the room. The twins looked up, and floating down from the ceiling was another sky-blue envelope, just like the day before. Once again, Xanthous flew up to retrieve it and read the new note from their grandmother in midair, away from the twins' curious eyes.

When he was finished reading he placed it on his shoulder and let it burn away before returning to the ground.

"We're leaving," Xanthous said and immediately had the twins' full attention. "Sir Lampton and I are being called back into our world."

"Why?" Alex asked.

Xanthous took a moment to compose his response.

"The Fairy Godmother needs us there more than she needs us here," he put simply. "But don't worry, she's sending in a replacement to watch over you."

Conner grunted. "Oh, great," he said with a massive eye roll. "Who's going to babysit us now? Bingo and the tooth fairy?"

"No. Mother Goose is replacing us," Xanthous said.

Alex and Conner stared blankly at him and then at each

other. Was he being serious? Xanthous didn't seem like he had much of a sense of humor.

"What?" Xanthous asked them, with no trace of sarcasm. "I'm serious. She's flying in from Europe tonight."

"*The* Mother Goose?" Conner asked. "As in the 'Jack and Jill went up the hill' Mother Goose?"

"Yes, of course *that* Mother Goose," Xanthous said and looked at him as if he had lost his mind. "Is there any *other* Mother Goose?"

"What is she doing in Europe?" Alex asked.

"Someone has to continue your grandmother's storytelling work while she deals with the crisis at home," Xanthous said. "But I wouldn't mention Jack and Jill to her, unless you want to hear her talk about conspiracies all night. Mother Goose has always been a bit of a . . . well . . . *handful*."

Mother Goose was the only member of the Happily Ever After Assembly the twins hadn't met in the Land of Stories, so they were looking forward to finally meeting her. However, the woman they expected her to be and the woman she actually was were very different *geese*.

A little past midnight, the twins were awoken by Lampton's shouts.

"She's here! She's here!" Lampton called through the house. "Mother Goose is landing!"

The twins met in the hall, rushed down the stairs together, and followed Xanthous and Lampton into the backyard. They looked up into the night sky but didn't see anything but stars and the moon.

"I don't see anything," Conner said.

"Trust me," Lampton said with his ears raised. "I can hear her."

Suddenly, a large silhouette flew past the moon. A large object was zooming toward them. The twins squinted, trying to see what it was. The closer it traveled, the more clearly they could see, riding on the back of a gigantic white goose, none other than Mother Goose herself.

"I have to admit, when you said she was flying in tonight, I wasn't expecting this," Conner said.

"Easy, Lester! Slow down, boy!" Mother Goose shouted in a raspy voice. She yanked on the reins of her large bird.

They were approaching so fast, the twins and Lampton dove under a patio table, taking cover. Xanthous remained exactly where he was, not deterred in the slightest—he had seen Mother Goose land before.

The goose landed hard on the ground with such a thud the entire house shook behind them. It felt like a mini-earthquake.

"Good lord, Lester! You call that a landing?!" Mother Goose reprimanded the horse-size goose. *"Meteors make softer impacts than that, you stupid gander!"*

Lester rolled his eyes, or at least the twins thought he did. His webbed feet were planted deep into the lawn, and he struggled to pull them out.

Mother Goose was a short, stout elderly woman. She had curly gray hair under a pointed black pilgrim hat that had a silver buckle on the front. She wore a baggy green dress with a white ruffled collar, large boots, and thick aviator goggles around her eyes.

"Are we even in the right place?" Mother Goose said, looking around. "I can't find my map—this is why I need to install a GPS in the back of your head."

Her goggles made her eyes appear enormous and obviously impaired her vision because she didn't see Xanthous standing directly in front of her.

"Hello, Mother Goose," Xanthous said with the little enthusiasm he could muster. "You're in the right place. Welcome to the Bailey home."

"Xanny, is that you?" Mother Goose asked and took off her goggles. Her face was red, weather-beaten from the flight. "Oh, Xanny, I am so glad to see you! I was worried Lester had taken us to Tijuana again. He loves Mexico."

Xanthous cringed at the nickname. "Besides the landing, I hope the rest of your flight went smoothly."

Mother Goose hopped down from Lester with difficulty. "Oh, it was fine, it was fine," she said. "Except when the *future pillow stuffing* here bumped into a 747 over Pittsburgh. *Stupid bird.*"

Lester slowly shook his head. Obviously, he had a different side of the story.

"Those damn planes have gotten so big they don't leave much sky for the rest of us," Mother Goose said. "I should have never encouraged the Wright brothers—biggest mistake of my life!"

She did a few windmill stretches and the joints in her back cracked like fireworks. Alex, Conner, and Lampton cautiously climbed out from under the table and approached her.

"Mother Goose, let me introduce the twins," Xanthous began. "This is Alex and Conner—"

"Yeah, yeah, yeah—I've met the squirts before," Mother Goose said. She put her hands on her hips and looked them up and down.

"You have?" Conner said.

"It was years ago, when you were babies. I visited you with your grandma," Mother Goose told them. She pointed to Alex and then to Conner. "If memory serves me right, *you* never stopped crying, and *you* peed all over me when I changed your diaper." She leaned close to them, eyeing them seriously. "I let it slide the first time, but history better not repeat itself."

Alex and Conner both gulped; now they knew what Xanthous had meant. Mother Goose's serious face broke into a giant smile and she cackled loudly.

"Relax, kids! I'm just yanking your tail feathers!" she said. Mother Goose turned to Lester and pulled a large basket off the goose's back. "Carry in my luggage for me, would you, boy?"

She shoved the heavy basket into Conner's arms and he grunted under its weight.

"And you," Mother Goose said to Alex. "Would you mind fetching Lester a bucket of vegetables? He needs to eat after such a long flight. Just no broccoli; it gives him gas."

The goose looked at her with large eyes and an open beak— appalled she would give out such personal information.

"Don't look at me like that, Lester, it does!" Mother Goose said.

"You want *me* to *feed* him?" Alex said nervously and backed away from the oversize bird.

"Don't be afraid of Lester, honey," Mother Goose assured her. "He's all squawk and no waddle."

Xanthous and Lampton escorted Mother Goose inside the house. Conner lugged the basket behind them; it was so heavy he almost threw out his back. Alex went into the kitchen and tossed all the vegetables she could find into a large bowl for Lester.

Mother Goose looked around the Baileys' rental house. "Not bad, not bad."

"It's just a rental house," Conner said. "We've only been here a couple years."

"I stayed with the old woman who lived in a shoe long before she had it renovated," Mother Goose told him. "Trust me, after that, anything else seems like a palace. I'll never forget that smell."

"It's become a bit of a prison for us recently," Conner said.

"Young man, I've *visited* many prisons and *been visited* in many prisons—this is not a prison," she said. "Put my basket by the fireplace, would you?"

Conner dragged the basket to the fireplace as he was ordered. Mother Goose reached inside it and pulled out an enormous wooden rocking chair. Conner couldn't believe his eyes; it was so much larger than the basket. He wondered what else she had magically stuffed inside there.

Mother Goose took a seat in the rocking chair and kicked off her boots. Her feet were surprisingly small for someone who wore such big shoes.

"Xanny, would you light this thing for me, please?" Mother Goose asked and nodded to the fireplace.

Xanthous reluctantly flicked a hand in its direction. A ball of fire shot out of his index finger and onto the log in the fireplace.

"Thank you, Xanny," Mother Goose said. "I suppose I can't convince either of you to rub my feet?"

Conner and Xanthous just stared at her with a look that said *definitely not*. Mother Goose shrugged. "Sorry I asked," she said.

Alex returned from feeding Lester and joined her brother.

Another bright flash filled the room; this time there was no envelope, but a white door appeared in the middle of the room. Alex and Conner eyed each other, knowing that it led to the fairy-tale world. They were tempted to make a run for it, but knew they'd be stopped if they did.

"That'll be for us," Xanthous said to Lampton. "Are you sure you can handle this, Mother Goose? I've been keeping the soldiers on a tight regimen. Two of them must be on guard in the house at all times while the rest rotate resting and guarding the outside of the house—"

"Yeah, yeah, yeah—I know the drill," Mother Goose said, rocking in her chair. "This isn't my first rodeo, Xanny. I've been doing lockdowns since you were just a little matchstick. I'll keep the munchkins safe, don't worry."

"Very well," Xanthous said in a disgruntled tone. His flames flickered faster than ever. "Come along, Sir Lampton."

The dog ran over to the door. "Good-bye, children," Sir Lampton said. "Please stay safe. I hope to see you soon."

Xanthous opened the door for Lampton and he ran through it. Xanthous stepped inside but looked back at the twins before closing it. "Respect your grandmother's wishes," he said and closed the door behind him.

The door vanished and the twins felt more despondent than ever.

Mother Goose waited until they were gone and then began digging around in her basket.

"Where did I put my bubbly?" she asked herself. Her entire arm was inside the basket searching for it. "Here it is," she said and withdrew a large metal thermos. She took a giant swig from it and let out a satisfied *"Ahhh."*

Alex and Conner looked at each other out of the corners of their eyes and slight smirks appeared on their faces.

"What are you two smirking at?" Mother Goose asked them.

"Nothing," Alex said and dropped her smile.

"You're just not what we expected," Conner said, and his smile grew twice as large.

"And what's that supposed to mean?" Mother Goose asked with a raised eyebrow.

Conner shrugged. "I sort of always expected you to be, well, a giant goose in a bonnet reading nursery rhymes to small children," he said.

"That's a common misconception," Mother Goose said and took another swig from her thermos. "Sometimes Lester likes to dress up in my bonnets; it makes him feel fancy but it messes with my image. *Don't look at me like that, Lester! Don't do it if you don't want people talking about it!*"

Lester was staring in at her through the window from the backyard. His bill was wide open and his eyes were squinting. Then he made himself comfortable on the grass and went to sleep, embarrassed enough for one day.

"He's so sensitive," Mother Goose said.

"Where'd you find a giant goose?" Alex asked.

"I've had him for years," Mother Goose said. "I was

gambling with a couple of ogres in the Dwarf Forests and won a giant golden egg in a game of cards. I was so excited—thought I was rich! You can imagine my disappointment when he hatched out of it the next day."

"Wow," Conner said. He didn't know what was more interesting, the fact that Lester hatched out of a golden egg or that Mother Goose was a gambler.

"Oh well," Mother Goose said and took another swig of bubbly. "I've put him to work over the years. He's been my main source of transportation. I hate flying commercial planes, I get too seasick to travel on ships, and my driver's license has been suspended for years."

The more she drank, the heavier her eyes became and the looser her neck seemed to become, because her head began to swivel. She held the thermos up to the twins. "Forgive me, did you want some?" she asked.

"I don't think we're legally allowed to have whatever's in there," Alex said.

"Suit yourself," Mother Goose said.

Alex was starting to have serious reservations about her. Conner stared up at her in awe; she was gradually becoming his favorite fairy-tale character *ever*.

He looked inside her basket. "What else is in there?" Conner asked. "Are those passports?"

Mother Goose quickly shut the lid of her basket and stared at him. He let out an apologetic laugh.

"Sorry," he said. "I didn't mean to invade your privacy, just wondering why you have so many?"

"Look, kids," she said, peeved. "When you've lived as long as I have and have traveled as much as I do, you make some enemies along the way. I'm not like your grandmother; I don't get along with everyone. Some cultures and countries that I'll refrain from naming don't appreciate a strongly opinionated dame such as myself."

Mother Goose nodded confidently to herself and took another swig. Alex and Conner nodded along with her, afraid to disagree.

"Always have a plan B and a friend with bail, and you're guaranteed to never fail," Mother Goose said and took another drink. "That's my motto."

Her words were starting to slur and her eyes began to flutter as they grew heavier.

"Where were you in Europe?" Alex asked, desperately trying to change the subject.

"I was at a children's hospital in Romania, then stopped by an orphanage in Albania," Mother Goose said.

The twins looked at each other to see if the other had noticed, but she seemed to be rhyming the more she drank.

"What stories did you read to them?" Conner asked, stopping her from slipping into unconsciousness. He was so amused he didn't want it to end.

"I read them 'Jack and Jill,' 'Little Miss Muffet'—the usual; they were a tough crowd, thought I was delusional." She yawned but kept her eyes open, excited by the new topic. *"Muffet can sometimes be a bit of a diva, but she can't help her severe arachnophobia."*

There was no denying it; Mother Goose was in full rhyming mode.

"Cool," Conner laughed. "What about Jack and Jill? I've always wondered what they were *really* doing on that hill."

Alex elbowed him. Mother Goose sat up in her rocking chair. Conner knew whatever she was about to tell them was going to be good. Alex wasn't sure if she wanted to hear it.

"Jack and Jill went up that hill, for a supposed pail of water," Mother Goose said. *"Jack fell down, broke his crown, 'cause Jill pushed him—but no one caught her!"*

"No way!" Conner said with an intrigued smile.

Mother Goose bobbed her head up and down, sloppily nodding.

"Why did Jill push Jack down the hill?" Alex asked.

Mother Goose chuckled to herself. *"Jack is nimble, Jack is quick—but Jack can be such a—"* She stopped herself from finishing the thought, perhaps remembering she was talking to thirteen-year-olds. "I think I've had enough bubbly for one night. It's time for bed anyway."

Mother Goose put her thermos in her basket and shooed the twins off. Her head touched her chest, her eyes closed, and she fell into a deep sleep in her rocking chair. She snored like a grizzly bear.

"I like her!" Conner said with a goofy grin, climbing up the stairs to bed.

"She's quite the gossip, isn't she?" Alex said.

"Sure is," he said. "And she really lets loose after a few sips of whatever she was drinking."

Alex paused halfway up the staircase and looked back at

their sleeping caretaker. "Yeah, she certainly does...." She began forming a plan in her head.

Alex tossed and turned all night long, having the worst nightmare of her life. It started off as the same dream she had been having for months; she and her brother ran happily through the woods only to be kept outside of their grandmother's cottage. However, this time when they peered through the window they didn't see their grandmother, but their mother. She was crying and whispered, *"Help me!"* over and over until Alex woke up.

Alex was shaking and sweaty and began crying. For all she knew, it wasn't just a dream. Her mother could be in serious danger or seriously hurt.

Alex couldn't live like this anymore. She needed to find out what was going on by any means possible.

Later, when the rest of the house had woken, Alex went downstairs and found Conner, Mother Goose, and Bob having breakfast.

"Good morning," Bob said. "How'd you sleep?"

"I didn't," Alex said.

"Sounds like we had similar nights," Conner said, looking at her with bags under his own eyes.

"I'll pour you some cereal," Mother Goose said. She went into the kitchen and poured milk and cereal from a box of Mother Goose Grits. A cartoon illustration of a much happier and smiling Mother Goose was displayed on the box.

She placed the bowl of cereal in front of Alex. "Goose grits?" Alex said. "Should I ask?"

"Don't judge me," Mother Goose said. "I usually hate the depictions of me in this world—they're normally so degrading. But I tried having an open mind about this cereal when they came out with it, and I've been addicted ever since."

Alex shrugged and took a bite—it wasn't half bad.

"Mother Goose was just explaining to Bob all about the fairy-tale world," Conner said.

"Fascinating stuff," Bob said. He was eager to continue their conversation. "Correct me if I'm wrong, but you and the other fairies have been around for hundreds of years traveling between worlds telling stories to children in need?"

"That's it in a golden eggshell," Mother Goose said.

"So you must be thousands of years old," Bob said.

Mother Goose shot him a dirty look. "Hold your horses there, cowboy," she said. "Don't get me wrong, I'm older than dirt, but I'm not as old as you think. This world used to run much faster than ours. You've had so many different eras and periods: the Middle Ages, the Renaissance, the Enlightenment, the Industrial Age, and now the Modern Age.... We've only had three or so that I can recall."

"What were they?" Alex asked, keen on learning a bit of the fairy-tale world's history.

"Let me think," Mother Goose said. "We had the Dragon Age, the Age of Magic, and we're currently in the Golden Age. Well, it used to be the Golden Age until all this drama happened."

"The Dragon Age?" Conner asked excitedly. "You mean there were dragons in the fairy-tale world?"

"Tons of them," Mother Goose said. "It was a mess! Disasters and barbecues left and right! They're extinct now, kind of like your dinosaurs."

"Did you ever see one?" Conner asked.

"I used to wrestle them, long before I took up magic and storytelling," Mother Goose said with a boastful smile.

Conner squinted at her. "Are you pulling my leg?" he asked.

Mother Goose rolled up her sleeve and showed Conner a large burn mark on her forearm. "*This* isn't from cooking, kid," she said.

Conner just stared at her with an open mouth. He had never been so impressed by someone in his entire life, and Mother Goose milked the admiration for all it was worth.

"You were around for the Middle Ages and the Renaissance?" Alex asked. "You must have seen so many people and places!"

"I started the Renaissance, honey," Mother Goose said, like it was a tea party she had thrown.

The twins felt they were both being led on now.

"I did!" Mother Goose said. "It was just me, your grandmother, Rosette, Skylene, and Violetta back then. We were so bored in the human world that one night I threw a big party. We had a great time. Next thing I know, we come back a few decades later and all of Europe had copied us."

"Our grandma was there?" Conner asked.

"Oh, yes," Mother Goose said. "She was a lot of fun back then. After she had your father she became so *motherly*. That's how she got her title, the Fairy Godmother—from being so sweet and maternal to everyone." Alex and Conner exchanged a look. However upset they were with their grandmother, she still became more amazing the more they learned about her.

"You know," Mother Goose continued, "Leonardo da Vinci and I had a bit of a fling."

Alex gasped. "I don't believe you! Now you're making things up!"

Mother Goose rolled her eyes and looked directly into Alex's, serious as can be. "Why do you think he tried building that flying machine? He was trying to keep up with me and Lester. *Hey, Lester, tell these kids I dated Leonardo! They don't believe me!*"

Lester appeared at the kitchen window. He nodded, confirming the news for the twins. They were astonished.

"Of course, I didn't go by Mother Goose back then," she said. "My code name was Mona Lisa."

"You're the *Mona Lisa*?" Conner asked.

"*The famous painting?*" Alex asked.

"Why do teenagers always think people are lying to them? I've got no reason to be dishonest with you," Mother Goose told them. "Leo, as I used to call him, made me laugh. But that's apparent in my portrait."

Alex and Conner glared at her with their mouths hanging open. They didn't know what to believe anymore.

"Why did you have a code name?" Conner asked.

"I told you, I've got enemies!" Mother Goose said. "I've had several aliases over the years...Guinevere, Mona Lisa, Lady Godiva, the Goose Flu...those were all me. But now I just simply go by Mother Goose. It fits me the best."

Bob was just as bewildered as the twins were. There he sat, a man of education and science, slowly losing faith in everything he thought he knew.

"So you and the fairies have been spreading the same fairy tales all this time?" Bob asked.

"We spread them as they happen," Mother Goose said. "Our more recent history has had the biggest impact on this world—the stories of Sleeping Beauty, Snow White, Cinderella, blah blah blah—that's why we call it the Golden Age. Unfortunately, the more this world began to develop, the faster it seemed to go by in comparison to our world. We were afraid the stories would get lost over time, so we recruited a few people in this world to help us."

"Like the Brothers Grimm?" Bob asked, starting to understand.

"The Brothers Grimm, Hans Christian Andersen, Walt Disney..." Mother Goose listed. "But we stopped recruiting protégés and mostly do it ourselves these days. There isn't a time difference to be worried about anymore. And things became so calm in our world after the Happily Ever After Assembly was formed, we needed something to do."

"The Happily Ever After Assembly?" Bob asked.

"It's sort of like their United Nations," Alex said. "All the kings and queens signed a treaty to regulate peace."

"All the kings and queens, the Fairy Godmother, the Fairy Council, and I make up the assembly. We've watched over the treaty since it was created," Mother Goose said. "It's been working out really well. Our world has stayed pretty peaceful... well, until *now*, that is."

Mother Goose eyed the twins—she had been told she wasn't supposed to bring up the current situation.

Bob nodded slightly. "I think I'm starting to understand it all," he said. "Except one thing: You said there *was* a time difference between the worlds? What happened?"

Mother Goose gestured to the twins. "These two showed up," she said with a smile. "They were the first children born of both worlds and somehow linked them together. Magic works in mysterious ways, always has."

Bob looked over at the twins with an impressed grin on his face.

"We're kind of a big deal," Conner said.

Bob smiled at him. "Well, you *think* you know someone, right, guys?" he said with a wink.

Bob left for work within the hour and the twins began another day of moping around the house with only their worries to entertain themselves with. They had grown very tired of the same concerns rotating in their heads.

The next couple days weren't as tense as the last week had been. Mother Goose wasn't as strict as Xanthous, and it was a huge relief for the twins. The soldiers had to wake her in the middle of her naps to remind her of the "gnoming shifts."

Alex's spirits were raised by seeing how much Conner bonded with Mother Goose. The two became practically inseparable. During the day they would sit at the window looking at the front of the house and play pranks on the mailman (Mother Goose would wiggle an ear and magically move the mailbox whenever he would turn his back). After dinner, if they weren't watching professional wrestling, Mother Goose and Conner would play cards with the soldiers. She even taught him how to hide an ace in his sleeve.

Alex didn't fill him in on the plan that had been forming in her head for days. She already felt guilty enough breaking her grandma's wishes alone; she didn't want to drag her brother into it.

One night Conner went to bed early and Alex stayed up, keeping an eye on Mother Goose. She was sitting at the kitchen table, thermos in hand, reminiscing about the fairy-tale world with the soldiers. Alex could tell she was having a little too much fun, because her eyes were glazed over and she was slurring and rhyming her words.

"I haven't had this much fun since I was so very young—and used to rub-a-dub-dub with the three men in the tub!" Mother Goose laughed and passed her thermos around the table. The soldiers each took a long swig and their eyes began to droop, too, as time went by.

"Mother Goose, may I confess something to you?" one of the soldiers said sadly. "I was one of the king's men who tried to put Humpty Dumpty back together again. I know you were very close; I'm so sorry we couldn't help him."

Mother Goose's eyes filled with tears as she was reminded of her late friend and the night he had his tragic accident.

"Humpty and I sat on that wall, Humpty and I had such a ball," she said. *"Humpty had a fall, right there and right then, because poor Humpty couldn't hold his gin.* I miss that egg so much!"

Mother Goose buried her face into her hands and cried drunken tears for a few minutes.

She woke a few moments later, collected her thermos, and took a seat in her rocking chair by the fireplace.

She snapped her fingers and a fire appeared in the fireplace. She went to take one last swig from her thermos but was disappointed to discover she and the soldiers had drunk it all. This was the moment Alex had been waiting for.

She snuck into the kitchen and retrieved the bottle of champagne that Bob had brought the night of the proposal. Alex hoped she could put it to good use tonight.

Mother Goose began to doze off again in her rocking chair when she was startled by a loud *pop*. Alex opened the champagne bottle right behind her.

"Care for a refill?" Alex asked and gestured to the empty thermos Mother Goose held in a tight grip.

"Oh, that's very kind," Mother Goose said, a little discombobulated. She held up her thermos and Alex filled it all the way to the top and set the champagne bottle aside.

"You've got a heavy pour; you're my kind of girl," Mother Goose said and took her first sip. "This is good stuff. Are you sure it isn't being saved for anything special?"

"Bob was saving it for when he was going to propose to my mom, but that all went out the window when she was kidnapped," Alex said restlessly and took a seat on the floor next to Mother Goose's chair.

"Kids as good as the two of you shouldn't go through what you've been through," Mother Goose said sadly and lovingly stroked Alex's hair. Her eyes were sad but grew heavier and glassier with every swig of the thermos she took. Alex almost had her where she wanted her—*almost*.

"Conner and I have been through so much together, and we've always been capable of handling anything that came our way," Alex said. "So you can imagine why it's so frustrating not knowing anything. It doesn't matter how fast we had to grow up; we're still being treated like children."

A loud snoring sound came from Mother Goose; she had dozed off. Alex tapped her until she was awake again.

"Hmmm?" Mother Goose said with one eye open. "What were you saying, honey?"

Alex thought fast. Mother Goose was somewhere between consciousness and dreamland, and Alex wanted to take full advantage of it.

"You were just telling me about how bad it is in the fairy-tale world," Alex said, nodding her head a little too convincingly.

Mother Goose bobbed her head up and down. *"Things are bad to say the very least—vines and thornbush still cover the East,"* she said and then looked around in a daze. "I think I've had too much bubbly, the room is spinning—"

"That's terrible," Alex said and immediately refilled Mother Goose's thermos. "But surely the Happily Ever After Assembly can handle vines and thornbushes, right?"

Alex pushed the thermos in her direction. Mother Goose took another sip from it.

"The vines and thorns are not what's awful—it's the magic behind them that's too darn powerful," Mother Goose said. *"They tried finding her before she struck—we ran out of time and out of luck."* Her head fell to her chest and she dozed off again. Alex shook her awake. It was more difficult this time.

"I'm sorry, dear, I don't mean to keep falling asleep in the middle of your sentences," Mother Goose said. She was practically cross-eyed from exhaustion. "What were you saying?"

Alex thought quickly again. "I was just saying I hope you find her, whoever you're looking for," she said.

Mother Goose nodded. She gently touched the side of Alex's face. *"Don't fret on the idea—they'll soon find Ezmia,"* Mother Goose said.

Alex had never heard the name before. *"Ezmia?"* she asked. "Who is Ezmia?"

Mother Goose's eyes grew twice in size. If she hadn't been so intoxicated she would have sat straight up in her seat. Alex knew this was some of the information that was supposed to be kept from her and her brother.

"Oh dear," Mother Goose said and hiccupped. "Please don't tell your grandmother what I've said."

"I won't, I swear," Alex said. Mother Goose slumped with relief. "As long as you tell me who she is," Alex added.

Mother Goose tensed up as much as she could with all the bubbly in her system. "I can't. I promised your grandmother that I wouldn't say a word!" she said.

"Then don't *say* it; *rhyme* it," Alex said. She stood up and looked closely into Mother Goose's eyes, more desperate for information than ever. "I'm going to find out eventually. It's only a matter of time—so please just tell me, who is Ezmia?"

Mother Goose looked around the house to make sure they were alone and took one final swig from her thermos. She looked away from Alex and into the fire, not wanting to make eye contact with Alex while she gave up the information she had sworn not to give.

"For years the world presumed she was dead—her where-abouts were unknown and left unsaid. In the shadows she stayed, quietly plotting, a vengeful wrath she planned on igniting. Driven by rage and centuries of sorrows, a suppressed fear shall soon be tomorrow's. After failing to curse a princess's death, she's now set her sights on the world's last breath. 'Happily ever after' will be a thing of the past—for the evil Enchantress has returned at last...."

Mother Goose closed her eyes, not from fatigue this time, but from shame. Alex had hung on to every word.

"The *Enchantress*?" Alex asked, putting together the pieces of her rhyme. "The evil Enchantress who tried killing Sleeping Beauty is *back*?"

"Yes," Mother Goose said. "Her name is Ezmia, and she has your *mother....*"

Her chin fell on her chest and she went into the deepest sleep Alex had ever seen. Her snores filled the silent house.

Alex's eyes darted around the room. Her heart was racing. She had to catch her breath, because learning this information knocked the wind out of her. It was as if Alex's brain had switched to autopilot. She immediately ran up the stairs and into her bedroom. She dumped all the schoolbooks and supplies out of her backpack and piled in as many clothes as she could fit. She threw a sweater over her head and put on her running shoes.

Alex ran down the stairs and into the kitchen. She stocked all the food and necessities she knew she would need on a long trip: knives, matches, water bottles, etc. She wasn't even that careful passing by the soldiers who were passed out at the table.

Even if she was caught making a run for it, she was so determined, she didn't think anyone or anything could stop her.

She went out the front door and steered her bike off the porch and into the street. She glanced back at all the gnomes, and while they remained completely still, she knew the soldiers inside were anything but.

"I know you can't stop me, because I'm not in any danger," Alex called out to the gnomes. "Yet," she said under her breath.

She pedaled off into the night as fast as she could, knowing it'd only be a matter of time before one of the soldiers or Mother Goose came after her. Alex didn't have much of a plan, but she knew where she was headed; she was going to her grandmother's cottage in the mountains.

The trips her family used to take when she and her brother were small to visit their grandmother always took a couple hours by car, so she knew she had a long journey ahead of her by bike. But if there was any place she would find something of her grandmother's to "set off" or "turn on" that gave her an entrance into the fairy-tale world, she knew it would be there.

Alex took one final look back at her house before it disappeared. A little voice inside her head told her it would be a long time before she saw it again, but she welcomed the feeling. She didn't care what her grandmother's wishes were; Alex was going to find a way into the Land of Stories and save her mom—even if she died trying.

Chapter Eight

THE COTTAGE

Alex woke up in a grassy field the next afternoon. She looked around and grunted to herself. She had been riding her bike all night and had just stopped to rest for a moment off the road. Clearly, that moment had lasted a few hours longer than she'd planned.

She was in the foothills leading up to the mountains where her grandmother's cottage was. It had been a great while since the last time she and her brother had gone, so it was difficult remembering the exact directions. As the foothills slowly rose into mountain terrain, she stopped at a tiny gas station and purchased a map. Navigating became harder as the roads wound and forked up into the mountains. She glanced back and forth at the map as she continued, making sure she was traveling northeast. She remembered her parents used to drive northeast until there were no more roads to take.

Alex felt guilty for leaving her brother at home but hadn't wanted to drag him into her spontaneous plan. Although, when night fell and Alex was forced to set up a small camp off the road by herself, she really wished her brother were there, keeping her company.

She couldn't make up her mind if it was more dangerous to be traveling in the woods of the fairy-tale world or her world. Even though there were no Big Bad Wolves to be worried about, she was sure there were still regular wolves around.

But if she couldn't handle a simple wolf now, how was she going to take down a powerful Enchantress when she found her? She doubted swinging a big stick would scare off the woman who'd cursed an entire kingdom for one hundred years.

The more she thought about it, the less it made sense. What did this Ezmia woman want with her mother anyway? How did she even get to her mom in the first place? If the fairies couldn't find her or her mother, what made Alex think she could?

Alex and her brother knew more about the Enchantress than others gave them credit for. During their encounter with the Evil Queen they discovered that the Enchantress had kidnapped the Evil Queen when she was a girl and used her in a scheme to take over the fairy-tale world.

Alex lay on the ground, using her backpack as a pillow, and let her troubled thoughts wander until she finally fell asleep.

Alex was back on her bike before sunrise the next day. She biked across windy road after windy road until the middle of the afternoon. She jolted forward and almost fell off her bike when her front tire hit a particularly sharp rock and went flat.

"You've got to be kidding me!" she said and angrily tossed her useless bike to the side of the road. She would have to travel by foot for the rest of her journey—however long that would be.

Her spirits rose an hour or so afterward when she saw a wooden bridge on the road ahead. When Alex and Conner were younger, seeing this bridge meant they were almost at their grandmother's house. Alex knew she was close.

She jogged toward the bridge in relief, but the closer she got, the less familiar it appeared. It seemed so small compared to the one in her memories. Was it just because she was so much smaller then? Also disheartening was how decrepit the bridge appeared to be. Every piece of wood was chipped and rotting like crazy.

Alex took a couple of steps onto the bridge and examined it closer. It didn't feel right. A car could never fit on the bridge. She looked over the side. Several hundred feet below was a dry and rocky riverbed. The bridge her family used to drive over was only a few feet higher than the stream that ran under it.

Alex sighed. She was lost.

She turned on her heels and started to head back when she heard a sudden crack. Before she could tell where the sound was coming from, Alex fell straight through the bridge, rotten wood splitting under her feet.

She screamed and grabbed hold of the bridge. She desperately tried pulling herself up, but it was no use; she could hear the wood cracking from the pressure.

"Help!" Alex screamed. *"Somebody help me!"*

Alex didn't know who she was yelling to. As far as she knew she was alone in the mountains and she was about to fall to her death.

"No! No! No!" Alex said to herself. *"It can't end like this! It can't end like this!"*

She struggled to pull herself up again. Another loud crack sounded and she slipped further through the bridge and toward the rocky ground below.

Alex felt two hands grab hers just in the nick of time. She looked up and saw a very familiar face looking down at her. At first she thought it was her dad but then realized it was Conner—it was a strange moment to notice how much he had grown up.

His face turned bright red as he struggled to hold his sister with all his might. *"Now, Lester! Pull us up, buddy!"* he grunted.

Conner and Alex were slowly dragged upward. Once Alex was above the bridge again, she could see Lester's bill tightly clutching Conner's pants, dragging him up while he dragged her. The giant goose pulled them across the bridge until they were safely on solid ground again.

The twins and Lester stayed on the ground until they all caught their breath.

"I hate you so much right now," Conner said between heavy pants.

"That's funny, because I've never loved you more," Alex said with a big smile and rolled over to give her brother a big hug. "Thank you. I owe you one!"

"Luckily, with the amount of trouble we get ourselves into, I know you'll have a chance to make it up to me," he said.

Lester squawked at them as if to say, *"Don't worry about me, I'm fine!"*

"She owes you one, too, Lester, don't worry!" Conner said.

The twins stood up and brushed themselves off. They were covered in splinters and chips of rotting wood. Lester got to his feet, too, and stretched out his neck and bill.

"How did you know where I was?" Alex asked.

"Lucky guess!" Conner said. "You can't even run away like a normal teenager. You're supposed to leave a note! There was only one place I figured you were going. Lester and I had been flying around looking for you all day when we finally spotted your bike down the road."

"Does Mother Goose know where I am?" Alex asked.

"I've been covering for you since I realized you were gone. I told Mother Goose you were sick and were vomiting all over your room. Then, when she wasn't looking, I hijacked her goose and came looking for you," Conner said.

"How did you manage that one?" Alex asked.

"Well, apparently he feels taken for granted and thought by helping me it would teach Mother Goose a lesson," Conner said. "I don't speak goose or anything, but I'm guessing that's the gist of it, right, boy?"

Conner turned to Lester and the giant goose nodded.

"Why didn't you take me with you?" he asked angrily. "How could you leave me locked up at home? Are you trying to do things solo now or something? Not cool, Alex."

Alex lowered her head shamefully. "Because Grandma's going to be mad enough at me when she finds out I took off, I

117

didn't want to drag you into it," she said. "And I found out who has Mom! I pried it out of Mother Goose."

"So that's why you took off so abruptly?" Conner said. "Well, who has her?! What did you learn?!"

Alex now understood why her grandmother had kept information from them. She felt horrible knowing she was about to make her brother as stressed as she was.

"Apparently the Enchantress is back," Alex told him. "The Enchantress who cursed Sleeping Beauty is terrorizing the fairy-tale world again and she has Mom."

"What?" he said in disbelief. "What does the Enchantress want with Mom?"

"I don't know," Alex said. "I've been trying to figure it out and can't think of anything."

"Wait, I thought the Enchantress was dead," Conner said. "The Evil Queen told us that she poisoned her and she ran off and died. Remember?"

"I guess she was wrong," Alex said. "Ezmia is her name— and she's very much alive."

"And that's why we hadn't seen Grandma in so long?" Conner said.

"I suppose," Alex said.

Conner paced around the mountain road, thinking.

"We've got to get into the fairy-tale world," Conner said. "We have to save Mom."

"I agree, but what are we going to do when we get there? What can we do to save her that the fairies can't?" Alex asked.

"We may not be able to do anything," Conner said. "But

two more people *trying* couldn't hurt. Besides, it sure beats sitting around and waiting for bad news."

A small smile appeared on Alex's face; she couldn't have agreed more.

"Let's try to get to Grandma's cottage before sundown," Alex said. "Do you know where we are? Are we even close?"

Conner looked around at the mountains surrounding them. "Yeah, we're close!" he said and then pointed to a flat mountain peak in the distance. "Grandma's cottage is just on the other side of that mountain peak! I remember seeing it when we were little and hoping it was a volcano!"

"Are you sure?" Alex asked.

"Positive," Conner said. "Let's go. Lester, can you take us in the direction of that mountain peak?"

Lester cocked his head in the direction Conner pointed, let out an exaggerated sigh, and then nodded.

Conner climbed onto Lester's back, then offered his hand to Alex. "Climb aboard," he said.

Alex hesitated. "Are you sure this is safe?" she asked.

Lester squawked, rather insulted.

"You've got to try this, Alex," Conner said enthusiastically. "I understand why O.M.G. travels this way."

"O.M.G.?" Alex asked.

"Old Mother Goose," Conner said. "It's my nickname for her—she calls me C-Dog."

Alex shrugged and took his hand. She swung a leg over the large goose and held tightly to her brother's waist.

Conner gripped the reins, ready for liftoff. "Let's fly, Lester!" he said.

Lester spread his wings; his wingspan was much more impressive in the daylight. He took a few steps back and then bolted into a fast waddle forward, flapping his wings as he went, and they rose higher and higher into the air.

Conner was right, it was an incredible experience. The mountains seemed much more majestic from a bird's perspective. The twins had never felt so free in their lives.

"I hope no one sees us," Alex said, fearfully looking down at all the roads and tiny towns underneath them.

"I just hope it isn't goose-hunting season," Conner said.

Lester squawked and looked back at him, terrified.

"I'm just kidding, Lester," Conner said. "Relax before you lay an egg!"

Lester headed in the direction of the peak. A few moments later, they were flying over it. Conner was a little disappointed to see it was in fact a flat mountaintop and there was no sign of molten lava inside of it.

"Keep an eye out for the cottage," he told his sister. "It should be coming up any moment now."

Alex scanned the ground below. It was hard to see anything but treetops and the occasional chimney. She saw a familiar bridge and her eyes followed the winding road that crossed over it and through the woods ahead. At the very end of the road, she could make out the roof of a storybook cottage.

"I see it! I see it!" Alex said and pointed to it. "It's Grandma's cottage!"

Lester landed in front of the cottage just as the sun began

setting. Alex and Conner climbed off the goose and observed their grandmother's old home.

"Whoa," Conner said.

"It's definitely not in the same condition we left it in," Alex said.

It was obvious that no one had lived in the cottage for a long time. The front lawn was partially dead and overgrown in some places; the flower beds were full of weeds and blades of grass were almost as tall as the twins. Ivy grew up the sides of the cottage and part of the roof had caved in.

Their grandmother's blue car was parked outside but hadn't been driven in years. A layer of dirt covered it, and a city of spiderwebs had been spun between the tires.

Although the cottage was used mostly as a prop, since their grandmother only lived here when the twins visited, it still was the location of the twins' happiest childhood memories. They were sad to see how abandoned it was.

Alex and Conner approached the front door apprehensively.

"Lester, bon appétit," Conner said and gestured to the overgrown grass. Lester squawked and happily went to town on it.

"Do you think it's locked?" Alex asked.

Conner twisted the handle and the door creaked open, answering her question.

The twins stepped inside and surveyed the interior. It was exactly how they remembered it, except dusty and covered in cobwebs. Grandma's rocking chair was still by the fireplace and faced a large rug the twins used to lie on when she read to them.

"It's so strange to see everything again," Alex said. "Grandma's chair, the fireplace, the kitchen table—I almost can't believe it's been here this whole time."

"Do you remember the forts we used to build with Dad under that thing?" Conner asked, pointing to the table.

"How could I forget?" Alex asked. "You always tried keeping me out, but Dad never let you."

"You know what's funny?" Conner said as he walked around. "Even though we know now that Grandma never actually lived here, whenever I picture Grandma I always imagine her in this place, baking cookies or reading by the fireplace."

"Me too," Alex said. "Most of our childhood was a front, but it was a happy front."

"You think we'll find something that can take us to the fairy-tale world in here?" Conner asked.

"We have to," Alex said simply. But she had her doubts. She wasn't sure what she was searching for, but knew she'd know what it was as soon as she saw it.

Conner looked at all the dusty frames on top of the fireplace mantel. They were mostly pictures of him and his sister at birthday parties and holidays with their family. In one picture the twins were three years old and sitting on Santa's lap. Conner was very chubby and had a big grin on his face; Alex was crying hysterically.

"Check out this picture of us with Santa." Conner laughed. "You look like he's about to eat you."

"I was preparing myself for the other fictional characters that *did* try to eat us," Alex said.

Conner snickered and picked up another photo. "No way!

Look how young Mom and Dad look in this photo! I don't think we were even born yet."

Alex walked over and looked at it for herself. "Conner, we look just like them," she said. "There's no denying that they're our parents."

"You're right," Conner said. "I came up with a whole adoption theory when I found out we were part fairy. But looking at this picture kind of tosses that out the window."

Alex went back to searching, confident something would pop up at any moment.

"Have you found anything that seems portal-worthy?" Conner asked her.

"Not yet," Alex said. "Well, except for maybe *this*."

Alex was staring up at a beautiful painting on the wall. She remembered it from when she was little, and, unlike the rest of the cottage, the painting had remained just as vibrant. It was a watercolor painting of a pond and had beautiful shades of greens and blues.

There was something about it that seemed more familiar now, as if they had been there.

"You think the painting could take us into the Land of Stories?" Conner asked.

"It worked in one of the Narnia books," Alex said.

She stepped closer to the painting and placed a hand on its frame.

"It's the Ugly Duckling Pond!" Alex said, recognizing it. "This is it! This has to be our way in! Why else would Grandma hang a picture of a pond in her cottage?"

"You think you can get it to work?" Conner said.

"I can try," Alex said.

She placed both of her hands on the golden frame and tried to will it to life. Nothing happened. She closed her eyes and took a deep breath, willing it even harder. Still, nothing happened.

Conner clapped his hands loudly, breaking his sister's concentration. "Clap on!" he said.

"What are you doing?" Alex asked him.

"Just thinking of other ways to turn it on," he said. "Is there a remote control or an on switch somewhere? Maybe it's like a plasma screen."

Alex ignored him and went back to focusing. She imagined all the places and people she had met during her first visit. She imagined all the castles and forests she and her brother had seen. She imagined all the dangerous animals and creatures they had encountered. But mostly, she thought of how desperately she wanted to see them again. Alex thought of her grandmother, her father, and her mother. She thought of the pond in the painting, the lily pads, the fireflies, and of its *water*.

To the twins' amazement, the painting began to glow.

"You did it!" Conner said and hugged his sister. "You set it off!"

"I did?" Alex asked—it was almost too good to be true. *"I did it! I did it!"*

The twins jumped up and down with excitement, but their excitement quickly faded into fear. The painting began to glow brighter and brighter, and the cottage began to rattle. It felt like a large train was passing directly below them.

"Exactly *how* did the Narnia kids travel through the painting?" Conner asked, slowly stepping away from theirs.

"Uh-oh."

The cottage stopped shaking and the painting dimmed, only now the painted pond was gone—the canvas was completely blank.

"Huh?" Alex said. "That's strange."

"A bit of a relief, though," Conner said. "I was worried for a second that water was going to spill out of the—"

CRASH! A tidal wave of water crashed through the windows by the front door. The twins screamed and ran to the back of the cottage. *CRASH!* Another tidal wave came rushing toward them from the back. *CRASH!* Water was gushing through every door and window and flooding the cottage.

"What is going on?!" Conner yelled. *"Did we hit an iceberg?!"*

He described it perfectly: They felt like they were sinking—and sinking fast. They were already waist-deep in water. The twins looked around in horror as their grandmother's former home was destroyed.

"What have we done?!" Alex shouted.

"I've always wanted a pool, but this is ridiculous!" Conner yelled.

The water poured into the house faster and faster. The twins couldn't keep their feet on the floor anymore. They treaded water as it lifted them toward the ceiling.

"We've got to swim out of here or we'll drown!" Conner said. *"Follow me!"*

He took a deep breath and dove underwater. Alex was quick to follow him. They swam across the cottage to the front door. There was an extremely strong current coming through the door, so the twins had to grab hold of anything they could to force themselves against it.

They pulled themselves past the front door and discovered the cottage was no longer in the mountains but in a large, murky body of water. It sank below them and disappeared into the dark, watery depths. The twins grabbed hold of each other and swam as hard as they could to the surface—*praying there would be a surface.*

Finally they saw a distorted night sky above them; *it was the surface!* The twins surfaced in the mysterious water, gasping for air. The air was freezing against their faces.

"What was *that* all about?!" Conner yelled.

Alex wasn't paying any attention to him. She saw large trees in the distance, with giant roots that sank into the ground. Fireflies filled the air and lily pads floated on the water around them. She knew exactly where they were.

"Conner!" Alex said and excitedly splashed her brother. *"We're in the Ugly Duckling Pond! We're here! We're back in the Land of Stories!"*

CHAPTER NINE

THE GATHERING IN THE WOODS

Alex and Conner slowly crawled out of the pond. They were soaked, muddy, and covered in lily pads. They shivered in the cool night air and held themselves tightly as they looked at the land around them.

The Ugly Duckling Pond was in the middle of a forest in the Northern Kingdom. The twins had passed it on their previous trip into the Land of Stories, but neither had expected to become so *acquainted* with it on their next visit.

"I cannot believe we just sank Grandma's house!" Conner

said through chattering teeth. "It takes a lot of talent to submerge something that isn't even close to water!"

Bits and pieces of their grandmother's cottage were still floating in the pond. Her rocking chair bobbed up and down in the water. Alex was so amazed, she didn't even care how dirty or cold she was.

"I sure hope Grandma has really good house insurance— *Alex, are you even listening to me?*" Conner asked.

She turned to face him. The excitement was practically glowing in her eyes. She didn't care how they had gotten there; they were finally there and that's all that mattered.

"We're *here*. . . . We're actually *here*. . . ." Alex said. Even a trembling jaw couldn't take the smile off her face. Despite the circumstances, it was the first time Alex had been happy in months.

"Congratulations, you managed to successfully and dangerously transport us into the fairy-tale world . . . *again*," Conner said with a smile of his own. "I've got to say, I prefer Grandma's methods of transportation to yours."

Alex's smile disappeared as the reality of it set in. She surveyed the forest around the pond more closely. "Something's wrong," she said.

"Of course something is wrong!" Conner said. "Grandma's cottage is at the bottom of a pond! How are we going to explain that one to her?"

"That's not what I mean," Alex said. "Listen. Do you hear that?"

Conner raised his eyebrows and looked from side to side. The pond and the forest around it were dead silent.

"I don't hear anything," Conner said.

"Exactly," Alex said. "We're standing at the edge of a pond and there are no sounds at all—no frogs or crickets or anything."

Conner nodded, understanding what she meant. It was so eerie he was surprised he hadn't noticed it before. "It's like everything is on mute," he said.

"Or *hiding*," Alex said.

Suddenly, on the other side of the pond, a dark figure emerged from the trees. It startled the twins at first until they saw it was small, barely the size of a dog. It was running very fast on four skinny legs and had something white trailing behind it.

Alex and Conner hid behind the closest tree and watched it from afar. The strange creature slowed into a fast and springy walk as it delicately approached the pond. It was wearing a dark cloak and lowered its hood with its front paws before taking a drink from the water.

The moonlight reflecting off the water illuminated the mysterious visitor, and the twins could make out what it was. It had dark red fur, pointy ears, and a long fluffy tail with a white tip.

"It's a fox!" Conner whispered to Alex.

The fox jerked his head up from the water and his bright yellow eyes stared in their direction. He must have had impeccable hearing.

The twins stayed still. The fox headed for the trees, in the opposite direction from where he had come.

"Where is he going?" Alex whispered to her brother.

"Do I look like an expert in cloaked mammals?" Conner said. The fox disappeared into the trees, but besides being the only living thing they had seen, there was something very intriguing about him. Neither of the twins wanted to let him out of their sight. "We should follow him," Conner said.

"Why?" Alex asked.

Conner shrugged. "Do we have another plan we're supposed to be following?" he said.

"Good point," Alex said. And without another moment to waste, the twins began chasing after the small fox, hoping he would lead them to someone or something that would help them find their mother.

Alex and Conner ran after the fox for a good while. He wasn't sticking to a path, so it was hard to see him between the trees ahead. He was incredibly fast for his size, too, so it was difficult to keep up with him. They were happy to run and warm their bodies, though. Their clothes began to dry the more they went.

"It looks like we're going into the Dwarf Forests," Alex whispered as she jogged.

"How can you tell?" Conner asked.

"The trees are getting thicker and it's getting harder to see the sky," Alex said. "Also, I'm feeling more anxious the farther we run—that's the biggest clue."

Conner gulped. The Dwarf Forests had never been a good place for the twins. The last time they had been in this part of the Land of Stories they had been chased by wolves and kidnapped by goblins.

The fox came into view ahead and the twins came to a belated stop, like cars with bad brakes. They hid behind the biggest tree they could find and each gestured for the other one to be quiet.

The fox was standing on his hind legs next to a stone well in the middle of a clearing. The moon illuminated the clearing like a spotlight. The fox stood very still, keeping a close watch on the trees around him. He was waiting, but for what the twins couldn't tell.

At one point the fox looked directly at the twins' hiding spot but didn't appear to see them. The twins wondered if they blended in with the rest of the forest because they were so dirty or just because it was so dark.

It was unnervingly quiet in the Dwarf Forests, too. It was surprising, since the twins had remembered hearing all kinds of troubling sounds coming from close by and afar the last time they were here.

A few twig snaps echoed into the night as someone or something made its way into the clearing. The fox jerked his head in the direction of the snaps and smiled, exposing several tiny sharp teeth. A sly expression came to his face—the twins couldn't tell if it was because he was pleased or just because he was a fox.

Three cloaked figures stepped into the clearing. They were all different shapes and sizes: One was enormous, another was only a little bigger than the twins, and the third was as tiny as the fox. A large raven swooped into the clearing, perching on the well next to the fox. It didn't need a cloak; its dark feathers were enough to camouflage it in the night.

The others surrounded the well, all facing the fox. The fox rubbed his small paws together. "So glad you all could make it," the fox said through his toothy grin.

The smallest of the cloaked figures lowered its hood. He had shiny black eyes, white stripes, and a short snout. It was a badger, and a paranoid one at that.

"It isn't safe for us to be out at night like this," the badger said and nervously looked around. "At least not anymore."

"Relax, Badger," the fox said. "If the Enchantress wanted to harm us, we would be dead by now."

"Get to the point, Fox," the raven squawked impatiently. "Why did you call us here tonight?"

The largest figure lowered its hood; it was a gigantic brown bear. "And make it fast, I've got cubs at home," the bear said with a booming and growly voice.

Alex and Conner had never seen so many talking animals in the same place. They hoped their presence would remain unnoticed.

"I've just returned from the Eastern Kingdom," the fox said. "I heard the Enchantress did a number on it but I wanted to see it with my own two eyes. The whole place is a disaster; it's covered in vines and thornbushes as far as the eye can see. It's worse than I ever imagined—it's as if the Thornbush Pit has taken over the entire kingdom!"

"Oh dear," the badger squealed and began nervously tapping his paws together. "Is it going to cross into other kingdoms?"

"I hate thorns," the raven said.

"That's the thing," the fox explained. "The plants grow perfectly along the border; they don't cross into the Northern Kingdom at all. I even tried provoking a plant with a stick but it only coiled around the edge that touched Eastern Kingdom ground. It takes very powerful magic to be *that* specific."

The animals exchanged worried expressions. The remaining hooded member of the group maintained his silence. Alex and Conner wondered what kind of creature was under the cloak.

"Why would the plants only stay in one kingdom?" the bear asked.

"I reckon the Enchantress is taking over the world in style," the fox said. "She's doing it one kingdom at a time, showing the world that the Happily Ever After Assembly is no match for her. It's only a matter of time before she takes over the Dwarf Forests, too . . . and we must be prepared."

"But what would she want with the Dwarf Forests?" the badger asked, shaking his head. "It's full of nothing but criminals and outcasts like us."

The fox's grin grew bigger. "Exactly why I called you all here tonight," he said. "I think we should pledge our allegiance to the Enchantress now, before she strikes."

The animals grunted and growled their protest.

"You're out of your rabbit-preying mind, Fox!" the bear said.

"We're already fugitives!" the raven said. "You want us to get locked away in Pinocchio Prison next?"

The fox raised his paws at them, calming their nerves.

"Hear me out before you disregard me entirely," he said. "Think about it: The reason we live in these parts is because none of us could fit in a Happily Ever After Assembly–regulated society. The Enchantress is going to change all that; the world of fairies and man is over. If we show loyalty to her now, then when she takes over, *and she will take over*, she may spare us."

The fox was slowly starting to convince the animals. They all remained quiet except the badger.

"We can't do that!" the badger said. "It's already bad enough living in exile! Can you imagine what they'd do to us if we sided with *her*?!"

"That's where you're mistaken, Badger," the fox said. "You're still in the happily-ever-after frame of mind. I saw what the Enchantress is capable of. Trust me; all the fairies in the world aren't going to be able to stop her this time. If they could, they would have done so already."

The animals looked back and forth to one another. All were afraid to be the first to express their interest.

"How would we show our allegiance?" the bear asked.

"You're not agreeing with him, are you?" the badger asked the bear.

The bear growled restlessly. "We're already castaways—what more can they do to us?" he said. "If the world is changing, why not change with it? Especially if there's something in it for us."

The raven bobbed up and down, contemplating. "What's your plan, Fox?" she asked.

"I've been asking around; I've got some ideas," the fox said. His mouth had dropped the smile but his eyes hadn't.

"What about you?" the raven squawked in the direction of the unidentified creature. "You've been awfully quiet."

"He's always quiet," the bear said. "I don't even know if he can speak."

The hooded creature looked around at his fellow animals and nodded his head. A simple and singular *ribbit* came from under his hood.

Alex and Conner both gasped. *Could it be?*

The badger must have heard the twins' reaction because he grew more timid than ever before. "We should get out of here before we get caught."

"Think it over!" the fox said. "You all know where to find me."

All of the animals put their hoods back over their heads and disappeared into the night. The fox took one last look around the forest before following the others. Perhaps the badger's paranoia had gotten to him.

The twins knew they wanted to follow the mysterious hooded creature. They made sure the other animals were a safe distance away, then bolted through the forest after their new target.

The forest became darker and darker as they went. The twins had been running for a few minutes, jumping over boulders and tree roots. They were cold, tired, and lost; it was almost nostalgic for them, reminding them of their last trip. But there was no sign of the hooded creature.

"I don't get it," Alex said. "He was *just* here."

"It's like he disappeared into thin-*AHHH*!" Conner screamed.

Alex turned to see what had startled her brother. Emerging from the trees directly behind them was the hooded creature.

He was much taller and more menacing than he had looked in the clearing. He began slowly walking toward the twins. They clutched each other in fear.

"We're sorry for following you!" Conner said. "We thought we might have known you."

"We didn't mean any harm!" Alex said. "We'll leave you alone now!"

The creature kept coming toward them.

"You better get away from us!" Conner said, taking another approach. "My sister knows magic! She just sank a house—*she'll mess you up*!"

Alex stared at her brother in disbelief. Did he think this was *helpful*?

The creature froze just a few feet away from them and looked the twins up and down and side to side.

Conner picked up a big stick on the ground and began swinging it in the hooded creature's direction.

"I played T-ball in elementary school!" he said. "I'm warning you!"

A soft chuckle came from under the creature's cloak.

"Come now, is that really how you're going to greet an old friend?" said a very familiar and proper voice. Its owner slowly removed his hood and the twins sighed with relief.

"Froggy!" the twins exclaimed. They jumped into a huge hug, violently embracing their old friend.

"Hello, Conner! Hello, Alex!" Froggy said and hugged them back. "I wish I could say it's a surprise seeing you two here, but you've always had a knack for being in danger."

Froggy was a tall, man-size frog with big bright eyes and a

wide mouth. He always dressed to impress; the twins noticed he was wearing a three-piece suit under his cloak.

"It's so good to see you, Froggy!" Conner said.

"We've missed you so much," Alex said.

"And I've missed you," Froggy said as he leaned down to look them both in the eye. "You've both grown so much! You're practically grown-ups!" His expression fell once he remembered where this reunion was taking place. "What on earth are you two doing here at a time like this? Does your grandmother know where you are?"

Alex and Conner exchanged guilty glances at each other.

"Er . . . not really," Conner said.

"Grandma doesn't know *exactly* where we are," Alex said, not looking him in the eye.

"I should certainly hope not," Froggy said. "The Dwarf Forests are still too dangerous for you to be in, especially these days and especially this late."

Alex and Conner gave each other another glance.

"I recognize that look," Froggy said. "What aren't you telling me? And why are you both so filthy?"

Alex and Conner considered lying to him for a second, but they knew they couldn't.

"Our grandma doesn't know we're in this world," Alex confessed.

Froggy's wide mouth fell open and he stared blankly at the twins. "How did you get here?"

"Alex sank our grandma's house—I wasn't kidding," Conner said. "That's why we're covered in swamp juice. It was horrifying and strangely awesome at the same time."

"You sank a house?" Froggy asked, dumbfounded. "You know, normally I would question such a possibility, but I don't with you two."

"It was an accident!" Alex said. "I activated another one of my grandma's portals."

"Your technique needs work," Conner said out of the side of his mouth.

Froggy looked around at the forest. They could tell knowing they had snuck into the fairy-tale world made him uneasy. "Children, you shouldn't be here," he said. "These are *very* dangerous times. An evil Enchantress is at large—"

"Ezmia," Alex said. "We know all about her. She's kidnapped our mom."

"What?!" Froggy said. "I'm so sorry."

"Not as sorry as we are," Conner said. "And our grandma practically imprisoned us trying to stop us from coming here."

"Clearly it worked," Froggy said with an eye roll. "Has she *met* you two? Are you even capable of sitting still?"

"Thank you," Conner said, glad of the validation.

"Wait," Alex said, noticing something for the first time. "Froggy . . . you're a *frog* again!"

"Oh yeah," Conner said. "What gives?"

Despite his transformation back into Prince Charlie, the long-lost Charming prince, Alex and Conner still imagined him as a frog whenever they thought of him. They had to remind themselves it wasn't his natural form.

"I'm undercover," Froggy said. "Your grandmother transformed me back into a frog so I could keep a watch over the animals and criminals living in the Dwarf Forests during this crisis. We figured they'd trust me more as an amphibian. Some of them even remember me from when I was living here."

"Are they really going to join the Enchantress?" Alex asked.

"I doubt it," Froggy said. "These are just a bunch of crooks trying to make the current situation work for them. I wouldn't worry too much about it. But still, the Happily Ever After Assembly wants to keep an eye on them just in case things change." Froggy folded his arms and looked between the twins. "I'm sure they'd be much more interested in knowing what you two are up to."

"Froggy, you can't tell anyone we're here," Conner said. "They'll send us back."

"We can't be stuck at home, not when we know our mom is in danger," Alex said.

They both looked up at him with large, pleading eyes.

"Children, you know I care about you deeply but—" Froggy started but was interrupted.

"WE'RE NOT CHILDREN!" Conner shouted. "Everyone keeps calling us that and I'm sick of it! We shouldn't have to prove ourselves after everything we've been through already. It's not like we're a couple of irresponsible kids sneaking into a party—we're two *young adults* trying to save our *mother's life*!"

"You can tell our grandmother if you have to," Alex said. "She can lock us up at home all she wants, but we'll just keep finding ways to get back here until our mom is safe."

"We *have* to find her, Froggy," Conner said. "We already

lost our dad; we can't lose our mom. We're not going to stop until we save her."

Froggy hopelessly looked back and forth between them with his big, glossy eyes. They had put him between a rock and a hard place.

"First things first," Froggy said. "We need to get out of the Dwarf Forests before anything else sees you. Let's get somewhere safe and we'll discuss it further."

Alex and Conner nodded, but they already knew there wouldn't be anything to discuss. His loyalty to them was much stronger than it was to their grandmother—he was their friend before he was her subject. Froggy placed his cloak over the twins and led them safely through the forest.

Alex and Conner were so relieved to have miraculously made contact with an ally so soon, but they knew the worst was yet to come in the uncertain days ahead.

Chapter Ten

RUMPELSTILTSKIN'S DEBT

Pinocchio Prison was home to the most dangerous criminals in all the kingdoms. It was a tall, dark fortress that sat in the center of a long peninsula that curved around Mermaid Bay in the southern part of the Eastern Kingdom. It was perched at the top of a high and rocky cliff with sharp spikes pointing inward and outward at every window so there was no possible way to escape or gain unauthorized entry.

Enchanted wooden soldiers patrolled the narrow stone halls, keeping watch on the lawbreakers behind bars. The majority of those locked away were typical sheep-stealing ogres, kidnapping witches, and man-eating animals that had been caught before they fled into the Dwarf Forests.

The prison was also the home of a great mystery. During the one-hundred-year sleeping curse the Eastern Kingdom had endured, the prison had been the only place in the kingdom that had been spared; all the soldiers and inmates inside had strangely remained conscious while the rest of the country had slumbered.

More recently, the mystery had developed when the prison also became the only place in the kingdom not covered in the Enchantress's demonic thornbushes and vines.

Whether it was a fluke or a miracle was the question. Many assumed the prison was just too far removed to be affected by the curses. However, unbeknownst to all the soldiers and inmates inside, the prison's exclusion from the kingdom's greatest woes was due to a high-profile prisoner who resided on the thirteenth floor.

Rumpelstiltskin was serving his one hundred and twenty-seventh year behind bars. He was a very small man with large baggy eyes, a button nose, and short hair that clung to his head like a helmet. He wore a large collared shirt, tight pants on his tiny legs, and pointed red shoes that jingled when he walked.

After his infamous failed attempt to take the firstborn child of the Eastern Kingdom's former queen, Rumpelstiltskin went into hiding. But after a few years of being at large, the small man couldn't live with the guilt of what he had almost done. So one hundred and twenty-seven years ago, he decided to turn himself in and had lived at Pinocchio Prison ever since.

Rumpelstiltskin had a tiny chamber all to himself. He had two barred windows, one on the heavy door of his cell and another on the wall facing Mermaid Bay. Both were too high for him to see out of unless he jumped, so the dark stones of his chamber floor and walls were all he had to look at every day.

His life had simplified greatly while in prison; he slept on a large stack of hay in the corner and ate on a tiny table pushed to the side with only one spoon and bowl in his possession. Although Rumpelstiltskin had many magical capabilities, he had decided to give them up when he went to prison, fearing magic would only lead him to trouble. He kept his quarters as simple as possible.

The first decade or so of imprisonment was incredibly lonely for the little man, but luckily for him, an unexpected roommate eventually moved in. One day a strong ocean breeze blew a seed into his chamber, and a week later a small daisy began to grow in between two rocks of the stone floor.

Rumpelstiltskin was amazed such a thing could happen. How could something so pleasant grow in such a miserable place? Of all the locations in the world, why did it decide to land here? He pondered the question for a great while, glad of something to distract him from his solitude and shame.

He ultimately decided the flower must have needed a friend as much as he did and that its presence in his cell had been purposeful. He took great care of the flower, impressively keeping it alive the entire time he had been in the prison. He shared his water with the daisy; he told it stories; and when it fell ill, he would stand on his tiptoes by the window with his spoon and reflect sunlight toward it until it regained its strength.

To the average person, having a flower as a companion may have seemed a little odd, but for Rumpelstiltskin, it was the best friend he had ever had.

The flower never *mocked* him for the clothes he wore like others had in his past. The flower never *judged* him for wanting the most out of life. The flower never *used* him for political gain. The flower never *condemned* him for the mistakes he made years before. The flower was only capable of doing one thing: sharing its beauty.

In a way, life in prison had been the best thing that ever happened to Rumpelstiltskin, giving him the most meaningful relationship he had ever had. However, his self-surrender hadn't only been a way for him to clear his conscience; it was also a way for him to protect himself from alliances he had made in his past. And unfortunately, after he'd spent so long hiding from his past, his past eventually found *him*.

It was just before sunset when a thunderous noise was heard outside the prison. It was an intense combination of snapping and crunching and popping that became louder and louder by the second.

The prison began to shake; his bowl and spoon rattled on his table. Whatever it was, it was getting closer.

Rumpelstiltskin jumped up and down at his window, trying to see what was causing the commotion. What he saw was the most terrifying sight he had seen in years. Like an enormous earthy stampede, a tsunami of angry thornbushes and vines traveled across the land, growing in the prison's direction.

"Oh no!" Rumpelstiltskin gasped. He clasped his hands

around his mouth and looked around his cell. There was only one person capable of such magic, and after one hundred and twenty-seven years he knew she had finally come for him.

The wooden soldiers rushed through the halls in a panic.

"Thornbushes and vines are headed for the prison!" one shouted.

"Prepare for an attack!" another yelled.

Rumpelstiltskin looked down at the daisy; it was quivering. "There, there, little flower," he said and gently stroked one of its leaves. "Everything is going to be all right. I'm going to hide you."

He quickly retrieved his bowl off the table and covered his friend with it.

The prison was hit by the plants and the impact made the whole fortress sway. The thornbushes and vines crawled up the sides of the structure, wrapping around it like an army of serpents, until all the windows were covered and the prison went dim inside.

After a few quiet moments, a series of soft rumbles pulsed through the prison like a giant heartbeat. Each rumble was stronger than the next and came from several floors below Rumpelstiltskin's cell. Something was slowly making its way higher and higher through the prison.

Rumpelstiltskin could hear all the wooden soldiers from above rushing down to fight off whatever was intruding below. The clanking of their weapons echoed as they tried fighting it off. They were definitely fighting off more than just plants.

Finally, Rumpelstiltskin heard the battle reach the thirteenth floor. He was too scared to move. He smelled things burning and smoke started to flow into his cell from under his cell door. Each soldier's scream was followed by a loud thud as their wooden bodies hit the floor one by one.

Once all the soldiers were gone, a pair of soft footsteps came down the hall and stopped at Rumpelstiltskin's cell door. He was trembling, afraid these were his last moments alive.

A bright flash of violet light blasted the cell door into smithereens. Rumpelstiltskin braced himself and was pelted by its debris. Once the smoke from the blast cleared, he finally saw who had been causing all the chaos.

Standing in the doorway of his cell was a tall and beautiful woman. She had long magenta hair that floated and rippled above her like slow-moving flames. Her eyes were violet with long feathered eyelashes like moths' antennae. She wore a long purple gown with matching gloves and a high collar. A ghostly cape flowed around her and through the hall like a thick sheet of smoke.

"Ezmia?" Rumpelstiltskin said in horror.

The Enchantress's bright red lips curved into a smirk. "Hello, Rumpy," Ezmia said in her playful, airy voice. "How I've missed you."

Ezmia stepped into Rumpelstiltskin's cell and examined the small chamber. Vines and thornbushes followed her, growing around the walls of the cell, covering the inside of the prison as she traveled through it.

"I love what you've done with the place," Ezmia said sarcastically, passing the stack of hay he used as a bed. "It doesn't fit a man of your *exquisite taste*, though, does it? I can't imagine why you'd abandon me to spend thirteen decades in *here*."

Rumpelstiltskin remained very still, knowing it wasn't wise to make sudden movements around dangerous creatures.

"Have you come to kill me?" he said with a quivering jaw.

The Enchantress forced out a theatrical laugh that did little to comfort him. "Why would I want to kill my oldest *friend*?" she said with a menacing smile. "Besides, if I wanted you dead I would have killed you ages ago." Her smile faded and her violet eyes glared down at him. "Why else do you think I've spared you from all the curses I've cast over the kingdom so far?"

Rumpelstiltskin had always wondered if the exceptions were because of him.

"If you aren't going to kill me, then what brings you here?" he asked, trembling even more. He was convinced she must have a fate worse than death planned for him.

"Look at you, Rumpy, you're just as helpless as the day I found you," Ezmia said pityingly. "When we met, you were just another miserable dwarf working in the mines. But I knew you and I were kindred spirits. We both wanted more than the world was offering us, and we both were ostracized because of it."

"I never meant to anger you," Rumpelstiltskin said and lowered his head. "I had to turn myself in—I couldn't live with what I had done."

"Or what you *failed* to do, that is," Ezmia said. "But all is forgiven."

Rumpelstiltskin knew her too well to believe her. Ezmia had something up her sleeve—she always did.

"What do you want from me?" he asked.

Ezmia went to the window. The vines and thornbushes covering the outside parted so she could see the view of the bay.

"Like it or not, we made a deal," she said. "I've come back so you can finally fulfill your end of our bargain. I saved you from a melancholy life in the mines, I made you my apprentice and taught you magic, and all I ever asked in exchange was for your *assistance*."

"You never said I would have to kidnap a child," Rumpelstiltskin said. "And a *princess*, no less!"

"I made it incredibly easy for you," Ezmia said sharply, her tone growing angry. "*I* bewitched the king into thinking he needed a wife who could spin hay into gold! *I* chose the village girl he ordered to do so! *I* planned the whole negotiation between the two of you! All *you* had to do was take the child that was owed to you!"

"You wanted me to do your dirty work," Rumpelstiltskin peeped. "You wanted *my* name to be tarnished if anything went wrong."

"Of course I did," she said unapologetically. "I was still in the Happily Ever After Assembly at the time. I couldn't get caught stealing an infant princess. As far as the fairies knew, I was still one of them."

"As far as *I* knew, you were still one of them, too!" Rumpelstiltskin said. "I thought I was going to be the apprentice of a great fairy, not an Enchantress who was secretly plotting to take over the world."

Ezmia took delight in remembering the deception. "Yes, *everyone* was surprised," she said. "Of course, that all changed when the rest of the fairies found out you were working for me and I wasn't invited to the child's christening. I lost my temper and cursed the whole kingdom to die. They would have, too, if the Fairy Godmother hadn't converted my curse into a pathetic *sleeping curse*."

The Enchantress closed her eyes and massaged the side of her head. "And since then, Sleeping Beauty has been my own personal nightmare," she said. "You should have seen her face when I attacked her in the forest, though. There she was, the martyr queen, trembling with fear.... It was *priceless*!"

Ezmia smiled to herself and let out a chuckle.

"You wanted me to kidnap her when she was a baby, then you cursed her for a hundred years, and now you've covered her kingdom in vines and thorns," Rumpelstiltskin said. "Why do you hate Queen Sleeping Beauty so much?"

Ezmia glanced at him sideways as she contemplated her honest answer and the answer she would give him. Whatever she said, there was always much more she *wasn't* saying.

"That's where everyone gets it wrong," Ezmia said. "I'll admit I take great satisfaction in seeing the Eastern Kingdom in a state of turmoil. My reputation was bruised when my fatal spell was reduced into an *extensive nap*, so there is an element of revenge I take great pleasure in. But the reason I've attacked the Eastern Kingdom again has nothing to do with Queen Sleeping Beauty."

"Then why are you causing all this chaos?" Rumpel-stiltskin asked, nervously looking at the vines and thornbushes outside.

"Everything has its purpose," Ezmia said with a proud and sinister gleam in her eyes. "It's been so long since my last public appearance, the world thought I was dead. I needed to show them that I was back and more powerful than ever. And when better than on a day they were celebrating the end of my last curse? It's *deliciously evil* of me, isn't it?"

Ezmia closed her eyes and a wide smile grew on her face.

"What part of our bargain do you want me to fulfill?" Rumpelstiltskin asked. "Surely you don't want me to kidnap Queen Sleeping Beauty now?"

"It was never Sleeping Beauty that I was after," Ezmia said and angrily paced around the chamber. "'Sleeping Beauty this...Sleeping Beauty that...' She wouldn't even have that ridiculous name if it weren't for me!"

This puzzled Rumpelstiltskin even more. "Then what were you after?" he asked.

"I was after a *child*," Ezmia confessed. "A child of royal blood, specifically; it's one of the many things I need to complete a *special project* I've been working on."

"A special project?" he asked. "You mean taking over the world, I assume? That's what you've always wanted, isn't it?"

Ezmia looked him straight in the eyes. "*Something* like that," she said. "And it's a lot harder than it looks. Shortly before I met you I figured out a way to do it. It's an enchantment of sorts—it's a very complex formula that requires certain properties to be claimed and special assets to obtain. Once I manage to gather all of them together, not even the Fairy Godmother herself can stop me."

"It's been more than a century since I last saw you," Rumpelstiltskin said. "Why have you decided to strike now after all this time?"

Ezmia waved a hand and the stones in the floor rose to form a large chair.

"You haven't been around, Rumpy," Ezmia said and took a seat. "While you've been locked away, I have had *quite* the century. It's not as if I've been lying around this whole time. I've been betrayed, I've been poisoned, and I've come back from the verge of death stronger and more powerful than ever."

"Poisoned?" Rumpelstiltskin asked. "By whom?"

"Evly." Ezmia said the name as if it were a disease.

"Evly?" Rumpelstiltskin said. "Who is that?"

"She was supposed to be my solution," Ezmia said. "However, she ended up being my greatest disappointment."

She waved her hand again and stones in the floor formed a stool for Rumpelstiltskin to sit on.

"It's a long story, so have a seat," Ezmia ordered.

Rumpelstiltskin didn't argue.

"After I cursed the Eastern Kingdom, I went into hiding," Ezmia explained. "I may have been the most powerful fairy in the world, but I was no match for all the other fairies put together. I knew I couldn't strike again until I was further along with my *project*—until I was past the point of no return. So I plotted in secret, keeping a watchful eye on all the kingdoms for the pieces I needed to continue my work.

"I assembled a quaint little castle in the Northeast where no one could find me, and plotted out what my next move would be. But it required so many elements outside my reach, I knew I would have to be patient. I brought many troubled souls into the castle, hoping to produce a proper apprentice, but they all failed me—each being a bigger disappointment than the last....

"Many years later, in the Charming Kingdom, when the late King Chester was just a prince, the palace had an unexpected visitor one night. A young maiden banged on the palace doors, seeking shelter from a horrible rainstorm. Chester instantly fell in love with her and asked his parents for permission to propose.

"Being the old-fashioned king and queen they were, Chester's parents said he could only marry the maiden if he could prove she was of royal blood. So the prince devised a plan to test the maiden's royal status; he made her a bed in the guest chambers with a stack of a dozen mattresses and placed a pea under the very bottom, convincing his parents that only a royal could feel the imperfection through the mattresses.

"The next morning the maiden complained about a restless night, and Chester was certain he had found his future wife. He asked for the maiden's hand in marriage but she refused his proposal. The maiden had a secret; she had tossed and turned with discomfort all night because she was *pregnant*, not because she was a princess.

"The maiden had been a simple peasant runaway, embarrassed to be with child out of wedlock. She disappeared from the palace as quickly as she came, and Prince Chester never saw her again. Naturally, when I heard about this so-called pregnant princess on the run, I was intrigued—knowing I needed a royal child. I tracked her down in the forest, where she was living on her own in a cave.

"To my delight, she was very much with child when I discovered her. I made her an offer she couldn't refuse; in exchange for her child I would give her a life of riches and luxury beyond her wildest dreams—*the usual*. She agreed and the deal was made. Unfortunately, she backed out of our agreement shortly before giving birth to the child. She ran into a neighboring village and died giving birth to a little girl, whom the villagers named Evly.

"I soon discovered that the maiden hadn't been a royal and Evly couldn't be the child I needed. I let the villagers raise her while I conceived *another* plan to get use out of Evly after all. I was going to train her to seduce and marry Prince White of the Northern Kingdom. Together they would produce an heir and I would finally have the child of royal blood that I desired.

"Unfortunately, when I returned for Evly in her adolescence, she had fallen madly in love with one of the village boys, a pathetic aspiring poet by the name of Mira. I took Evly to my castle in the Northeast to begin training, but all she did was cry and whine every day and night about how much she missed Mira. So I brought the boy to her, imprisoning him inside a Magic Mirror.

"I thought it had been a kind gesture on my part, but it only caused Evly to grow more spiteful. She conducted a plan of her own against me. She broke into my room of potions and concocted a poison so strong that when a few drops touched the ground outside her window, all the trees and plants for miles around were killed.

"Evly laced a small dagger with the poison and stabbed me

with it. The poison almost killed me; I shriveled down to the state of a dying human—I lost all my power, all my beauty, and all hope that I would fulfill my plans for the future. I ran as far away as I could, fearing Evly would try to finish me off, but the stupid girl was so consumed with trying to free Mira she forgot all about me.

"An old witch named Hagatha found me in the woods, barely alive. She recognized me and the effects of the poison. She brought me to her small hut in the Dwarf Forests and nursed me back to health. I became her apprentice but she treated me horribly, taking advantage of the person I once was. She sent me out on the most gruesome errands and forced me to sleep outside like an animal.

"Ironically, the poison is also what saved me. The Happily Ever After Assembly had been looking for me since I cursed the Eastern Kingdom; they didn't recognize me in my frail state and decided I was dead.

"But one day, a few decades later, Hagatha and I were collecting plants from the Thornbush Pit that she planted around her hut. She was forcing me to do all the work and my hands were scraped and scratched from all the thorns. I remember feeling more angry than I had ever felt in my life. I was furious that I, the woman who had once been more powerful than anyone else, had become a witch's slave.

"And with this anger I felt something different. Suddenly, I felt *alive* again—like a candle had been relit inside of me. After many long years, my body had finally recovered from the effects of the poison and my powers had come back.

"It's true what they say, what doesn't kill you makes you stronger; I'm living proof. I was more powerful than ever before. My powers were different, too; my magic had always come from a happily-ever-after source, coming from a life among fairies—that's why every curse I created could be broken with a kiss or token of affection—but not anymore. This time my magic had no limits.

"I pushed Hagatha into the pit and cursed the vines and thornbushes to trap anything that came close to it," Ezmia confessed.

"*You* pushed her into the Thornbush Pit?" Rumpelstiltskin asked. "All this time, that's been *your* magic festering in that godless place?"

"Indeed," the Enchantress said with a boastful shrug. "Believe me, I wanted to take the credit for it, but I still had work to do before I went public again. I returned to the castle and collected all my belongings, ready to complete what I had started so long ago.

"But I knew that I would have to continue being patient. The kingdoms were experiencing a golden age: Cinderella and Prince Charming were married; Sleeping Beauty had just awoken; Snow White was crowned Queen. . . . I knew if I waited until the right moment, my return would have a much bigger impact, and now it has."

Rumpelstiltskin feared what her newfound strength would mean for the future of the kingdoms. "I've never understood you," he said. "You used to be so admired and loved by the whole world—why wasn't that enough? When did it all go wrong?"

The Enchantress looked to the floor with a snide expression. "People only love you as long as they're getting something out of you, but the minute you say something they don't want to hear or do something they don't want to see, all the admiration drains from their hearts."

"But why this obsession with power?" Rumpelstiltskin asked as cautiously as possible. "Why do you need the world, Ezmia?"

Ezmia let out a long sigh. "I have my reasons," she said sharply. "And quite frankly, I don't give a damn if you or anyone else understands."

A tension grew in the room, but it wasn't between Ezmia and Rumpelstiltskin; it was between Ezmia and the world.

"But where do I fit in?" Rumpelstiltskin asked. "If you're so powerful now, why do you need me?"

"Well, that's simple," Ezmia said. "Out of all my apprentices over the years, you have been the most loyal to me, Rumpy. You actually *started* what I asked of you, and now I'm going to let you finish it. Besides, it'll be nice to have a friend around once I take over."

They exchanged a weighty glance, both aware that this was nothing close to a friendship.

"There is another child, isn't there?" Rumpelstiltskin asked with a heavy heart, already knowing the answer. "You want me to kidnap another child."

"Precisely," the Enchantress said.

Rumpelstiltskin lowered his head and closed his eyes. He knew he wouldn't have a choice this time; refusal would mean death.

"Well, that's enough catching up for one day," Ezmia said and glided toward the door with a newfound spring in her step. "Come along, Rumpy. There is much work to be done. I've waited almost two centuries for this, so as you can imagine, I've grown very impatient."

The stones sank back into the ground and Rumpelstiltskin fell on his behind.

"Where are we going?" he asked.

"Hagatha's old hut," the Enchantress said. "It's where I've been spending most of my time since my castle was destroyed a year ago. You should see what I've done with the place! A little magic goes a long way in the Dwarf Forests."

Rumpelstiltskin nostalgically looked around at his tiny cell; it had never seemed so much like home until he was being forced to leave it.

"I just have to say good-bye," Rumpelstiltskin said sadly.

Ezmia raised an eyebrow, not knowing who on earth he was talking about. Perhaps prison had been harder on her small friend than she'd imagined?

Rumpelstiltskin got on the floor and took the bowl off of the daisy. "I have to go now," he said, fighting back tears. "Please don't look at me like that. You'll be all right." He lightly stroked one of its white petals. "Good-bye, little flower. Please take care of yourself."

Rumpelstiltskin stood and walked through the door-way, leaving his cell for the first time in one hundred and twenty-seven years, but stepping into a world of even harsher imprisonment.

Ezmia lingered in the doorway, glaring down at the flower. She couldn't believe something so small and inferior could be so important...so protected...or so *loved*. It ignited a fire inside of her.

The Enchantress waved a hand in its direction and the daisy withered away, crumbling into bits of nothing. A smile appeared on her face—so satisfied to destroy something even so small.

CHAPTER ELEVEN

THE QUEEN AND THE FROG

It was the final moments before dawn, and the stars were slowly fading away as the sky began to brighten. Froggy and the twins had been traveling through the Dwarf Forests for the majority of the night, covering ground as quickly and quietly as possible.

Even after all they had been through together, the twins had never seen Froggy so tense. He constantly watched the path ahead and glanced behind them every few steps to make sure they weren't being followed.

"You seem stressed, dude," Conner said, looking up at his green friend.

"These times are definitely worthy of concern," Froggy said. "By the way, what's a 'dude'?"

Conner shrugged. "It's lingo from our world, nothing important," he said. "Sorry, I forgot where I was for a second."

Alex moved closer to Froggy as they walked, keen to have a more serious conversation. "How bad is it really?" she asked. "We've only heard from those animals in the forest and Mother Goose. What's your take on it?"

Froggy sighed. "I can't recall a time that's been so troubling," he said. "Even when the Evil Queen was at large, people went on with their lives. Now that the Enchantress is back, it's as if the world has stopped. Everyone stays indoors, too afraid to come outside until the Happily Ever After Assembly can do something."

"And have they done anything?" Conner asked. "Have they figured out any way to stop her?"

"I'm afraid not," Froggy said. "They tried unenchanting the plants covering the Eastern Kingdom, but it was no use— the magic is too strong. Ezmia has grown more powerful than anyone ever thought possible."

"Besides covering the Eastern Kingdom in plants, has the Enchantress attacked anything else?" Alex asked.

"That's all for now," Froggy said. "Which means she's likely to strike again at any moment."

"Why is everyone calling it the Eastern Kingdom now?" Conner asked. "Did I miss something? What happened to the Sleeping Kingdom?"

"Because the kingdom had finally been restored to its

former glory before the sleeping curse," Froggy explained. "Queen Sleeping Beauty wanted to celebrate the kingdom's restoration by reclaiming its former title. They were having a huge celebration on the night the Enchantress attacked. Those poor people, they weren't even expecting it."

"I wonder if my rubber-band trick helped," Conner said to himself.

"Why has Ezmia covered the kingdom in plants of all things?" Alex asked. "If the Happily Ever After Assembly can't stop her magic anymore, why not curse Sleeping Beauty to die again?"

Like everyone else in the fairy-tale world, Froggy could only guess. "The symbolism, I'm assuming," Froggy said and rubbed his tired eyes. "During the sleeping curse, the entire kingdom was covered in thornbushes and vines because no one was taking care of the grounds. I'm sure Ezmia is taking pleasure in seeing all their hard work go to waste by covering it again. She's getting more use out of hostages than casualties—making people suffer is crueler than killing them, if you ask me."

Alex and Conner were a tiny bit relieved to hear this. If hostages were what the Enchantress was collecting, then maybe their mom's life wasn't in jeopardy. They just hoped she wasn't suffering.

"And now the plants are keeping people prisoner there, just like in the Thornbush Pit," Alex said to herself, trying to make sense of it all.

"Exactly," Froggy said. "Although no one has been able to make a connection between the two."

"What about Queen Sleeping Beauty and King Chase? Are they all right?" Alex asked.

"King Chase is still stuck in the Eastern Kingdom as far as anyone knows," Froggy said. "Queen Sleeping Beauty barely made it out. She was attacked while making a run for the border. All of her soldiers were killed, but she survived, thankfully. Soldiers from the Charming Kingdom found her in the forest and brought her back to the Charming Palace."

"That's horrible," Alex said with a sigh. "Even though she took our mom, after what we learned about the Evil Queen I'm trying to come up with a reason the Enchantress may just be misunderstood, too. But it's difficult."

Conner grunted. "Not for me," he said. "I don't care what her excuse is—if she hurts Mom in any way, I'll make sure it's the last thing she does."

The sun started to rise and the land around them became more visible. In the distance the twins were taken back to see a familiar wall made of gray brick that stretched across the entire horizon.

"Isn't that the wall surrounding the Red Riding Hood Kingdom?" Alex asked.

"Oh yeah," Conner said, recognizing it, too. "Wait—why are we headed there? I thought you were taking us back to your place, Froggy?"

"I am," Froggy reassured.

"What happened to your hole in the ground?" Conner asked.

"I moved," Froggy said. "I live in the castle now...with Queen Red."

Froggy blushed a shade of dark green and went silent. Alex and Conner looked at each other with *did you just hear that?* written on their faces. Froggy walked ahead of them, crossing through the western gate of the Red Riding Hood Kingdom's famous wall.

"Good morning, fellas!" Froggy said with a nod to the guards monitoring the gate.

"Morning, sir," they said back, bowing slightly as he walked past them.

The twins ran through the gate and caught up with Froggy on the other side.

"Wait a minute," Conner said with a laugh. "You're living with Red? Are you guys like a couple or something?"

Froggy turned even darker green. "Well, I suppose so," he said, too bashful to look them in the eye.

"I wasn't expecting that," Alex said with raised eyebrows.

"How the heck did that happen?" Conner asked, with a confused grin on his face. "I mean, you're so worldly and she's so . . . *not.*"

"Conner, don't be rude!" Alex said and nudged him.

"No, it's quite all right," Froggy said. "It's very simple how it all happened. Shortly after I was transformed back into a human by your grandmother, and her castle was rebuilt from the fire, Queen Red invited me over for some tea one afternoon. She wanted to thank me again for saving her life during the battle against the Evil Queen and the Big Bad Wolf Pack. It was only supposed to last an hour or so, but we ended up talking all day—well, she talked and I listened—but we really connected. And since then our friendship has taken a more romantic turn."

Their mouths hung wide open, not helping Froggy in the slightest.

"And how does she feel about you being in your frog form again?" Alex asked.

"It was challenging at first—she was afraid to touch me and wouldn't let me sit on the furniture—but she's come a long way and knows it's for the greater good, even if it does put a pause in our relationship for now," Froggy said. "Red's really an exceptional woman; you just have to get to know her."

"Is she still hung up on Jack?" Conner asked. Alex gave him a dirty look.

The dark green coloring faded from Froggy's face. "We're working on that," he said. "I don't think anyone can ever *stop* loving someone entirely. Sometimes love turns to hate, but I'm not sure it's possible to ever stop *feeling* for them. Despite whatever feelings she has left over for Jack, I have no doubts about her affection toward me."

Froggy smiled and nodded to himself. Alex and Conner shrugged to each other. Relationships always seemed complicated to them, but they seemed almost impossible to understand under these circumstances.

"Does it bother you, though?" Alex asked. "Knowing how much she cared about someone else in the past?"

Froggy shook his head confidently. "I figure if Red is willing to accept me, flawed and frogged, then I can do the same for her regardless of what baggage she brings," he said. "And in time, the longer Jack and Goldilocks are out of the picture, the better it will be for her. Out of sight, out of mind."

"Uh-huh," Conner said with a snort, looking at him through the corner of his eye. "Whatever happened to Jack and Goldilocks? Has anyone heard from them?"

"Very little, actually," Froggy said. "Occasionally they'll be spotted on the outskirts of the kingdom and a villager will alert the castle guards, but they've kept pretty quiet, and for my and Red's sake, I'm not complaining."

The twins were happy to hear Jack and Goldilocks were still together and on the run, relieved that at least something had stayed constant while the rest of the world was in chaos.

They walked through the rolling hills of Bo Peep Family Farms and soon reached the picturesque town in the center of the kingdom. The twins were delighted to see all the dainty cottage homes and brick buildings with pointed hay roofs again. They smiled at seeing Henny Penny Bank, the Shoe Inn, and shops like Pat-a-Cake Bakery and Jack Horner's Pie Shop all exactly the same as their last visit.

One thing was visibly different. The town that had once been full of farmers and shepherds hauling their livestock around was deserted.

"It's so empty," Alex said.

"Remember how crowded the town was last time?" Conner said. "It was like Take Your Goat to Work Day or something if I remember correctly."

Froggy let out a sad sigh. "It's a sign of the times, I'm afraid," he said. "It's like this in all the villages in all the kingdoms. No one leaves their home unless it's absolutely necessary."

They walked through the park in the center of the town and

were pleased to see the Humpty Dumpty and the Little Boy Who Cried Wolf memorials and Jack and Jill Hill. The twins couldn't help but look at them a little differently, though, considering the information they had learned from Mother Goose.

"Whoa," Conner said, looking across the park. "Check out the renovation."

At the edge of the park, facing the twins, was Red Riding Hood's castle—her *new* castle. It stood twice as tall and sat twice as wide as the previous one. It had several towers, each higher than the next, a large dome in the center, and a gigantic clock just above the newly built front steps.

Alex and Conner both tilted their heads and squinted at the new castle; there was something rather peculiar about it.

"Looks familiar," Alex said.

"Sure does," Conner said. "It almost looks like all the other castles and palaces mixed together, doesn't it?"

"Just wait until you see the inside," Froggy said. "Red built me my very own library! It's just splendid! Hundreds and hundreds of books and they're all mine."

"That's wonderful!" Alex said, sharing his enthusiastic smile.

"Don't worry," Froggy said. "I kept all the books you gave me. They have their own special section."

He winked at her and Alex grinned. She remembered the books they had bonded over the first time they met.

The trio made their way up the castle's front steps and two guards opened the impressively large red doors for them to enter.

"Good morning, sir," the guards said to Froggy and bowed like the previous set of guards had.

"Morning, gentlemen," Froggy said.

"Does every guard know you or something?" Conner asked him.

"Well, I'm not exactly easy to forget," Froggy said. "I don't fit in around here, looking like this. I'm just glad the villagers stopped fainting when they see me . . . most of them, at least."

They took their first steps into the castle and the twins gasped. There was a marble floor under their feet, golden pillars to their sides, and an enormous grand staircase in front of them. And to no one's surprise, every wall was covered in a portrait of Queen Red in different glamorized positions.

"She certainly spared no expense," Conner said, eyeing everything around him. He looked down at the floor and noticed tiny basket-shaped tiles connecting the corners of the marble tiles.

"It sort of reminds me of Cinderella's ballroom," Alex said. "Except Red-ified."

A short and plump handmaiden was descending the stairs with an empty tea tray. Her cheeks were pink and she was wheezing from the effort. Alex and Conner hid behind Froggy, remembering that their last encounter with her hadn't been a pleasant one.

"Welcome back, Prince Charlie," the handmaiden called out to Froggy. It was strange for the twins to hear him addressed by his real name. "The queen is in the library; I just served her some breakfast."

"Thank you, I'm headed there now," he called back to her.

"Would you like me to bring you up some lily-pad tea?"

"That would be wonderful, thank you. Three flies in mine, please. Would you like any tea, Alex? Conner?"

"Sure, what the heck?" Conner said. "It wouldn't be a visit without some lily-pad tea."

The twins followed Froggy up the stairs, passing the hand-maiden, who stopped in her tracks and stared at them peculiarly, not being able to recall exactly where she knew them from, but clearly remembering that it hadn't been a good experience.

They reached the top of the stairs, made a right, and traveled down another impeccably decorated hallway also lined with portraits of Queen Red. They found a pair of golden doors with *Library, Place of Books* carved into the wall above it.

Conner pointed out the carving to his sister. "I bet you anything it's so she doesn't forget what's inside!" he quietly snickered into her ear.

"Here we are!" Froggy said and pushed open the doors.

The twins stepped inside and were awestruck once again. It was the most elegant library they had ever seen, beating even the one in Snow White's palace. Alex almost teared up; Conner nodded with raised eyebrows.

"It's beautiful!" Alex said and placed a hand over her heart.

"Not bad," Conner said.

Shelves stretched to the tops of the very high ceiling, with ladders and balconies on various levels. A group of armchairs and sofas was placed in the center of the room near a large fireplace with a gigantic wolfskin rug (that had once been the Big Bad Wolf himself) spread across the floor in front of it. A beautiful chandelier hung in the center of the room, giving an abundance of light perfect for reading.

There were many portraits of Queen Red hung around the library, but an especially large painting was hung over the fireplace of Red reading a book in one of the armchairs. The twins had to do a double take, because just below the portrait was the real Queen Red Riding Hood seated in an armchair reading a book in the identical position as in the portrait.

She looked up as soon as she heard the doors open. *"You're back!"* Red said when she saw Froggy. She tossed aside the book, which was thin and mostly pictures, and ran to her beau. They collided into a giant embrace.

Queen Red Riding Hood was a beautiful young woman with blonde hair and bright blue eyes. She was always dressed to the nines in red gowns and a hooded cape, but the twins noticed something different about Red. She wasn't wearing nearly as much makeup or jewelry as she had been before. Perhaps her relationship with Froggy had simplified the young queen's need to impress.

Froggy tried kissing her but Red pulled away. "No kisses, remember?" Red said. "I love you to death, darling, but I just find you repulsive at the moment. There's nothing worse than a cold and clammy kiss—*you two*!"

Red's full attention was diverted to the twins once she spotted them. She stared at them as if Froggy had brought a poisonous snake into the castle.

"Red, do you remember Alex and Conner?" Froggy asked.

"*Remember?* How could I *forget?*" Red said, not looking away from them.

"Hi, Red," Alex said politely.

"How's it going?" Conner said nicely.

"Forgive me, I don't mean to be rude," Red said to the twins. "It's just every time I see you two I'm heartbroken, kidnapped, or homeless."

The twins couldn't argue. She was right.

"No worries," Conner said.

Red eyed them nervously for a minute before saying anything else. "So what brings you back to this world?" she asked. "Vacation? Visiting your grandmother?"

"Not exactly," Alex said.

"We were lost in the woods," Conner said. "Surprise, surprise."

"Thank goodness we saw Froggy in the forest, otherwise who knows where we would have ended up," Alex added.

Red glanced back and forth between them and then to Froggy. "So you brought them *here?*" she said through a forced smile. *"Lovely."*

"They had nowhere else to go," Froggy said. "I couldn't let them wander around alone at a time like this."

Red looked back at the twins, still anxious. "No, I suppose not," she said.

The twins tried to break the awkward tension. "Your new castle is beautiful," Alex said.

"I feel so at home—at *many* homes, actually," Conner said. "Was there a theme you were going for?"

"*Inspiration*, mostly," Red said blankly.

"Ah," Conner said. "Well, it certainly feels . . . *inspired*."

The handmaiden knocked on the door and entered the library carrying tea for Froggy and the twins.

"Oh, wonderful, why don't we catch up over some tea," Red said. Her tone didn't match her enthusiastic words.

The handmaiden set the tea tray down on a table by the armchairs and left the room. The twins took a seat across from Froggy and Red and the impromptu tea party began. Froggy held Red's hand lovingly.

"Is this all right?" Froggy asked her.

"Of course it is; I'm wearing gloves," Red said.

It was silent for a couple of moments, with only the sounds of their spoons clanking against their teacups filling the awkward tension in the room.

"So how old are you two now?" Red asked. "You look like you've grown."

"We're thirteen," Conner said.

"Oh, that's nice," Red said. "That's how old I was when I was elected queen. Of course, I had my granny to help me."

"How is your granny?" Alex asked.

"Retired, actually," Red said. "She lives at the Shoe Inn now. So I've taken over all responsibilities as queen."

"How's queenship treating you?" Conner asked. He sipped his lily-pad tea and then spit it out immediately.

"It's been difficult," Red said. "There's much more to being a queen than people realize—it's not all about jewels, fabulous dresses, and an abundance of affection. There are lots of decisions to be made every day about peasants and farmers and their needs and whatnot. Luckily I've had Charlie to help me."

"That's nice," Alex said. "Have you passed any new laws or anything worth mentioning recently?"

Red looked up at the ceiling trying to recall what her latest act as queen had been. "I raised taxes," she said happily, but then her smile faded into a frown. "But the people didn't like that at all so I quickly lowered them—my mistake, didn't realize they would take it so personally. Apparently my kingdom has a strong ecology, so there was no need to anyway."

"A strong *economy*, dear," Froggy corrected her.

"Oh yes, *economy*, forgive me," Red said. "We grow so much food and produce so much wool that our trades are very strong with the other kingdoms. The Red Riding Hood Kingdom is the breadbasket of this world, no pun intended."

The twins politely nodded along but were in shock someone like Red was still allowed to lead a kingdom. Froggy decided to save the twins from the conversation and escorted them to the corner of the room.

"I want to show you something special," Froggy said and pointed to a special shelf where all of Alex's old books were kept. "Here's where I keep all of your books, Alex."

"They look very happy there," she said with a smile. Her eyes fell on the titles of the books just below them.

"*Around the World in Eighty Days, 20,000 Leagues Under the Sea, Frankenstein...*" She discovered with delight. "Froggy, these are all the classics from our world! Where did you get all of them?"

"Your grandmother, actually," Froggy said. "She wanted to thank me again for helping you the last time you were here. I must say, the people in your world definitely know how to tell stories!"

Alex smiled at the thought, knowing most of the authors of her world had been inspired by the stories of his world.

"I've read a few myself," Red said, trying to stay relevant in the room. "What's that heavy one that I enjoy so much, Charlie? With that funny little language? *The Complete Works of Shakeyfruit*, was it?"

"*The Complete Works of Shakespeare*, my dear," Froggy corrected her.

"Oh yes, that's the one!" Red said. "It was a lovely read—one story is so pleasant and then the next is so tragic—took me nearly a year to get through them all. I hope he's still writing in your world; he has a lot of potential, if you ask me."

Conner laughed but made it look like a sneeze. "Don't worry, he's around," Conner said. He wondered what Shakespeare would have thought about Red's endorsement.

Alex was looking through all the other books in the library. Some of the titles that caught her eye were *Royal Romances Through the Ages*, *History of the Age of Magic*, *Mammals of the Northern Kingdom*, and *The Extinction of Dragons*. She knew she could easily spend a month in Froggy's library reading everything in it.

"Look at this one," Froggy said, pulling a book from a high shelf. "I think you two would appreciate it."

He handed it to the twins and they read the title together. It had a dark red cover and illustrations pasted on pages inside.

"*Myths, Legends, and Collecting Spells*," Alex read with surprise. "Is it about the Wishing Spell?"

"That and many others," Froggy said. "There are all kinds of gathering folklores in there. I had no idea there were so many, but who knows which ones are real and which are not?"

They flipped through the pages, skimming past chapters about various legends of the fairy-tale world. A few caught their eye as they searched: The Sorcerer's Sword was a weapon believed to have gone missing during the Dragon Age and allegedly could cut through anything. The Wand of Wonderment was a magic wand built from the most treasured items of the most hated people in the world and made whoever possessed it invincible. The Vanity Crown was made of the most valuable jewels in all the kingdoms and was rumored to transform whoever wore it into the most attractive person alive.

They came across a section devoted to the Wishing Spell, and Alex read aloud as Conner followed.

The Wishing Spell is a legendary spell, mostly told to children to inspire a work ethic, that grants one wish to whoever collects a series of special objects. Several people have died trying to test the theory of the Wishing Spell, but due to all that is unknown about the spell, it is highly unlikely that the spell exists, and it is thought to be only a childish story.

"If I had a nickel for every time we proved a childish story was true..." Conner said under his breath.

There was a knock on the door and the handmaiden poked her head inside the library.

"A message from the Charming Kingdom has just arrived for you, Your Majesty," she said.

"Oh?" Red asked. "Let's see it."

The handmaiden walked in and handed Red the letter. It was in a white envelope that had a golden glass slipper wax seal on the back.

"I wonder what this is about," Red said as she opened it. "I doubt Chance and Cinderella are throwing a ball at a time like this." She read the letter and her eyes grew wide. She placed a hand over her mouth. "Oh my . . ." she said.

"What is it, my dear?" Froggy asked.

"Pinocchio Prison has been attacked by the Enchantress," Red said, looking up from the envelope. "The Charmings are hosting a meeting for the Happily Ever After Assembly."

Red handed him the envelope and Froggy read with the twins looking over his shoulder.

To Her Majesty, Queen Red Riding Hood,

We regretfully inform you that late yesterday evening, the Enchantress attacked Pinocchio Prison, consuming it with her enchanted plants. There is still no word of any survivors.

Your presence is requested tomorrow evening at the Charming Palace, where a meeting will be held with all heads of state and the Happily Ever After

Assembly to discuss the current situation. Your attendance will be expected unless other word is received.

Sincerely,
Their Royal Majesties,
King Chance and Queen Cinderella

Red sighed and nodded her head. "I'll need to leave at once," Red told the handmaiden. "Please prepare a carriage for us to travel in and another carriage for my overnight luggage."

The handmaiden nodded and hurried out of the library with her instructions. Alex and Conner looked to each other, knowing they were thinking the same thing.

"We have to go to this meeting, Froggy," Alex said. "We have to know what's going on."

"And why is that?" Red asked.

"The Enchantress has our mother," Conner said. "We need to figure out a way to save her."

"Well, what does your grandmother say?" Red asked.

Alex and Conner looked at each other cautiously, wanting to break the news to Red gently.

"She doesn't even know we're here," Conner said.

"She doesn't want us to know anything," Alex said.

Red cocked her head sideways and glared at Froggy. "Hold on a second," she said. "Are you telling me the Fairy Godmother's runaway grandchildren are hiding in *my castle*?!"

Froggy turned a shade of light green. "Like I said...I

couldn't leave them wandering alone in the forest," he said with an apologetic laugh.

Red turned the same color as her clothing. *"Do you know how much trouble we could get into if the Fairy Council finds them here?!"* Red yelled.

"It doesn't matter, because no one is going to tell her where we are," Conner said sternly.

"Excuse me, but who died and elected you my successor?" Red said. "I should have you both thrown out of here!"

Conner raised an eyebrow and crossed his arms. "But you won't," he said snidely. "Because you know what's worse than *involuntarily housing* the Fairy Godmother's runaway grandchildren? *Voluntarily kicking out* the Fairy Godmother's runaway grandchildren!"

Red made a couple high-pitched grunts as she looked between the twins and Froggy. She hated being compromised in her own home.

"How are you going to get inside that meeting?" Froggy asked the twins. "It's for the heads of state only—it's very exclusive. Besides, your grandmother is going to be there. How would you hide from her?"

Alex sighed, thinking of how they were going to pull it off.

"We'll need to hide in something," she said. "Something large enough to fit both of us inside it, but not suspicious looking."

Conner's eyes lit up and he looked around the room, searching for something he had seen when they came in. He walked across the room and pulled a portrait of Red off of the wall and brought it to her.

"Hey, Red," Conner said, "do you still have this dress?"

Alex and Froggy walked to Red's chair to take a look at what he was referring to. In the portrait, Red was wearing an enormous ball gown that protruded from her waist and flowed to the floor.

"I believe so, actually," Red said. "It was one of the only dresses that was saved in the fire—*wait a second, you're not thinking what I think you're thinking, are you?*"

Conner looked up at Froggy and his sister with a giant smirk on his face. It didn't take them long to figure out what he was planning, and once they did, matching grins appeared on their faces.

"It's perfect!" Alex said.

"I have to admit, it's very clever," Froggy said.

Red was appalled.

"Have you all gone mad?" Red said. "You expect me to waltz into a meeting with the Happily Ever After Assembly with two brats under my dress? Absolutely not! I will not have any part in this whatsoever."

Alex and Conner looked to each other and their grins disappeared. Each gestured for the other to do or say something to convince her.

"Red," Alex said, leaning down by her side. "Our mom is in danger. We need to know what's going on so we can figure out a way to save her."

Conner leaned down on Red's other side, taking his sister's lead.

"She's all we have, Red," Conner said. "If anything happens to her, we'll be orphans."

Red was accosted by their pleading faces. She knew she couldn't say no to that—even *she* wasn't that selfish.

"All right, all right, all right!" Red said. "I'll help you out this one time, but after this, I'm done!"

Large smiles appeared on the twins' faces. Red rubbed the sides of her head, wondering how on earth she had gotten so involved so easily—it had been such a quiet day until the twins showed up.

"Thanks, Red," Alex said.

"You won't regret it," Conner added.

Red sank into her chair. "Can I get that in writing?" she asked.

Chapter Twelve

A NOT-SO-CHARMING EVENING

The twins left with Froggy and Red shortly after receiving the letter about the Happily Ever After Assembly. The four of them rode in one carriage while all of Red's "necessary" luggage was carried in a separate carriage behind them. The twins felt sorry for the horses pulling the second carriage—it seemed like a heavy heave.

They had half a dozen soldiers surrounding them as they traveled, which Froggy insisted was the perfect amount for safety but not enough to cause any unwanted attention.

Halfway there they came to a stop so Red could change into the enormous gown their scheme required. They pulled into a tiny field between two large oak trees and Red transformed the first carriage into a dressing room. She kicked Conner and Froggy out and made Alex stay inside to help her dress.

It was definitely a challenge, as the gown was much bigger than the inside of the carriage.

"I'd just like to point out that Queen Snow White never has to change on the side of the road," Red said, struggling to pull the heavy dress over her head. "I suppose that's what I get for being an *elected queen*."

"It must be some consolation to know you were *wanted*," Alex said, trying to help Red move through the dress. "They actually *chose* you to lead their kingdom. It wasn't just handed to you."

"Not really," Red said. "After the C.R.A.W.L. revolution, it was between me and the *third* Little Pig—and he didn't even want the job. He was a total recluse. He barely came out of that brick house he was so proud of."

And with one last effort, Red pushed herself up through the center of the gown.

"There we go!" she said, out of breath.

The boys rejoined them inside the carriage and the procession continued to the Charming Palace. There was physically no room for anything else inside the carriage with the four bodies and the mound of endless red fabric crammed inside.

"Oh no," Red said after they had been on the move for less than five minutes.

"What is it?" Conner asked with his face pressed against the window.

"Now I have to tinkle," Red peeped. Everyone else in the carriage groaned.

The following evening, Queen Red's party arrived at the Charming Palace. The twins couldn't resist ogling all the storybook estates and villages they passed on the way to the palace's front steps.

Something seemed different about the Charming Kingdom, though the twins couldn't put their finger on it. Even beyond the lack of villagers parading through the streets and trading in the shops, there was a very gloomy vibe that floated through the whole kingdom.

The carriages rolled up to the bottom of the lengthy staircase leading up to the palace's entrance, and the twins were relieved to finally be getting out of the compact carriage—they didn't care how crammed they would be under Red's dress.

They were greeted by a palace footman. Froggy immediately jumped out of the carriage and busied him with unloading the luggage in the second carriage.

The twins both hopped out of the carriage and crouched on the ground. Red was next to hop out and landed directly in the middle of them. Her gown exploded out of the carriage and securely covered the twins below her. *It was perfect!*

"So far so good," Alex whispered under Red's dress.

"Nice bloomers, Red," Conner said, chuckling about the knee-length undershorts she had strategically put on.

Red grunted and kneed Alex in the head.

"Ouch! That was me, Red!" Alex said.

"Apologies," Red said and then kneed Conner in the head.

"Ouch!" Conner yelled.

Froggy walked back to find Red and the twins perfectly in position. "Are we ready for this?" Froggy asked.

"I think so," Alex said.

"Roger, Roger!" Conner said.

"That's reassuring," Froggy said and used a handkerchief to wipe the beads of sweat on his forehead. "Because *I* most certainly am not."

"Take a chill pill, Frog," Conner said. "No one is gonna know we're under here."

The footman glanced over suspiciously from the second carriage, positive he had just heard voices come from bodies that weren't visible.

"Make sure you two stay as silent as possible under there," Froggy said and gulped so hard he croaked. "Let's make our way into the palace, shall we?"

Red took a step forward the twins weren't ready for.

"Red, we can't see anything; you're going to have to guide us," Conner whispered up at her.

"And how am I supposed to do that?" Red whispered down at them.

"Narrate what you're doing," Alex said.

Red closed her eyes and took a deep breath, mentally preparing herself for the evening she was in for.

"Fine, I'm *walking* toward the stairs," Red informed them, and they moved with her. She was walking too fast for them to keep up.

"Take baby steps," Conner whispered. "We're crouched down here like chimpanzees."

Red's nostrils flared. "Sure," she said sharply. "Now I'm walking *slowly* up the stairs."

The first few steps were a disaster—Froggy kept gasping every time he saw one of their sneakers peeking out from under the gown. Slowly but surely, they managed to get the hang of it, and smoothly made their way up the enormous flight of steps.

Back at the carriages, the footman could have sworn he saw three pairs of feet under Red's dress out of the corner of his eye. But when he double-checked, they were gone. The footman continued unloading the second carriage, deciding he just needed glasses—or to retire.

Alex's and Conner's backs were starting to ache from crawling up the steps like monkeys, but it only got worse when they reached the top of the stairs and the ground became flat, causing them to slouch even more.

"And now I'm walking toward the palace entrance, no more steps," Red said out loud.

A few of the Charming Kingdom guards patrolling the entrance looked at her funny. After all, she was walking at a snail's pace and talking to herself.

"You certainly are!" Froggy said to Red and patted her back, trying to reduce the awkwardness.

"Prince Charlie, welcome back, sir," the twins heard a familiar voice say.

"Sir Lampton," Froggy clarified for them. "Good to see you, although I wish the visit were for a different occasion."

Alex and Conner tensed up knowing Sir Lampton was just a few feet away from them. They held their breath, afraid he'd hear even that.

"Now I'm *walking* inside the Charming Palace," Red said to the twins, but was caught by Sir Lampton. "Um...*and I can't believe it*! Feels like I was home just a minute ago—such a quick trip."

It was a decent cover, but from under the gown the twins could feel the suspicious gaze Lampton was giving Red.

"Are you feeling all right, Your Majesty?" Lampton asked her. "You're walking so slowly—are you ill?"

Alex and Conner exchanged a glance, wondering how Red was going to cover up this one.

"Perfectly fine, Sir Lampton," Red said. "I just selected the wrong pair of shoes to travel in. My feet are killing me."

Alex and Conner sighed with relief. Conner gave Red a thank-you pat on her knee. She quickly slapped his head through the gown and Conner bit his fist to silence a scream.

"Just an itch," Red said with a tight smile.

"How are things here?" Froggy asked, trying to distract Lampton.

"Terrible," he said. "Have you not heard?"

"I'm guessing not," Froggy said. "What happened?"

Lampton let out the most troubled sigh the twins had ever heard. "Princess Hope was kidnapped last night."

The twins gasped, unable to contain their shock, but it was covered by the gasps coming from Red and Froggy.

"What?" Froggy said, devastated by the news about his only niece. *"What do you mean, kidnapped? By whom?"*

"Rumpelstiltskin," Sir Lampton said. "It looks like he's working for the Enchantress again, only this time he succeeded."

It grew quiet. The whole world seemed to be falling apart for everyone.

A few moments later, after traveling across the red-carpeted interior of the Charming Palace's entrance hall, the twins knew they had arrived inside the ballroom, recognizing the golden dance floor beneath them. The room was filled with troubled voices and impatient footsteps milling about.

"Here, Your Majesty, please have a seat," the twins heard Sir Lampton say.

"Thank you," Red said. "I'm now going to *slowly sit* on the stool I've so graciously been provided with...."

The twins cringed from the inelegance of Red's statement, but thankfully everyone else in the room was too occupied to have even noticed Red and Froggy enter the room. She slowly sat on the stool placed behind her, giving the twins enough time to adjust themselves to her seated position, sitting on the floor beside her. It was a relief to all their joints.

The twins could hear small conversations from all corners of the room. They wished they could put faces to the voices they heard.

Conner nudged Alex and quietly gestured to a loose seam he'd found in Red's dress. He carefully pulled the seam apart even more and created a small hole to peek out of. Alex did the same on her side and they were finally able to see outside the gown.

Although they knew everyone in the room, there was so much heartache and hopelessness worn on all the faces, the kings and queens were almost unrecognizable. It was hard for the twins to see them all like this; their lives had always been perfect examples of happiness, but here they were now, the most distraught group of people they'd ever seen.

Queen Cinderella was seated on her throne, devastated beyond belief. Her hands covered her swollen eyes as tears rolled down her face. She was comforted by Queen Snow White and Queen Rapunzel, who used the tip of her remarkably long braid to dry Cinderella's tears.

The men paced around in the corner of the ballroom. King Chance never stopped moving, furious that his daughter had been taken from him. King Chandler and Rapunzel's husband stood near him, unable to do anything but watch. Froggy joined them, lending his support with his presence.

"Last night I heard her crying," Cinderella told the women at her throne. "I got out of bed and went to her room. A few of the maids were on their way inside, but I insisted on checking on her myself. When I opened the door the first thing I saw were the curtains blowing inside. I thought it was strange—I didn't remember leaving her window open—and that's when I saw him . . . *that horrid little man holding my daughter*!"

Heavy streams of tears flowed down the queen's face. Rapunzel rubbed her back and Snow White held her hand tightly.

"Breathe, Cinderella, breathe," Snow White told her.

Cinderella caught her breath and continued. "Then he looked me right in the eye and hopped out of the window. I screamed and ran to the windowsill, trying to see if I could see them below, but they were gone," she said. "That disgusting man disappeared with my baby!" Snow White held her and she cried into her shoulder.

"This is all my fault," said a soft voice across the room. Queen Sleeping Beauty stood at the window in the back of the ballroom, listlessly staring at the land outside.

"I'm the one she wants, I'm the one she's after," Sleeping Beauty said in a daze. "Why doesn't she just take me? Why does she have to make everyone else suffer?"

"This isn't your fault," Rapunzel said.

"You can't blame yourself for this," Snow White agreed.

King Chance grew tired of pacing and groaned angrily. He needed *someone* to blame. "Where are those useless fairies?" he demanded. "And why haven't they done something about this yet?!"

A soft breeze blew through the ballroom, and twinkling lights of all the colors of the rainbow floated through the room. The Fairy Council slowly appeared out of thin air.

Emerelda was first to appear. "We're doing everything in our power," she said. She was tall, black, and beautiful. She wore a long emerald gown that matched her eyes and jewelry. Emerelda always had a soft but authoritative presence; she was someone you could trust but never wanted to cross.

Xanthous was next to arrive and was followed by Skylene,

the blue fairy. She had pale skin, hair the color of the sky, and robes the color of the ocean. Tangerina appeared shortly after her. She was the orange fairy and actual bees flew around her beehive. Violetta, the purple fairy and oldest of the council, popped up close to where Red and the twins were sitting.

Rosette, the short, plump, and rosy-cheeked red fairy, appeared next. Coral, the youngest and the pink fairy, showed up shortly after that, hovering in the air thanks to her tiny wings. The fairies' colorful arrivals were a beautiful sight, but not beautiful enough to raise the spirits in the room.

"Well, it's not enough," Chance yelled at them. "The Enchantress is one of you, isn't she? You outnumber her—why can't you handle this?"

"We are greater than her in size, but not in strength," said Skylene in her dreamlike voice.

"She's managed to grow more powerful than we ever imagined," Xanthous said. "I'm afraid even the Fairy Godmother is no match for her."

"Speaking of the Fairy Godmother, has she or Mother Goose arrived yet?" Emerelda asked, looking around the ballroom. "We need to begin."

Another soft breeze blew through the room, this time carrying white sparkling lights that circled into a vortex in the center of the room. A moment later, the twins' grandmother appeared with her crystal wand raised.

The twins looked nervously at each other. Now that their grandmother was here they were *officially* in the same room as everyone they wanted to avoid.

"Forgive me for being late," the Fairy Godmother said and politely acknowledged everyone in the room with a comforting nod. "There was a bit of an issue in the Otherworld."

The twins had never heard their world referred to as anything else but *home* before; it was odd to hear it have a name of its own, although not entirely surprising. What else had the fairies been calling it this entire time?

"Red Riding Hood, my word, that is *quite* a dress you're wearing," the Fairy Godmother said when she saw Red sitting in the oversize gown.

Alex and Conner could hear each other's heartbeats and were terrified they were about to be discovered.

"Well," Red said nervously, thinking as quickly as possible. "It's important to dress your best when the world is at its worst . . . to raise morale."

"Yes, I suppose that is true," the Fairy Godmother said, though she didn't sound fully convinced.

"With all due respect, I don't believe this is the proper time to be talking about dresses and the Otherworld," King Chance said, his frustration building every second spent without his daughter.

"Will Mother Goose be joining us?" Emerelda asked, getting the meeting back on track.

The twins' grandmother dropped the subject of Red's dress. "No, she stayed behind in the Otherworld," she said. "My grandchildren are missing, so she agreed to continue searching for them while we have our discussion."

"That's *horrible*," Red said, shaking her head a tad too much. "I hope they're all right, I just *loved* those two so much."

Alex and Conner shared a mutual eye roll.

"Is everyone else here?" the Fairy Godmother asked, still eyeing Red strangely.

"Everyone but the elves, ma'am," Sir Lampton informed her from the side of the room. "We sent word of our meeting to the Elf Empire, but they have chosen to miss it, feeling the current situation has nothing to do with them."

King Chandler sighed. "Typical," he said. "The elves never get involved unless they have to."

"Thank you, Sir Lampton," the Fairy Godmother said. "Then let's begin."

King Chance stormed up to her. "Tell us why the Enchantress can't be stopped! Why are all of you so incompetent?" he shouted.

The Fairy Godmother looked at him with her trademark compassion. "Chance, I'm afraid I don't have your answers. Ezmia is just as big a mystery to me as she is to all of you."

"Then tell us what you know," Chance ordered. "Where did this monster come from? What is she after now?"

Sleeping Beauty took a few steps toward the Fairy Godmother. "I'm willing to give myself up to her if that's what she's after," she said.

"My dear, you are not responsible for any of this," the Fairy Godmother said. "I'm afraid I'm the one who is entirely to blame. Ezmia wouldn't be here if it weren't for me."

All the fairies lowered their heads, knowing the Fairy Godmother was telling the truth.

"What do you mean, Fairy Godmother?" Cinderella asked.

"Surely someone like you couldn't be accountable for a creature like that?"

The Fairy Godmother closed her eyes and took a deep breath, deciding where to begin. There was so much to tell and not enough time to tell it.

"It all started centuries ago, on one of my first visits to the Otherworld," the Fairy Godmother explained. "It was a horrible time for that world; there was plague and war everywhere you looked. Today they refer to that period as the *Dark Ages*, and there couldn't be a better description. Sometimes the air would be filled with so much smoke from all the destruction the sun would be hidden for days at a time.

"I discovered a little girl all alone in the middle of the forest, no more than five years old. She was crying and was covered in ash and dirt. She told me that her name was Ezmia and that she had lived in a village nearby. Like many of the villages at the time, hers had been invaded by a group of barbaric soldiers. They swept through the village and killed everyone in their path, including her family.

"The soldiers discovered Ezmia hiding in a barn. However, when they tried harming her, the girl was able to defend herself using *magic*. She told me she had started a giant fire with just her hands and that it consumed her entire village and all the soldiers with it. The girl took me to her village so I could see the damage for myself, and it was devastating. Not only had the villagers perished, but all the land around the town for acres was destroyed. I knew then that this girl was no ordinary child.

"Magic has always been a mysterious thing, but I'm abso-

192

lutely astonished that a child in the middle of another dimension could have such capabilities. But for whatever reason, magic had found this girl and had saved her life, and I believe my discovering her was no accident.

"I didn't think she would survive the Otherworld on her own so I brought her back to our world. I knew she was special because when we arrived in the Fairy Kingdom, the unicorns bowed," the Fairy Godmother said.

Conner looked at his sister. The unicorns had bowed to them when they first traveled to the Fairy Kingdom—what did it mean?

"Ezmia was raised there," the Fairy Godmother continued. "We taught her how to use her magic and she became a fairy. Her powers grew with time and she proved herself to be one of the most gifted fairies the Fairy Kingdom had ever seen.

"Ezmia was also the kindest, most honest, loving young woman I had ever known. She was so thankful I had brought her to live in our world and received so much joy from helping others. I loved her like a daughter and she became my apprentice. I was certain when my time came to an end I could leave this world safely in her hands. I was positive she would be the next Fairy Godmother. We created the Happily Ever After Assembly in hopes that Ezmia would lead it someday.

"But as Ezmia grew into adulthood, she changed. Things were going on beyond our knowledge—things we couldn't see—and she became another person altogether. She became aggressive and mean-spirited; her interest in fairy life faded completely. Helping people became a chore for her and she started abusing her magic.

"It was during our first official meeting as the Happily Ever After Assembly that I knew Ezmia was no longer the little girl I saved in the Otherworld. We hadn't officially appointed a leader of the assembly yet, so I was presiding. The trolls and goblins had just been sanctioned to their own territory but they were still enslaving innocent people from other kingdoms—I asked the rest of the assembly what the best solution was.

"Ezmia blurted out, *'Why don't we just drown them all? Thumbelina Stream practically runs through their territory; just break a dam and be done with them. We can make it look like an accident.'* She almost seemed amused by the idea.

"Naturally, after an outburst like that we couldn't appoint her head of the assembly as planned. We appointed Emerelda and the Fairy Council instead. When Ezmia found out she had been replaced she was enraged. She went on a tirade, dissociating herself from the assembly and the Fairy Kingdom altogether. She changed her entire appearance and refused to be known as a fairy, deeming herself an *enchantress* instead.

"The next time we crossed paths with Ezmia was at Sleeping Beauty's christening. She was uninvited, but we knew she would come anyway. We discovered Rumpelstiltskin had been working for her when he tried kidnapping Sleeping Beauty and we confronted her about it. Ezmia lost control and went on a rampage, cursing the princess to die after pricking her finger on the spindle of a spinning wheel.

"However, I knew that the curse wasn't only going to affect Sleeping Beauty; Ezmia's powers were too strong for that amount of rage to be aimed at just an innocent child. Luckily, I was able to convert the curse into a harmless sleeping spell, and when she pricked her finger on a spinning wheel as planned the entire kingdom was affected, confirming my suspicions.

"Ezmia disappeared after the christening and we never saw her again. We searched everywhere but found no trace of her. Later, word reached us that she had been poisoned by the same toxins that left the upper Eastern Kingdom bare—we figured she must have died and stopped our search. Unfortunately, we were wrong.

"A year ago, my grandchildren accidentally found a way into this world and went missing. While I was searching for them I made a troubling discovery; small weeds started to grow in the Northeast where the flowers and grass had grown: The land had revived itself from the poison—except the poison had obliterated everything good that had come from the soil and the weeds had taken its place.

"I knew then it would only be a matter of time before Ezmia resurfaced. I alerted the Fairy Council at once and we spent the last year actively searching for her but found nothing to lead us in the right direction. It wasn't until her recent attack on the Eastern Kingdom that we were positive she had returned."

The crowd in the ballroom was even tenser after hearing Ezmia's story.

"And why can't we stop her *now*?" King Chance demanded. "If her spells could be converted back then, why can't we get a grip on them anymore?"

"That's what I'm trying to tell you," the Fairy Godmother said. "We taught her everything she knows—we taught her how to use magic from her heart; we had trained her to channel it from a good source—that's why every spell she ever cast could be altered. But when she was poisoned, anything good that was left in her soul was killed. Now Ezmia's powers come from a place of darkness and anger, forces that we fairies don't stand a chance against—and believe me, Ezmia has a lot of anger to feed off of."

Alex and Conner couldn't believe what she was saying. Was their grandmother insinuating that the Enchantress was *unstoppable*?

"So . . . what are we to do?" Snow White asked.

The Fairy Godmother lowered her eyes and looked down at the floor, hating to say it as much as they hated hearing it. "I don't know," she said softly.

And with that, whatever hope had survived was obliterated. It was if the Fairy Godmother had told them the world was over.

Suddenly, all the windows burst open and a monstrous wind blew inside the ballroom, knocking Sleeping Beauty to the ground. A gigantic bolt of lightning hit the floor so hard the entire palace buckled, and in its blinding flash the Enchantress appeared.

She was the most majestic person the twins had ever seen. Her hair and cape flowed through the ballroom, and although her mouth was still, her eyes smiled evilly through her long lashes.

"Hope I'm not late," Ezmia said. "I do love a good story, especially when it's mine."

Alex and Conner clutched on to each other under Red's dress. Everyone in the room was frozen in fear.

"Don't tell me you're having another party without inviting me," Ezmia said, glaring at all the royals and fairies around her. "You'd think you'd have learned your lesson from the last time you didn't include me."

A smirk appeared on her face. Cinderella was the only person to move. She jumped out of her throne and ran straight toward the Enchantress with fists raised. King Chandler and Froggy were quick to grab hold of her, but she lunged with such determination Rapunzel's husband had to join them in holding her back.

"You horrible witch!" Cinderella screamed, struggling against her brothers-in-law. *"Magic or no magic, I'll pull you apart limb from limb if you hurt my daughter!"*

Ezmia just laughed at her.

"What have you done with our daughter, you monster?!" Chance yelled. Emerelda and Skylene placed their hands on his shoulders to keep him from charging toward her.

"She's alive . . . for now," Ezmia said and casually examined her nails. "I hope there are no hard feelings. I'll give her back to you once I'm done with her . . . maybe."

"What do you want with Princess Hope, Ezmia?" the Fairy Godmother demanded.

Ezmia squinted at the Fairy Godmother and walked in a circle around her, closely examining her former teacher. "Why, if it isn't the big *F.G.* herself," she said. "You're looking rather old, *Grams*. Is something on your mind? Is something troubling you?"

"Don't be cheeky, Ezmia, it's a shade you never wore well," the Fairy Godmother said.

Ezmia frowned at her playfully. "You're good at putting on this noble façade, but I know better," she said. "Have you told *them* what I took from you yet? Or have you left that part of your story out because you were afraid they would worry more knowing *you're* just as terrified as the rest of them?"

The Fairy Godmother kept her silence, not giving in to Ezmia's games.

"Fine, I'll tell them," Ezmia said and faced the rest of the room. "I have her *granddaughter*."

Everyone in the room gasped, including the twins. *What was she talking about?* Alex wondered. The Fairy Godmother looked puzzled as well, wondering if the Enchantress had managed to get hold of Alex as well as Charlotte.

"My *granddaughter*?" the Fairy Godmother asked.

Ezmia rolled her eyes. "Oh, don't look surprised," she said. "I took her weeks ago—you had to have known. I left you plenty of clues."

The Fairy Godmother looked at Ezmia with the most neutral face she could muster. "How did you get to her?" she asked.

"It was simple, as most things are for me," Ezmia said with a small shrug. "I stole that book of yours, the old one with all our history in it, *the portal*. I cast a tiny spell on it and was able to pluck her straight out of the Otherworld. I said, *'Bring me the Bailey girl from the place where the Fairy Godmother's precious Bailey family resides'* and that was all. Stupid woman, she didn't even pretend to be someone else—she told me exactly who she was right from the beginning."

Alex grabbed Conner's hand and they locked eyes.

"She thinks Mom is me!" Alex whispered to her brother.

"And Mom must be going along with it!" Conner whispered back. *"But why was she taken instead of you?"*

Alex clutched Conner's shoulder as the answer came to her. "Conner, I was in my honors class when Mom went missing. *I was in the next town—I wasn't in the place where we reside! That's why she got Mom instead!"*

The Fairy Godmother began nodding her head, coming to the same conclusion as the twins. She looked over to Red and stared down at her huge gown again. The twins could have sworn she was looking straight at them—did she know they were under there? Whatever she did or didn't know, it made the Fairy Godmother stand a little taller knowing the Enchantress had made a grave mistake.

"I'll admit you have our attention now," the Fairy Godmother said, quickly looking back to Ezmia. "So what is it that you want from us? Why have you graced us with your presence tonight?"

A menacing smile grew on the Enchantress's face; this was the part she had been waiting two centuries to tell them.

"As you may have guessed, I've decided to take over the world," Ezmia said matter-of-factly with a small yawn. "But rather than continuing to show you examples of my powerful wrath, I've decided to give you an opportunity that will make all our lives easier. I want you all to renounce your thrones and hand over your kingdoms to me *willingly*."

The entire room erupted in outrage. The men had to restrain Cinderella once again.

"Never!" Chance shouted, speaking for everyone in the room.

"Even with an entire kingdom consumed and a young princess's life at stake there is *still* some hesitation?" Ezmia said, shaking her head. "I'm going to take over—it's unpreventable. I'm giving you a chance to accept your defeat with dignity; you'd be wise to take it."

No one moved or made a sound under Ezmia's heavy glare. She turned to Sleeping Beauty, who was still on the floor, trembling under the Enchantress's gaze.

"Why don't you do it first, *Sleeping Beauty*?" Ezmia said. "Show your fellow rulers how easy it is. Your kingdom has been through enough already, wouldn't you agree? Ease their sufferings—do it for your *people*, for your *husband*. If you hand me over your kingdom, I'll release it from my enchanted plants. Do we have a deal?"

All was quiet while Sleeping Beauty contemplated the impossible decision. Snow White and Rapunzel shook their heads, urging her not to give in. Finally, Sleeping Beauty stood up and slowly walked over to stand behind the Fairy Godmother.

"Any partnership I make will be made against you," Sleeping Beauty said. "And my people would expect nothing less."

All the monarchs and fairies looked to one another, inspired by Sleeping Beauty's bravery. One by one, they walked across the ballroom and stood behind the Fairy Godmother, showing the Enchantress where their loyalties would remain.

Ezmia was beside herself with rage. The twins were positive they could see small flames flickering from her eyes. "You're all making the greatest mistake of your reigns," she said. "But don't worry—they'll be ending soon."

The Fairy Godmother took a few confident steps toward Ezmia. "No one in this room may be able to stop you, Ezmia," the Fairy Godmother said and then glanced in the twins' direction. "But I have nothing but the highest confidence someone *unrevealed* will find a way."

Alex and Conner looked to each other. Her words were so carefully chosen—*was she talking about them?*

Ezmia's anger turned to amusement and she let out a long laugh. "I see," she said. "You all think you're safe standing behind your precious Fairy Godmother. Well, in case you think her promising words alone can save you ... *allow me to clarify!*"

Ezmia reached an open hand toward the Fairy Godmother and a gigantic bolt of lightning erupted from it. It hit the Fairy Godmother and she disappeared. A turquoise jar appeared in the Enchantress's hand and a ghostly version of the Fairy Godmother appeared inside of it.

"What will the rest of you do now that I have the Fairy Godmother's *soul*?!" Ezmia asked the room.

Alex and Conner squirmed frantically around in Red's gown. Alex had to hold her brother back as he tried running toward the Enchantress like Cinderella.

"She's got Grandma!" Conner whispered, begging his sister to let him go. *"She's got Grandma!"*

"She can't know we're here, Conner!" Alex whispered back to him.

"Consider this my final warning," Ezmia declared to the crowd. "My attacks on your kingdoms will continue until you surrender to me. We'll see where you stand when all your people are begging you to make the suffering end. Your days of happily-ever-after are over."

Another gigantic bolt of lightning hit the palace and the Enchantress disappeared, taking the Fairy Godmother with her.

Everyone in the room was as pale as Snow White. The twins froze inside Red's gown with their hearts broken. No one knew what to do. All the kings, queens, and fairies searched for some sign of optimism in one another's eyes, but there was none to be found.

For the first time in history, the leaders of the fairy-tale world were helpless.

CHAPTER THIRTEEN

JARS OF SOULS

Deep in the heart of the Dwarf Forests, where the trees and shrubbery grew the thickest, was a small hut unseen by all who passed it. A witch named Hagatha had lived in the hut many years ago and strategically planted a wall of thornbushes around her home, making it virtually impossible to find. And although the witch was long dead, the hut had more residents now than ever before.

The Enchantress had turned the hut into her new home following the restoration of her powers. It still looked the same on the outside, with only two windows and a hay roof, but it had

been charmed to become a spacious manor the moment someone walked through the door.

It had large rooms with high ceilings and black stone walls.
A wide fireplace was made of amethyst stones, within which a
fire of purple flames burned a collection of skulls like firewood.
The furniture was made of exotic porcupine and salamander
animal skins. A chandelier made of various species' teeth hung
from the ceiling but gave no light.

It was usually a quiet place, but tonight the piercing cries of
a child echoed through its halls.

"Please be quiet, little Princess," said Rumpelstiltskin.
Princess Hope was more than half his size, but he still rocked
the one-year-old back and forth, trying to soothe her.

"Mama," the princess cried. *"Mama!"*

"You can't have your mama, I'm afraid," Rumpelstiltskin
told the child, and she bawled harder than before.

"She's been crying for more than a day," said Charlotte Bailey from the back of the room. "Would you please just give her
to me?" The twins' mother was imprisoned in a large birdcage
that swung a few feet above the ground.

"What makes you think you can get her to stop crying?"
Rumpelstiltskin said. He was exhausted from having to care
for the child the last day.

"I'm a nurse—it's what I do," she said.

Charlotte was still dressed in her nursing scrubs. She had
just finished a shift at the children's hospital when a mysterious
blanket of light wrapped around her and transported her into
the fairy-tale world. It didn't take long for Charlotte to realize

that the Enchantress who had summoned her there was after her daughter, and so for Alex's protection, Charlotte had pretended to be her daughter.

It didn't appear that Princess Hope would calm down anytime soon. Against his better judgment, Rumpelstiltskin handed the young princess to Charlotte through the bars of the cage. He didn't care how angry Ezmia would be to find the child with the other prisoner; he just wanted the crying to stop. Rumpelstiltskin had never been good with kids.

"There, there, baby girl," Charlotte said and stroked Hope's auburn curls. "It's all going to be okay, it's all going to be okay."

Slowly but surely, Princess Hope calmed down in Charlotte's maternal embrace, sleeping for the first time since she had been taken. All the young princess needed was a mother's touch.

Rumpelstiltskin was so relieved to have silence; he could have slept for three days if he were allowed. Charlotte studied the little man. Nothing about him was malicious like his master. He seemed like such a gentle and kind man.

"So you're Rumpelstiltskin?" she asked him.

"Yes," he said with a remorseful shrug, ashamed of the reputation that came with his name.

"Did you really spin hay into gold for the maiden, like the story says?" Charlotte asked.

"That I did," Rumpelstiltskin admitted.

"And did you really try to take her firstborn child away from her?" Charlotte said, finding it hard to believe.

Rumpelstiltskin let out a heavy sigh. "That's what *Ezmia* wanted me to do," he said. "But I couldn't go through with it. I told the maiden—well, she was a queen by that point—that I would dismiss her end of our bargain if she could guess my name."

"And she did, if I recall," Charlotte said. It had been a while since she'd heard the story.

"I made sure she did," Rumpelstiltskin confessed. "I caught one of her soldiers following me. I danced around a fire, proclaiming my name to the whole forest as loud as I could."

"So you intentionally made it easy for her," she said. "That was very kind of you."

A tiny smile grew on Rumpelstiltskin's face, but it quickly faded. "I thought so, too," he said. "Unfortunately, no one will ever know that part of the story."

"People are quick to judge," Charlotte said. "And I'm no exception. I never wondered why you did all of those things; my mind was just made up that you were a . . . a—"

"Villain?" Rumpelstiltskin asked, unfazed. It was what he had been known as the majority of his life.

"Yes . . . a *villain*," Charlotte admitted.

Rumpelstiltskin was growing very comfortable talking to Charlotte—too comfortable. Had he not been so tired, he might have kept his guard up, but he couldn't deny there was something trustworthy about Charlotte. They were both good people stuck in a bad situation.

"How did someone like you get mixed up with someone like *her*?" Charlotte asked, shaking her head.

"Because I had the misfortune of being born a dreamer," he

said sadly. "A dwarf is born with one option: *Become a miner.* A life spent in dark tunnels under the ground was never what I wanted for myself. I always loved being outside with the plants and animals; I used to daydream about being a shepherd or a farmer. My brothers used to scold me day and night for it. They said being a miner was an honor and that I was lucky. Then one day Ezmia came to me with an offer to be her apprentice."

Rumpelstiltskin rubbed his eyes and took a seat on a porcupine-skin chair, too fatigued to mind the needles poking him.

"It's funny," he said. "I didn't think twice about saying yes, but I've regretted it every day of my life."

Charlotte couldn't help but feel sorry for him. She realized there were *three* prisoners under this roof.

"Anyone would have said yes if they were in your shoes," she said.

"Back then, perhaps," Rumpelstiltskin agreed. "But *now* no one would ever admit to it."

A strong breeze blew through the room. "Why is the child with *her*?" said a booming voice that made Charlotte and Rumpelstiltskin jump. Ezmia had suddenly appeared.

The Enchantress seemed tired. Her posture wasn't quite as straight and her hair didn't flow as freely as it had before. Ezmia had been planning this night for a long time, and it hadn't ended the way she wanted.

Rumpelstiltskin immediately hopped out of the chair. "Princess Hope wouldn't stop crying," he said. "And I wanted you to have a silent home to return to."

Ezmia scowled at Charlotte and she held on to the princess even tighter. The Enchantress moved toward the cage and peered in at them through the bars like a preying hawk.

"You're awfully good with children, aren't you?" Ezmia said suspiciously.

"I told you, I'm a nurse, it's my job," Charlotte said, shifting uncomfortably under the Enchantress's gaze. "I take care of sick children at a hospital."

Ezmia raised an eyebrow. "Interesting," she said. "I never expected the Fairy Godmother's granddaughter would be so *old*."

"Well, not all of us have magic holding us up," Charlotte retorted.

"You've got spirit, I'll give you that," Ezmia said. "Perhaps *this* will humble you."

Ezmia placed the glass jar she had been carrying on a small table close to Charlotte's cage. Charlotte was horrifed to see a miniature ghostly version of the Fairy Godmother trapped inside.

"That's my . . . my . . . *grandmother*!" Charlotte said, almost forgetting she was still pretending to be her own daughter. "What have you done to her?"

A smile appeared on Ezmia's face, matching the satisfaction in her eyes. "I captured her soul," she said.

The thought almost made Charlotte sick. She'd had no idea such a thing was possible, even in the fairy-tale world.

"What do you want with her soul?" Charlotte asked.

"It's a bit of a hobby of mine, actually," Ezmia said and walked to her fireplace. Displayed proudly on the mantel were five other turquoise jars, each containing a ghostly substance.

"You're a *soul collector*?" Charlotte asked. "Is it to make up for being soulless?"

"What a clever play on words," Ezmia said mockingly. "You know that phrase *forgive and forget*? Well, I always disagreed with it—I found it impossible, actually. People would do me wrong and then *forget* about me, as if their actions didn't matter—because *I* didn't matter. How was I supposed to *forgive* people like that?"

"So you imprisoned their souls instead of forgiving?" Charlotte said.

"Precisely," Ezmia said. "I found taking away their life force to be much more appealing than simply *forgiving*. To forgive would be to allow them to continue living their lives, free of consequence. But by taking their souls and preventing them from all future happiness, I could heal and find peace."

Charlotte couldn't believe what she was hearing.

"Do you honestly expect anyone to sympathize with that?" Charlotte asked her.

Ezmia stared into the fire at the burning skulls, almost in a trance. "I don't want the world to *understand*; I want it to *grovel*," she said.

The confession made Charlotte's heart heavier. She wondered if she would ever escape the clutches of a person who thought like this. But thinking about her children, Bob, and the life she had been stolen from gave Charlotte the strength to survive the Enchantress's imprisonment.

"I find it hard to believe that the Fairy Godmother, who is known for her generosity, would harm you in any way," Charlotte said.

"Sometimes help can be just as destructive as harm," Ezmia said. "But I imagine someone who *helps* for a profession couldn't comprehend that."

"Enlighten me," Charlotte challenged.

The Enchantress raised her eyebrows. "The Fairy Godmother found me in the Otherworld when I was just a girl," Ezmia said. "I was alone, orphaned, and starving. She brought me here to live with the fairies in the Fairy Kingdom. They gave me a home, taught me to use magic in a productive manner, and in time trained me to become one of the greatest fairies in the kingdom."

Charlotte shook her head as though she had misunderstood. "That doesn't sound like something to begrudge," she said.

"Success can scar you as much as failure," Ezmia continued. "The more I surpassed the other fairies with my talents, the more they resented me. Fairies are incredibly jealous creatures, although no one ever talks about it, because it would tamper with their image.

"When the Fairy Godmother declared me her protégé, all the other fairies distanced themselves from me. I had never asked for the attention, but they targeted their frustrations on me as if I had done something to personally offend them. Every spell I cast and every enchantment I performed was subject to an unjustified amount of criticism.

"Even though I was accomplishing incredible things left and right, my achievements were ignored because of the special treatment I received. I became ashamed of my gifts and mediocrity became my new goal—wanting to be in the same league as the others. Lowering my standards only aggravated them more, and by the time I reached adolescence I was alone and starving again, but this time for *affection*."

The Enchantress gestured to the jars displayed on her mantel.

"Which brings us to these," she said. "Now this section of the story is very close to my heart, you see, because inside the jars on my mantel are the souls of five men who unwisely broke it. One man who never loved me, one man who couldn't love me, one man who loved me too much, one man who loved me in secret, and one man who didn't love me enough . . ."

Ezmia picked up the jar farthest to the left and looked inside it. A figure of a young man wearing an apron appeared in the ghostly substance inside.

"The Baker was my first love," the Enchantress said. "He lived in a small village in the Charming Kingdom and worked in his family's bakery. He was the first person besides the Fairy Godmother to ever ask me if I was having a good day. I was so young and vulnerable—all it took was a shared smile to make me fall madly in love with him. We became very close and I confessed my deepest secrets and desires to him. I was positive our love would last forever.

"Unfortunately for me, I learned his intentions were anything but genuine. I had been the subject of a practical joke— the Baker had pretended to have feelings for me only to report back to the other village youths everything that I had confessed to him. He had been playing a game with my heart the whole time.

"I went back to the Fairy Kingdom in tears. I was hoping for some kind of sympathy from them, some sort of compassion—but instead they just laughed at me. They were happy to see something topple me from the pedestal I had never asked to be placed on. You see, I had broken an unwritten rule: Apparently, a person of privilege is never allowed to complain about anything.

"With no one to confide in and no shoulder to cry on, I ran into the forest and collapsed onto the roots of a tree. I lay there for hours and cried my heart out into its bark. That tree was the only thing that ever comforted me from the pain...and I visited that tree quite a bit over the years.

"Over time I tried *forgiving* the Baker, but it only angered me more. I returned to his bakery and demanded an apology. He refused, saying the whole thing had been a childish prank. So I cast a spell on a gingerbread man he was baking. It jumped up from the tray and ran away from him. It became quite the ordeal; the entire village chased after it with no success.

"The Baker and his family became the laughingstock of the village and they lost their bakery...but it made *me* feel *so much better*. That's when I learned that taking the high road would never give the same satisfaction as getting even."

The Enchantress set aside the Baker's jar and moved on to the one next to it. A man holding a hammer with a chain draped over his shoulder appeared in the jar.

"The *Locksmith* was a troubled man," Ezmia said and shook her head. "A testament to his profession, he liked keeping his properties locked down, and I was no exception. I fell for him mostly out of convenience—needing something to repair my heart from the damage left by the Baker. He was such a quiet man, he barely said a word to me. He never looked me in the eye and when he touched me . . . it was rarely out of affection.

"He definitely left his mark on me—*several*, actually. And, like a fool, I stayed, thinking it might be the only type of love I would ever receive. When I finally told him I was leaving him he didn't even blink. He had so many demons already I didn't feel the need to cause him more distress when we parted. I felt more anger toward myself than I did toward him for *letting* him harm me. I kept him as a reminder—to never let myself sink to such pitiful depths again."

Charlotte and Rumpelstiltskin looked sideways at each other. They couldn't believe the Enchantress was telling them so much, but Ezmia had completely lost herself in a stroll through the most painful memories of her past.

The trip down memory lane wasn't entirely for them, however. Telling her captives the stories of her former loves appeared to gradually rejuvenate her from her long night. She stood taller and her hair flowed more vigorously above her. The purple flames in Ezmia's fireplace even grew the more she reminisced. It was undeniable; the Enchantress was fueled by the pain of her past.

Ezmia picked up the third jar in the center of the mantel. A man playing a pipe appeared in the cloudy substance.

"The Musician was the lover I thought I had been waiting for," Ezmia confessed. "I was so taken by his charm. He constantly serenaded me with songs and sonnets. He was so eager to confess our love to the world—*too eager*. I soon realized that it wasn't *me* he was in love with—it was the *idea of me*. He wanted the world to know he was connected to *the future Fairy Godmother*, not *Ezmia*. He was using me like a ladder.

"However, I stayed with him despite knowing his true intentions, dreading the thought of being alone. I showered him with gifts—in particular, an infamous pipe he used to magically clear a town of rats. I had enchanted the pipe myself and had hoped it would equalize our statuses. I thought if I gave him something that made him feel as important as me, he would learn to love me for me and not my title.

"Sadly, the only thing that grew following his victory was his ego, and it led him to infidelity as easily as he had led the rats to the river. I transformed his new lover into an instrument, so he could forever play her in the same way he had played with me."

The Enchantress picked up the fourth jar on the mantel. She stared inside at the soul of a man dressed from head to toe in armor.

"The Soldier was a very guarded man," Ezmia said. "He kept our relationship a total secret. It was refreshing to be with someone so private after the Musician. Later I discovered his discretion was not to protect me but to protect himself. The Soldier was *ashamed* of our relationship. He thought if word broke that he was courting a fairy it would damage his career and he would never be promoted to a general.

"I cast a spell on him that flattened his feet and stiffened his joints. He spent the rest of his days guarding the entrance to a kitchen and never received any promotion at all."

The Enchantress moved on to the final jar on the mantel. A handsome young man wearing robes and a crown appeared inside of it. Ezmia looked at him differently than she had all the others—it was clearly the hardest memory to relive.

"The King hurt me more than anyone," the Enchantress confessed. "Unlike all the others, the King treated me with the compassion all the rest failed to. He was my best friend and the only person who I felt loved me back. Perhaps that common kinship is what made me fall for him more than the others and is why it still hurts to this day. However, he never loved me as much as I loved him. Friendship was the only thing he wanted from me.

"I visited him every day hoping he would change his mind. One day he caught me trying to give him a love potion. I had never seen him so angry; he shouted for the entire castle to hear that he would never love me the same way I loved him, even with all the love potions in the world.

"I lost my temper and I cursed the King to live as a hideous beast, turning him into the monster I thought he was. Eventually he found a girl to love him despite his animalistic features, and my curse was broken. The story of Beauty and the Beast has been exaggerated over time, but the King never told a soul I was the one who cursed him—he was still a friend after everything I had done to him.

"The King's rejection was the final break my heart could take. I thought if the *King* was incapable of loving me, then no one could. The Fairy Godmother says I changed over that period of time, and she's right. I represented 'happily ever after' but couldn't find a happily-ever-after for myself. Everywhere I went I was expected to solve problems, but I couldn't salvage my own. I began hating the world I stood for—I hated the fairies, I hated the pathetic people they helped, and I hated myself for being one of them.

"I stopped pretending I belonged among them. For the first time I began to say and do what *I* wanted to, rather than what I was *expected* to. If the other fairies were going to condemn me regardless of what I did, I figured I might as well give them valid reasons to.

"When they replaced me on the Happily Ever After Assembly and gave my seat to Emerelda, I can't say I was surprised. I was furious and hurt, but I knew the fairies had secretly been waiting for an excuse to take something away from me. Emerelda had never been as gifted as me, but she had always been so *loved* by everyone she met—the fairies knew appointing her would hurt me the most.

"I ran into the forest and found my trustworthy tree to cry into. I stayed and cried for days and days—I felt as if my soul had finally been crushed, as if my entire life had been a cruel experiment to see how much heartbreak I could withstand.

"When I finally dried my tears I looked up at the tree—it was significantly taller than all the other trees in the forest. After all the tears I had shed over the years into its roots, the tree had surpassed all the others surrounding it. I was so ashamed of myself; I couldn't believe what I had let the world do to me. I cast a spell on the tree, causing it to curve and loop like a vine, until it was the same height as all the other trees and the evidence of my heartache was gone.

"That's the moment that the fragile heartbroken fairy inside of me died and the Enchantress was born. I decided from then on if the world was going to speak of my name it would be whispered in fear rather than mocked with envy. If the world was going to take all the joy from me, I would simply *take away all the joy from the world.*"

Ezmia had almost forgotten she wasn't alone. All the pain from her past was what had created the person she was today, so it was difficult for her to realign herself with the present.

"Everyone goes through heartache," Charlotte said. "I've been through my own share of loss, but I got over it. I never plotted a ruthless revenge scheme or held the world responsible for it."

Ezmia jerked her head toward her. *"Really?"* she said angrily. "Have *you* ever felt loneliness so strong that it hollowed your soul with every heartbeat? Have *you* ever hated the sun for rising and forcing another day of solitude upon you?"

"I suppose not," Charlotte said. "No one ever had trouble loving *me.*"

Rumpelstiltskin gasped at Charlotte's bold statement. Ezmia was almost impressed by Charlotte's fearlessness.

"Careful," Ezmia warned her. "There's a thin line between bravery and stupidity."

Charlotte turned away, unable to look at her anymore. Ezmia placed the jar containing the king's soul back on the mantel. "I should retire for the night," she said. "I know I make it look so effortless, but world domination is exhausting. I'm going to rest for a bit before continuing my attacks across the kingdoms. I want to be at my best when I cause the world's worst."

Ezmia headed toward her chambers for the night, but Rumpelstiltskin stopped her before she left the room.

"Ezmia?" Rumpelstiltskin asked, carefully filtering any judgment in his tone. "Are you sure you'll ever find peace? Even after taking over the world, are you certain you'll be satisfied?"

Charlotte turned back, interested to hear the answer. A malevolent smile appeared on the Enchantress's face.

"Silly Rumpy," Ezmia said with a laugh. "Who said I only wanted *this* world?"

CHAPTER FOURTEEN

THE WAND OF WONDERMENT

The carriage ride back into the Red Riding Hood Kingdom was a difficult trip to make. Witnessing the Enchantress take their grandmother's soul was the most devastating thing the twins had ever seen.

Alex cried into her brother's shoulder for most of the trip back to Red's castle.

"She has *Mom*, she has *Grandma*, and soon she'll have the whole *fairy-tale world*!" Alex sobbed. "She's taken everything from us!"

"Not everything, Alex," Conner said. His was the only

reassuring voice in the carriage. "We have each other—and we'll figure out a way to get them back."

Although they appreciated his optimism, Froggy and Red couldn't help but have doubts. The world had been counting on the Fairy Godmother for a solution, and now that she was gone, nothing seemed powerful enough to stand against the Enchantress.

"I'm not sure we can fight this one, Conner," Alex said with tears spilling out of her eyes like a leaky faucet. "For the first time, I think the bad guy may win this story."

The despair grew inside the carriage with every mile it traveled. The twins, Froggy, and Red racked their brains for a solution but couldn't come up with anything. After a day and a half of traveling and worrying, they were very eager to reach Red's castle.

"That's funny," Red said, looking out the window. "I would have expected to be past the wall by now."

Froggy and the twins looked out the window, too. They were surprised there was no sign of the wall in the distance. It did seem to be taking longer than usual to get back to the Red Riding Hood Kingdom.

"Wait a minute..." Conner said and squinted at something in the distance. "Does that say what I think it says?"

The others looked out the window to what he was referring to. The carriage slowly passed a sign that made their stomachs turn.

BO PEEP FAMILY FARMS

"How is that possible?" Red said, and her eyes grew twice in size. "The Bo Peep farms are inside my kingdom. Where was the wall?"

Froggy and the twins stared out at the rural hills surrounding them, wondering the same thing. A few moments later they discovered a group of Red Riding Hood's soldiers standing at the side of the road. They scratched their heads and looked around in bewilderment, just as confused as they were.

Froggy opened the door and poked his head out of the carriage as they passed them. "Excuse me, good sirs? What is going on? Where is the wall?"

"There is no wall, sir," one of the soldiers said in disbelief.

"What do you mean, there is *no wall*?" Froggy asked.

"I mean, there is no wall *anymore*, sir," the soldier said. "The whole thing disappeared earlier this morning."

"What?" Red gasped.

"We were guarding the southern entrance when a bright flash came out of nowhere," another soldier explained. "The next thing we knew, the whole wall was gone!"

Alex and Conner turned to each other, each thinking the same thing.

"The Enchantress," Alex said. *"She's started her attacks!"*

Red placed a hand over her chest, trying to calm her uncontrollably beating heart. Even after hearing the Enchantress's warnings firsthand, she'd never thought *her* home would be targeted.

"Were there any casualties?" Froggy asked the soldiers.

"No, sir," one replied. "Just a lot of confusion."

Froggy shut the carriage door and sank into his seat across from the twins. "So it begins," he said sadly to himself.

It was dusk by the time the carriages approached Red's castle. They felt so exposed without the wall. And as they looked around the town, it was apparent the villagers felt the same. Everywhere they looked, wooden boards were nailed over doors and windows of the homes and shops, as if the residents were preparing for a storm.

"I haven't seen people this frightened since the Big Bad Wolf was around," Red said. "It reminds me of the days before the C.R.A.W.L. Revolution."

Froggy took Red's hand in his; her mind was too preoccupied to notice its cold, slimy texture. "Ezmia could have done much worse," Froggy said. "Thankfully, it was just the wall."

His words had the opposite effect of what he'd intended. Red pulled her hand out from his and her eyes became watery.

"It's not *just* a wall," Red yelled. "That wall is what separates us from the rest of the world! It represents our safety and victory after years of struggling! The Big Bad Wolf and his succeeding pack may be gone, but that wall has always been a symbol of peace to my people."

Red wiped away the few tears that had escaped, embarrassed by her outburst. "As soon as we get back to my castle I'm going to order a line of soldiers to surround the town at once," Red said and nodded to herself. "We may not have a wall, but we *will* be protected."

Froggy and the twins nodded along with her. The twins liked seeing Red give an official and selfless order as queen.

Maybe Froggy had been right about her. Maybe there was much more to Red than they had ever considered.

They eventually reached the castle, and as soon as Red gave her orders to the soldiers, the four of them headed into the library for a much-needed quiet and recuperative evening. But as they walked in, they were shocked to discover a surprise visitor who had been awaiting their arrival.

"Jack!" Red yelled.

The infamous Jack of beanstalk fame was nonchalantly sitting in one of the armchairs. He was tall and handsome, with broad shoulders, exactly how the twins remembered him. He wore suspenders, and his trusty axe hung from his belt.

"Hello, Red!" Jack said and stood to greet the group.

Red went pale and stiff as a statue. *"What . . . what . . . what* are you doing here?" she managed.

"Visiting, obviously," Jack said with a smile.

The young queen could only make a couple high-pitched squeals as she attempted to form another question. Froggy's eyes went back and forth between Red and Jack—he couldn't decide if the surprise was good or bad.

"Well, this is . . . *unexpected*," Froggy said and chose to smile.

Jack's face lit up when he saw the twins. "I remember you two," he said.

"Hi, Jack," Alex said.

"Hey, man," Conner said.

Despite everything else on their minds, the twins were glad to see him. Red grew anxious quickly and she began looking around the library.

"Wait, Jack, if *you're* here then that means—"

SLAM! The library doors shut with gusto. They all turned to see Goldilocks standing behind them.

"YOU!" Red said and pointed at her. She quickly backed away from her old nemesis.

"Hello, Red," Goldilocks said with a fake smile. She wore tall leather boots and a long maroon knitted sweater. A silver sword swung from her side. She had golden curls and was just as beautiful as the last time the twins had seen her.

There was something different about Goldilocks and Jack that the twins noticed; they both looked much *happier* now that they were on the run together.

"Goldilocks!" Alex said, and she and her brother ran to give Goldilocks a hug.

"What a wonderful surprise," Goldilocks said, and a proud smirk appeared on her face. "I would say, 'It's nice to see you again, children,' but you're hardly *children* anymore."

Conner nodded. "Thank you!" he said. "That's what we've been trying to tell everyone!"

Goldilocks playfully rubbed his head. "I had at least four warrants for my arrest by the time I was your age," she said and then winked at Jack.

Jack smiled at her. "I'm a late-blooming bandit myself, but I'm catching up," he said and winked back. They lovingly stared at each other as if no one else were in the room.

"YOU!" Red said, still pointing at Goldilocks. She looked like a teapot whose spout had been corked.

"Oh, relax, Red," Goldilocks said. "We aren't here to cause any trouble. I'm not going to hurt you."

Red snorted. "You bet your porridge-loving indecisive behind you won't be harming me! This is my castle!" she said. "You're both wanted fugitives! How did you get inside?"

"We used the front door," Jack said blankly. "They let us in without any trouble. I grew up with most of the guards, remember?"

Red looked back and forth between Jack and Goldilocks, not wanting to believe the statement was true. It was frustrating to feel so disrespected in her own home.

"Does the word *queen* mean anything to anyone?!" Red shouted. "Shouldn't my *safety* be a *priority* in *my* castle?"

Froggy decided to break the tension. "Forgive us—we weren't expecting company and have had a rough few days," he explained, still a little on edge himself. "Why don't we have a seat and catch up?"

No one argued. Everyone took a seat around the Big Bad Wolf floor rug. It took a minute for Red to gather her thoughts and join them. She sat next to Froggy but left a noticeable space between them. Jack and Goldilocks sat across from them, sitting so close to each other they looked joined at the hip. Alex and Conner shared an armchair adjacent to the couples.

"You just returned from the Happily Ever After Assembly meeting, I take it?" Goldilocks asked.

"Indeed," Red said with her nose raised slightly. "Because that's what we *law-abiding rulers* do: We meet *publicly* and discuss things that *benefit the greater good*."

Her words didn't affect Goldilocks in the slightest. "Where's the fun in that?" Goldilocks said, happy to get under Red's skin.

"How did it go?" Jack asked.

"It was awful," Conner said. "The Enchantress showed up and kidnapped our grandmother! And she already has our mom!"

Jack and Goldilocks looked to each other with the same inquisitive expression. "What could she want with your mother and grandmother?" Goldilocks asked the twins.

Alex and Conner had forgotten Jack and Goldilocks had made a run for it long before they discovered who their grandmother was.

"Our grandmother is the Fairy Godmother," Alex said with a shrug that said *"surprise."*

Jack and Goldilocks looked rather impressed. "Well, how about that?" Jack said.

The twins told them all about how they were from another world and their grandmother had traveled back and forth for centuries sharing the stories of the fairy-tale world with theirs. Once Jack and Goldilocks had processed the information, the twins continued to tell them how their father had used the Wishing Spell to be reunited with their mother in the Otherworld and how they had discovered the fairy-tale world by traveling through their grandmother's old storybook.

"Yes, yes, yes—and it was very touching," Red said, waving her hands. "They learned the Fairy Godmother was their grandmother and then all three of them disappeared through a door that led into a different world, blah blah blah—*you still haven't told me what you two are doing in my castle*?"

The twins could tell Jack and Goldilocks were interested in

hearing more of the story but knew they'd better appease Red before her head exploded.

"We wanted to see if any progress had been made with the Enchantress," Jack said.

"Nope, there hasn't been any, sorry—you both can leave now," Red replied quickly.

Froggy placed his hand on her knee. "Darling, let's not be rude," Froggy said. "They may be emotionally distressing wanted fugitives, but they're still our guests."

The twins were eager to tell Jack and Goldilocks about the meeting from the previous night and didn't wait for Froggy or Red to get to it. They told them all about Princess Hope being kidnapped and how the Enchantress had taken their grandmother and was starting to attack the kingdoms.

"And there's nothing that can be done to stop her?" Jack said, shaking his head in the same disbelief the twins had felt for days.

"Unfortunately not," Froggy said.

"I don't know how the situation concerns the two of you," Red said and crossed her arms.

"This affects us, too," Goldilocks said. "We don't want to live in a world ruled by her, either. We thought we could help."

"*Help?*" Red said and laughed at the idea. "And what are you going to do, Goldilocks? Steal her jewels? Pick her locks? Test all her furniture until it's *just right*?"

Goldilocks stood and glared down at Red. It made the queen squirm in her seat. She looked to the others for help, but she was on her own.

"Is there something you want to say to my face, *Grandma's girl*?" Goldilocks asked.

"No, I'd much rather say it behind your back," Red said.

"I thought after helping me escape you had changed," Goldilocks said. "But apparently I was wrong."

"Well, I thought helping you would make me feel better, but I suppose I was wrong, too," Red admitted and sheepishly glanced over at Jack.

Froggy raised his green index finger. "Moving back to more important matters," he said, "the fairies and monarchs don't have any clue what to do. The Fairy Godmother has always been able to just wave her wand and make things better, but unfortunately she can't this time. So now we're all waiting for a solution to arise . . . if there is one."

The twins nodded. Goldilocks sat back down next to Jack and held his hand. The room was reunited with the hopelessness they had tried leaving in the carriage.

Suddenly, Conner cocked his head like a puppy.

"Froggy, what did you just say?" he asked, pointing at his amphibious friend.

"I said no one knows what to do," Froggy said, not sure how he could have made it clearer.

"No, before that," Conner said. "What did you say about the Fairy Godmother?"

Froggy looked at him peculiarly, wondering why he wanted the horrible news to be repeated. "I said the Fairy Godmother usually just waves her wand and makes everything better," he said.

"Bingo!" Conner said and immediately jumped out of the armchair and ran toward the bookshelves.

"Conner, what's gotten into you?" Alex asked.

"Hey, Froggy," Conner asked, completely in his own world. "Where is that book we were looking at the other day? The one that had the chapter about the Wishing Spell in it?"

It took a moment for Froggy to remember. *"Myths, Legends, and Collecting Spells?"* he asked. "It should be on the shelf two over and one below the books from your sister. I'm very specific about where my books are kept."

Conner scanned the shelves until he found it. "Gotcha," he said with a satisfied jump. He sat back down next to his sister and flipped through the pages. "I think the answer we're looking for is in this book!"

"Are you talking about using the Wishing Spell again?" Froggy asked.

"Could we use it on the Enchantress?" Jack asked.

"Trust me, wishing someone away never works," Red said and raised an eyebrow in Goldilocks's direction. Goldilocks placed a hand on her sword as a warning.

"We couldn't use the Wishing Spell even if we wanted to," Alex said. "The spell could only be used twice, and the Evil Queen was the second person to use it."

"I'm not talking about the Wishing Spell," Conner said, his eyes still glued to the pages he was searching. "I'm thinking about something even bigger and better and—*found it!*"

Conner turned the book around to the section he was referring to.

" 'The Wand of Wonderment'?" the room read together. Conner nodded enthusiastically, expecting them all to share his excitement. Unfortunately, everyone else just exchanged pitying looks with one another.

"Why are you all looking at me like I want to take my pet rock for a walk?" Conner asked. "This book says that whoever holds the Wand of Wonderment is *invincible*. Whoever gets their hands on it *could potentially stop the Enchantress*!"

Froggy looked at him regretfully. "That isn't real, Conner," Froggy said. "That's just a childish legend like all the other subjects in that book."

"Okay, says the *giant talking frog*!" Conner said with an eye roll. "This book talks about the Wishing Spell, too, and we've proven that *that* wasn't just a myth. I bet most of the stuff in this book is real, too.

" 'The Wand of Wonderment,' " he read aloud from the book. " 'Many believe that possessing the Wand of Wonderment gives the beholder the gift of invincibility. It is said that the Wand is formed when combining the six most prized possessions of the six most hated people in the world. Although the idea is dubious, the legend of the Wand may have some truth to it considering the materials needed are most likely of a magic background. Unlike most collections, the materials required for making the Wand of Wonderment may change with the times.' "

Conner took a breath and looked up at the others, who still looked ambivalent.

"Oh, come on," Conner said to the stubborn group. "You've got to admit that it doesn't seem like too much of a stretch."

Everyone was on the fence about it. Conner was frustrated that they weren't as convinced as he was.

"My sister and I are from *another dimension*," he said and then pointed to Froggy. "*This guy* has been magically transformed into a giant amphibian *twice*! What part about the Wand of Wonderment is hard for any of you to believe in?"

Conner made a valid point. What about this Wand was so hard for them to believe after all the other things they had witnessed? At least it was an *option*, and an option gave them *hope*. Alex silently stared down at the book with a growing eagerness in her eyes.

"Just out of curiosity's sake," Alex said, "who are the six most hated people in this world?"

Red looked up at Goldilocks and opened her mouth to answer.

"By the *world*, Red, not by you," Alex clarified and Red went silent.

"I'd say the Evil Queen is a candidate," Froggy said, and the others nodded in agreement.

"The giant," Jack said. "And I'm not speaking from personal experience—people were terrified of him."

"The Snow Queen," Goldilocks mentioned. "Her historic reign over the Northern Kingdom still sends shivers down people's spines."

Conner was all ears, making mental notes of their suggestions. "Who else?" he said.

"You know, I've personally never cared for Miss Muffet," Red said, as if she was confessing a horrid secret. "I mean, it was just a spider! Get over it!"

Everyone in the room stared at Red for a moment and then went on with their brainstorming.

"What about the Sea Witch, who traded with the Little Mermaid?" Alex said. "I was always scared of her as a kid."

"Oh yeah! I bet all the fish in the sea are afraid of her!" Conner said.

Froggy sat straight up in his seat as another idea came to him. "Cinderella's *wicked stepmother*!" he said. "The whole Charming Kingdom despises her."

"This is great," Conner said. "So far we have the Evil Queen, the giant, the Snow Queen, the Sea Witch, and the wicked stepmother. We just need one more."

They all went silent and their eyes wandered around the room.

"Well, isn't it obvious?" Red said. "It's the *Enchantress*."

Lumps grew in everyone's throats; Red was right.

"Well, the Wand of Wonderment was a good *idea*," Goldilocks said, as if it were obvious it was no longer possible. Everyone slumped in their seats, but Conner wouldn't accept defeat.

"What's wrong with you guys?" he said. "We can't let confronting Ezmia get in the way. This may be our only chance at stopping her!"

He desperately looked to everyone in the room, hoping for someone to agree with him, but no one said anything. Conner leaped to his feet, deciding actions would have to speak louder than words if he wanted to get through to them. He walked around the room collecting random books off the shelves.

"What are you doing?" Alex asked him.

He didn't respond. He took a portrait of Red off the wall

and added a couple candlesticks to his pile. He walked to the fireplace and promptly dumped everything into the fire.

"*Conner!*" Alex said.

"*Those are mine!*" Red said.

"*Have you gone mad?*" Froggy asked him.

Conner stood in front of the fireplace with his hands on his hips. The fire slowly consumed the pile of stuff behind him.

"You won't need them anymore," Conner said. "Don't you get it? If we just sit around and wait, the Enchantress is going to take over! *Everything* we love will be gone!"

Alex wanted to share her brother's passion, but she couldn't get her head past the odds. "Conner, it's just too dangerous. It's practically a death wish," she said.

Her lack of faith was about to make Conner jump out of his skin. "Doing *nothing* is a death wish!" he said. "If building this Wand of Wonderment thing offers us a chance at saving the world, we'd be idiots not to try it!"

Conner was practically in tears trying to convince them. Everyone looked back and forth between him and the objects burning in the fireplace. A decision had to be made. However, one thing was certain; whatever they did, they risked losing it all.

Froggy stood up abruptly. "I agree with Conner," he said with his head held high. "We know the outcome of doing nothing, so I'd rather die fighting."

Froggy's words had a rallying effect.

"I've never been good at just sitting around," Goldilocks said, standing with Froggy. "Besides, you'll need someone who's good with a sword out there."

Jack stood next to Goldilocks. "If the Enchantress thinks she's taking over without a fight, she's mistaken," he said.

Their determination made Alex's heart skip a beat.

"This is a *really* big decision to make," she told them. "Once we make it, there's no looking back; we can't give up if the stakes become too high. We won't be able to do it unless we agree on that. No matter what, we can't give up."

Froggy looked to Jack, Jack looked to Goldilocks, and Goldilocks looked to Conner. The same confident smile appeared on their faces.

"I'm up for the challenge," Conner said, looking to his sister.

Alex nodded and stood, too. "Then count me in," she said and smiled.

"Me too!" Red exclaimed, the last to stand. "I have no additional point to make, but I support this venture completely! No one takes my wall away from me and gets away with it!"

Conner went to a desk in the corner of the library and quickly retrieved a piece of parchment and a quill.

"Let's make a list of the things we'll need to make the Wand of Wonderment!" he said. "We've narrowed it down to the six most hated people in the world—now, what are those people's most prized possessions?"

Everyone sat down and began planning out the expedition.

"Everyone knows the Snow Queen's scepter is her most prized possession," Goldilocks said. "It's where her magic comes from."

"Snow Queen—magic scepter," Conner said and wrote the information down.

"I imagine the wicked stepmother's most valued possession has something to do with her family. An heirloom for her atrocious daughters perhaps," Froggy proposed. "She won't be hard to get to. She still lives in the same home Queen Cinderella grew up in."

"Wicked stepmother—family heirloom," Conner said and made a note of it.

"The giant's favorite item shouldn't be difficult to figure out, either," Jack said. "There weren't many things in his castle when I traveled there as a boy. It's difficult finding material things that size."

"Giant—to be determined," Conner said.

"The Evil Queen's would have to be her Magic Mirror," Red suggested. "Think about all she went through to free that creepy bald man from it."

"Evil Queen—Magic Mirror," Conner said. "And just when I thought our Evil Queen days were behind us."

"It's in pieces at the bottom of castle ruins but it shouldn't be hard to retrieve," Alex said, trying to comfort him.

"What about the Sea Witch?" Red asked. "What could she not live without?"

"Her jewels!" Goldilocks said without hesitation. "It's what she collects in exchange for favors. Unless she bargains for something greater."

"Sea Witch—loves her bling," Conner said and scribbled it down.

"All we have left is the Enchantress," Alex said and the room unanimously took a deep breath. "What is Ezmia's most prized possession?"

Everyone drew a blank. They all knew the Enchantress loved power, but how would that manifest as an object?

"We'll have to come back to it. I'll put a question mark by her name for now," Conner said.

Goldilocks looked over his shoulder at the list they'd compiled.

"These people live far and wide across the kingdoms," she said. "How are we going to get around?"

Jack looked over the list, too. "Not to mention a group of travelers would look awfully suspicious at a time like this," he said.

"And we'll need to travel fast, too," Alex said. "The Enchantress said herself she's grown impatient."

The room was filled with a low humming sound as Froggy thought on it. "We'll need something to travel in quickly and discreetly across the land," he said, rubbing his chin. "Let me propose we forget about traveling on land and suggest we travel above it!"

Froggy hopped to the other side of the library and returned with a book. Alex recognized the title and instantly knew what Froggy was getting at.

"We'll travel by *balloon*!" Froggy said excitedly. "Just like the travelers did in *Around the World in 80 Days*! I have to admit, I've been waiting for a situation to arise that offered an excuse to build something like it since I read the book."

"Froggy, that's very . . . *ambitious*," Alex said.

"But it just might work!" Conner said. "The Enchantress isn't going to be expecting people in the sky! This world is centuries away from aviation!"

"Precisely," Froggy said and flipped through the book. He quickly grabbed the quill out of Conner's hand and began sketching something on the back of their list. "Now, in the story there were only three travelers, so all they needed was a large basket to travel in. But I propose we go even further—we need something to glide across the sky *and* sail across the sea— so let's build a *ship*!"

Froggy finished his drawing and showed it to the room. His proposal was a modest boat-shaped vessel with sails on the sides of a large balloon above it.

"Can we build something that extravagant in time?" Goldilocks asked.

Jack took the sketch and examined it himself, rubbing the side of his head. "It's not the construction I'm worried about, it's the amount of supplies needed to build it," he said. The twins remembered he was a very talented carpenter, so they took his words to heart.

Red took a closer look at the drawing. "Exactly what kind of supplies would be needed?" she asked with a raised eyebrow.

Froggy looked down at the drawing. "Lumber, very sturdy fabric, and a lot of lamp oil," he said.

Red squinted and quietly nodded, counting things off in her head. "Yup, I have all of those things here in the castle," she said with a big smile.

Everyone did a double take at her. "Where?" Conner asked.

"We can weave the ship out of all the wood from my basket collection," Red said. "I think my collection of summer dresses would provide enough fabric for the balloon and the sails—they were made with the finest fabric in the kingdom. As for the lamp oil, they keep barrels and barrels of it in the castle just to warm the water for my baths. And I take a *lot* of baths."

"Didn't you lose all your baskets in the fire?" Alex asked.

"Most of them," Red said. "But I've had plenty of birthdays and holidays since then. My collection is practically complete again."

The twins couldn't argue. If the dress Red had worn to the Happily Ever After Assembly meeting was any indication, the queen definitely had enough supplies to go around.

"I think it may work," Jack said. "I can have some better plans drawn up by tomorrow morning. Red, can you send for the best builders in the kingdom? We'll need as many as we can get."

"Absolutely," Red said. "The third Little Pig happens to be one of the best builders in the kingdom, and he actually owes me a favor—he accidentally built part of his brick house on Bo Peep property and I pardoned him."

"How long will it take to build?" Goldilocks asked Jack.

"Four or five days if we work diligently," Jack said. "Three days if we work around the clock."

"Terrific," Froggy said.

"It's really a great idea, Froggy," Conner said.

Froggy smiled. "I think so, too," he said. "It'll make traveling a lot easier, not having to trek through the northern mountains to the Snow Queen or up a beanstalk to the giant's castle."

Jack cleared his throat. "Unfortunately, we'll still need to climb the beanstalk," he said.

"Why?" Alex asked.

"The beanstalk is what summons the giant's castle," Jack said. "It won't appear unless the beanstalk grows to a certain height."

Conner scrunched his forehead. "Where is the beanstalk, anyway? I don't think we've seen it since we've been here," he asked.

Red went silent and stared at the floor.

"Red, did you do something with Jack's beanstalk?" Goldilocks asked, noticing her not-so-subtle bashfulness.

Red looked around the room with guilty eyes. "I may have had it *removed*," she confessed.

"Removed?!" Jack yelled. "Why would you do that?!"

"Because it was an *eyesore*!" Red said defensively. "Besides, it was hard waking up every day and having *that* staring down at me—you know—after all of *this*." She gestured to herself, Jack, and Goldilocks.

"Oh, great," Goldilocks said. "Now what are we going to do?"

Jack sighed. "I'll have to find the Traveling Tradesman again," he said. "Hopefully he'll have more magic beans or know where to get them. I'll leave as soon as I get the builders set up tomorrow."

"Then it's settled," Froggy said with a clap. "The five of us will leave as soon as the ship is ready."

Red looked at him sideways. "What do you mean *five* of you?" she asked.

Goldilocks's mouth fell open. "Don't tell me you were planning on coming?" she said.

239

"Of course I'm coming," Red said. "I'm supplying every-thing for it, aren't I?"

"With all due respect, Red," Conner said, "this trip may not be suitable for a queen."

"Excuse me?" Red said, horribly offended. "If mem-ory serves me right, the last time we were all together I had been kidnapped twice, thrown into a pit of demonic plants, and almost mauled to death all in the same day! Are you tell-ing me my life can only be in danger when it's convenient for *you?*"

Red crossed her arms even tighter and looked away from the others. There was no changing her mind.

"Darling?" Froggy asked. "Do you think that's the best idea, given the *history* of everyone traveling?"

"I'm coming!" Red declared. "I'm not sitting around here and letting the five of you take credit for saving the world with-out me. I should start packing immediately! I've never packed for an adventure before!"

Red giddily got to her feet and ran out of the library. The others shot Froggy a dirty look.

"I'm going to go talk to her and explain the situation a bit more," he said and quickly followed the excited young queen out of the room.

Jack went to the desk and began outlining better plans for the ship. Goldilocks stayed with the twins by the fire. A proud smile came to her face as she looked at them.

"What is it?" Alex asked her.

"Nothing," Goldilocks said with a shrug. "I just recall a

time when I told the two of you to be brave, and now look who's doing the convincing."

Alex and Conner exchanged a smile. They had grown a lot since their last trip.

"I should feed Porridge," Goldilocks said. "I had to put her in the castle stables and she's never gotten along very well with other horses."

Goldilocks left the library, gently tapping the twins on their shoulders on the way out. It grew very quiet in the library, except for the flames flickering in the fireplace and the strokes of Jack's quill as he worked on the ship's designs.

"You almost lost me there," Alex told her brother. "I felt so defeated—thanks for pulling me back."

"Any time," Conner said. "Thanks for helping me cheat on my tests in sixth grade."

Alex let out a noise that was half gasp and half laugh. "How did you know about that?" she asked.

Conner looked at her. "The only C or B that belonged on my tests were my initials," he said.

Alex laughed for the first time in two days. She missed the times when passing tests was their biggest concern.

"Are you sure you're up for this?" Alex asked him.

Conner thought about it. "You mean another dangerous adventure through the fairy-tale world collecting various items with potential life-or-death stakes?" he asked with a sly grin.

Alex snickered. "Yes, that's what I'm referring to."

Conner thought about it for a moment and then nodded to himself. "Bring it on," he said.

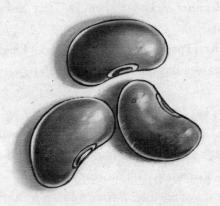

CHAPTER FIFTEEN

BEAN THERE, DONE THAT

The balcony doors burst open and Queen Red Riding Hood emerged from the castle. She was dressed in her best gown and was covered in her finest jewelry. Red always dressed to impress when speaking to her people.

"Fellow Hoodians," Red said with raised arms. "Thank you for joining me today!"

She glanced down at her observers and was disappointed by the lack of attendance. Although the entire kingdom had been invited to hear a message from the queen, only a crowd of roughly two dozen had gathered outside—including two sheep and a goat.

Red swallowed her pride and went on with her announcement.

"I'm assuming many people are too frightened to leave their homes, especially after the disappearance of our beloved wall, so please pass this message along," Red said. "However challenging the current times may be, I have called you all here to encourage your strength and bravery—we have faced great threats in the past and have always overcome them together as a kingdom! And as I look around at your faces I can see that courage in your eyes! The Enchantress may have taken our wall, but she will never take away our spirit!"

Red posed for applause but there was none to accept.

"Furthermore," she continued, "if there is one thing the people of the Red Riding Hood Kingdom know how to do— with the exception of the Boy Who Cried Wolf—it's survive!"

Red caught her breath. She had forgotten the rest of her speech.

"What was the other point I was going to make, darling?" The young queen spoke out of the side of her mouth. Luckily for Red, Froggy was standing inside the castle just on the other side of the balcony doors.

"We're going to rebuild the wall!" Froggy whispered to her.

"Oh yes, that's right! Thank you," Red said and then refaced her people. "We are going to rebuild our wall!"

Red struck another pose of grandeur. This time she didn't continue until she heard clapping from the people below.

"But before we do that, I'd like to invite all the carpenters in the kingdom to my castle this afternoon to work on something else—I know it's short notice, but it would mean so much to me," she said. "Thank you for joining me today, Hoodians! I wish you all peace and poverty!"

"Prosperity, my dear! Prosperity!" Froggy corrected her.

"I mean peace and prosperity!" Red declared and then quickly went back inside the castle. As soon as the doors shut behind her Red began taking off her jewelry and passing it to her handmaiden.

"Tough crowd," Red said with a sigh. "At least I got all the 'queen words' in there."

The twins had been listening to Red's speech with Froggy.

" 'Queen words'?" Alex asked.

"Yes—*strength, bravery, courage, spirit*—the four words essential to making a good speech as queen," Red said and then quickly changed the subject. "Have all the baskets and dresses been taken down to the courtyard yet?"

"Yes, Your Majesty," the handmaiden said.

The twins had awoken that morning excited to see that the castle's courtyard had been transformed into a workstation. Red's servants piled thousands and thousands of baskets from her collection in one corner of the courtyard and hundreds of her summer dresses in another.

Jack had spent the entire night drawing up detailed plans for their flying ship. The blueprints were posted on an enormous board in the center of the courtyard for all to see.

"That should do it," Jack said with a huge yawn. "How soon can we expect the builders?"

"A few have already arrived but the rest should be here by noon," Froggy said.

Goldilocks scanned the courtyard. "I think we have a problem," she said and gestured to the pile of dresses. "Who is supposed to make the ship's balloon and sails?"

Alex and Conner looked at each other, each hoping the other would have an answer.

"Don't look at me," Conner said. "I barely passed Home Economics. I almost set the school on fire pouring cereal, remember?"

"I'm not very good with a needle," Alex said. "Do you know of any good seamstresses in the kingdom?"

"I've already asked Granny," Red said, happily charging into the courtyard.

No one said a word at first, but they were all thinking the same thing.

"Are you sure your grandmother is capable of stitching together a balloon and sails for a flying ship, dear?" Froggy bravely asked.

"Of course she is!" Red said without a sliver of doubt. "She and the Little Old Woman who manages the Shoe Inn will be here later to work on it. They were delighted by the request. Granny's been making my clothes since I was a toddler. Trust me—if there's anyone who can do it, it's her."

Within the hour, Red's granny and the Little Old Woman arrived at the castle with their needles and thread ready. Unlike Mother Goose, these ladies were exactly how the twins had always pictured them. They both had gray hair wrapped into tight buns on the top of their heads and reading glasses placed on the tips of their noses. The Little Old Woman walked with a cane and Granny carried a large purse full of yarn and thread.

"Thank you so much for coming, Granny!" Red said and hugged her grandmother.

"No problem at all, sweetheart," Granny said. Her voice was soft, slow, and soothing. "It's rather nice to take a break from retirement. We can only play cards and watch the grass grow for so many hours in a day before it gets tiresome."

"*What?!*" the Little Old Woman asked loudly. Obviously, she was a little hard of hearing. And if the way she was squinting was any indication, she was also hard of seeing.

Granny spoke directly in her ear. "I was telling Red that we're happy to be out of the Shoe Inn."

"*Who's dead?!*" the Little Old Woman asked.

"Not dead—*Red*, my granddaughter," Granny said.

"*Your granddaughter's dead?!*" the Little Old Woman said, aghast.

Granny turned back to Red. "Don't mind her, sweetheart. She has more than two hundred grandchildren—her ears aren't what they used to be."

Froggy, Goldilocks, Jack, and the twins were growing more pessimistic by the second. Could these elderly hands be given such a daunting task?

"*This* is what we're trying to build," Red said and showed the old women the blueprints on the board. "Do you think you'll be able to make it?"

"Let's see," Granny said and pushed up her glasses for a better look. "Looks like you got a balloon and sails of some kind, huh? Are you kids going on an adventure?"

"It just so happens we are!" Red said with her head raised high. "We're going to save the world!"

"That's very nice, sweetheart," Granny said and patted her on the back. She didn't seem too invested in what Red had to say, as if a little girl had told her she was going to the moon. "Do you have fabric or should I run to the shop?"

"We should have everything we need here," Red said and gestured to the mountain of her dresses piled in the corner.

"Well, look at you, being thrifty," Granny said. She took one last glance at the board and at the pile of dresses and nodded. "Yes, I think we'll manage just fine."

Red jumped and clapped. The others looked more skeptical than ever.

"Are you positive you can manage?" Jack asked. Before he could get an answer the old women had sat themselves on stools near the pile of dresses and begun ripping their seams apart.

"Oh, this is nothing," Granny said. "Remember that summer *you* ballooned, Red? Poor dear, you gained so much weight I had to make you new clothes every week."

The twins had to bite their fists to keep from laughing. Goldilocks didn't even try to shield her chuckle.

"You don't say?" Goldilocks said with a sly smile.

Red blushed a deep shade of her name. "Granny, I don't think this is an appropriate time to—"

"That's why I made her the red cloak she's so famous for," Granny said, oblivious to her granddaughter's embarrassment. "It was the only thing that fit her longer than a week! She used to show up to my house with empty baskets every time I fell ill. I never understood why her mother was sending them to me; then I figured out Red was eating all the baked goods inside them on her way to my house."

No one in the courtyard could hide their laughter after hearing this. Even Froggy let a snicker escape.

"I was an emotional eater!" Red declared in her own defense. "I had a lot of things on my mind at the time." She unintentionally glanced toward Jack. "Thankfully, like all my clothes, I grew out of that phase."

"Yes, sweetheart," Granny said. "We all were thankful for that—except for the fabric store."

Granny and the Little Old Woman both ripped impressively long seams at the same time. The sound made Red cringe even more. Although it had been her idea, Red couldn't bear to watch her dresses be torn apart—or to stick around for her granny to share any more embarrassing memories.

"If you all will please excuse me," Red said and headed out of the courtyard. "I think I'm going to lie down for a minute. My life has suddenly become a Shakeyfruit play."

Word must have spread through the kingdom, because by noon the courtyard was filled with dozens of builders and carpenters alike, eager to help their young queen. The third Little Pig was the last to arrive, pulling a toolbox half his size behind him.

"I huffed and I puffed and I dragged this all the way from home," he told the others. "Serves me right for being in the red with Queen Red."

Jack stood on one of the larger baskets to address the room. "Welcome, and thank you all so much for coming! I'm afraid the task is large and our time is short, so forgive me for speaking hastily. The queen has put together a small mission in hopes of salvaging what's left after the Enchantress's return. The mission involves a special ship, designed to sail across the clouds rather than the sea, and it must be built in record time."

Jack walked across the room to the blueprints.

"If you could all gather round and take a look," Jack instructed. "Our supplies are scarce but I believe if we follow these plans precisely we could build this in a matter of days. I won't lecture you with the reasons this project must remain an absolute secret, I'll only repeat that your involvement may finally free the world from the Enchantress's grip. So if you all could be so kind as to lend us your labor, your strength, and your devotion, we can get started immediately and put a stop to this madness once and for all."

None of the carpenters objected—his words had encouraged them past the point of questioning. Half of them began stripping the baskets into usable pieces while the others aligned them and started crafting them together to form the ship's bow.

Jack was beaming. For the first time in a long time, he was taking charge of something productive—and he was a great leader.

"He's really good at this sort of thing," Alex said to Goldilocks.

"Quite good," Goldilocks said with a bittersweet smile. "He doesn't get many opportunities to be a hero anymore."

Her face was full of pride, but as she watched him command the carpenters, the pride was replaced with guilt. Jack had been such a respected and valued member of the Hoodian society—he had thrown it all away in his decision to go on the run with her. Although Goldilocks knew it had been his own choice, she couldn't help but feel a bit responsible.

"Ouch!" Conner shrieked. He had joined the carpenters and kept getting splinters as he stripped the baskets apart. "How are you doing this so easily?"

The third Little Pig stayed silent and simply showed him his hooves.

"Gotcha," Conner said. "I've always thought thumbs were overrated."

The day flew by as the carpenters worked tirelessly on the ship. Jack was growing anxious, knowing he still had to track down the Traveling Tradesman. He left Froggy and the third Little Pig in charge of overseeing the construction after carefully going over his blueprints inch by inch.

"This is going to be better than I imagined!" Froggy said with a happy hop. "What do you call this contraption?"

The third Little Pig rolled his eyes. "That's a hammer," he said.

"So *this* is a hammer! Interesting," Froggy said and carefully examined it. Despite all that he had been through, he was still a prince at heart.

"On second thought, maybe I shouldn't leave," Jack said.

"They'll be fine," Goldilocks said and started to drag Jack away from the carpenters. "You're a terrific instructor."

Goldilocks and Jack were stopped before they could leave the courtyard.

"You two!" Red called down from an open window. She

was holding a freshly opened white envelope in her hand. "Take the twins with you! I just received word that fairies are coming to inspect our missing wall and I don't want *those* two hanging around when they do!"

"Ah, man," Conner said. "I was hoping to help with the ship!"

"Then you should definitely leave," the third Little Pig said and yanked a piece of basket out of his hands.

"Very well," Goldilocks said. "They can help us track down the Traveling Tradesman."

Alex and Conner had to admit they were a bit excited to go on the hunt.

"What am I supposed to tell the fairies when they see all of this construction going on?" Red asked.

Alex was quick to answer. "Tell them you decided to combine all your baskets into one big basket," she said.

Red scrunched her forehead. "Would anyone believe I'd do something like that?"

"Yes," the entire courtyard said in unison. Even the carpenters and the old women were in agreement.

Red grunted. "Fine," she said and promptly shut the window behind her.

"We're going to need another horse if the twins are traveling with us," Goldilocks said.

"Not to worry," Froggy said. "We have plenty of horses in the stables. You can have your pick of the lot."

The twins eagerly ran up to their rooms and collected the things they thought they'd need searching for the Traveling

Tradesman. They met Jack and Goldilocks in the castle stables, where they were busy packing supplies onto Goldilocks's infamous cream-colored horse, Porridge.

Porridge glanced uneasily at all the other horses. Goldilocks hadn't been exaggerating; her horse really didn't care for other horses. And as the twins also glanced around at the perfectly groomed ponies, it wasn't hard to understand why. While Porridge had been out in the world running from the law with her mistress, all these horses had spent their days in their comfortable stalls—no wonder they didn't get along.

"Which horse should we take?" Alex asked.

"Um . . . *that one*," Conner said and pointed to a large brown stallion in the very back of the stables.

"Why that one?" Alex asked.

"Because he's the only one that doesn't have bows in his mane," Conner said.

"That's Buckle," a stable hand told the twins. "Are you sure you want that one? He can be a tad aggressive."

Conner did a lap around the stable to make sure. "Positive," he said. "All the other ones look like they belong in the doll aisle at a toy store."

"Suit yourself," the stable hand said. "But don't say I didn't warn you." He threw a saddle with the largest silver buckles the twins had ever seen over the horse.

"Is that why you call him Buckle?" Alex asked.

"Partially," the stable hand said. "You'll see."

A few minutes later Jack, Goldilocks, and the twins were

off. Jack and Goldilocks led the way on Porridge while Alex and Conner rode on Buckle a few yards behind them. It didn't take long to figure out why the horse had been given his name—he bucked aggressively every few feet and neighed loudly as he did. Clearly, the silver buckles on the saddle were the only fasteners strong enough to keep the saddle on the horse.

"How do you turn this thing off?!" Conner yelled, clutching the reins as hard as he could.

"I think I'm going to be sick!" Alex said. Her arms were wrapped around her brother's ribs as tightly as possible without crushing them.

Goldilocks steered Porridge around to face Buckle.

"Porridge, tell the show-off to stop," Goldilocks said to her horse. Porridge neighed disapprovingly at Buckle, and he stopped bucking immediately.

Porridge rolled her eyes at Buckle. Buckle snorted at Porridge almost flirtatiously. It made the twins a little uncomfortable—obviously there was a history with the horses, a history they weren't interested in learning.

The twins followed Porridge out of the Red Riding Hood Kingdom and into a forest that rested along the Charming Kingdom and Fairy Kingdom border. Jack and Goldilocks were extra wary—the Enchantress had turned the entire world into the Dwarf Forests.

Before they knew it, nightfall was upon them, and they set up a small camp to the side of the path. Alex and Conner laid out some blankets on the ground to sleep on.

"This discomfort is almost comforting," Conner said once

he stretched out on the hard ground. "I think I actually missed sleeping in strange forests."

"Get used to it," Alex told him. "We've got a lot of adventure ahead of us."

"True," Conner said. "But at least this time we'll have friends."

Unlike her brother, Alex couldn't sleep. After tossing and turning, she got up and had a seat next to Goldilocks, who was sharpening her sword by a tiny campfire. She kept an eye out while the others slept.

"You're not like any other woman I've ever met," Alex told her.

"Why is that?" Goldilocks asked.

"You're just so confident and self-sufficient," Alex said. "So many girls—especially in my world—are so insecure and jealous. We rely so much on one another, but we're so mean to each other at the same time. We could use more women like you to look up to."

Goldilocks was sad to hear it. "I was all those things once," she said. "But after being on the run I've learned a life spent creating enemies isn't worth leading. Having allies is the best advantage in the world. Jealousy is just a reminder of the frustrations you have with yourself. Who has time to only concentrate on that?"

Alex smiled. "That's powerful," she said. "I wish the girls at school could hear that."

"Bring a sword to school. Trust me—those girls will leave you alone," Goldilocks said.

"Oh, I couldn't do that," Alex said. "Violence is frowned upon in my world. It's not like it is here; it's not *needed*."

Goldilocks liked the sound of that. "Then find out what *your* sword is—find your own *advantage*—and wear it proudly. Beat those girls at their own game by seeming perfectly content in your own life," she said. "Then again, I'm a wanted fugitive. I may not be the best person to give advice."

Alex laughed. It was some of the best advice she had ever been given, even if it was by a crook.

Everyone was up by sunrise the following morning. To pass the time as they searched, Jack and Goldilocks told the twins all about their escapades over the last year on the lam.

"I knew Goldie could fight, but I had no idea what a warrior she was," Jack said. "There I was in the Corner Kingdom, surrounded by twenty soldiers. I had just been caught stealing a loaf of bread from a bakery. I didn't have my axe, a sword, or anything! I was helpless! Then, like a cannonball, Goldie and Porridge burst through the doors and Goldie fought off all of the soldiers single-handedly!"

"No way!" Conner said.

"He's embellishing; there were only a dozen soldiers," Goldilocks said with a modest shrug.

"Where did you learn to fight, Goldilocks?" Conner asked. "And could you teach me? I've always wanted to be a good swordsman."

"When I was younger I realized no one was going to fight for me, so I picked up a sword and taught myself," Goldilocks said. "I can show you a few tricks if you'd like."

"Awesome!" Conner said. "I've got really good hand-eye coordination! I have the second highest score on Pac-Man at the arcade."

Jack and Goldilocks had no idea if this was supposed to be impressive.

"Jack isn't so bad himself, you know," Goldilocks boasted. "Once he saved me from a trio of ogres! I was tied above a large boiling cauldron—they would have made a soup out of me if Jack hadn't gotten there in time!"

Jack let out an indifferent laugh. "I only distracted them long enough for you to untie the knots," he said. "She took care of them once she was free."

"But it's the thought that counts," Goldilocks said and hugged his neck.

The Tradesman-bound group traveled up and down every path they found, looking everywhere for any sign of him.

"He should be in this area," Jack said. "It's where I found him as a kid. They call him the Traveling Tradesman, but he never goes far."

"Wait a second," Goldilocks said. She hopped off Porridge and scanned the dirt path. There were two sets of identical bird tracks on the ground that stretched a good distance behind and ahead of them.

"What kind of birds walk for this long?" Goldilocks asked.

Jack's eyes lit up. The twins didn't know what they were on to but knew they were making progress. Goldilocks remounted Porridge and their group charged down the path as fast as the horses could gallop, following the tracks into the forest ahead.

The group eventually discovered an old covered wagon parked to the side of the path. A small chimney poked out of the wagon's roof. The wagon's mule was resting and tied to a nearby tree.

"Look at the tracks!" Alex said and pointed to the ground. The bird tracks led right up to the back of the wagon. It had bird foot–shaped spurs around its wheels—the wagon was leaving bird prints as it traveled down the path! It was an incredibly clever way to cover one's tracks.

"Tradesman?" Jack called out. "Is that you in there?"

All was silent at first. Then a hurried shuffle came from inside the wagon and it rocked from side to side. The top half of the wagon's door burst open and the Traveling Tradesman peeked outside.

"Are you a friend or a foe?" the Tradesman asked. He was an elderly man with a long gray beard, tattered clothing, and a wandering eye. He had aged a bit since the last time the twins saw him, but he was just as kooky as ever.

"Friends!" Conner happily exclaimed. "Old friends, actually! Do you remember us?"

The Tradesman studied their faces.

"My boy, I remember every trade I have ever made," the Tradesman said. "But my mind has grown weary in my old age, and the faces attached have been lost in my memory."

Jack, Goldilocks, and the twins climbed down from their horses and walked closer so he could view them better.

"You helped us escape the Troll and Goblin Territory a year ago," Alex said. "We met you in the dungeons and you traded your freedom for ours. You told us about the Wishing Spell."

The Tradesman stroked his beard, brushing crumbs off of it. He must have been in the middle of a meal.

"Ah yes," he said with one squinted eye. "I do admit a small sprinkling of familiarity sweeping through me. I wish I had a memory of *you*," he said to Goldilocks. "But *you*—I think I remember *you*," he said to Jack.

"It's been a long time since we were last face-to-face," Jack said. "Perhaps you remember a lad you traded magic beans to in exchange for a cow?"

The Tradesman's eyes and mouth grew wide with delight. "Well, I'll be darned as a legless goat," he said and clapped his hands together. "If it isn't Jack, my favorite customer!"

Jack happily nodded up at him. "It's me, old man!" he said. "It's good to see you again!"

"Come on in, my boy!" the Tradesman said and opened the lower half of the wagon door. "I've just made some pheasant pudding!"

He disappeared in his wagon and the others took that as their cue to follow him inside.

The small wagon was very cramped. A bed was pushed in the back, a tiny table was in the center, and the interior was lined with cabinets and shelves and cages. Canteens, brooms, buckets, daggers, and more were displayed on the shelves and in the cabinets. The twins knew the objects most likely held some gimmicky value and were waiting to be traded. Geese, ducks, and pigs were locked in the cages—no doubt what the Tradesman had profited from his recent trades.

"Have a seat, have a seat," the Tradesman said. Jack, Goldilocks, and the twins forced themselves around the table. The Tradesman handed them each a plate of his pheasant pudding (which was bits and pieces of unplucked birds floating in mysterious gravy) and a loaf of stale bread. The twins had to hold their noses so they didn't become sick.

"So what brings you to my neck of the woods, old boy?" the Tradesman asked Jack with a pat on the back.

"We've been searching for you, actually," Jack said.

"And to what do I owe the honor of being the subject of such a quest?" the Tradesman said.

Conner had to replay this sentence in his head before he understood what the Tradesman was asking. Jack cautiously looked to the others before confessing.

"I was wondering if you had any more magic beans?" he asked. "Like the ones you gave to me as a boy."

The Tradesman's good eye darted around the room. He was honestly surprised by the request.

"Why would you need *more* magic beans?" he asked. "Surely the first batch gave you enough adventure for a lifetime."

"Indeed they did," Jack said. "It's not an adventure we're after but a way back to the giant's castle. The beanstalk has been removed and we are hoping to grow another one."

The Tradesman's good eye studied each of their faces. "But why would you need to revisit the giant's castle at a time like this?" he asked.

The group looked across the table at one another. Alex decided they didn't have time to beat around the bush and got straight to the point.

"Have you ever heard of the Wand of Wonderment?" Alex asked.

"The Wand of Wonderment?" the Tradesman asked.

Conner began explaining. "It's a Wand that you build out of the six most prized possessions of the six most hated people in the world."

The Tradesman raised a hand to silence him. "Young man, I've known what the Wand of Wonderment is for longer than you've been alive," he said. "I just find it hard to comprehend why *that* would be at the top of your agenda, things being as they are."

"That's just the thing, Mr. Tradesman—if I may call you Mr. Tradesman," Alex said. "We're trying to build it so we can fix the way things are now. We're trying to stop the Enchantress, and it's the only way we know how."

The wagon went silent. Everyone sat on edge, questioning Alex's decision to blurt out the truth. Would spilling the beans get them closer to obtaining magical ones?

The Tradesman sat back in his chair and stroked his beard, gazing back and forth between Alex and Conner. "I remember you now," he said softly. "I don't recall the exact whereabouts or whenabouts, but I do remember the faces of two youngsters on an extraordinary quest. They were so ambitious in their pursuit, but they were completely selfless in their attempt—it wasn't glory they were after but harmony, rather. I decided to help them because I knew our paths would cross again one day."

The twins didn't know what to say. His saving them had been such a kind gesture it still humbled them.

"I guess your intuition was right," Conner said. "Only now we're trying to save the world."

The Tradesman observed them for only a moment more. He stood up and went to one of the cabinets. He dug through it for a while, pulling out strangely shaped plates and goblets and tools and gadgets before finally removing a small brown bag.

The Tradesman poured the contents of the little bag onto the table, and the twins found themselves staring down at three beans. They were round and wide like lima beans but were black and bounced livelily on the table.

"Magic beans!" Jack said excitedly. "You still have some!"

"They're the last I have in my possession," the Tradesman said. "They aren't easy to come across, either. Magic beans have to be plucked from a plant that grows in ground fertilized by unicorn manure and watered with the tears of a witch. But they're my gift to you."

Everyone sat up in their seats. "Are you sure?" Goldilocks said. "We were prepared to pay you."

She pulled a handful of diamonds from out of the side of her boot.

"Goldie, where did you get those?" Jack asked.

"I stole them from Red when she wasn't looking—she won't miss them," Goldilocks said. "I was assuming we would have to make a trade of some kind."

The Tradesman scooped the beans up, put them back into the bag, and handed it to Jack.

"Consider it my little contribution to the people brave enough to take on the evil Enchantress," the Tradesman said.

"That was easy," Conner said. He couldn't believe the luck they had so far. "Maybe making this wand won't be so difficult after all."

"There will be plenty of dangers to be found, I'm afraid," the Tradesman said. "Especially when pursuing the Wand of Wonderment. I would know. I tried building it for myself when I was a young man."

"You did?" Alex asked, unable to contain her surprise. "So does that mean it's real?"

"Oh yes, it's very real, I can assure you," he told her. "Much like the Wishing Spell you were after previously, many fools have attempted to create it themselves and have died trying. It was during my own pursuit I became the tradesman you see today. I discovered selling trinkets of interest was more profitable than searching for them."

"Do you know what we should expect, then?" Conner asked.

"I can only imagine," the Tradesman said. "Just remember that even the tamest of places will surprise you with what is lurking in its shadows—and these beans are no exception! Although the giant is dead, there are still dangers waiting for you at his castle."

Conner gulped loudly. "Do you care to specify?" he asked.

"Young man, if it was in my nature to be specific I wouldn't be able to look in two directions at all times," the Tradesman said and his good eye glared at Conner.

"Well, we can't thank you enough," Jack said. "Kindness is a rare thing to come across in the forest."

"But it's I who should be thanking you," the Tradesman said. "After giving you those beans my sales went through the roof! You gave me my career, old boy! You'll always be like a son to me, Jack."

Conner cleared his throat. "The kind of son you rip off in a trade that sends him on a life-threatening adventure?" he asked.

The Tradesman rethought his words. "More like a nephew, then," he said. He looked through the wagon door at the darkening evening sky. "Where did the time go? You must excuse me now. I must be off before sunset. I never stay more than a day in one place—sake of the trade, sake of the name." He winked with his good eye, although none could figure out who it was meant for. "Good luck, my friends."

Jack, Goldilocks, and the twins left the wagon and found their horses. The Tradesman hitched up his mule and rode off into the forest just as the sun began to set. The twins wondered what very special circumstance would be required for them to cross paths with him again.

"What do you think he meant when he said there are other dangers waiting for us at the giant's castle?" Conner asked. "The giant didn't leave behind a crazy widow or anything, did he?"

"It's been so long since I was there," Jack said, climbing astride Porridge. "The giant was the only terrifying thing I can remember being in the castle. That, of course, and the golden harp's singing."

The twins and Goldilocks remounted their horses and rode off in the opposite direction of the Tradesman, heading back to the Red Riding Hood Kingdom. They rode the entire night and arrived the next afternoon to find amazing progress had been made on the flying ship.

Red, Froggy, and the third Little Pig were huddled around the blueprints.

"Did you find the Tradesman?" Froggy asked as soon as he saw them arrive.

Conner held up the small bag of magic beans. "Our first of hopefully many victories," he said. "By the way, Froggy, after seeing what that guy ate, I'll never pick on you about lily-pad tea again!"

"This looks incredible!" Alex said. More than half the ship looked ready.

"It should be completed the day after tomorrow," the third Little Pig said.

Jack was hesitant to give his own praise. "It looks so much *bigger* than what my plans proposed," he said.

"Yes, about that . . ." Froggy said with an apologetic laugh.

"Queen Red made a few revisions to your plans," the third Little Pig said.

"Revisions?" Jack said and looked at Red.

"Well, I figured since I was going to be traveling with you I would need my own chambers," Red said matter-of-factly. "I added a lower deck for me and my things—but don't worry, there's plenty of room for the rest of you on the upper deck."

Jack sighed and rubbed his eyes. Goldilocks looked like she was going to strangle someone, so the twins decided to excuse themselves before she did. They could hear Goldilocks and Red arguing as they climbed the stairs to their bedrooms.

The sun was about to set on another day and the twins fell asleep the instant they made contact with their beds. They knew the days ahead would be difficult, but the Wand of Wonderment had finally been confirmed as a real tool for overthrowing the Enchantress, so they focused on that and let that triumphant feeling ease them to sleep.

At an hour or so after midnight, Conner awoke with a troubling sensation. He couldn't fight off the feeling he was being watched as he slept. His eyes fluttered open and as they slowly focused his heart dropped. Standing at the foot of his bed, intently staring at him, was a *woman*.

She was beautiful and transparent. She had long, flowing hair with a single rose behind her ear. She wore a long nightgown under a robe that was tied at the waist. Although Conner was certain he had never seen her before, she looked oddly familiar.

"W-w-w-who are you?" Conner stuttered.

The woman didn't respond. She glided to the window and pointed to the land in the distance. She looked back at him with a grave expression.

"W-w-w-what do you want?" Conner muttered.

The woman said nothing. She held her somber stare and slowly disappeared.

Conner's jaw fell open. There was no denying it—he had just seen a *ghost*.

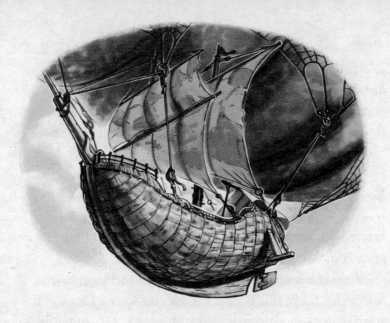

CHAPTER SIXTEEN

FLIGHT OF THE *GRANNY*

Alex couldn't find her brother anywhere. "Have you seen Conner?" she asked Froggy. "He wasn't at breakfast this morning and he isn't in the courtyard."

"I haven't seen him since yesterday," Froggy said. "Have you checked his room? Maybe he fell ill?"

Alex hoped this wasn't the case, as they were on the eve of their expedition. She climbed the stairs to his bedroom to check on him, praying he wasn't sick.

"Conner?" Alex said and knocked on the door. "Are you in here?"

There was no response, so she twisted the handle and pushed open the door without an invitation. Conner was sitting straight up on his bed. He stared off into the distance, lost in thought. A small dribble of drool spilled from the corner of his mouth.

"Are you feeling all right?" Alex asked.

"What?" Conner said with a jump. He hadn't noticed the door open.

"You don't look well," Alex said. "Are you sick?"

Conner had to think about it. "No," he decided. "At least, I don't think I am." His gaze drifted off again toward his bedroom window.

"Then what's the matter?" Alex said. "You look like you've just seen a—"

Conner's face jerked in her direction. He looked absolutely horrified and didn't make a sound. Alex's figure of speech had accidentally uncovered the truth.

"Wait a second," Alex said. "Did you actually see a ghost?"

Conner's eyes darted around the room. He didn't know how to explain.

"It happened last night—I woke up and it was standing there just staring at me!" Conner proclaimed with bombastic gestures.

"Who was staring at you?" Alex asked.

"A ghost!" he said. "She was *right there*!"

"I was being sarcastic!" Alex said. "Are you telling me you saw an actual *ghost*?"

267

"Yes!" Conner said and placed his hand on his face. "I mean—she was see-through, quiet, and disappeared into thin air—all signs point to it!"

"Are you sure you weren't dreaming?" Alex said.

"You have to wake up from a dream," he said. "And I've been wide awake ever since it happened! I've been too afraid to move."

Alex tried to come up with a logical explanation but she couldn't. His hysterics made it hard for her to doubt him.

"Maybe this castle is haunted?" she suggested.

"Who haunts a new castle? That's like holding a grudge against a baby!" Conner said. "It was so strange. She *waited* for me to see her. And once I did she went over to the window and just pointed outside. It was the creepiest thing I've ever seen."

"And you have no idea who she was?" Alex asked.

"No clue," he said and shook his head. "But what's even stranger is that she looked familiar. I could swear I've seen her before."

Alex took a seat on Conner's bed. Their days were already full of mystery; the last thing they needed to add to the mix was a ghost sighting. A moment later, Red's handmaiden knocked on the open door and peeked her head inside.

"There you two are," the handmaiden said. "Her Majesty is looking for you two. She wants to see you in her chambers."

The handmaiden hurried away as soon as she was finished giving her message.

"I wouldn't mention the ghost to anyone if I were you," Alex said. "I think everyone has enough on their plates as it is."

Conner couldn't have agreed more. "Trust me, the last thing I want people to know is that I'm seeing dead people," he said.

Alex sat with her brother until he gained the courage to leave his bed. He got dressed and the twins walked across the castle to meet Red in her chambers.

Queen Red's new bedroom was twice the size of the twins' rental house. There was a diamond chandelier hanging from the ceiling; large, colorful, and cushiony furniture lined the room; and the biggest four-poster bed the twins had ever seen—large enough to sleep ten comfortably—was on its own platform in the back of the room.

"Yoo-hoo, we're in here!" Red called from a doorway to the side.

The twins followed her voice and found themselves stepping into a long hall of mirrors. It was almost as big as the bedroom itself. The hall was incredibly bright and had several chandeliers and wooden floors, and weeping willow trees were painted on the walls.

"This is beautiful, Red!" Alex said. "Is this your ballroom?"

"Ballroom?" Red said with a laugh. "Good heavens, no. This is my closet."

The twins did a double take. In between every two mirrors was a large chest of drawers built into the wall. A collection of golden chests lined the far side of the room. Thousands and thousands of clothes and accessories must have been kept in here.

Red was standing on a stool facing a mirror, with a large gray fur coat around her shoulders. Her handmaiden took measurements and put pins along the sides of it, fitting it perfectly to the slender queen.

"Nice coat," Conner said.

"Thank you!" Red said. "It's for our voyage. I figured it might get chilly flying around the sky, especially in the Northern Mountains, where the Snow Queen lives. Did either of you bring a proper coat?"

Alex and Conner shook their heads.

"Luckily I'm always thinking ahead," Red said. "I had two coats whipped up for you with the extra material."

The Handmaiden tossed two fur coats to the twins and they tried them on. They weren't quite as stylishly cut as the one Red was getting fitted for, but they would do just fine. The twins couldn't deny it was a very kind gesture on Red's part—she kept surprising them.

"Thanks, Red," Alex said.

Conner looked down at the coat suspiciously. "What is this?" he said. "Or should I ask what *was* this?"

"It used to be the rug in the library," Red said.

Alex and Conner suddenly grew very uncomfortable.

"Are you telling me that we're wearing *the Big Bad Wolf*?" Conner asked.

"Yes," Red said, without a crumb of remorse. "Soft, wasn't he?"

The twins grew very stiff, as if what they were wearing was still alive.

"I don't know what to say—thank you so much for thinking of us," Alex said through her teeth.

"No trouble at all," Red said and stepped off the stool. "Now step up and have it fitted properly. Saving the world is not an excuse to wear ill-fitting clothes."

Alex was first to step on the stool and get her coat tailored by the handmaiden.

"Speaking of things that used to be alive," Conner said, "I was wondering, has anyone ever died in this castle?"

Alex shot him a sharp look. Conner didn't make eye contact with her.

"No, thank heavens," Red said. "Why would you ask such a question?"

Conner shrugged innocently. "No reason," he said. "If someone had, though, would you even know about it?"

Red glared at him peculiarly. "Are you making plans to be the first?" she asked.

"Of course not," Conner said. "I was just curious. Forget I mentioned it."

The handmaiden finished pinning Alex's coat, and Conner was next. Goldilocks entered the closet a few moments later. Her eyes had to adjust from the light.

"Where am I?" Goldilocks said, shielding her face from the chandeliers.

"You're in my closet," Red said with an eye roll. "Poor thing has been living like an animal for so long she can't even recognize one," she whispered to the twins.

"For a moment I thought I had stepped onto the sun," Goldilocks said. "The ship is almost complete and we'll be loading it soon. We need a chest. Froggy said I could find one here."

"Did he?" Red said, a little annoyed Froggy would point Goldilocks in the direction of her room. "He was mistaken, I'm afraid. All the chests up here are full."

Goldilocks ignored her. She saw the line of them in the back of the hall and headed toward one. "Perfect!" Goldilocks said. She opened it and dumped a pile of high-heeled shoes out of it.

"Excuse me!? I need that!" Red said.

"Well, *we* need it now," Goldilocks said and started dragging the empty chest out of the closet.

"For what?" Red said.

"We're going to fill it with supplies," Goldilocks said. "Weapons, lanterns, ropes—things we *actually* need for the trip. Your shoes will just have to be homeless for the time being."

Goldilocks dragged the chest out of sight. Red looked after her for a moment with a puzzled expression on her face. "Sometimes when I talk to her I feel as if I'm not speaking to another woman, but to another species altogether," she said.

That afternoon the twins decided to go with Jack to plant the magic beans. Jack figured it was best to plant the beans in the same soil as the previous beanstalk, so they walked through the village and headed to his former home just on the outskirts of town. Jack carried a shovel over his shoulder and held the bag of magic beans tightly in his hand.

"The ship is coming along splendidly," Jack said. "The men are finishing up some final touches, but it'll be ready by sunset."

"When do we leave?" Conner asked.

"Tonight at midnight," Jack said.

The twins were half excited and half nervous to hear this.

"We have five places to stop—six including wherever the Enchantress keeps her most prized possession," Alex counted. "Where are we going first?"

"It's important that our course isn't predictable," Jack said. "I reckon by our second or third stop word will reach the Enchantress about our little escapade—we have to keep her guessing where we'll be headed. We should start with the Snow Queen first, begin our adventure with a bang. Then we'll go south to the wicked stepmother's estate. By then the beanstalk should be grown and we'll come back here for the giant's castle. Then we'll head northeast to collect pieces of the Evil Queen's mirror and then south again for the Sea Witch's jewels."

"Oh, is that all?" Conner said sarcastically.

"Hopefully we'll figure out what Ezmia's most prized possession is before we get to the Sea Witch," Alex said.

"Yeah, hopefully," Conner said.

They walked for a bit longer and Jack's old house appeared in the distance—both of them. A wooden shack Jack lived in with his mother when they were poor sat in front of a large and elegant manor they had built after acquiring the riches from the giant.

Jack stopped walking when he saw his old homes.

"What's wrong?" Alex asked, looking back at him.

"Nothing," he said quietly. "I just haven't been back in a really long time."

"We know how you feel," Conner said. "Alex and I used to walk home every day from school and pass our old house. It used to make us so sad—"

"That's just the thing," Jack said, and a small grin grew on his nostalgic face. "I was expecting to be sad—I was expecting it to make me feel blue, but I feel quite the opposite. Every minute I remember spending here was a minute missing or worrying about Goldilocks. I don't suppose I could consider anyplace home without her."

He continued walking with a cheerful hop in his step, patting the twins on the shoulders as he passed them. Alex smiled to herself, knowing how happy Goldilocks would be to hear this.

Jack walked to the edge of a large hole in the ground that the previous beanstalk had grown out of.

"I'll plant the beans here," Jack said. He dug a small hole and dropped the three magic beans into the ground. "The last beanstalk took less than a day to grow."

"Should someone keep an eye on it while we're away? To make sure nothing disturbs its growth?" Alex asked.

Jack contemplated this for a moment. "I have the perfect person for the job," he said and headed toward the manor.

Before he reached the large home, two windows in the front of the house burst open. Standing behind them was the beautiful and golden magic harp. She sang with a soprano voice and the strings connected to her back played along with her voice.

"Oh, another day has come at last,
What once was today is now the past,
As the sun slowly sets and disappears,
I've been at this window for too many years—Jack!"

"Hello, Harper!" Jack said, happy to see his old friend.

"Oh my goodness gracious!" the harp said, completely overwhelmed. "Is it really you, or are my eyes deceiving me?!"

"I'm here, Harper," Jack said bashfully. "I'm so sorry I haven't written or visited. I couldn't risk being seen."

The harp instantly burst into a triumphant song.

"Oh, Jack, my Jack, the Jack is back,
You almost gave this harp a heart attack,
But now I no longer need to be concerned,
For Jack, my Jack, the Jack has finally returned."

The twins couldn't help but applaud—she was a one-woman show.

"I remember you two!" the harp said. "It's been ages since I last saw you!"

"It's been a year," Conner said.

"Only a year?" the harp said in amazement. "I could have sworn it was decades! Time goes by so much slower when you have nothing to look at but grass and an old shack and only the squirrels to keep you company."

One of the harp's eyes began twitching. Alex and Conner had felt sorry for her when Jack lived in the house with her—they couldn't imagine what complete isolation had been like for her.

The harp's strings played the opening chords of a sad ballad.

"A lonely, lonely life I lead,
As lonely, lonely as a seed,
A tree with lonely, lonely leaves,
But just how lonely no one believes!"

Alex and Conner clapped again for her, though not as vigorously.

"But you look great!" Conner said, trying to break the sad tension.

"I'm sorry you've been so lonely, Harper. Truly I am. If it had been safe to come back to visit you, I would have," Jack said.

"All is forgotten, dear," the harp said. "Today is a happy day! You've come home at last! I'm sad to tell you the house is an absolute mess inside. I would have tidied up had I known you were coming back home—and if I had legs."

"I'm not coming back, I'm afraid," Jack said. "We're just passing through."

"Oh, I see," the harp said. Her strings played a sad little melody as her spirits sank.

"But we were wondering if you could do us a favor," Jack said.

The harp's tempo sped up as her hopes were raised again.

"A favor?" the harp asked and her eyes fluttered. "What's your request, my boy? Is there a party you wish for me to perform at? A celebration you'd like me to serenade? A funeral you'd like me to give a farewell aria at?"

"Not exactly," Jack said sheepishly. "I just planted some magic beans. Would you mind keeping an eye on the beanstalk that grows while we're away for a few days?"

The harp's hopeful chords came to an abrupt stop.

"Pardon?" the harp asked and her eye began to twitch more severely.

"We're hoping you can keep an eye on the beanstalk," Conner reiterated.

The harp's nostrils flared and the eyebrow above her twitching eye rose so high it almost touched her hairline.

"I have performed for kings and queens and aristocrats!" the harp said, horribly insulted "And you're asking me to *watch a plant grow for you*?!"

The three of them took a couple steps back from her.

"Do you have anything else better to do?" Conner asked. He wasn't helping matters at all. The harp's strings started to play a fast and angry theme behind her.

"Harper, are you aware of what's happening in the world?" Jack asked.

"Unless it's happened directly in front of this house, I haven't heard about it," the harp said and folded her arms.

Jack sighed and rubbed his neck, not knowing where to begin.

"Well, I don't mean to worry you, but the world is in a bit of a crisis," he said. "We're going on a trip that will hopefully restore it. So if you could keep an eye on the beanstalk as it grows, we would be so appreciative."

The harp snorted and looked away from them. "I suppose this is my new life now," she said over-dramatically. "The former renowned entertainer for the royal and rich is now a *plant sitter*. My, how far I've fallen."

A clever smile appeared on Jack's face as an idea came to him. "In exchange," Jack said, "I'll have you moved to Queen Red Riding Hood's Castle. You could perform for the queen and all her servants all day long."

Conner laughed into his fist, poorly disguising it as a cough. The harp tried her best to conceal her intrigue, but it was obviously the most exciting proposal she had received in a decade. A symphony of exhilaration was coming from her strings.

"I will have to consider," the harp said with half a smile, but they all knew her answer. "I will let you know if I decide to move into Queen Red's castle when you return, but for now I'll keep an eye on your beanstalk. *Now if you'll excuse me, I must practice my scales!*"

The harp quickly shut the window and went to work on her vocal exercises.

"Way to go," Conner said and patted Jack on the back.

"Aside from rescuing her from the giant, you probably just made her century!" Alex said.

Jack chuckled to himself. "I'm not sure who I feel worse

for," he said. "Harper, for leaving her alone for so long—or Red, for sending Harper to live with her."

The twins laughed and the three headed back to the castle.

The twins packed all their things and met the others downstairs in the courtyard at midnight. Conner was too scared to be by himself, so he didn't let Alex out of his sight. He was afraid if he was alone the ghost would pay him another visit.

The flying ship had come a very long way from the sketches in the library. The enormous vessel filled the entire courtyard, made of woven pieces of wood—it looked like a giant ship-shaped basket. The carpenters had the ship on its side and were attaching the balloon and sails to the top of it.

"Oh, Granny! The balloon and sails look terrific!" Red said. She was right: Although it was deflated, the twins couldn't deny that Granny and the Little Old Woman had stitched together an impressively durable balloon. In fact, the balloon looked sturdier than the actual ship.

"Oh, thank you, sweetheart," Granny said. "We were so honored to be a part of it."

"Who's a tart?" the Little Old Woman asked.

Once the carpenters were finished attaching the balloon and sails, they ignited a large lamp-like object in the center of the ship. Carefully, with Jack's commands, the balloon and sails were filled with hot air and the ship was pulled upright.

Goldilocks dragged the chest she had filled with supplies onto the ship. Once she climbed aboard she was surprised to discover the entire deck had been filled with dozens of other chests and trunks.

"What is all of this?" Goldilocks called down.

"Those are Queen Red's supplies," the third Little Pig said.

"What supplies?" Goldilocks said with an irritated glare.

"Oh, relax, Goldie," Red yelled up to her. "I wasn't sure how long we'd be gone for so I made sure to bring plenty of wardrobe options."

Goldilocks visibly bit back her frustration and made sure everything was properly tied down for their launch. Froggy hadn't brought anything onto the ship except a tall stack of his favorite library books.

"Just something to pass the time," Froggy said. "Everyone is welcome to share if they'd like."

It was getting later and anticipation was rising. The twins and Jack joined Froggy and Goldilocks aboard the ship.

"Where's Red?" Jack asked after doing a head count.

"Just a second, just a second," Red said. She had quickly run back to her chambers to change for the third time that night—she wanted her outfit to be perfect for their maiden voyage. A basket hung from her arm like a purse and she pulled out a fancy bottle of champagne from inside.

Red cleared her throat. "I would like to make an announcement," she said. *"Would you mind?"*

Before he could agree to it, Red stepped on top of the third Little Pig so she could get a nicer view of all the carpenters in the room.

"Make it quick, Red, we have to be as far away as possible

by sunrise," Goldilocks called down to her. Red waved her off like she was a hovering insect.

"I wanted to thank all of the men, women, and pigs alike for working tirelessly around the clock to build this ship. You have made your kingdom and your queen very proud. It is an honor to be among citizens of your *courage*, *strength*, *bravery*, and *spirit*!" Red said, and the courtyard erupted in applause.

"It wouldn't be a proper launch without a proper christening," she went on, raising the bottle. "I'd like to dedicate this ship in the name of my grandmother. May it forever be known as the HMS *Granny*."

She smacked the bottle on the side of the ship and it burst into a fizzy explosion. Granny smiled, touched by her granddaughter's dedication.

Red wiped her hand on the third Little Pig. "Now someone clean that up, please," she ordered and finally boarded the ship.

"Everyone brace yourselves for takeoff!" Jack shouted. He pulled a lever near the flame and it grew four times in size. Goldilocks and the twins gripped the banister. Froggy took hold of the large steering wheel. He gulped and his thin frog legs trembled, but he was ready.

The *Granny*, as Red had just declared it, smoothly rose higher and higher through the courtyard. The carpenters cheered from below. The twins held their breath, hoping nothing would go wrong on their first ascent. Within moments they were rising past the tops of the castle's highest towers and into the open night sky.

"We did it! We did it!" the twins shouted. "We're flying! We're flying!"

It was so peaceful and serene. A cool night breeze blew past them as the Red Riding Hood Kingdom grew smaller and smaller.

Froggy delicately turned the steering wheel and the sails positioned the ship in a northern direction. The twins couldn't fight off the proud smiles they shared with the others. Their vision had become a reality, and their flight had officially begun.

CHAPTER SEVENTEEN

THE SNOW QUEEN

The *Granny* sailed steadily through the night sky. They had been flying for a few hours now and the initial excitement had worn off and been replaced with anticipation for the journey ahead. They were flying somewhere above the Northern Kingdom, and the snowy Northern Mountains came into view on the horizon.

The farther north they traveled, the colder it became. The twins were so thankful Red had given them fur coats to wear, despite whom the fur used to belong to.

Froggy was still clutching the steering wheel. He looked

like a little boy—too excited to let it go. Red leaned on the banister facing west. She kept looking over her shoulder, as if to ask someone a question.

"Are you all right, my love?" Froggy asked her.

"Yes, darling, I'll be fine," Red said. "I keep thinking of things for my handmaiden to do for me and forget she's not here. I forgot what it was like to go without *help*."

Jack and Goldilocks were seated near the front of the ship. Goldilocks sharpened her sword and Jack sharpened his axe as the twins joined them.

"So what can you tell us about the Snow Queen?" Conner said. "On a scale of kitten to tiger, what kind of danger are we talking?"

"It's hard to say," Jack said. "The Snow Queen has been out of the public eye for so long—no one has seen her in decades."

"Really?" Alex asked, always eager for a good story. "I'm not very familiar with her."

Jack went into full-throttle storytelling mode, dramatically retelling the events that had made the Snow Queen a household name.

"Many years ago, the Snow Queen was just a weather witch from deep in the mountains. She befriended the king of the Northern Kingdom by granting him wishes and gained his trust by giving him prophecies about the kingdom. The king made her his royal advisor, but she was evil and secretly plotted to take over the kingdom for herself. Eventually, she overthrew the king and imprisoned the entire kingdom in an everlasting winter. All the trees and plants, most of the animals, and some of the people died—not able to survive the cold," Jack said.

"So what happened?" Conner asked.

"Wise Prince White, Snow White's grandfather, rallied up an army to overthrow the Snow Queen," Jack said. "They took back their kingdom and banished the evil Snow Queen to live the rest of her days deep in the Northern Mountains."

"Whatever became of her?" Alex asked.

"Some people say she started an army of snowmen and is waiting for the right time to unleash them. Others say she was so distraught after losing the kingdom she cried until her eyes froze and they melted away. Nothing is certain, because no one ever saw her again, but her icy wrath still sends chills down people's spines whenever her name is mentioned," Jack said.

"So how do people know she's alive?" Alex asked.

"Oh, she's alive, believe me," Goldilocks said. "The Snow Queen sends vengeful blizzards through the kingdom when she's feeling particularly angry—just to let people know she's still around."

Alex and Conner gulped at the same time.

"And this scepter of hers that we need," Conner said. "I'm guessing we're going to have to steal it, right? She's not just going to hand it over willingly."

In response, Jack and Goldilocks simply continued sharpening their weapons.

"Speaking of cold," Goldilocks said and gestured to Red, who had been staring at the four of them for some time. Red quickly turned away from them, embarrassed to be caught.

A week ago, Red had been certain she was in love with Froggy. But as soon as Jack returned to her life, all the old feelings she had for him slowly started to return as well. She tried to fight them off, telling herself it was just her mind playing tricks on her heart, but tonight, as she watched him tell the twins about the Snow Queen, she couldn't deny that feelings had definitely resurfaced.

Froggy, despite his current state, was perfect for her, and everyone she knew agreed. She loved him with all of her heart—but wasn't that how she felt about Jack, too? Could she be in love with two people at once? Or worse—could she be in love with one of them and just in denial about how she felt toward the other?

But which was which? What would it take for her to be certain? All the thinking gave Red a headache.

"It looks like things are about to get bumpy for us," Froggy said to Red.

"Excuse me?" Red asked in shock, terrified he could read her mind.

Froggy cleared his throat to get Jack's and Goldilocks's attention. "I don't mean to put a damper on the night, but I believe we may be headed to a certain death unless we do something about it."

Everyone's head shot to the front of the ship. The *Granny* was headed straight into the sharp and snowy peaks of the Northern Mountains—and unless they gained altitude quickly, *they were going to crash.*

Red sighed to herself, relieved Froggy hadn't been referring to her thoughts, but her relief turned into a series of screams as she realized what was happening.

Jack leaped up and pulled on the lever by the flame. The flame grew and the *Granny* rose, but not high enough. The mountain peaks were getting closer, certain to rip a hole right through the ship. Jack pulled on the lever as hard as he could, but the flame was as big as it was going to get. The *Granny* wasn't getting any higher.

"Oh no!" Alex said.

"What are we going to do?" Conner asked.

Goldilocks looked around the deck. She ran over to the trunks and chests Red had insisted on bringing and sliced through the ropes that held them down with her sword. One by one, Goldilocks began chucking the chests and trunks overboard.

"What are you doing? Are you crazy?" Red said. She ran over to her beloved items and threw herself on top of them.

"Don't tempt me to throw you overboard, too!" Goldilocks said.

"These are my things! You can't just toss them overboard! I need them!" Red yelled. They both grabbed on to the handles of a chest and played tug-of-war with it. Goldilocks managed to get it over the edge of the ship, but Red wouldn't let it go.

"Red, you need to listen to me," Goldilocks said, looking her directly in the eyes. "You've got too much baggage! You need to let it go or we'll crash!"

Red froze. Had *Goldilocks* heard her thoughts moments before? Had she been thinking out loud and not realized it?

"Red, we can't go on with all of this weighing us down! Do you understand?" Goldilocks pleaded with her.

"I have to let go?" Red said to herself. "I have to let go..." She looked up at Jack, down to the chest, back at Jack, and slowly let the chest slip out of her grasp and fall to the earth below. She watched it fall until she couldn't see it anymore.

Goldilocks wasted no time. She eagerly (almost too eagerly) began hoisting all of Red's trunks and chests over the side of the ship. Jack and the twins joined her. The more they tossed overboard, the higher the *Granny* rose.

"*Almost... almost...*" Froggy said. His green hands were almost white from clutching the steering wheel. He was doing his best to navigate the *Granny* around the sharp peaks, but there was still one more to fly over—and it was exceptionally high.

There was only one more trunk to get rid of. It took Jack, Goldilocks, and the twins all their strength to push it up and over the side of the ship. They flung it over just in time and the *Granny* glided over the mountain peak, inches away from its jagged edge.

Jack, Goldilocks, and the twins fell to the deck floor—their hearts were pounding and they were breathing heavily. Red was leaning on the banister, her eyes fixed on the ground, trying to see where her things had landed, but they were too high up for her to tell.

"*I need to let go...*" Red quietly sniffled to herself. "*I need to let go.*"

After a few moments, the four caught their breath and got to their feet. Red was devastated and wiped away tiny tears that had formed in the corners of her eyes.

"I'm so sorry we had to throw all of your clothes overboard," Alex said.

"Clothes?" Red said. "Oh no, those weren't my clothes—those were just my hats and jewelry. All my clothes are packed in the trunks downstairs."

Everyone glared at her as if she were responsible for everything wrong in the world.

"Does this ship have a plank?!" Goldilocks asked. She jumped toward Red—Jack and the twins had to hold her back.

"My dear, for your safety I think it's best if you go to bed," Froggy told Red. She didn't argue and climbed down the steps to the lower deck.

The *Granny* bobbed gracefully above the rocky Northern Mountains. The sun had risen hours ago but no one could tell through the thick, cloudy sky. The ground looked menacing below. There were no trees or villages, only snow. The twins couldn't imagine anything living this far north—anything except a Snow Queen.

The wind suddenly picked up and the ship rocked harder than it ever had. The cold had become almost unbearable, and the twins wrapped their coats even tighter around themselves.

"We're getting closer," Jack said. "Look!"

He pointed to the dark sky in the distance. Bright northern lights circled into a vortex above a particularly jagged cluster of mountain peaks.

"We found her! She should be just under those lights," Goldilocks said.

"Charlie, let's put the *Granny* down gently over there," Jack said and gestured to a large snow bed they were approaching. Froggy nodded and steered the ship in its direction. Jack lowered the lever by the flame and the ship descended, settling onto the snowy ground.

Red poked her head up from the lower deck. "Are we here?" she said with a big yawn, just waking up from a nap.

"We'll travel the rest of the way by foot," Jack said. "A large ship hovering over her lair may cause some attention."

Goldilocks opened the trunk she had brought onto the ship. She and Jack began tucking away as many weapons as possible: daggers in their boots, knives in their belts, rope around their waists. They both took a lantern and handed one to the twins.

"Are you two sure you're ready for this?" Jack asked. He was very businesslike, but the twins could sense a paternal hesitation in his voice.

Alex and Conner took a deep breath and nodded. "We're ready," they said in unison.

"I don't think I packed any *snow heels*; I may have to sit this one out," Red said.

"Great," Jack said. It was the best news he had heard all day. "Charlie, you should stay with the ship. If we're not back in a day, come looking for us."

"Yes, sir," Froggy said.

Jack looked at Goldilocks and the twins. "All right," he said. "Follow me."

They climbed off the ship and headed in the direction of the northern lights. It was hard for Alex and Conner to keep up with Jack and Goldilocks—partially because the snow was hard to walk in and partially because they weren't used to trekking through the wilderness like Jack and Goldilocks were.

As they continued farther north, the wind became stronger and stronger. It almost knocked them down and the sounds were piercing, like screaming—the Snow Queen's screaming. Perhaps this was part of that wrathful blizzard they had been warned about.

After a long while of traveling by foot the twins looked up and saw the northern lights circling the sky directly above them. Jack led them into a small opening between two enormous glaciers, and the harsh winds were blocked. It was like walking in a narrow hallway without a ceiling.

"I think it's this way," Jack said to his three followers.

They traveled between the glaciers, farther into the mountains of the Snow Queen's lair. The opening between the glaciers zigzagged through the mountains like an icy labyrinth, twisting and turning every few feet. Alex and Conner couldn't tell which direction they were walking in anymore. They were afraid they would get lost but saw Goldilocks scraping the glacier wall with a dagger as they traveled, marking the way back out.

They started to hear voices echo through the glacier maze. Jack gestured for them to be as quiet as possible as they walked farther.

The group found themselves entering a large crater in the

middle of the mountains. A frozen river circled the bottom like a snowy floor, and a frozen waterfall spilled inside from the mountain above. There were several pillars of ice surrounding the frozen river.

Everything was white so it was hard to make out what they were seeing at first. But as her eyes began to focus, Alex had to stifle a scream. At the base of the frozen waterfall, the ice flowed into a gigantic chair on which the Snow Queen herself was sitting. They were on the edge of an icy throne room.

Upon seeing her, Jack and Goldilocks dove behind one ice pillar and the twins hid behind another.

The Snow Queen was a tall woman with a large white fur coat, a snowflake crown, and a cloth wrapped around her eyes. Her skin was so pale and frostbitten it was practically blue. She had a very strong jaw and tiny jagged teeth. She clutched a long icicle scepter in one hand, and her other hand was being stroked by something enormous and fluffy kneeling before her... *it was a polar bear.* He blended so well into the rest of the crater the twins had barely noticed him.

"Bear!" Goldilocks gasped. It was the first time the twins had ever seen her *afraid* of anything.

"You're afraid of bears?" Alex whispered to her.

Goldilocks nodded but her eyes never left the polar bear. "Ever since I was a girl and went inside the Three Bears' house by mistake," she said.

The polar bear gently caressed the Snow Queen's hand—a faithful and obedient servant.

"How many people are there outside?" the Snow Queen

asked him hoarsely. One of the rumors Jack had told the twins was true; she was definitely blind.

"Thousands and thousands have come today, Your Majesty," the polar bear said in a deep, growly voice.

"What have they come for?" the Snow Queen asked.

"They've come to bow and grovel at your feet and witness your beauty," the polar bear said.

A snide smile came to the Snow Queen's face and a slow, rattling laugh came from deep inside of her.

"Do I still control all the neighboring kingdoms?" the Snow Queen asked.

"All of them, Your Majesty," the bear said. "The whole world is covered in your snowy wrath—just as it was before."

The Snow Queen's smile grew wider. "What gifts does my army have for me today?" she asked.

"I'll call for them, Your Majesty," he said.

The polar bear let out a booming growl. A few moments later another polar bear appeared. He carried two long poles with several pairs of boots tied to them. He raised the poles and lowered them to the ground as he walked, giving the Snow Queen the illusion that dozens of soldiers were marching into the crater.

"My faithful army has returned," the pleased Snow Queen said. "What have you brought me this time?"

"Jewels, My Queen," the second polar bear said. He set the poles aside and carefully dropped a handful of average rocks into her hands. "Rubies, diamonds, and sapphires—all Your Majesty's favorites."

The Snow Queen gasped. "These are the biggest jewels I've ever held!" she said. "You've made your queen very proud."

The polar bears looked to each other, relieved to have pulled off another hoax. The second polar bear retrieved the poles and walked off behind the waterfall, marching the boots along with him.

"Everything she believes is a lie!" Conner whispered to his sister.

"I wonder how long those polar bears have been fooling her for," Alex whispered back.

"Pssst," Jack said, getting the twins' attention. "I'm going to distract the bear. The three of you get the scepter."

They all nodded.

Jack picked up a chunk of ice and threw it to the other side of the crater's rim. The polar bear jerked his head toward the sound. He scowled, waiting for it to happen again, and then looked back at the Snow Queen when it didn't.

Jack threw an even bigger chunk of ice in the same direction—the polar bear looked toward it and sniffed the air. He let out a low growl and bared his teeth—he knew they had company.

"What is it?" the Snow Queen asked.

"Nothing, Your Majesty," the polar bear said. "Please excuse me for a moment." The polar bear walked off to inspect the sound and disappeared from view behind the pillars on the other side of the crater.

"I'm going to keep him busy," Jack mouthed to Goldilocks, and the twins and followed the bear.

The Snow Queen was all alone. Now was their chance.

"I say we just go over there and tackle her," Conner suggested.

"No, I'm going to try to steal it on my own first," Goldilocks said. "Stay here and keep a lookout. Whistle if you see anything."

Goldilocks carefully stepped onto the frozen lake and made her way to the Snow Queen's throne. As one would expect from a master thief, she was very agile, barely making a sound.

Goldilocks was halfway there. The twins crossed their fingers; they were watching her so intently they forgot to keep an eye on the rest of the crater. Just when she was a few feet away from the Snow Queen, a small piece of ice crunched loudly under her foot.

"Who's there?" the Snow Queen yelled and raised her scepter.

Suddenly, the polar bear reappeared from behind the pillars and charged toward Goldilocks. With one swipe of his paw, he knocked Goldilocks to the ground and she slid to the center of the frozen lake.

"Goldilocks!" Jack screamed, emerging from behind the pillars himself. He raced toward the polar bear with his axe raised high.

The Snow Queen heard him and pointed her scepter directly at him. A bright icy blast erupted from its tip and hit Jack. He flew across the crater and crashed into a pillar. He scrambled to his feet but was hit again by another icy blast from the Snow Queen—this time a sheet of thick ice pinned his hands and chest to the pillar behind him. Jack struggled with all his might, but he was stuck.

Although she was blind, the Snow Queen apparently had impeccable hearing.

"Who dares disturb my *palace*?!" the Snow Queen demanded.

Goldilocks was hyperventilating on the ground—terrified of the polar bear before her. The Snow Queen glided toward her.

"Leave her alone!" Jack yelled from across the crater, desperately struggling to free himself.

The Snow Queen raised her scepter in Goldilocks's direction. But just then, a giant snowball came out of nowhere and hit the Snow Queen square in the face.

"Hey, abominable snow-woman! Over here!" Conner yelled at her.

The Snow Queen let out a furious moan and the twins could see her breath in the cold air. The polar bear roared and lunged toward them, but the Snow Queen stopped him.

"*No*, you stay here," she ordered. "I want to kill them myself!"

The twins didn't waste a beat and took off running. The Snow Queen went after them, following the sounds of their footsteps. They ran behind the frozen waterfall and found themselves entering a large cavern.

The polar bear slowly walked toward Goldilocks. His sharp teeth were exposed and drool was dripping from his salivating mouth. "No one disturbs the Snow Queen and lives to see another day!" the polar bear growled.

"Goldie, get up!" Jack yelled. "You have to get up!"

"I-I-I can't!" she whimpered, sliding away from the approaching bear as fast as she could.

"What's the matter?" the polar bear asked her. "Am I too close for comfort?"

"Actually," Goldilocks said, *"you're exactly where I want you!"*

Goldilocks retrieved her sword and hit the frozen lake as hard as she could. A large crack bolted across the lake straight to the polar bear. The ice under his feet caved, and the polar bear fell straight through into the freezing water below.

"That's my girl!" Jack hollered proudly. *"Woo-hoo!"*

Goldilocks got to her feet and caught her breath. It was very rare for her heart to race this fast. She carefully looked down at the hole in the ice, waiting for the polar bear to resurface, but the water refroze before he had the chance.

Goldilocks ran over to Jack. She reached into her boot, pulled out a few matches, and struck them against her belt. She held the small flames against the ice trapping him.

"We have to hurry!" Goldilocks said. "The twins are in trouble!"

Alex and Conner ran through the cavern with the Snow Queen hot on their trail. They were barely avoiding the icy blasts she sent toward them.

"Come back here!" she demanded.

The cavern was full of enormous icicles protruding from both the ceiling and the floor—as if the twins had discovered the mountain's teeth. There was very little light but the ice was extremely reflective. The twins could see themselves everywhere they looked.

As if the situation couldn't get worse, the twins ran smack into the second polar bear. He was standing at a long ice table sorting through a collection of props: pots and pans, bells and whistles, pieces of metal, and blocks of wood—everything the bears needed to keep the Snow Queen's ears believing their charade.

The polar bear sneered down at the twins, and they bolted in the opposite direction.

"How dare you intrude upon my palace!" the Snow Queen screamed, blasting icicles into pieces near the twins.

"You're not in a palace! The bears have been lying to you!" Alex shouted back at her.

"You live in the mountains! You haven't conquered anything!" Conner added.

"They're liars, My Queen," the polar bear proclaimed. "We would never do something like that to you—*to your left, My Queen*!"

The Snow Queen pointed her scepter to her left, and an icy beam hit the icicle directly to the twins' left. Thankfully, the polar bear had mistaken their reflection for the real twins.

"To your right, My Queen!" the polar bear shouted, acting as her eyes.

The Snow Queen blasted away the icicle directly to the twins' right, missing them by inches.

"Conner, I hate to say this, but I think it might be smart to—"

"Split up?" Conner said, finishing his sister's sentence.

They separated and ran in different directions. It looked like there were dozens of Alexes and Conners running through the cavern now.

"Ahead of you, My Queen!" the polar bear shouted.

The Snow Queen followed his instructions and fired icy blasts in every direction he told her.

"To your right! Behind you! To your left! To your front! Behind you again! To your side!" the polar bear instructed. Alex and Conner were running circles around them. The Snow Queen was going to blast the entire cavern away if she wasn't careful.

"Now to your side! Turn around! One is right behind you! He's getting away! Quickly, to your left!" the polar bear yelled.

The Snow Queen shot a strong blast to her left and the cavern went silent.

"Well?" the Snow Queen grunted. "Where are they?!"

Alex and Conner looked back—the polar bear was frozen in a block of ice. In her attempts to shoot them, the Snow Queen had hit him.

The Snow Queen grew frustrated and yelled so loudly the entire cavern started to shake. The cavern rumbled and the twins looked up to see a massive avalanche rolling straight toward them.

Conner dived behind an icicle. Alex hid under the ice table. The avalanche swept through the cavern and engulfed the Snow Queen. She screamed as it crashed into her. The wave of snow settled and the cavern was dead silent.

Alex peeked her head up from the table. The Snow Queen was lying on the ground, covered in a mound of snow. Her crown had been knocked off and her scepter was lying nearby.

Alex cautiously walked over to her. Was she dead? Could she hear her approaching?

Alex leaned down and picked up the scepter. Just as her hand wrapped around it, the Snow Queen grabbed on to Alex's forearm and pulled her in close. The cloth slid off of her lids and Alex was staring into two bright lights instead of eyes.

"Of the four travelers, one will not return..." the Snow Queen rasped. Then the lights faded into nothing but empty eye sockets. The Snow Queen's hand around Alex went limp and she fell unconscious.

Alex didn't understand what had just happened. Had the Snow Queen just given her a prophecy?

"You got it!" Conner said excitedly and ran up to his sister. He was covered in snow but was jumping for joy.

"Yeah, I did," Alex said—still unsure of how to process what the Snow Queen had just told her.

Jack and Goldilocks charged into the cavern. They were so relieved to see the twins. They took one look at the frozen polar bear and at the trapped Snow Queen and laughed.

Jack playfully nudged Goldilocks. "And *you* were worried they were in danger," he said.

"Jack, look out!" Conner yelled. Jack ducked just in time to miss being slashed with a claw. The other polar bear had managed to get out of the frozen lake and appeared behind

them—he was soaked and furious. He leaped toward Jack and Goldilocks, ready to tear them apart.

Alex pointed the scepter at the polar bear and an icy beam hit him in the chest. He froze in midair and hit the ground, trapped in ice.

"Well, I'm ready for this snow day to be over," Conner said.

"Let's get out of here before the bears thaw out," Goldilocks said.

The group found the opening in the glaciers they had entered through and followed the marks Goldilocks left back into the harsh winds. They traveled south until they found the *Granny* right where they had left it.

"You're back! You're back!" Froggy said and literally leaped for joy as they climbed aboard the ship. "Well, how'd it go? Did you get the scepter?"

Alex showed him the Snow Queen's scepter. "Boy, do we have a story for you!" she said.

But before Alex could even start, Red emerged from the lower deck. "Oh good, you're all back! You won't believe what happened to me while you were gone!" she said.

"*We* won't believe what happened to *you*?" Conner asked, wondering what could top defeating polar bears and a Snow Queen.

Red was cradling something in her arms like a baby. As she neared the others, they could see it was furry and had four paws.

"I got a puppy!" Red said and happily showed them the small dog sleeping in her arms.

"Where did you get a puppy?" Alex asked.

"I grew a little impatient waiting for you to return—*oh, I see you got the scepter! Well done*—anyway, I went for a walk to pass the time and I found this little guy wandering around the snow alone! He was helpless, starving, and adorable, so I decided to adopt him!" Red explained.

No one knew what to say. Anything they could have said about retrieving the scepter wouldn't have been nearly as interesting to her as the pup in her arms.

"Did you name him?" Conner asked.

"I named him Claudius," Red informed them. "I named him after one of the characters from my favorite Shakeyfruit play, *Hamhead*."

Froggy hit his forehead with an open hand. "*Hamlet*, my dear," he corrected her.

"Yes, that's the one," she said. "But I'm going to spell it with a *w*. Wouldn't that be divine? Clawdius, with a *w*! Do you get it?"

Everyone nodded along with her like she was a three-year-old child—except for Goldilocks. She was staring daggers at Red.

"You probably don't get it," Red said and explained it to her further. "If I spell it with a *w*, the word *claw* will be in his name, like an animal claw. Get it now? Say it with me, Goldie—*Clawdius*."

Goldilocks looked down at the small dog and then back up at Red with a smile. "He's very cute, congratulations."

The others did a double take. They had never seen Goldilocks collect herself so effortlessly before.

"Thank you," Red said. She climbed the steps back down to the lower deck, rocking her new pet as she went. "Oh my, what cute little paws you have, Clawdius! Oh my, what precious little eyes you have. Oh my, what pointy little ears you have..."

Goldilocks began unloading all her weapons, chuckling as she did.

"That was big of you," Conner said to her.

"What's so amusing?" Jack asked.

"Red is in for a rude awakening," Goldilocks said.

"Oh, dear," Froggy said. "Why is that?"

A sly smile came to Goldilocks's face. "I'd recognize one of those anywhere. That's not a *puppy*—it's a *wolf cub*."

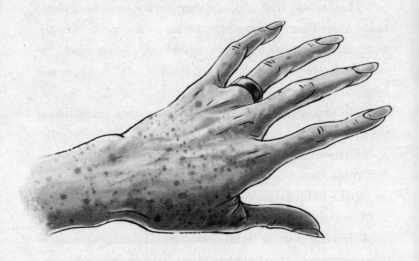

CHAPTER EIGHTEEN

THE WICKED STEPMOTHER

Red was insufferably inseparable from her new pet. While the others rested in the lower deck after their encounter with the Snow Queen, the sounds of Red playing fetch with Clawdius kept them tossing and turning in their cots.

"Fetch, Clawdius!" Red encouraged in a loud and high-pitched voice. "Go on, boy! Go get the stick! Bring it back to Mommy!"

Since they had decided it was best for the *Granny* to fly covertly at night, everyone on board was struggling to adjust to the nocturnal traveling schedule, getting sleep whenever they could—and Red wasn't helping matters.

A loud clank came from the upper deck that caused everyone to jolt.

"That's it!" Goldilocks said, jumping out of her cot. She ran up the steps to the upper deck and was mortified by what she saw—*Red was using the ice scepter to play fetch with Clawdius.*

"Are you insane!?" Goldilocks said, yanking the scepter out of the pup's mouth.

"What? He likes it," Red said.

The twins could hear their conversation as clear as a bell below, and they worried these moments would be Red's last.

"You're really not helping my urge to throw you and that mutt off this ship!" Goldilocks said.

Red ignored her. She hummed a tune to herself and took a seat on the other side of the deck. Clawdius curled up in Red's lap and went to sleep as she stroked his bushy gray fur.

"Hoods have always suited me so well, and motherhood is no exception," Red said. "Isn't it amazing how quickly we've bonded? What are the chances a poor dog would be stranded in the wilderness and rescued by a fabulous queen? I feel like we're living in a story!"

Goldilocks had had enough. It was time to burst Red's bubble.

"He treats you like you're his mother because *he actually thinks you're his mother*," Goldilocks said. "He's bonding with your coat, Red, not you! Clawdius is a wolf!"

"What?" Red said with a laugh, as if it was the most

preposterous thing she had ever heard in her life. "That's ridiculous! There's no way Clawdius is a..." Her voice trailed off. She looked down and saw Clawdius sucking on one of the buttons of her coat—disappointed no milk was coming from it.

Red was suddenly aware of the familiarity of his teeth, his ears, his snout, and his fur—she had seen all these features before, just on a larger scale.

A piercing scream erupted from the back of Red's throat. *"WOLF!"* She jumped to her feet and pushed Clawdius to the ground. *"Get it away from me! Get it away from me!"*

Jack, Froggy, and the twins climbed to the upper deck when they heard the screaming. They were afraid Goldilocks might have finally lost her patience and tried to murder Red, but Goldilocks was leaning on the banister watching Clawdius chase Red around the deck with a huge smile on her face.

"Don't just stand there! Help me!" Red yelled at Jack and the twins. She was running in circles and Clawdius was playfully barking up at her, thinking they were playing another game.

"Darling, please calm down!" Froggy said. "He's just a tiny little—"

"He's a bloodthirsty killer!" Red screamed. *"Just look at him! He's probably been plotting to kill me in my sleep since he came aboard!"*

"He's not the only one," Goldilocks said.

"Get away from me, you ferocious beast!" Red yelled over her shoulder at the baby wolf. The twins found her choice of words to be a bit extreme. The wolf cub didn't seem threaten-

ing in the slightest, especially as Clawdius was now chasing his own tail.

"Perhaps you could raise him to be *unferocious*, my love?" Froggy suggested.

"Name one example of *that* method working!" Red yelled. Froggy drew a blank. "That's because you can take the wolf out of the wilderness but you can't take the wilderness out of the wolf!"

Red stood on the banister and Clawdius jumped up at her, trying to join her on the ship's edge. He grew tired of jumping up for Red's affection and sat on the floor just below her with his oversize paws spread in front of him.

"Don't look at me like that," Red said. "I can't be your mother if I'm constantly worried you're going to maul me to death, now can I?"

A singular sad yelp came out of the pup and he looked at her sideways.

"I have a history with wolves, you know," Red said. "One almost gobbled me and my grandmother up when I was a little girl! A wall was built around my kingdom to keep out the likes of you. Surely you can understand the inconvenience?"

Clawdius whimpered, somehow understanding the young queen. He moped over to Froggy, feeling like he had been abandoned for a second time.

"There, there, old chap," Froggy said and picked up the tiny wolf. "We'll find you a nice home, don't you worry."

Red stayed on the banister for the majority of the day, too afraid to move.

That night, as soon as the sun set, Jack fired up the ship and Froggy steered it south. It sailed through the clouds of the Northern Kingdom to their next destination—Cinderella's wicked stepmother's estate.

Jack and Froggy took shifts through the night navigating the *Granny*. The twins tried to sleep, but it was difficult with the *Granny* rocking along the midnight sky and because Red was talking in her sleep.

"Oh my, what soft fur you have, little Clawdius," Red said, and stroked an imaginary dog in her bed. "Oh my, what small nonthreatening teeth you have.... Oh my, what strong non-growing bones you have.... Oh my, what a delicate little diet of fruits and vegetables you have...."

Goldilocks had successfully blocked out the noises with a pillow wrapped around her head. Alex wasn't so lucky. Not only did she have Red talking in her sleep to drown out but also the fear of what the Snow Queen had told her in the cavern.

Out of the four travelers, one would not return. What did it mean? Was she referring to the twins, Jack, and Goldilocks? Was she telling Alex that one of them was going to die? Had she actually made a true prophecy or was she just trying to get into Alex's head?

Alex wondered if anyone had literally worried themselves to death, because if not, she was probably going to be the first. Her thoughts were overwhelming and Alex finally gave up on the idea of sleep. She got up from her cot and discovered her brother had done the same. She climbed up to the upper deck and found him leaning on the banister facing the East. He held a quill, and a stack of parchment was spread in front of him.

It was quiet out here. Only the sounds of the *Granny*'s sails flapping in the wind and the flickering of the central flame could be heard.

"You couldn't sleep, either?" Alex asked.

"I don't think someone comatose could sleep through all of that," he said.

"What are you doing?" Alex asked, gesturing to his quill and parchment. "Not homework, I hope. I think you'll be allowed to turn in a couple late assignments given the circumstances."

"No, I'm just writing," Conner said. "I'm making notes of all the things we've seen and the places we've been so far. I don't want to forget anything. I may want to make a couple short stories out of it. The Snow Queen's polar bear servants, Red having a pet wolf, *pheasant pudding* . . . It's all good stuff."

"That's great," Alex said. "I hope you get to use them—"

Alex said it without thinking. Conner stopped writing and took a deep breath.

"Alex, we're gonna save Mom," he said firmly.

Alex didn't know what to say. "I hope so—"

"No, I need to hear you say it. We won't be able to do it unless we both believe it."

Alex found the confidence in her brother's eyes contagious. "We're going to save Mom," Alex said, this time fully believing it.

Conner smiled. "Good," he said. "Thanks for that."

"What keeps you so positive? Usually I'm the one giving the pep talks, but you've been boosting my morale since we got here."

"What are our options? If I have the choice of being doubtful or being hopeful, I'm going to choose hopeful. It takes less work to be positive."

Alex smiled at him. "That's a nice way to see things."

"And," Conner added, "you know once we save Mom's life there's no way she'll ever be able to say no to us again!"

Alex laughed and covered her mouth, forgetting the rest of the ship was asleep. "Okay, *now* you're getting your hopes up way too much!"

The twins savored the thought. Conner was right; it was much easier than letting their minds fill with doubt.

A cool breeze suddenly blew past the ship and shivers went down their spines.

"Do you feel that?" Alex asked.

"Yeah, what's going on?"

Alex looked over her shoulder and gasped. *"Conner, look!"* She turned her brother in the direction she was facing.

Slowly gliding toward them was the ghost Conner had seen in Red's castle. There was something so majestic, so regal, and yet so frightening about her all at the same time.

"It's the ghost!" Conner whispered. "That's the one I was telling you about!"

The ghost's gaze grew more serious as she approached them.

"Say something to it!" Alex elbowed her brother.

310

"What am I supposed to say? I don't speak ghost!"

The spirit stopped and hovered a few feet in front of them. She never blinked or looked away from the twins. Whoever she was, she was a very serious spirit.

"Who are you?" Alex peeped.

The ghost remained silent and still as ever.

"What do you want from us?" Conner squeaked.

The ghost raised her hand and simply pointed into the distance. And as the *Granny* passed through a weak cloud and a veil of mist brushed past them, the ghost vanished.

The twins' hearts were racing. "Who was that?" Alex asked.

"I wish I knew," Conner said. "Why is she following me?"

Alex thought about it. The spirit had looked so familiar to her, but she couldn't put her finger on why. "She's trying to tell us something."

The *Granny* settled into the countryside of the Charming Kingdom just before sunup. Luckily, only a few grazing cows witnessed the large ship descending from the sky, and they weren't the least bit interested in it.

The twins kept the second ghost sighting to themselves, not wanting to cause any further worry.

"So what's our plan?" Conner asked the others. "How are we going to discover and steal the stepmother's most prized possession?"

Goldilocks and Jack looked to each other and both shrugged. Froggy stepped forward and cleared his throat with a small croak.

"If I may, I believe I'll be quite useful at organizing this scheme—I *am* from the Charming Kingdom, after all," he said.

"By all means," Alex said and gestured for the frog to take the floor.

"The stepmother," Froggy declared with a finger raised, as if he were giving them a history lesson, "has always been obsessed with titles and social status—remember how desperately she wanted her daughters to marry my brother? If we want to get into her home and discover what her most prized possession is, we'll have to do it in a very formal manner—and I think I know just how to do it."

Froggy turned to Red. "Me?" she asked. "What do I have to do with anything?"

"You're a queen, my dear," Froggy said. "The stepmother would never resist the chance at having a royal in her home."

Red rolled her eyes and folded her arms. "Oh, *now* I'm a queen? *Now* you're all respecting my rank?" she said.

"Precisely," Froggy said. "You'll go to her home and request a sitting with her. Have a look around and pocket whatever you see she values the most."

"Request a sitting for what?" Red asked. "What could I possibly need to talk to her about?"

Conner was quick to come up with an answer. "Tell her you're designing a country home and Cinderella told you to look at her old house for inspiration," he said.

Alex patted him on the shoulder. "Good one," she said.

Red looked from side to side. They could tell the idea was marinating in her head. "Yes, that is a rather good idea... a splendid idea, in fact! I've always wanted a country home, actually. This may not be such a lie after all," she said and happily clapped her hands. "Am I going alone?"

Froggy looked around at the others. "I'm afraid everyone here would look a bit suspicious if any of us were to go with you," he said.

"We can go with you, Red," Alex said. "We'll pretend to be your cousins."

Red looked the twins up and down and her face scrunched up disapprovingly. "Can we be second cousins? Our bone structures are just so different I'm not sure anyone would believe it."

A dagger flew through the air and stabbed into the wall a few inches away from Red's head. She screamed and fell to the floor. Everyone turned to Goldilocks—her hand was still extended from the throw.

"Sorry, it slipped," Goldilocks said with a shrug.

Once Red recovered from Goldilocks's "accident" she dressed herself for the day's mission. She wore a red fascinator and an exceptionally fluffy red dress. Apparently Red had been saving this outfit for a special occasion on their trip and figured this was the best place to show it off.

Jack and Goldilocks stayed to keep an eye on the ship. Froggy escorted Red and the twins through the Charming countryside. He wore one of Red's scarves around his head to conceal his amphibian skin. Red complained about her shoes the entire time as they walked, but the twins had grown so accustomed to her complaining it didn't bother them.

Large storybook estates began popping up on the sides of the path as they walked farther into the kingdom. Some were made of brick; others were covered in ivy; and many had pointed straw roofs, just like the twins' grandmother's cottage. Farther off in the distance they could make out the tops of Cinderella's palace towers. It was the nicest neighborhood the twins had ever walked through in the fairy-tale world.

"This is making me so excited to plan my country house!" Red said.

The twins rolled their eyes. At least Red didn't have a cover to blow.

"What's that over there?" Conner asked and pointed ahead of them.

A large display was gated off to the side of the path. They walked to the edge of the gate and looked inside. A very old and large decaying pumpkin was on the ground—it was like a jack-o'-lantern that had been left outside for far too long after Halloween.

"Read this!" Alex said, and pointed to the plaque placed in the ground.

THE ROYAL PUMPKIN REMAINS

THESE ARE THE REMAINS
OF THE CARRIAGE THAT

ESCORTED QUEEN CINDERELLA
TO THE RENOWNED BALL
ON THE NIGHT SHE MET
KING CHARMING.
THE PUMPKIN WAS MAGICALLY
TRANSFORMED INTO A CARRIAGE BY
THE FAIRY GODMOTHER,
BUT AT MIDNIGHT
THE SPELL WAS BROKEN
AND THE PUMPKIN TURNED
BACK INTO ITS ORIGINAL FORM.
IT HAS RESTED HERE EVER SINCE
CINDERELLA'S LEGENDARY DASH.

"Our grandma *would* be behind the most famous curfew in history, wouldn't she?" Conner said to his sister.

Red squinted at the rotten pumpkin. "She swept floors, rode in a pumpkin, and was friends with mice . . . and somehow Cinderella sets the bar for all the other queens," she said to herself. "I'll never understand that."

"This means we're very close," Froggy said. "The stepmother's estate should only be a little ways farther down the path. I don't want her to recognize me so I'll wait for you here. Best of luck!"

Red air-kissed him and she and the twins continued down the path. After a few minutes they reached the stepmother's estate—and it was not what they had been expecting.

Had the twins not known any better they would have

thought the estate was abandoned. The house sat on the top of a tall hill and was in desperate need of repair. It was very dark, with tall windows, a steeple, and pointed gables. All the windows needed to be washed and most of them were broken. Half of the steps leading to the front door had caved in.

Everything on the property was either dead or overgrown. The entire estate was surrounded by a tall iron fence. Two suited guards patrolled the only entrance at the front.

"Whoa," Conner said. "This may be trickier than we thought."

The trio walked up to the guards in a very friendly, non-thief-like manner.

"Excuse me," Alex said to one of the guards. "Is this where Cinderella's stepmother lives?"

The guard glanced over to the other guard with an irritated look on his face. "This is the residence of *Lady Iris* and her daughters," the guard said. "And yes, she is the queen's stepmother."

"Why is it so protected?" Conner asked.

The other guard made a face at him. "You're not from around here, are you?" he said. "Lady Iris is not liked around these parts. The fence is for her protection from people who vandalize her home. Lady Iris doesn't even bother fixing things anymore—there's no point."

Alex looked up at the house with a heavy heart. Even with knowing how poorly the stepmother had treated Cinderella, she couldn't help but feel sorry for her. One of the higher windows was open and she saw white drapes flicker inside—someone was watching them from the house.

"Can we meet her?" Alex asked.

"What did you say? *Meet Lady Iris?*" the guard asked with a rude laugh. "No, I'm afraid not. Lady Iris never takes any visitors."

"Run along now back to wherever you came from," the other guard said.

Conner nudged Red—this was her cue. She cleared her throat and looked up at them with large, bright eyes.

"Gentlemen, I know it's hard to recognize me without a proper hood over my shoulders, but I'll give you another chance before I grow weary," Red said with a haughty smile.

The guards said nothing. They didn't recognize her at all. Red became frustrated and her cheeks turned pink.

"I'm Queen Red Riding Hood of the Red Riding Hood Kingdom," she said.

A guard raised an eyebrow and looked at her sideways. "If you're Red Riding Hood, where's your staff and sheep?" he said, half laughing as he spoke.

"That's Little Bo Peep!" Red yelled and stomped her foot. The twins were growing frustrated, too. They hadn't planned on this setback.

"Let them in," said a frail voice from the high window at the house.

The guards were surprised by the command. Clearly this had never happened before.

"All right, the lady says you can go inside," the guard said. He opened the screechy gate behind him and Red and the twins went through it. They carefully walked up the front steps and Conner knocked on the door with enormous spade-shaped knockers. They heard frantic whispering and hurried footsteps inside. It took a moment for anyone to answer the door.

The large door swung open and two awkward women cautiously peered from behind it.

"Hello?" Alex said. "May we come inside?"

The two women decided Red and the twins were safe and stepped out from behind the door. They were both very plain and plump (although one was shorter and heavier than the other). Each had curly brown hair and thin lips. They were the kind of women who had the potential to be pretty but had let themselves go over the years.

They fidgeted with their lacy dresses—as if they had gotten ready in a hurry. Alex nudged Conner; they both knew without a doubt they were facing Cinderella's ugly stepsisters.

"Please come in," the taller of the two said with an overdramatic gesture.

The twins and Red took a step inside to the house's entrance hall. A large staircase curved up and above them. The entire house was an absolute mess. The floors were dirty, the windows were dusty, and a foul odor lingered in the air. The twins wondered if Cinderella had been the last person to clean the house.

"Forgive the mess," the shorter of the two said. "We weren't expecting company."

"Shocking," Red said under her breath.

"No worries," Alex said. "It's just very—*lived in.*"

A loud creak came from above them. "Girls, girls, don't be rude," said a voice. "Introduce yourselves."

Red and the twins looked up to see the infamous wicked stepmother herself standing at the top of the stairs. She was very thin and her hair was graying and done up in an impressively high bun. Her makeup was splotchy and smeared as if she had freshened herself in a rush. She held a cane as she wobbled down the stairs.

"Welcome to our home! I'm Lady Iris and these are my daughters, Petunia and Rosemary," she said, and the taller one curtsied, followed by the shorter one. The stairs creaked so loudly beneath her it was hard to hear what she was saying.

"Hello, Lady Iris," Red said. "I'm Queen Red Riding Hood and these are my second cousins, Hamlet and Ophelia."

The twins cringed at the sound of their aliases. "Pleasure," Conner said and gave Red a dirty look.

The stepmother nodded cordially but her eyes held many questions. "Yes, I recognized you from Princess Hope's first birthday celebration at the palace," Lady Iris said.

"Oh yes, of course!" Red said, surprised to share the memory. "I remember meeting you there as well!"

"We didn't stay very long," Lady Iris explained. "It's hard leaving home when people boo and hiss at you wherever you go." She laughed even though no one found it funny. "Won't you please join us in our sitting room, Your Majesty?"

Red and the twins followed the stepmother and her daughters into the next room. The stepsisters tried picking up the house as they went, but there was so much clutter the twins didn't see why they bothered.

The sitting room had blue walls and white seats. It would

have looked like a bright blue sky had it not been covered in a thick layer of grime; as it was, it resembled an overcast day. They all sat down and dust filled the air. Conner held a cough the best he could.

"You must forgive the state the house is in," Lady Iris apologized. "My girls and I are useless when it comes to housework and it's hard to find help when you have a history like ours."

"I imagine," Conner said.

"So what brings you to our humble abode, Your Majesty?" Lady Iris asked.

Red had no idea where to start. Saying that she wanted to build a country home that resembled the one they sat in would have been an obvious lie.

"Well, I...I...I..." Red said. "Ophelia? Why don't you explain?"

Red and Conner turned to Alex, completely putting her on the hot seat. Alex looked up at the stepmother with a lie forming in her head, but she was distracted by several paintings of animals that lined the walls.

"What beautiful paintings!" Alex said, changing the subject. "Whose work are they?"

Petunia's mouth fell open; she wasn't used to being complimented. "*I* painted those," she said with large, excited eyes.

"Petunia is quite the gifted painter," Lady Iris bragged. "She does animal portraits mostly but she's been working on landscapes." Her voice was smooth and dreamy, as if she were a saleswoman.

"I like animals," Petunia said enthusiastically, so happy to talk about herself. "I usually paint the ones I see outside my window—sometimes they're pets, sometimes they're pests—animals have always liked me, too; there's something trusting about me, I guess. Anyway, it gives me something to do."

Red and the twins nodded politely.

"Well, that's *exactly* why I'm here!" Red said. "I've recently adopted a *wol*—excuse me—a dog, and I was hoping you could paint a portrait of him."

Alex and Conner were sort of relieved and sort of mortified by Red's sudden ad lib. Petunia's bottom lip quivered. "Really?" she asked. "I would love to!"

"I LIKE TO BAKE!" Rosemary yelled—desperate for attention herself. The outburst caused the others to jump in their seats. "Sorry, I didn't mean to shout! I just like to cook and would love to cook for you if you'd let me...."

"Rosemary is an exceptional baker," Lady Iris boasted. "She cooks all our meals at the house."

"Well, someone has to, otherwise we'd starve," Rosemary said with a laugh, although it wasn't funny. Laughing through misery must have been a family trait.

Both of the stepsisters were so excited to show off their talents they could barely sit still. Lady Iris, however, was still looking at her three guests skeptically.

"What do you usually bake?" Conner asked Rosemary.

"Rosemary, why don't you go prepare a batch of your mushroom biscuits for our guests? And Petunia, why don't you go to your room and gather other samples of your paintings to show Her Majesty?" Lady Iris said.

The stepsisters leaped to their feet and collided into each other, running opposite directions in the house. They could hear the stairs creaking as Petunia ran up to her room. Rosemary disappeared behind a swinging door into the kitchen—for a split second the twins caught sight of the stacks of dirty dishes piled inside.

Once her daughters had left, Lady Iris dropped her cordial face and glared at Red and the twins with a suspicious stare.

"You have such lovely daughters," Red said with a tight smile.

"Save it," the stepmother said sharply. "I've lived in this house alone with my daughters for years—I know Petunia is a lousy painter and Rosemary is an even worse cook. Why have you *actually* come here today?"

They didn't answer her. Red and the twins didn't have to look at one another to know they were all sporting the same doe-eyed expression.

"I see," Lady Iris said after they didn't respond. "You've come to mock an old woman and her daughters, then, have you? Come to laugh at the black sheep of the kingdom? How dare you, especially at a time like this."

Lady Iris struggled to get to her feet so she could escort them out. "I'll show you to the door," she said.

"Why did you do it?" Alex asked abruptly.

Lady Iris turned back to her. "Excuse me?" she said.

"I bet that's not a question you hear very often, but I've always wondered why you were so cruel to Cinderella," Alex said. "Why did you dislike her so much?"

"Alex, how is this helping our cause?" Conner whispered to her, but she waved him off. Lady Iris stared her down, searching for a malicious motive behind her question, but Alex didn't have a malicious bone in her body. Lady Iris went to the side of the room to a small fireplace. A very dusty portrait was hung over it. Lady Iris took a deep breath and blew the dust off the painting. It was of a very attractive and dignified man with auburn hair and a full beard.

"Who is that?" Alex asked.

"My late husband," Lady Iris said. She stared up at him with her back to the twins. "Does he look familiar?"

The resemblance was so blatant they didn't have to think twice; Cinderella was the spitting image of her father.

"Ella has always looked just like her father," Lady Iris said. "Her father nicknamed her Cinderella when she was a toddler because she loved playing in the fireplace—she would cover herself in so much soot and ash she was unrecognizable. When her father died I found it unbearable to look at her face. I forced her to do countless filthy chores around the house, covering her appearance so she wasn't a constant reminder of what I had lost. Now the face I had spent so many years trying to hide is one of the most recognizable faces in the world."

The stepmother slowly caressed the wedding ring she still wore on her left hand. Red looked at the twins out of the corner of her eye. They were all three thinking the same thing: *They had found her most prized possession.*

"So you don't *hate* her, then," Alex thought out loud. "It wasn't jealousy, it was *heartache.*"

Lady Iris lowered her head. "I'm twice the widow but half the woman Cinderella is," she said. "When the way I treated her was revealed to the rest of the kingdom and my daughters and I became hated across the land, Cinderella had the fence built and had the guards placed around our home so we'd be protected. She visited and apologized to *us*. Can you believe that? After all we had done to her, she felt guilty about what her marriage to Prince Chance had done to *us*."

"In your defense, it seems like the story has been exaggerated a bit," Conner said. "Your daughters aren't *ugly*, for example; they're just average looking."

The stepmother sat back down across from them. "Indeed," she said. "The kingdom has always loved mocking us. I heard a rumor that after the ball when the prince visited, my girls tried cutting off parts of their feet to get them to fit inside the glass slipper. *Such nonsense!*"

Lady Iris looked at them vacantly—she had nothing else to tell them.

"Well, is that all you were after, then? An old woman's useless confession?" she asked.

"Not to add salt to the wound, but that hatred is actually why we're here," Conner said. "This is going to sound crazy, but we're on a bit of a quest—"

"Conner, I don't think it's smart to tell—" Alex tried to say.

"Why not? It's not like we've got anything to lose at this point," he said and continued with his explanation. "We think we've found a way to defeat the Enchantress. It requires us to go on a bit of a treasure hunt. Your ring is one of the items we need."

"*Excuse me?*" the stepmother asked, appalled by the request.

"Your granddaughter's life is in danger," Alex said. "Don't you want to help her?"

Lady Iris looked away to hide the shame in her eyes. This was evidently a sore subject for her. "*Grandmother* is not a title I consider myself worthy of," she said. "A *grandmother* is the mother of a child's mother—and I have never been a mother to Cinderella."

The room went quiet. The stepmother had to calm herself down from the emotional declaration.

"Well, it's not too late," Red said. "Giving us your ring would be quite the noble act. It'd be the most *Cinderellian* thing you could do. Your status in the community may change when people find out you helped us."

With this said, the twins could see a spark ignite in Lady Iris's eyes. They knew if they could speak with her for a little while longer they might be able to convince her. Unfortunately, the kitchen door swung open and Rosemary brought a tray of her mushroom biscuits into the room, bringing the conversation to a halt.

"Who wants mushroom biscuits?!" Rosemary asked happily. The energy had completely changed in the room since she left it and she couldn't figure out why.

Lady Iris stood again. "You'll have to wrap them up, Rosemary," she said. "Our guests were just leaving."

"Leaving?" said Petunia, walking into the room with several rolled-up portraits under her arms. "But I just found my best paintings."

Red and the twins rose to their feet, too.

"No, your mother is right. We better get going," Red said. "After further consideration, I think I may be getting rid of my dog—I have a suspicion he may be a wolf. *It's a long story*. We'll be in touch about the portrait if I should acquire another pet."

The stepsisters' faces clouded over with disappointment. Petunia threw her portraits to the floor. Rosemary went back to the kitchen and dumped the biscuits into a brown sack for them to take.

"Here," Rosemary said through an enormous frown as she shoved the sack into Conner's chest. "Eat them soon. They spoil after the first hour."

Lady Iris walked Red and the twins back through the entrance hall to the front door. The twins kept glancing at each other, waiting for the other to do something. Alex thought her brother's method of tackling her might be their only option.

Lady Iris opened the door for her visitors but blocked them from leaving. "Wait," she said to the twins as they passed her. She slipped her wedding ring off her hand and placed it into Alex's. "Make sure to tell Cinderella I gave it to you."

Red and the twins couldn't believe their eyes, but their spirits soared.

"We will!" Alex promised her.

"Thank you!" Conner said.

"I'm going to personally issue a statement to let people know you aren't the mean old tart everyone thinks you are!" Red said and hugged her.

The stepmother forced a smile. "Unfortunately, some sins are forgiven and others are never forgotten," she said. "I'm afraid the only place we could live free of judgment would be another world completely. But one day, long after I am gone, I hope Cinderella can tell her daughter I did something to help her."

"She will," Alex said. "Thank you."

Lady Iris gave a shallow bow, not completely sure she had made a good decision. She shut the door behind them and the twins jumped with joy. Red and the twins passed the guards, who didn't understand why the three of them looked so happy after spending an afternoon in *that* house.

Red and the twins walked down the path and found Froggy waiting for them at the Royal Pumpkin Remains exhibit.

"Well?" he asked. "How did it go?"

Alex opened her hand and showed him the ring.

"We got it! We got it! We got it!" Conner shouted. "We got the ring!"

An incredibly wide smile lit up Froggy's face. He picked them both up and swung them around. "Well done, children!" he said and Conner shot him a look. "Forgive me, *young adults*."

Red was quietly waiting for praise of her own but none came. "I wasn't too bad myself!" she said.

"Of course you weren't, my darling," Froggy said and air-kissed her cheek. "Now let's get back to the *Granny* and share the victory with the others."

Froggy led the way back through the countryside to their flying ship. Goldilocks was thrilled to hear of their success, but Jack was nowhere to be found.

"He went into town to pick up some supplies," Goldilocks said. "He'll be back soon. But in the meantime let's see if the Wand of Wonderment is all it's cracked up to be."

They placed the Snow Queen's ice scepter in the center of the lower-deck floor. Alex was still gripping the stepmother's ring so tightly it dug into her palm.

"How is this supposed to work?" Alex asked. "Is it like the Wishing Spell? Do we need all the items together for anything to happen?"

Conner shrugged. "Let's find out," he said.

Alex carefully placed the ring on the floor beside the scepter. The five of them waited impatiently for something—anything—to occur. Anticipation was even getting the best of Clawdius, who was curled up in the corner watching from afar.

"Well?" Red said.

"Shhhh!" Goldilocks silenced her.

The ring started to quiver. The scepter began to move as well. Suddenly, the ring magically attached itself to the tip of the scepter as if it had been magnetically pulled.

The room cheered. Alex and Conner hugged each other. Clawdius barked up at them happily, although he wasn't sure what the celebration was about. It was a small occurrence, but it was the most meaningful part of their journey so far. All their efforts hadn't been a waste—*they were building the Wand!*

Jack emerged down the steps to the lower deck a second later. He had just returned from his trip into town and carried a bag full of vegetables and bread.

"Jack! The wand is working!" Conner said. "Wait—what's wrong?"

They had been so immersed in celebration they hadn't noticed Jack's long face.

"Jack, what's happened?" Goldilocks asked him.

"While I was in town I heard some troubling news," he said. The room grew very quiet.

"What is it?" Froggy asked.

"The Enchantress has attacked the Corner Kingdom," Jack said. "She's knocked down Rapunzel's tower."

Alex and Red gasped. Froggy's large mouth fell open. Conner was still listening, expecting to hear more.

"So?" Conner asked. "It's just a tower—what's the big deal?"

He glanced over to his sister and saw tears running down her face.

"Am I missing something?" Conner asked. "It could have been so much worse. Thankfully, no one is dead."

Froggy cleared his throat, emotion building up inside of him. "Much like the Hoodians' wall, the tower is very sacred to the people of the Corner Kingdom," he explained. "It represents their queen and the beginning of their country. It symbolizes their history and their spirit."

Alex dried her tears and thought to herself: Of all the awful things to do, why was Ezmia picking off things that were *symbolically* valuable to the kingdoms? Why was she attacking people's spirit, of all things?

"I just realized something," Alex said. "Everything Ezmia has done—the tower, the wall, the plants, the kidnappings— it's all been an attack on people's spirits. It's not casualties the Enchantress wants, it's *souls*."

CHAPTER NINETEEN

THE CASTLE IN THE SKY

The *Granny* sailed across the night sky over the Charming Kingdom, determined to beat the sun into the Red Riding Hood Kingdom. The news of Rapunzel's tower had left everyone in a somber mood, but the fact that they were successfully building the Wand of Wonderment kept them moving.

Jack and Froggy rolled a barrel of oil across the deck and loaded it under the ship's flame. Goldilocks was manning the steering wheel and carefully piloting the *Granny* between the clouds. Red was avoiding Clawdius as much as possible.

The twins were at the front of the ship watching the ground move below them. They wondered if they had flown over the place their mother was being kept.

"It's amazing how different the world looks from up here," Jack said cheerfully, walking up behind the twins. "I remember thinking that when I climbed the beanstalk. Very few people get a chance to see the world from a different point of view."

Red was eavesdropping and snuck into the conversation. "I know exactly what you mean," she said. "Once you start looking down on people it's hard to look at them any other way again."

The twins and Jack rolled their eyes. Red had shown great potential for rejoining the real world over the course of their trip, but she still had a long way to go.

"No, Red," Jack said. "I meant it really puts the world into perspective. Your whole life may exist between two streets, but then you realize those streets are just tiny veins in the body of the world. It makes you feel very small."

Red's head bobbed up and down as she followed along with what he was saying. For a second the twins thought she had understood what Jack meant.

"Oh dear," Red said and shook her head. "I don't believe anything could ever make me feel like *that*."

Jack and the twins weren't shy about their exasperation with the young queen and slowly walked away. Red leaned on the rail and let out a sigh, not understanding why it was so challenging to identify with them.

Froggy joined Red at the front of the ship, not wanting her

to feel completely isolated after the exchange. While the others were constantly annoyed by Red's vain statements and lack of empathy, it just made Froggy love her even more. He had lived in hiding for years because he was afraid of how the world would treat a prince-turned-frog, but Red was the kind of person who would never lose confidence no matter what anyone or anything said to her. It was the trait he admired most about her.

"Are you all right, my love?" Froggy asked her.

"Yes, thank you," Red said and wearily looked down at the land beneath them.

Although he knew better, Froggy took her remoteness personally. "Are *we* all right, darling?" he asked. "I know having Jack and Goldilocks around is distressing for you, but if there was ever anything besides their company bothering you, you would tell me, right?"

Red still hadn't figured out what exactly was bothering her yet. It had been a thorn in her side since they left.

"Yes, of course, darling," Red said simply, although neither of them believed it.

Froggy's mouth smiled but his eyes remained blank. "Very well," he said and let her be.

Although she had insisted she could handle the situation, Froggy knew having Jack around would weigh heavily on her. Red wasn't hard to read—and the long stares at Jack from across the ship, her lengthy sighs when no one was looking, the way she ignored Froggy more and more as they traveled didn't go unnoticed. It didn't take a genius to figure out what Red was so conflicted about.

Unfortunately for Froggy, his human-turned-amphibian heart

belonged wholly to Red, and he hoped hers still belonged to him underneath all her uneasiness. Until she told him otherwise, he would remain true to his affections for her.

"Look ahead!" Red called out to the others. "It's my kingdom! Oh my, how adorable it looks from up here! It's unfortunate the weather is so gloomy."

"I don't think that's just gloomy weather," Goldilocks said from the steering wheel. Thick clouds were circling the kingdom like a whirlpool. As they sailed closer, they could make out a tall beanstalk penetrating the cloud's vortex.

No one had ever seen such a thing . . . except for Jack.

"What's all that about?" Froggy asked.

"It means the beanstalk is ready," Jack said with an eager smile.

Conner placed a hand on his sister's shoulder. *So were they.*

The crew began to descend the *Granny* toward the beanstalk. The sun started to rise and both of Jack's old houses came into view. Only one thing was wrong—*the* Granny *was going way too fast.*

"Steady . . . steady . . ." Jack told Goldilocks. "Charlie, shut all the sails! Everyone else, brace yourselves! This is going to be a bumpy landing!"

Froggy yanked the ship's ropes and securely shut the sails. Alex and Conner held on to Clawdius and the banister, Jack and Goldilocks held on to the steering wheel, and Red held on to Froggy.

"Everyone bend your knees!" Jack said, and they all followed his advice. The *Granny* glided down, headed straight for Jack's manor. The front windows of the manor opened and the twins saw the magic harp blissfully welcoming the new day, unaware of the flying ship headed straight toward her.

> *"Oh the day is here and so am I,*
> *To wistfully dream of birds that fly,*
> *Soon I will be moved far far away,*
> *And Queen Red Riding Hood's castle is where I shall—*
> *AAAAAAH!"*

The *Granny* crashed into the ground and bumped across the grassy earth. Chunks of dirt flew into the air, and the ship left a large furrow in the land as it came to an overdue stop *feet away from the manor*.

The harp's mouth and eyes were wide open, and although she was made of solid gold, the twins could have sworn she went pale.

"Good morning, Harper!" Jack called down with an apologetic laugh.

The harp was so stunned one of the strings on her back snapped. The twins couldn't blame her. After years of looking outside at nothing, she had just witnessed a flying ship crash in her front yard.

"What in the name of Mother Goose is going on?" the harp yelled.

"We've been traveling, just like I told you," Jack said and climbed down from the *Granny*. "Did I mention we were traveling by *flying ship*?"

"You left out that minor detail," the harp said, starting to recover feeling in her golden body.

"Thank you for keeping an eye on the beanstalk. It looks terrific!" Jack said.

"You're very welcome," the harp said. "You'll be pleased to know I have thought it over and will accept your offer to be moved to Red's castle. Although I hope you give me a few days for my strings to recover from the fright you just gave me. I don't want my first ballad in the castle to be pitchy."

"What? What did you say?" Red asked from the ship. "Did I hear you say something about being moved to my castle?"

Alex and Conner looked to each other—this was going to be awkward.

"Yes. Jack promised I would be moved in exchange for watching the beanstalk," the harp said.

"Did he?!" Red said through her teeth. "This trip keeps getting better and better, doesn't it?"

"Oh yes, I've been practicing for days! It's been so long since I had a proper audience to perform for!" the harp said. "After spending more than a century with that awful giant, it'll be such a treat to sing songs that aren't about eating sheep and stepping on villages."

The others climbed down from the ship and joined Jack at the front of the manor.

"Hey, Harper," Conner said. "When you were up there, did you ever notice if the giant had a favorite item?"

"Not that I can recall," the harp said. "I have no idea why you'd want to go back to that awful place."

Jack inspected the beanstalk. He circled around the base and scanned it from top to bottom, kicking it in different places as he went.

"It's ready!" he called to the others. "I'm going to climb it and return as quickly as I can."

"Pardon?" Goldilocks asked with raised eyebrows. "Do you actually think you're going without me?"

"He's got to be kidding himself if he thinks we're not going along, too," Conner said to Alex.

Jack hadn't meant to offend anyone. "Forgive me, I wasn't sure anyone else would be up for it," he said.

"It's not every day one gets to see a castle in the clouds," Froggy said. "Count me in as well."

"Fine, then," Jack said. "I'll take the lead. However, it's important that you climb exactly as I climb and step exactly where I step. It's harder than it looks."

Goldilocks retrieved a long rope and tied it around Jack's waist, then around her own, Froggy's, and the twins. She went to tie it around Red's, but the queen nervously blocked her from doing so.

"What do you think you're doing?" Red asked.

"It's just for safety," Goldilocks said. "In case one of us falls."

"Falls? From up there?" Red said and pointed to the endless stalk. "Is that likely?"

"As likely as climbing anything else, I imagine," Goldilocks said. "This will also discourage me from throwing you off of it."

Red looked up and down the beanstalk with large, fearful eyes. "You know what, I think I'm going to sit this one out," she said. "I'm exhausted after my sitting with the stepmother and want to conserve my strength for our next stop," she said.

"Suit yourself," Goldilocks said and promptly cut the rope after securely tying it around Alex.

"Are you sure, Red? The giant died a long time ago," Jack said. "There's nothing to worry about."

"What about what the Tradesman said?" Alex said. "He said there would be other dangers waiting for us up there."

"The man was eating *pheasant pudding*," Conner said. "Are you really going to take his word?"

"Good point," Alex said.

Red pretended to consider it for a moment, but her mind was made up. "I still think I'll be the most useful staying with the ship," Red said.

"Fine by me," Jack said. "Then if we're all ready, *let's climb*."

Jack placed his hands on the stem of the closest leaf and pulled himself up and over it. *The climb had begun.* He enjoyed it more than he would admit and cheerfully led the others up the beanstalk and toward the sky.

Jack and Goldilocks once again set a quick pace for Froggy and the twins to follow—although Froggy hopped his way up the stalk more than actually climbed it. The twins were glad to be the caboose of the climbing crusade; they had the least responsibility if someone fell.

"Let me know what the castle looks like in case I need to rebuild anything in the future!" Red called up at them.

Jack had been right; the beanstalk was tricky to climb. It didn't have the sturdy branches that a tree would, so the stems of the leaves were all they had to grab hold of and step on. After some time had passed, the twins were thankful Red had opted to stay behind—it was difficult enough without her.

They were making great time in their ascent and Jack looked back to congratulate his fellow climbers. "You're doing great," Jack said. "But whatever you do, don't look—"

"*AHHHHHH!*" Froggy yelled.

"Down," Jack finished.

"Sorry, I won't make that mistake again!" Froggy assured them, trembling a bit as they continued. The twins didn't know how high up they were and didn't want to—ignorance was bliss in this scenario.

After only a couple short breaks here and there, the group reached the top of the beanstalk by noon. The twins' bodies were aching already and they just hoped the trip back down would be easier.

"This thing is getting harder and harder to climb," Conner said.

"It doesn't help that the air is getting thinner," Alex said.

"We should start wearing skinny jeans," Conner said. "We'd both look great in them after this workout."

Everything became foggy as they reached the top of the beanstalk. They felt the cool moisture of the clouds against their skin until they finally emerged above the clouds. It was as if they had surfaced in another world completely; for miles and miles around, a sea of fluffy clouds surrounded them. They felt closer to the sun, and its rays illuminated this world to perfection.

"It's beautiful," Goldilocks said. The twins had never seen her so moved by something before.

"Extraordinary," Froggy said breathlessly. "I've read so

many descriptions of such a thing, but that's never as good as seeing it with my own eyes."

The top of the beanstalk curled into the open sky above them. They all waited for instructions.

"Whoa," Conner said and pointed into the distance. "Check it out!"

An enormous medieval-looking castle sat on the cloudy horizon. It had huge stone bricks, several flat towers, and a gigantic wooden door.

"Is that the giant's castle?" Alex asked.

"I'm assuming," Conner said. "Unless Mary Poppins moved into the neighborhood."

"Who?" Froggy asked.

"Never mind," Conner said.

Jack carefully placed a foot on top of one of the clouds. It sank down but eventually came to a stop. He took a wobbly first step onto the cloud and the others gasped.

"Oh my God!" Alex yelled and covered her mouth.

"No way!" Conner shouted.

Jack was beside himself with the joy of standing on a cloud again, but he put on a serious face before turning back to the others.

"Carefully step off the beanstalk and onto the cloud, but don't put your weight on it until you know your foot has stopped sinking," he instructed them. "Be gentle. If you move too fast, you'll fall straight through."

Goldilocks was first, followed by Froggy, and the twins joined them after—it was like walking in fluffy quicksand. With each step, the twins waited for their feet to eventually stop, never certain at what point it would, or if it would. Sometimes their legs would sink ankle-deep into the clouds; other times they would sink down to their knees.

"This is the weirdest thing we've ever done!" Conner said. "Or it's at least near the top of the list."

The cloud crusaders headed across the sky to the castle. To their relief, a stony path came into view that curved through the clouds all the way up to the castle's entrance. They were grateful to be walking on something solid again and removed the rope that had been connecting them.

"I really wish I could turn off my brain sometimes," Alex said. "I keep trying to come up with a scientific theory that explains how we're walking on a road through the sky, but nothing is coming to mind."

Conner cleared his throat. "To quote a girl I know, 'My most scientific analysis, with all means of science and technology in mind, is that it's magic,'" he said.

Alex laughed. "How do you remember that?" she asked.

"It was my favorite thing you've ever said," Conner said.

It was taking them much longer than they'd anticipated to reach the castle. It didn't matter how long they walked; the castle didn't seem to be getting any closer.

"Is it moving away from us?" Conner asked.

"No," Jack said. "It just seems that way because it's so gigantic."

After what seemed like miles and miles of stony road, the group finally came face-to-face with the giant's castle. It would have been big at a normal scale, but Jack, Goldilocks, Froggy, and the twins stood before the wooden door dwarfed like a pack of mice.

"Sure, it's *big enough*, but look at the *location*!" Conner said and chuckled to himself. No one laughed with him—they were too overwhelmed by the castle's magnitude.

"Remember what you were telling us earlier about feeling small, Jack?" Alex said. "I think if Red saw this, she'd understand what you were talking about."

"Thankfully, she's not here," Froggy said. "Otherwise she might try to re-create it somehow."

They stayed staring up at the massive structure for a minute longer.

"Well, we can't stand out here all day. Let's go inside," Goldilocks said.

"How do we get in?" Alex asked.

"Is there a doorbell Froggy could jump up to?" Conner asked.

"We'll have to crawl—*follow me*," Jack said. He got on his hands and knees and squeezed into the space between the door and the ground, barely fitting. "This was easier when I was a boy."

They followed him under the door, each moving uncomfortably through the small space. They got to their feet on the other side, finding themselves in an entrance hall the size of a football field. The stones that made up the stone floor were the size of swimming pools. A staircase soared above them like a dozen connected skyscrapers, each higher than the next.

"What is that awful smell?" Alex asked and covered her nose with her shirt.

Goldilocks heard a loud *crunch* under her boot and looked down. Scattered across the entrance hall floor were hundreds and hundreds of bird skeletons. They belonged to normal-size birds but were large even so—the twins assumed they were the remains of hawks and eagles. Perhaps they had flown too close to the castle and had been scooped up by something.

"Did the giant like birds?" Conner asked Jack.

"Not that I remember," he said. "Let's keep moving. Everyone keep an eye out for something the giant would have valued above anything else."

Jack led the group to the right and they entered an enormous dining room. A rug that could have carpeted a dozen regular homes was under a gigantic table and chairs. A large portrait hanging on the wall took them by surprise—it was a painting of *the magic harp*.

"I'd say the giant fancied the magic harp a great deal," Froggy said.

"Yes, he *certainly* did," Goldilocks added, scanning the room in its entirety. The portrait was just one of several different artworks inspired by the magic harp. There were statues and sculptures of her displayed around the room; oil and finger paintings of her covered the walls. Even the backs of the chairs had the harp's silhouette carved into them.

"Is anyone else thinking what I'm thinking?" Conner asked.

"Was *Harper* the giant's most prized possession?" Alex asked.

No one wanted to believe they had traveled all this way for nothing, but as they looked around the giant's dining room and discovered more and more harp-inspired pieces of art, it was difficult coming up with an alternative theory.

"I know he loved her very much—I just wish I could have remembered all of this," Jack said. "I remember walking through this very room and hearing a *psst*. I looked up and saw the harp standing on the top of the table. She was looking down at me and said, *'Hey, kid, get me out of here, would you? I'm going stir-crazy in this place.'* I took her, and when the giant noticed she was gone, he came after me."

"At least we know how to convince Red to let Harper into her castle," Conner pointed out. "We'll tell her she was all the rage with giant decoration. Who knew she'd be the epitome of *fee fi fo feng shui*!"

The twins laughed but their laugh was cut short when a loud jingle sounded through the room.

"What was that?" Goldilocks asked.

The jingle sounded again, only this time it was much louder.

"Jack, didn't you say the giant was dead?" Froggy asked, nervously adjusting his tie.

"He is," Jack said. "And he didn't have any family to speak of."

Conner turned toward the direction they had just come from—and stood stock-still.

"Hey—hey—hey, Jack?" Conner peeped. "Did the giant have any *pets*?"

Everyone turned around and froze. Standing directly behind them was a cat the size of a house.

"Mew," the cat squeaked so loudly they all had to cover their ears. The giant's cat was obese, with gray fur, black stripes, and white paws. It blinked its large green eyes slowly and stared down at them in a flirtatiously fatal manner. A red band was wrapped around its neck, and a bell the size of one of their heads swung from it.

"Guess we know where the bird skeletons came from," Alex said under her breath.

A low rumbling sound filled the room as the cat began to purr. It licked its lips, its eyes grew, and its narrow pupils shrank. Goldilocks retrieved her sword and Jack pulled out his axe.

"No one move," Jack said. "On the count of three we're all going to run under the table and split up to try confusing it. Ready? One...two...*three!*"

The five bolted under the table and spread out. The cat leaped after them, trying to grab hold of as many of them as it could. They ran through the table and chair legs, dodging the claws coming at them from all angles.

"This is why I'm a dog person!" Conner yelled.

The cat was so excited it didn't know whom to start with first. It eventually became most fascinated with Froggy, who out of all of them looked the most like a giant cat toy. He was hopping around like a maniac, barely missing the cat's claws and snapping teeth.

"Somebody help me!" Froggy shouted.

Jack grabbed hold of the cat's tail—the twins didn't know what he expected to accomplish by this, because he immediately flew through the air, whipping around and hanging on for dear life. The cat's belly swung almost more dangerously than its claws and knocked the twins to the floor as it passed by them.

Goldilocks saw a large knife peeking over the top of the table above her. She climbed up the chair leg and then jumped from the seat and grabbed on to the top of the table. She pulled herself up and went to the large knife—but it was too heavy to lift.

The cat violently jerked its tail and Jack was thrown across the room. Froggy was screaming like the twins had never heard him scream before. He hadn't been injured yet, but his clothing had been shredded by the cat's claws. The cat cornered Froggy and crouched down, about to pounce.

"Not the frog! Not the frog!" Froggy tried to persuade the giant feline. *"I won't taste good, trust me!"*

Goldilocks whistled from the top of the table. "Here, kitty, kitty," she called down. She had managed to get the knife on its side and was reflecting light to the other side of the room. The cat left Froggy alone and began chasing the reflection around the room.

Alex and Conner helped each other to their feet.

"Are you okay?" he asked her.

"Yes, I'll be all right," she said.

"Alex! Conner! Charlie! I've got a plan and could use a hand!" Jack called for them. He was standing in front of the giant's cupboard. "Let's get this open and we'll trap the cat inside!"

The twins ran over and helped him pull the large cupboard doors open.

"What am I going to do?" Froggy asked, completely out of breath.

"Stand in front of it," Jack said. "When the cat goes in for the kill—jump out of the way!"

"Oh, thank goodness," Froggy said with fake relief. "For a minute I thought it was going to be *dangerous*!"

The cat quickly became bored with chasing the reflection. It looked up and saw Goldilocks on top of the table—*she* was what it wanted now.

"Oh no," Goldilocks said to herself. The cat ran toward her, jumping onto the top of the table in one leap. Goldilocks dove under the tablecloth—she moved around like a bug under a rug, and it drove the cat crazy.

"Mew," the cat squeaked, trying to grab her through the tablecloth. *"Mew."*

"Hey, whiskers!" Froggy shouted. "Care for some frog legs?" He did a little degrading dance to get the cat's attention.

"Mew?" The cat considered. *"Mew,"* the cat decided and jumped down from the table toward the frog.

"Now, Charlie!" Jack shouted. The twins watched in horror as if it were happening in slow motion. The cat was zooming toward Froggy, ready to sink its teeth and claws into him. Froggy hopped out of its way at the very last second, narrowly avoiding its outstretched claws. The cat slammed into the

cupboard, and Jack and the twins shut the doors behind it. Froggy joined them and together they fought against the cat, trying to keep it inside.

A heavy grunt came from the top of the table. Goldilocks pushed a giant spoon over the edge, and it hit the floor with a thud. She slid down the table leg like it was a pole in a firehouse. The twins ran to her and helped her carry the spoon to the cupboard. They slid the spoon between the handles of the cupboard and the cat was trapped—*for now.*

"Raaaaaar!" the cat angrily growled from inside the cupboard. *"Raaaaaar!"*

"Let's get out of here!" Jack ordered. "The spoon won't hold it in there forever!"

The five of them made a mad dash through the dining room and back into the entrance hall. The cat banged violently against the cupboard doors, bending the spoon ever so slightly with every push.

Jack and Goldilocks ran toward the door at full speed. They hit the floor with perfect momentum and slid under the door. Conner tried copying them but only tripped himself and had to climb under the door the regular way with his sister and Froggy.

Once they were all outside, the five of them took off running as fast as they possibly could down the stony path.

"The cat isn't going to follow us outside, right?" Conner asked the others as they ran.

They all glanced back, praying they wouldn't see the cat emerging from the castle behind them. What they hadn't seen until now was a giant cat door cut into the castle's door and a furious cat poking its head through it.

"Oh come on!" Conner shouted.

The cat chased after them like a fat and furry torpedo. Thankfully its weight slowed it down, so it took a while for it to catch up with them.

The stony path ended and the group of five carefully moved through the clouds at a sluggish speed. The cat was apprehensive about stepping onto the clouds, but it was too determined to stop now. Luckily, it had just as much trouble walking on the clouds as they did, but the cat still tried clawing at whoever was closest to them.

"We've got to get down!" Goldilocks shouted. *"Everyone crawl the rest of the way to the beanstalk!"*

They all fell to their hands and knees and were covered by the clouds. They couldn't see where they were crawling, but at least the cat couldn't, either. It tried digging them out of the clouds, sending large cloudy chunks into the air, but it never found anyone.

One by one, Jack, Goldilocks, Froggy, and the twins found the beanstalk and started their descent back to the ground. They didn't even bother with ropes this time—in fact, they were practically throwing themselves down the beanstalk. Leaf by leaf, they bounced closer and closer to the ground below.

"The cat's not going to follow us down the beanstalk, is it?" Conner asked, but just as he did, the cat poked its huge head through the clouds above them.

"Mew!" the cat said, delighted to finally find them.

"GOD, I HATE THIS FLIPPING CAT!" Conner yelled.

The cat was descending the beanstalk behind them now. It looked like an elephant climbing down a tightrope. It was timid from the height, moving at a lazily cautious pace. It clearly hadn't thought this plan through.

Goldilocks started slicing down the beanstalk's leaves as they passed them, making it more difficult for the cat to follow.

"What in the world—?" a voice shouted up at them. Red was staring up at the beanstalk, watching her five friends being chased by an enormous cat. *"Am I actually seeing this or did I bump my head when we landed earlier?"*

"You're actually seeing it, my dear!" Froggy yelled down at her.

Clawdius was going nuts, too. He barked up at the colossal cat in the sky and pulled against his restraints. The tiny wolf made the enormous cat very nervous and it stopped, now stuck on the upper part of the beanstalk.

"Red! You need to cut down the beanstalk!" Jack yelled down at her.

"Excuse me?" Red asked.

"You need to cut it down before the cat reaches the bottom!" he yelled. *"There should be an axe in my shack—get it and start chopping!"*

Red looked around for someone else to do it instead, but there was no one to be found.

"Red, we need you!" Alex said.

Red mustered up all the determination she had. "I'll do it!" she yelled. She ran straight into the shack—but quickly ran back out a moment later. *"Wait—which one is the axe again?"*

Goldilocks slapped an open palm against her head.

"The one that looks like this!" Jack said, raising his own.

"Got it!" Red said and ran back into the shack. She ran out, dragging a large axe behind her as if it weighed more than her.

"Now chop it down!" Jack yelled.

Red nodded. She lifted the axe, which took all the strength she possessed, and swung it toward the beanstalk. She missed it by several inches and the swing spun her to the ground.

"Come on, Red! You can do this!" Alex cheered down at her.

"We believe in you, darling!" Froggy called down.

Red looked at her reflection in the axe and fixed a strand of her hair that had fallen. She took another swing at it, and this time she hit the beanstalk but only left a tiny dent in it.

"I hit it! I hit it!" Red said and jumped up and down, so proud of herself.

"You're going to need to hit it about a thousand times harder than that!" Goldilocks yelled.

The cat grew agitated, seeing the five of them getting closer and closer to the ground. It started to climb down again, moving faster than ever, its bright green eyes fixed on them. Red took another swing at the beanstalk, barely leaving a larger mark.

"I can't do this!" Red said through sniffles.

"Yes you can, Red! Do it for your country! Do it for your granny! Do it for me!" Froggy encouraged her.

"PRETEND THE BEANSTALK IS GOLDILOCKS!" Conner shouted.

Everyone on the beanstalk froze and just stared at Conner.

Red looked down at the axe more determinedly than ever—Conner had done the trick. With one confident swing, Red sliced through the entire base of the beanstalk with practically inhuman strength.

Everyone was shocked, but not as shocked as Red. Even the cat looked surprised.

The beanstalk began to teeter. *"Everyone get to this side of the beanstalk!"* Jack yelled, and they all swung themselves to the side of the beanstalk that wasn't going to hit the ground.

The beanstalk slowly began to fall . . . faster and faster and faster. . . . The cat, however, wasn't ready for its quest to conclude. It sank one front paw into the beanstalk and a back paw into the clouds above it, holding it in place.

"Now what?" Alex yelled.

Clawdius broke his restraints on the deck of the *Granny* and ran down to the base of the beanstalk. He barked up at the gigantic cat dangling in the sky.

"Raaaaaar!" the giant cat yipped fearfully. In one giant leap, it let go of the beanstalk and soared back into the cloudy world above.

"Timber!" Jack yelled.

The beanstalk fell toward the ground like a giant whip. It crashed into the manor, splitting it in half like a knife slicing a birthday cake.

Jack, Goldilocks, Froggy, and the twins looked up at one another—they were all surprised they had survived the ordeal. There was a moment of silence before they heard an earth-shattering scream. They all looked toward the manor—the beanstalk had missed the golden harp by inches.

"That's the second time I almost died today and it isn't even dusk!" the harp shouted.

The team climbed down from the beanstalk and brushed themselves off. Froggy gave Red an enormous hug.

"You saved our lives!" Froggy said and twirled her around.

Goldilocks avoided making eye contact with Red. "Nice one," she said begrudgingly, and then quickly walked away.

The twins lay on the grass and caught their breath. The clouds began to part now that the beanstalk was gone and revealed a beautiful bright blue sky.

"I *never* want to do that again," Conner said.

"Never," Alex agreed.

Jack walked over to the newly destroyed manor.

"Hey, Harper," he said, with an apologetic hesitance in his voice. "I've got good news and bad news. *Good news*—you're still moving! *Bad news*—you're coming with us."

CHAPTER TWENTY

THE REFLECTION

L et me get this straight," the magic harp said. "You're on a *quest*, collecting the most *prized possessions* of the most *hated people* in the world to build a powerful *wand* that you hope will overthrow the *Enchantress*? And *I* happen to be one of those possessions?"

Conner shrugged. "That's right," he said. "Although it sounds lame when you say it like that."

It took Jack, Froggy, and Conner to move the harp of solid gold into the lower deck of the *Granny*. Once they got her there, the men and the women of the ship surrounded her and told her all about their mission and her newly discovered relevance to it.

"I don't understand. How am I supposed to be a part of that wand?" the harp asked and gestured to the ice scepter Goldilocks had been showing her moments before.

Froggy had to agree. "I don't see how you fit into this, either," he said. "You're awfully big to be a part of a wand."

"I beg your pardon?" the harp snapped at him.

"My apologies," Froggy said. "I just meant, everything else has been small material items. We've yet to have—well— whatever it is that you are."

"Whatever it is I am?" the harp said. "That's rich, coming from a *giant frog man*!"

Froggy took a step back and bowed out of the conversation completely.

"What if we cut off one of her fingers or something?" Conner suggested.

"What?" the harp yelled.

"Conner, that's so barbaric!" Alex said and hit him in the shoulder. "Why would you even mention such a thing?"

"It was only an idea," he said.

"But what would happen if she came in contact with the Wand?" Goldilocks asked. "Will she shrink? Will the Wand blend into her somehow? *Would she die?*"

The harp went berserk and desperately tried to jump out of the ship, but she was too heavy to lift herself.

"Harper, calm down," Jack said to the overly excited instrument. "No one is going to harm you."

"But I'm still your prisoner, aren't I?" the harp said. The strings on her back played the opening chords to a dramatic ballad.

> *"Right when it teased me,*
> *The cruel world deceived me,*
> *No hope now for freedom,*
> *No stars now to wish upon,*
> *Born for imprisonment am I,*
> *Can't be free until I die—"*

"Enough, Harper," Goldilocks said. "You're not our prisoner. We're just going to keep you around for a while until we can figure out what to do—then you'll be free to live your exciting life of watching grass grow and entertaining people against their will."

The harp squinted at Goldilocks and raised a golden eyebrow. "So *you're* the girl Jack ran off with, eh?" she said. "No wonder he can't be seen with you in public—I wouldn't want to be, either."

The twins both made *ooh*ing sounds. Jack and Froggy had to hold Goldilocks back. A high-pitched laugh erupted from Red's mouth and she slapped the side of her leg.

"You know, I think having Harper around my castle won't be such a bad thing after all," she said.

That evening at sundown they fired up the *Granny*'s flame and steered the ship northeast. Their next stop would be the ruins of the old abandoned castle for the Evil Queen's Magic

Mirror. Alex and Conner slept most of the way—the journey up and down the beanstalk had taken a toll on them and they were so tired they slept through most of Red's sleep-talking and the harp's self-pitying songs.

The twins woke just before sunrise the next day and made their way to the upper deck. Red was already there when they arrived. She was cradling Clawdius again and the young wolf slept soundly in her arms.

"Reunited?" Conner asked her and she nodded happily.

"I had a nice long think to myself," Red explained. "If it weren't for Clawdius, a giant man-eating cat would be wreaking havoc on my kingdom right now. He's not a killer after all! On the contrary—he's a savior!"

"So the fact that he's a wolf doesn't bother you anymore?" Alex asked. She didn't speak "Red" fluently yet.

"Not at all," Red said. "What kind of mother would I be if I let something as simple as *species* get in the way of love? I'm courting a giant frog, after all! I'll just raise Clawdius to be a loving and compassionate animal. If a wolf has never been capable of possessing such qualities before, then Clawdius will be the first. But if he tries eating me, Mama's getting a new coat."

They appeased her with fake agreeing smiles and left her with her pet.

The twins went to the front of the ship and looked at the ground below—what they saw horrified them. The entire Eastern Kingdom had been devoured by thornbushes and vines. The plants wrapped around every building below. Even though they had been told about it countless times, Alex and Conner could have never imagined what they were seeing.

"It's just like the fox said in the Dwarf Forests," Alex said. "The entire kingdom is covered!"

"I don't think I realized just how powerful the Enchantress was until now," Conner said with a gulp. "Seeing this really raises the stakes, doesn't it?"

The thornbushes and vines began to thin out the farther northeast the *Granny* traveled. The overgrown terrain was replaced with the dry, deserted land the region was known for, and soon the ruins of the old abandoned castle could be seen in the distance.

What had once been an imposing structure was just a massive pile of stone bricks and pieces of wood now.

Jack, Goldilocks, Froggy, and Red joined the twins at the front of the ship and shivered. It was like seeing the remains of a large monster they had killed, but instead of a carcass, they felt as if they were nearing its sleeping body. Something about the castle still seemed very much alive.

The *Granny* landed gently beside the moat.

"How much of the mirror do we need to gather?" Conner asked the others. "Do we just need a piece of it or the whole thing?"

"It's going to take a while to retrieve every piece of it if that's the case," Alex said.

Goldilocks removed the Wand from under her cot, where she stashed it for safekeeping. "We'll take the Wand with us," she said.

The six travelers headed out of the *Granny* and toward the destroyed castle.

"The Enchantress lived here once," Alex said. "You don't think there's any part of her lingering, do you?"

Conner took a look around at the dead land surrounding them. "I don't think there's any life lingering around here whatsoever," Conner said. "We're all just spooked because of what happened here a year ago. There isn't anything in that dump except a bunch of broken castle junk."

One by one, Froggy helped the others across the moat. Once they were on the other side they came to a halt and stared at the rubble in dismay.

"How do we get in?" Conner asked.

No one had an answer. There didn't appear to be a practical way of getting inside the ruins. They circled the rubble for a few minutes, looking.

"Over here!" Red called out. "I found a way in." The others ran to her and she pointed to a small opening between two stone blocks that led deeper into the debris.

Froggy attempted to crawl through it. "We won't fit," he said. "It's too narrow."

"The twins will," Goldilocks said.

"You want us to go in there alone?" Alex asked.

"It may be the only way," Jack said, looking around the rubble. "I don't see another option."

The twins shared an anxious glance. Goldilocks placed her hands on their shoulders.

"We wouldn't be here if it weren't for you two," she said.

"You said it yourself: There's nothing in there to be worried about. Go inside and try to collect as much of the Magic Mirror as possible. We'll be right outside. Take this with you."

Goldilocks handed Conner the Wand. He let it hang from the belt loop of his jeans.

"We're all counting on you," Red said, and then received dirty looks from the others. "I mean—*you can do it*!"

"Be careful, children," Froggy said. "Try not to move anything while you're in there. The stones have settled, but you don't want them caving in anymore."

Froggy seemed so concerned the twins didn't even mind being referred to as children. Alex and Conner stepped up to the opening and gently squeezed through the stones, scraping their sides as they went. Inside, it was like an obstacle course made of debris. The twins carefully climbed over and under and through broken pieces of wood and stone. Everywhere they looked was a broken piece of the castle that triggered a not-so-happy memory of their last visit: a wooden beam, a cell door, a stair railing, an occasional smashed chair or table.

They climbed farther into the endless wreckage and soon entered a large clearing. They assumed they had reached what used to be the castle's great hall—the place they had seen the Magic Mirror shatter.

"Alex, this whole place is covered in glass," Conner said. "How do we know which pieces of glass came from what?"

Everywhere they looked they saw shards of glass. It was scattered across the ground and all over the mounds of rubble around them. Some fragments were bigger than others, and the twins could see their reflections in them, but it was impossible to determine which parts were the Magic Mirror and which were the windows or something else.

"Look!" Alex said and picked up a small piece. "It's a piece of the Mirror of Truth." She happily stared into the small piece, and the little reflection she could see of herself changed—the Alex in the reflection wore a long golden gown and had a pair of enormous sparkly wings behind her back.

"Let me see," Conner said and looked into the piece of glass in his sister's hand. His reflection also changed—the Conner in the reflection was wearing a golden suit and had a giant pair of shimmering wings behind him.

Conner stuck his tongue out. "Gross, put that thing away!" he said.

Alex tucked it into her pocket safely. She figured she might need a reminder of who she was in the days to come.

"How are we going to sort through all of this?" Alex asked.

Conner pulled the wand out of his belt loop. He held it into the air and a series of small scraping sounds came from all around the wreckage. Little by little, pieces of glass inched closer to the wand, pulled magnetically by a magical force.

"I think I have an idea," Conner said. He placed the wand in the center of the ground and quickly pulled Alex behind a large piece of wood. They watched as tiny bits of glass flew from all over the debris and attached themselves to the wand until it looked as if it were covered in silver sequins.

"Amazing!" Conner said and went to pick up the wand. "It almost looks futuristic, doesn't it?"

Suddenly, the twins were both hit with an unsettling feeling. They both felt it at the same time, and each turned to the other, knowing it was mutual.

"Conner, do you feel that?" Alex asked.

"Yeah, what's going on?" he said.

"I feel like someone's watching us," Alex said.

Conner looked around at the rubble. "How could anything be in here but us?" he asked.

Something began moving around them through the piles of rubble. They kept catching it in their peripheral vision, but it would disappear before they could get a proper look.

"*Conner!* Look into the glass!" Alex panted.

Gracefully gliding around them in the larger pieces of glass among the debris was the reflection of a young woman. She was pretty and wore a long white gown and had long raven hair. The reflection playfully circled them, giggling to herself as it did. Alex and Conner felt like they were in a reverse aquarium where *they* were the ones on display.

"Hello," the reflection said and smiled. The woman's voice was smooth and inviting, and it echoed from each piece of glass she moved through. "Who are you?"

There was something incredibly familiar about her. The twins were positive they had seen her before.

"I'm Alex and this is my brother, Conner," Alex said and took a step closer to her. The reflection shot across to the other side and appeared in the glass behind the twins.

"Such funny names," the reflection said. "Have you seen *Mira*?"

Conner grabbed Alex's arm. *"Oh my God! Alex, it's—"*

"He's always hiding from me!" the reflection said and twirled around inside the pieces of mirror. "Mira? Oh, *Miiiiiira*?! Where are you?"

It settled in a large shard of glass, and Alex stepped closer to it. *"Evly? Is that you?"* she asked the reflection. It instantly looked up at her at the sound of the name.

"How do you know my name?" Evly asked with a big curious smile. "Have we met before?" As soon as she asked, her curious expression faded and she began to recognize them as well.

"Yes, we have," Conner said. "Last year in this castle."

Alex looked around at the castle remains and a horrible thought came to her. "You've been trapped in the mirror this entire time, haven't you?" Alex asked her.

"Have you seen Mira?" Evly asked as if she hadn't heard Alex. "I can't find him anywhere."

Alex felt her heart drop into the pit of her stomach. "She's been trapped and it's starting to affect her just like it affected Mira," she whispered back to her brother.

"Miiiiiira? Where are you?" Evly said musically, floating through the glass around the room.

"Mira's dead, Evly," Alex said. "Don't you remember? You tried freeing him with the Wishing Spell but it was too late."

Evly looked to Alex and just stared at her, as if she was deciding whether or not to believe it. She began circling them more frantically.

"Mira? It's not funny anymore—please come out now,"

Evly asked, her voice growing more desperate by the second. "Where are you?"

It was hard for the twins to watch. Evly wasn't just in denial; she was *cursed*.

"Evly, do you remember anything that happened to you?" Alex asked her. "Do you remember the Magic Mirror? Do you remember Snow White? Do you remember being *the Evil Queen*?"

Evly's eyes grew and she gasped at the sound of her old sobriquet. *"I—I—"* Evly stuttered. Her reflection gradually aged and transformed into that of the Evil Queen the twins had known, as the memories of who she was and what she had done resurfaced in her mind.

"I remember..." the Evil Queen said, and her eyes filled with tears. "I remember everything...oh no, what have I done? How did I get here?"

"We tried to warn you but you wouldn't listen to us," Conner said. "The mirror fell on top of you and you vanished. There was nothing we could do."

Tears rolled down the Evil Queen's face as her mind filled with more memories of her heartless life.

"I was such a monster," she sobbed. The Evil Queen collapsed with grief and her reflection appeared in pieces of glass near the ground. "I poisoned my own daughter....I harmed innocent people....I kidnapped children."

Alex kneeled down to her. She wished she could reach through the glass to console her. "But it wasn't your fault," she said. "You had your heart cut out and turned into stone, remember? You didn't know what you were doing."

The Evil Queen nodded. "I was in so much pain—I didn't know what else to do," she said. "Pain will drive you mad if it's strong enough; it'll change you into something you're not. It'll turn you *evil*."

"We know," Alex said. "But that's all in the past now."

"You must forgive me, children," the Evil Queen begged. "Forgiveness is what we all need to forget the past, even if we don't deserve to."

Alex and Conner nodded to her, willing to do anything they could that would give her consolation.

"Of course," Alex said. "We forgive you."

The Evil Queen smiled at them through her tears of shame. "Thank you," she said. "I'm afraid I'll never forgive myself, though. I spent my entire life trying to free him from this prison, and now I'm doomed to spend eternity in here without him. I couldn't think of a worse punishment."

"We could try to free you if you'd like," Conner said. "We're building a wand—a powerful wand. Maybe we could use it to get you out of there."

The Evil Queen dried her tears and shook her head. "No, let me be," she said. "I deserve this fate....I deserve to be inside here...."

Her head tilted and she stared at the twins, as if someone was whispering something about them into her ear. "You're on a quest, aren't you?" she asked them.

"Yes, how did you know?" Alex asked.

"I can see many things from inside here," she explained. "I can reflect on the world in ways I never could before. I see a large ship waiting outside these castle ruins.... I see a kingdom imprisoned by plants.... I see a whole world in fear.... I see—*I see Ezmia!*"

The Evil Queen shuddered at the thought of her former mistress.

"But how can this be? I thought she was dead."

"You didn't kill her like you thought," Alex said, sorry to break the news to her.

"And now she's back and she's taking over the world," Conner said.

The Evil Queen covered her mouth. "Oh no. I made the poison as strong as possible—it killed life outside the castle for miles—but even that wasn't strong enough, evidently."

Conner kneeled down next to his sister. "We're trying to stop her. We need to know what her most prized possession was in order to do so. Would you happen to know what that might be?"

The reflection thought on it. "Ezmia's most prized possession was always *herself*, and I don't need magic insight to tell you that."

"Oh boy," Conner said. "That's going to be difficult to retrieve."

The Evil Queen grew very still as another troubling realization came to her. "Someone is following you...."

"In here?" Conner asked.

"No, across the land as you travel."

"Who? The Enchantress?" Alex asked.

The Evil Queen looked off into the distance as if she was

trying to see something far away. "No, it's neither a person nor a thing, but an entity."

"The ghost!" Conner said. "We've been wondering what her deal is! Can you tell us who she is?"

"They call her the Lady of the East."

The twins were stunned to learn the ghost's name. They tried to remember if they had ever heard of the Lady of the East before.

"The east!" Conner said. "Every time I've seen her she has always pointed to the east! That's what she was pointing at through my window in Red's castle! And that's the direction she pointed to when we were on the ship."

"You must leave now," the Evil Queen told them. "The Enchantress grows stronger as we speak—she plans on attacking again very soon. You must hurry if you want to defeat her before it's too late!"

"But—" Alex started, but the Evil Queen's reflection turned away from them.

"I'm afraid I can't help you anymore, children," the Evil Queen said. "I feel myself fading away more and more as every second passes...."

"Wait! Please, you have to tell us more! Who is the Lady of the East and why is she following us?" Alex pleaded.

"Where is Ezmia going to attack next?" Conner asked, but the Evil Queen ignored them. "Hello? Can you hear us?"

The Evil Queen turned to them, but her reflection had morphed back into that of a happy and smiling Evly.

"Have either of you seen Mira?" Evly asked with a laugh. "I can't find him anywhere!"

Alex and Conner sighed hopelessly. They knew they had gotten as much information out of the reflection as possible. They didn't want to leave Evly there but knew it wouldn't be long before the curse of the Magic Mirror took over her soul completely, just as it had Mira's.

"Good-bye, Evly," Alex said sadly. The twins headed out of the castle ruins as Evly continued her never-ending search for her long-lost love.

"Mira? *Oh, Miiiiiira?!* Where have you gone?"

CHAPTER TWENTY-ONE

THE SEA WITCH

The others were thrilled by the twins' triumphant return from the castle ruins.

"Well done," Froggy said and patted them on the back with a relieved smile.

"We knew you could do it," Goldilocks said and winked at them.

Red took the wand from Conner—she was mesmerized by it. "It's so shiny!" she said, although the twins weren't positive she was impressed by the accomplishment so much as by the fact that they had returned with something *else* she could view herself in.

"Was everything all right in there?" Jack asked them. The twins looked to each other and both fell silent.

"Not exactly," Conner said. "We saw the Evil Queen."

"She's been trapped in the Magic Mirror ever since she used the Wishing Spell," Alex said.

Everyone was just as shocked as the twins had been to discover this. "How horrible," Goldilocks said quietly to herself.

"There's no hope of getting her out now, I suppose," Jack said.

Conner shook his head. "She doesn't want to be rescued. She thinks she deserves to be in there. There's not much left of her to save anyway."

"Well, speaking as one of the victims she kidnapped and almost fed to wolves, I'm not sure I feel sorry for her," Red confessed.

"There's more bad news," Alex said. "We asked her about the Enchantress—she probably knew her better than anyone."

"What did she say?" Froggy asked, and they all leaned closer to hear the answer.

"She said Ezmia's most prized possession is *herself*," Alex said.

Jack, Goldilocks, and Froggy looked to one another with the same exasperated expression.

"It doesn't make any sense," Froggy said. "How can living things make up the wand? I understand how the harp could be considered a prized item, but not the Enchantress herself."

Red scrunched her lips and hummed, thinking on the subject. "I think the Evil Queen is mistaken. I'm not a stranger to loving myself, but that self-admiration *comes* from something. For example, if you took away my beauty or my incredible ability to match dresses with tiaras, I wouldn't value myself half as much as I do now."

The others weren't sure how to gauge the outburst. Red was always very coherent or not at all; there was rarely an in-between.

"What are you saying, Red?" Goldilocks asked.

"I'm saying it's not the actual *woman* we should be concerned about getting," Red explained. "We need to find *what* the Enchantress values the most about herself and take it away from her."

Everyone thought about it and their heads slowly moved in a mutual nod. This was the first moment any of them were happy Red had demanded to come along on the trip.

"That's so insightful, Red!" Conner said. "*Shallow*, but insightful!"

"How do we retrieve it for the Wand?" Jack asked.

No one could come up with an immediate answer. What was the one quality Ezmia prized above the rest? There were so many things she obviously cherished. Her *beauty*? Her *power*? Her *ruthlessness*? Or perhaps it was a combination of all three? And whatever it was, how would they take it away from her?

"Well, we knew it would be a challenge," Goldilocks said and let out a long sigh.

The six headed over the moat and back to the *Granny*. They returned to a furious harp, whose strings played an angry chord as she pouted.

"Harper? What's the matter?" Jack asked her.

"That *thing* peed on me!" the harp exclaimed and pointed to Clawdius, who was crouching shamefacedly in the corner of the lower deck.

"That's my fault; I forgot to take him out before we left!" Red said. "My apologies—*mother in training*." She scooped him up and carried him off the ship.

The crew waited until nightfall before firing up the ship and steering it south.

"Next stop, Mermaid Bay!" Jack called out.

"Does the Sea Witch live in the bay?" Conner asked.

"From what I read, she lives in the ocean waters just outside it," Froggy said.

"How do we find her?" Goldilocks asked.

"I'm a good swimmer, believe it or not," Froggy said. "I can have a look around the ocean floor and report back to you. We'll have to be very careful once we get there—the Sea Witch is known for being very sneaky with her trades."

"We'll have to outsmart her, then," Alex said. "If her jewels are her most valued possession, we'll have to trade her something in exchange for them."

"What's the most valuable item we have in *our* possession?" Conner asked. "What do we have to trade with her?"

"The harp?" Red asked a little hopefully.

"No, we need to keep her until we can figure out how to incorporate her into the wand," Jack said.

Goldilocks's face suddenly lit up as if an actual lightbulb had appeared over her head. "I think we're all forgetting something in our possession that's even more valuable," she said.

"What's that?" Alex asked. They all stared at her, completely puzzled.

"*Red,*" Goldilocks said. "We have an actual *queen* on our ship."

Everyone immediately turned to look at Red. As expected, the young queen was appalled by the idea.

"You want to trade *me* to the Sea Witch like some farm animal?" Red said. "Absolutely not! Out of the question!"

"It is a good *option,*" Jack said, defending Goldilocks's idea.

Red grunted and her nostrils flared. "Now you listen to me, *giant chaser,*" she said and pointed her finger at all of them. "So far I've built us a ship, lost half of my wardrobe, adopted a killer animal, snuck into the wicked stepmother's estate, and supplied something nice to look at during this escapade. If you ask me, I've gone above and beyond what a *normal queen* would do! Do you see Cinderella flying a mile above the ground? No! Is Snow White risking her life for the greater good? No! Is Rapunzel braiding her hair to restore peace and harmony? No!"

Everyone slumped. They couldn't argue, but they also didn't have much to work with.

"*I'll* do it, then," Goldilocks said.

"What?" Jack gasped.

"I'll pretend to be Red," Goldilocks said plainly. "You can trade me for the jewels and the Sea Witch will never be the wiser."

"We most certainly will not!" Jack protested, outraged by just the suggestion of it.

"It's the best way," Goldilocks said. "After you collect

the jewels, you'll only have one more thing to complete the Wand. Once you defeat the Enchantress you can come back for me—until then I'll keep my cover and make the Sea Witch happy."

Jack was shaking his head. He couldn't imagine leaving the woman he loved the most in the world in the hands of someone so horrible.

"Oh, Jack," Goldilocks said, flattered by how worked up he had become. "You know I'll be able to handle a little old sea witch. I've been stuck in worse situations before."

Jack held her close, looking deeply into her eyes. "What if, for whatever reason, we can't come back for you?" he said.

Goldilocks looked down at the floor, knowing what he meant. "If I get anxious, I'll find a way out," she said and returned his loving gaze. "You have to trust me."

It was an incredible sacrifice to make, but no one could persuade her otherwise.

"Red, I never thought I would ever say this, but I'm going to need to borrow a dress," Goldilocks said.

"I doubt anything of mine will fit you," Red said.

Froggy cleared his throat. "Darling, don't be rude," he said.

"That is—I'm sure I can make something work," Red said and gave in. She grabbed Goldilocks's hand and dragged her down to the lower deck to play dress-up.

Jack went to the steering wheel and looked ahead of them to the horizon, but his thoughts were anywhere but with the ship. Froggy played tug-of-war with Clawdius while Alex and Conner sat on the deck floor near the bow of the *Granny*.

Alex rested her head on her hand and stared off into space, having her own reservations about their plan.

"What's on your mind?" Conner asked Alex. "You look troubled."

Alex sighed. "It's just a little concerning to think about leaving Goldilocks with the Sea Witch," she said.

"I know, but what else can we do? It's a great idea," Conner said.

"I guess," Alex said. Something had been on her mind, and she felt it was time to tell her brother before her head exploded. "Conner, when we were back in the Northern Mountains the Snow Queen said something to me—I didn't think much of it then, but it's really starting to worry me now."

"What did she tell you?" Conner asked.

"She said, *'Of the four travelers, one will not return,'*" Alex said. "I thought it was just nonsense—I mean, an avalanche had just fallen on the woman—but now I wonder if she was making a prophecy. I wonder if she was talking about *Goldilocks*."

"But there's six of us traveling," Conner said. "Seven including the mutt and eight counting the harp."

"I know, it doesn't make sense," Alex said and rubbed her tired eyes. "But I'm still worried there may have been some truth to it. We've been really lucky so far, but what if one of us doesn't survive this trip?"

Conner surprised her with his reaction—he didn't recipro-cate her fear but met it with a calmness that reminded her of their dad.

"Alex, we all knew what we were getting into," he said. "Just because you and I are spearheading this mission doesn't mean it's our fault if anything goes wrong. We're all trying to save the world, and as awful as it sounds, if one of us doesn't make it in the process... I can't think of a better way to die than being a hero."

She let a long, exasperated breath escape her lungs. "There are worse fates, I suppose," Alex said. "I'd hate to lose some-one for no reason, though—I don't know if I could live with myself."

"We'll just have to make sure we succeed, then," Conner said.

Within the hour, Red climbed up from the lower deck with a proud smile on her face. "Eh-hem," she said, getting all of their attention. "Lady, wolf, and gentlemen—I would like to introduce to you my latest creation. She may be a rough-porridge-eating-fugitive by day, but tonight I would like to introduce you to the new and improved *Goldilocks*!"

Goldilocks walked up the steps behind her. She was wearing one of Red's corsets with a long red gown, a hooded cape, and matching gloves. Red had even put her hair up in a stylish do similar to her own and had painted some rouge on her cheeks. There was no doubt about it—Goldilocks looked stunning.

"Goldie..." Jack said. "You look...you look...*gorgeous*." He looked like a teenager in love.

"Thank you," Goldilocks said and blushed. She didn't get too many opportunities to look pretty for him.

"You're welcome," Red said and swayed happily. "The cor-set is a little small for her. Poor thing, her waist isn't quite as slender as mine."

"That's because I'm hiding three daggers under here," Goldilocks said. She had trouble balancing in a pair of Red's high heels. "I don't know how you walk in these shoes—they're completely impractical."

"I don't know how you walk in them, either; they're meant for feet almost half the size of yours—*I'm only teasing, Goldie, put that knife away*!" Red said and ran to the other side of the ship.

The harp grew bored below them and began to play a soft melody for herself that could be heard on the upper deck. Jack grabbed Goldilocks's waist.

"Care to dance?" he asked.

"Oh, Jack." Goldilocks laughed.

"Come on, when's the last time we got to dance?" Jack asked.

"The last time I believe involved a witch throwing hot stones at our feet," she said.

Jack chuckled at the memory and spun her around. They danced to the harp's tune under the starry night sky, gazing into each other's eyes.

"Would you do me the honor?" Froggy asked Red, and offered her his hand with an overly pronounced bow.

"I'd be delighted!" Red said. They didn't dance quite as smoothly as Jack and Goldilocks—Red kept stepping on Froggy's large webbed feet—but both couples enjoyed the time for all it was worth. The twins smiled as they looked on, knowing this would be something they'd remember forever.

It was a few minutes before dawn and the *Granny* was still a ways away from Mermaid Bay.

"We're not going to make it to the bay before sunrise," Jack said from behind the steering wheel. "We need to put the ship down before we're caught."

"We can travel the rest of the way by water," Goldilocks said. "We'll land it in the Sleepy River and then sail down the river into the bay."

"That's brilliant!" Froggy said.

"Very well," Jack said. "Everyone prepare the ship for a water landing!"

Goldilocks took over the steering wheel. Froggy grabbed hold of the sail's ropes and flattened them to the sides of the balloon. Jack pulled the lever under the ship's flame and it diminished. The *Granny* began to descend. Goldilocks aligned the ship with the wide river flowing on the ground below. The twins weren't sure what to expect. Would a water landing be rougher or easier?

In a few moments they had their answer. The ship dove into the water, coming to a painful, abrupt stop and nearly submerging itself completely on impact. The entire deck and its crew were drenched.

Conner spat out a mouthful of water. "Thank goodness that was easy," he said sarcastically.

"I'm on my side and can't get up!" the harp called up from the lower deck. "The wolf is licking my face! Can someone please help me before he gets any other ideas?"

Froggy hopped down the steps to assist her. Red wrung her

wet dress over the side of the ship; she was not enjoying life at that moment.

The ship sailed peacefully down the river as the sun rose farther into the sky. Not long after, Mermaid Bay came into view ahead. The ship was just about to spill into the bay from the river when it came to another abrupt stop, knocking everyone to the deck floor.

Jack jumped to his feet and ran to the front of the ship to look overboard. "The ship is stuck in the delta!" he said. The twins joined him and had a look for themselves. The *Granny* was only feet away from fully being in the bay but was stuck in a very narrow channel.

"Oh, great," Conner grunted. "Now what?"

Just as the others were about to panic, something very colorful caught Alex's eye. "Look!" she said and excitedly pointed down at the water. The thing swam under the ship and disappeared from sight.

"Where did it go?" Jack asked.

"Alex! Conner! Jack!" Froggy yelled from the back of the ship. "Take a look at this!"

They joined him at the back of the ship and gazed into the river below. It was difficult to make out what was happening through the ripples of the water, but Alex and Conner recognized it right away. Dozens of mermaids had gathered behind the *Granny* and were slowly pushing the ship through the delta.

They had pale skin and long, colorful tails that matched their long, beautiful hair—just as the twins had remembered.

The ship began to move through the channel little by little, thanks to the mermaids' efforts.

"Well, I'll be darned," Froggy said, amazed at what he was witnessing.

The *Granny* edged forward bit by bit, finally squeezing through the channel and splashing into the bay.

"That was so kind of them," Alex said.

"Why were they helping us?" Conner asked.

Goldilocks whistled from behind the steering wheel. "Speaking of mysteries, what is *that*?" She nodded to something ahead of them.

In the distance, hovering majestically in the misty bay air, was a large cluster of sea foam. It was shaped in the silhouette of a mermaid and shimmered in the sunlight, continuously rejuvenating itself.

Alex grabbed Conner's arm. "It's the Sea Foam Spirit!" she said.

"Come again?" Froggy asked.

"It's the Little Mermaid," Conner explained to the others. "Or at least it used to be. I wonder what she's doing here."

"You think she knows we're going to visit the Sea Witch?" Alex asked.

The *Granny* sailed closer to the foam until it hovered directly in front of the ship. "Hello, Alex. Hello, Conner," the Sea Foam Spirit said. The others were shocked to hear her speak.

Red rubbed her eyes—she didn't believe what she was seeing. "Is this clump of bubbles a friend of yours?" she asked the twins, as if she was making a judgment against their character.

"What are you doing here?" Alex asked the Sea Foam Spirit.

"I've come to speak with you," the Sea Foam Spirit said.

"You're trying to stop us from going to visit the Sea Witch, aren't you?" Conner said.

"On the contrary, I've come to assist you," the spirit said. "I may be the world's greatest cautionary tale when it comes to matters of the Sea Witch, but I've come to offer you help. I've heard about your quest—we *all* have."

The spirit gestured to the water below, where all the mermaids had gathered. The bay looked like a colorful koi pond.

"Who told you about our quest?" Alex asked.

"No one told me; I heard your thoughts," the Sea Foam Spirit said.

"I thought you could only hear and feel thoughts expressed in or near the water," Conner said, remembering what he had learned during their last encounter.

"As the snow melts down the mountains and pours into rivers that lead to the sea, it brings with it the thoughts of those who have traveled across it."

Conner hooted. "So much for privacy," he said.

"How can you help us?" Alex asked the spirit. "Can you take us to the Sea Witch?"

"I cannot leave the bay," the Sea Foam Spirit said. "But I have asked an old friend to escort you to the depths of the sea where the Sea Witch dwells."

"That would be terrific! Thanks!" Conner said. "Who is your friend? Are they solid, at least?"

"Very," the Sea Foam Spirit said.

Suddenly, a gigantic splash erupted from the bay and a sea turtle of epic proportions emerged from the water. He was as big as their ship. The entire crew was flabbergasted and their eyes grew to the size of tennis balls.

Conner leaned closely to Froggy. "I never thought I'd see a reptile as big as you," he whispered.

"The Great Sea Turtle is very old," the Sea Foam Spirit said. "He can't hear very well, but he will escort you to the Sea Witch."

"How far away is the Sea Witch's lair?" Jack asked.

"It's a day's journey to the bottom of the ocean," the Sea Foam Spirit said. "But the Great Sea Turtle can get you there in a quarter of the time."

"How are we supposed to breathe?" Goldilocks asked.

The Sea Foam Spirit extended both of her hands and six white scallop shells appeared. They each had a seaweed band around them, like they were oceanic surgical masks. The Sea Foam Spirit passed them to the men and women aboard the ship.

"These will supply you with air while you're under the water," she said.

"Do they come in pink?" Red asked.

Froggy passed on his shell. "I'll be fine," he said. "Being a frog has its perks, you know." He took a very deep breath and his throat expanded into a large bubble.

"Awesome." Conner chuckled and poked it.

The Sea Foam Spirit nodded to the Great Sea Turtle. "It's time," she instructed.

The turtle drifted toward the ship and placed his front flipper gently on the bow like a drawbridge. Jack and Froggy armed themselves with daggers and rope, then led the others over the turtle's flipper and onto his shell. They gathered at the front of his shell and each held tightly to the edge.

"Good luck. May all the spirits of the sea be with you," the Sea Foam Spirit said; then she disappeared.

The turtle drifted away from the *Granny* and gradually sank into the water. The water was colder than they expected, and they all gave small yelps.

It was very strange to breathe from the shells. They inhaled normally but a trail of tiny bubbles fluttered above them every time they exhaled. It was like they were magically scuba diving. And just like with regular scuba diving, there was plenty to see.

The entire bay floor was covered in bright coral and plants. Mermaids and fish of all colors and sizes swam through it like it was a vast underwater city, their bodies shimmering in the rippled sunlight from above. It was a beautiful sight and the twins made sure to seize every moment of it.

Soon they left the bay and the Great Sea Turtle traveled deeper into the endless ocean ahead. The ocean floor wasn't nearly as colorful as the bottom of the bay. It was very bare, with nothing but rocks and seaweed spread across it.

An enormous underwater canyon was ahead of them, and the turtle dived down into it. It had jagged edges and sharp rocks along its sides, and the canyon floor was littered with ghostly empty shells—it was like an underwater graveyard. They knew they were close.

The turtle swam through the canyon, and the twins saw a wide entrance to an underwater cave ahead. The cave was surrounded with small glowing lights, inviting and decorative. However, as they got closer, the twins realized the lights were the glowing antennae of a school of anglerfish surrounding the entrance to the cave. They were terrifying, with their sharp, toothy overbites and the spikes down their spines—they were the monsters of the sea.

The anglerfish glared at them as the turtle passed into the cave. To their discomfort, the inside of the cave was filled with even more of the scary-looking fish. They peered out from behind stalagmites and stalactites. Their antennae gave off the only light in the cave.

Imprisoned behind nets and rock cages throughout the cave were other sea creatures. Swordfish, sea horses, octopi, manatees, and whales all looked somberly at the passing turtle, hoping it wouldn't suffer the same fate. The anglerfish watched over the creatures like prison guards.

The turtle arrived at the entrance to a long tunnel. As if the twins hadn't seen enough to give them nightmares for years after, the tunnel was being watched over by a group of great white sharks. They lingered eerily in the water, staring sinisterly at the turtle and his passengers.

The sea turtle moaned at the sharks. Nothing happened. The turtle moaned again and the sharks slowly separated and let him pass into the tunnel. They turned chillingly as he passed; all they needed was one threatening gesture and the sharks would have food for a week.

They traveled through the tunnel for a few moments and then surfaced in a cave within the cave. To their astonishment, this cave was filled with air.

"We can breathe down here!" Alex said, and they all took off their shell masks.

"The Sea Witch has to appeal to her human customers, too," Froggy said, and his throat deflated to normal.

They climbed off the turtle and walked across the floor in single file. They all shivered terribly—their bodies were so confused as to what temperature to be.

"Good turtle, stay!" Conner said to the Great Sea Turtle. The turtle squinted at him and then spat a stream of water in his face. "Sorry, didn't mean to patronize."

"Oh my lord!" Red gasped and tears filled her eyes. "Look up there!"

She pointed above them to one of the most gruesome sights the twins had ever seen. Dozens of mermaids were hung upside down from their tails across the dome-shaped cave ceiling. They were all weak and frail; some breathed heavily while others didn't breathe at all; some were just skeletons, while others were close to becoming one.

"What are they doing up there?" Alex said, covering her mouth in horror. She wanted to save them all but knew it wouldn't be possible, at least not today.

"Those are probably the Sea Witch's customers who couldn't fulfill their bargains," Froggy said.

Jack was wide-eyed and white-faced, terrified they would be leaving Goldilocks to suffer in the same conditions. She implored him to stick to their plan in spite of what they saw, even though they could all tell she was hesitant herself.

The group traveled farther into the cave. A whale's rib cage was positioned like a grand staircase leading up to *another*, smaller cave. Jellyfish carcasses covered the entrance like a curtain. A large rocky platform at the base of the ribs acted like a small stage—the Sea Witch must have enjoyed looking down on her customers.

"Are you ready for this?" Conner asked Goldilocks.

She nodded, mustering up as much bravery as she could. Jack kissed her as though it would be the last time. The passionate display normally would have made the twins look away, but they all shared Jack's reluctance as he said good-bye to the woman he loved.

"I love you," he whispered into her ear.

"Likewise," Goldilocks said and winked at him.

The team huddled together, reiterating their course of action.

"All right, *we* are ruthless pirates who have kidnapped Queen Red," Froggy said and gestured to the twins. "I have been cursed to live out my days as a frog and you have been cursed to remain adolescents."

The twins nodded. "Aye aye, captain," Conner said and saluted.

"How fun! It's like a little play!" Red said and excitedly clapped her hands. "Who will I be?"

"You'll be hiding behind, with me," Jack said. "We'll be backup in case they run into any problems. Let's hide back here," Jack said and pulled the young queen behind a large rock. "It's always best to have backup."

"Let's make this a little more believable," Froggy said, taking the rope off his shoulder and tying it loosely around Goldilocks. She legitimately looked like a prisoner now. "Shall we?"

The four of them traveled up to the rocky platform while Jack and Red hid behind a large rock.

"Hello?" Froggy called up the whale ribs. *"Sea Witch? We've come to make a trade!"*

Their anticipation made time go by incredibly slowly as they waited for the Sea Witch to appear. Just when they began wondering if she would ever show her face, they heard horrible scraping noises from beyond the jellyfish curtain. A series of heavy footsteps—*several footsteps*—sounded through the cave, like a giant spider was approaching.

The Sea Witch appeared through the jellyfish curtain. Her skin was pale turquoise and scaled. Tall blades of seaweed grew straight out of her head like hair. She had a wide face, with wide turquoise lips and round insect-like black eyes. She wore a gown made of dark shell that had several mussels and sea polyps growing on it. She walked on six legs, and a pair of claws peeked out from under her gown, as though she were part crustacean.

She cuddled a plump cuttlefish in her arms, stroking it like it was a small slimy pet.

"Customers," the Sea Witch hissed in a snake-like voice. "Welcome, fellow vertebrates, to my underwater underworld."

The twins were shivering from being so cold, the Sea Witch didn't notice they were trembling from fear as well.

"Get me out of here!" Goldilocks yelled, playing the part of a captive Red. *"It smells so nasty in here! I want to go home! I want to be back in my castle!"*

"And who might we have *here*?" inquired the Sea Witch, interested by the choice of words.

"We have brought you Queen—" Froggy started, but Goldilocks interrupted him.

"I'll introduce myself, thank you!" she said, playing the part impressively well. "I am Queen Red Riding Hood of the Red Riding Hood Kingdom! And if you don't release me at once I will have my soldiers swim down here and make ink of you all!"

The Sea Witch's eyes widened. Not only was she buying it, she was intrigued.

"A captured queen, you say?" she asked. "And you wish to trade her for what?"

"We've come for your jewels," Froggy said.

The Sea Witch let out a long, hissing laugh that sounded like it might have come from a dying cat. "You insult me with your offer," she said. "I'll make a deal with you; I will give you one of my pearls in exchange for the queen."

She gently placed her hand over the pearl necklace wrapped around her neck. Each pearl was black, and they were all of different sizes and shades.

"Witch, please!" Conner said. "We've got a living, breathing *queen*! We're the ones who should be requesting more from you!"

The Sea Witch eyed him—she didn't like being beaten at

her own game. "You are just a large frog and two children. Tell me how you acquired a *queen*," she hissed.

Conner laughed a little too hard. "We only appear as a frog and children because that's how we've been cursed to spend eternity!" He pointed to his sister. "This *girl* used to be a six-foot man with the hairiest chest in all the kingdoms!"

Alex closed her eyes and assembled enough pretenses to go along with her brother's ridiculous backstory. *"Grrr, I miss me man body,"* she said in her best impression of a pirate's voice.

The Sea Witch looked down at them peculiarly—she had been hanging on every word they said until this point.

"I was on my royal boat when they scooped me up and brought me here!" Goldilocks cried, trying to authenticate their tale.

"Do we have a trade, Sea Witch?" Froggy called up to her. "Or shall we take the queen back to the land and sell her to the ogres?"

The Sea Witch thought on it, stroking the cuttlefish as she did. "Very well," she said. "I believe we have a deal."

The Sea Witch climbed down the whale ribs toward them. They got a better glimpse of her black pearl necklace, and their hearts fluttered with the knowledge that it was exactly what they needed. But the twins' eyes fell to a familiar ring she wore on her turquoise finger. It was silver and had two diamonds, one blue and the other pink.

Alex and Conner looked back and forth between the ring and each other. Was it just a coincidence, or had their worlds collided more than they realized?

"That ring!" Alex gasped. "Where did you get it?"

The Sea Witch glanced at her ring and then suspiciously down to Alex.

"The same place I get all my jewelry," she hissed. "From people like *you*, and creatures like *them*." She jerked her head toward the ceiling where all the mermaids hung. "Do you want to make a trade or not?"

"Yes!" Froggy said, getting the twins back on the subject.

A conniving smile stretched across the Sea Witch's face. "Hand over the queen first and I'll give you the jewels," she said.

"Nice try," Conner said. "Give us the jewels and we'll hand you the queen."

The tensions between them grew.

"As you wish," the Sea Witch said through a frown. She raised her arms and two crabs crawled out from under her dress. They crawled around her body, collecting all the jewelry she wore. The crabs climbed down the platform and stood in front of the twins.

Froggy untied Goldilocks and pushed her up the platform toward the Sea Witch. A long black-and-white-striped sea snake slithered out of the Sea Witch's gown and toward her.

"On the count of three we'll make the exchange," the Sea Witch said. "One . . . two . . . *three*."

The twins took the jewels from the crabs and the snake wrapped around Goldilocks like a living rope. Alex and Conner pocketed the pearls and the other jewels. They were happy the trade had been made, but they desperately didn't want to leave Goldilocks behind.

"This has been splendid," Froggy said with a nod and slowly backed away from the platform. "Pleasure doing business with you—"

"Not so fast!" the Sea Witch hissed. The crabs jumped to the other side of Froggy and the twins, blocking their way out. "Did you think I would let you go without checking to make sure the trade was truthful?"

The Sea Witch reached into her gown and pulled a dried-up blowfish from inside of it. She broke off one of the blowfish's needles and pricked Goldilocks's finger with it. She raised her cuttlefish toward the bleeding finger and it stuck out its tongue from between its legs and tasted it.

Froggy and the twins were so anxious they could hear one another's hearts beat. They hadn't been planning on *this*. The cuttlefish turned bright blue. The Sea Witch frowned angrily and knocked Goldilocks to the ground with one of her claws.

"*Liars!* My cuttlefish has turned blue! He did not taste royal blood!" she screamed.

"Uh-oh," Alex said.

The crabs leaped onto the twins. The Sea Witch threw her cuttlefish and it hit Froggy, wrapping its legs around his face. All three frantically fought off the sea creatures attacking them, but it was no use.

The crabs pinched and poked the twins, scratching them and drawing blood. Jack ran to the twins' side and, with two quick blows of his axe, chopped both of the crabs in half.

"Mmmmmm! Mmmmmm!" Froggy mumbled from under the cuttlefish.

Red ran to help Froggy. She took a good look at the cuttle-fish and then, not wanting to touch it, took off her shoe and began hitting the cuttlefish with it.

"Not helping, darling," Froggy mumbled under the cuttle-fish's clasp. She was mostly hitting him in the head.

Across the lair, Goldilocks pulled one of her arms free from under the snake and grabbed its head. With one tug, she pulled the serpent off her body. The Sea Witch was livid over such an easy escape; she stretched her legs and grew twice in height. She lunged toward Goldilocks, her claws snapping as loudly as gunshots in her direction.

"Goldilocks! Behind you!" Jack screamed.

Goldilocks swung the snake around, cracking it like a whip, and fought the Sea Witch off like a lion tamer. She jumped and tumbled on the ground, barely avoiding fatal pinches. The twins had to cover their eyes, fearing they were about to wit-ness the Snow Queen's prophecy come true.

Red gave the cuttlefish one final smack with her shoe and the tentacled creature fell on the ground. Jack ran up to it and kicked it across the cave. The cuttlefish flew across the cave and hit the Sea Witch square in the face and wrapped itself tightly around her head. They could hear a loud, muffled scream as the Sea Witch struggled to free herself—a prisoner to her own pet.

"Let's get out of here!" Jack yelled.

Goldilocks jumped off the platform, somersaulting through the air, and landed near the others. The group ran through the cave and back toward where they had left the Great Sea

Turtle. They retrieved their scallop shells and strapped them over their faces; then they jumped onto the turtle's back and grabbed hold of him.

"*Go, turtle, go!*" Conner yelled. The Great Sea Turtle might not have heard him, but he could clearly tell by their panicked faces that they needed to get out of there fast.

The turtle dove into the water and swam as fast as he could down the tunnel. He bolted past the group of sharks waiting at its entrance before they knew something was wrong. He passed all the anglerfish they had seen on their way into the cave. Their fins began to move a little quicker as they floated in the water; they could tell something wasn't right but were just waiting on orders to intervene.

The turtle swam through the canyon faster than they had ever seen a turtle swim before. For a moment the twins felt relieved—they had narrowly escaped death once again. But then a high-pitched sound boomed through the ocean, causing a ripple to travel through the water. It sounded like a scream— *the Sea Witch must have freed herself from the cuttlefish.*

Conner looked back at the canyon and had to blink twice. The Sea Witch's army of anglerfish and sharks erupted from the canyon and headed toward them like a swarm of underwater wasps. It wasn't long before the terrifying swarm caught up to them.

A few of the sharks zeroed in on the turtle. Jack was quick to punch one in the nose as it tried biting the turtle's flipper. Froggy kicked another one and it crashed into yet another— it was like an underwater car chase. A moment later the Sea

Witch's creatures had gained speed and the turtle was surrounded. *They needed a miracle if they wanted to escape.*

Suddenly, a series of colorful blurs zoomed past the turtle, taking the sharks and anglerfish with them. The twins looked at each other, each making sure the other had seen it, too. More colorful blurs jetted past them one by one, picking off the creatures trying to harm the turtle. *The mermaids had come to the rescue.*

As if they were moving through a colorful meteor shower, the twins saw hundreds of mermaids shooting through the ocean and tackling the harmful fish around them. Some mermaids carried spears and shields; others shared nets. The twins found themselves in the middle of a massive underwater battle.

The turtle and his passengers had made it back into the bay. They could see the *Granny*'s belly floating on the surface above. The Great Sea Turtle surfaced next to it and Froggy quickly escorted everyone from the back of the turtle to the deck of the ship.

"Thank you!" Alex said to the giant turtle. It dipped its head slightly to her and then disappeared again beneath the water.

Alex and Conner ran down the steps to the lower deck.

"Where's the fire?" the harp asked them, but they ignored her.

Alex and Conner retrieved the Wand of Wonderment from under Goldilocks's cot. They put it on the floor and dumped out all the Sea Witch's jewels beside it. The black pearls instantly coiled around the base of the scepter, creating a handle.

"It's working! We did it!" Conner said, but his sister didn't join him in celebration. "Alex, what's wrong?"

Alex was staring down at the floor at a piece of jewelry that hadn't connected itself to the wand. She picked up the ring with the pink and blue diamonds on it that they had seen the Sea Witch wearing.

"It's the ring!" she said. *"It's the ring Bob got Mom!"*

"How do you know it's the same ring and not just a similar one?" Conner asked.

"I'm a thirteen-year-old girl—I know a ring when I see one!" Alex exclaimed.

"Does this mean *Bob* is in the Land of Stories?!" Conner asked.

A thunderous set of footsteps flew down the steps from the upper deck—it was Jack.

"Hey, you two!" Jack said. "We could use a hand up here!"

The twins put the Wand away and joined the others on the upper deck.

Just when they thought they were safe, anglerfish were jumping out of the water and landing on the ship. They snapped their massive jaws at their ankles. The twins joined Red in kicking the hideous fish overboard. Goldilocks picked up her sword and began a gruesome game of baseball with the fish flying up from the water.

Jack and Froggy tried starting up the ship, releasing the sails and firing up the flame as high as it could go.

"We've got to get away from the water as quickly as possible!" Jack yelled.

The *Granny* rose higher and higher above the bay.

"We're getting away!" Red cheered, still kicking unwelcome fish off of the deck.

The ship was gaining height at a steady speed. Just when they could finally sigh with relief, an anglerfish Red and the twins had missed on the deck flopped high into the air and tore through the *Granny*'s balloon and sails with its huge teeth.

The ship began to descend out of the sky, spinning out of control. The shredded sails above them acted more as a floppy parachute than as a balloon. They couldn't tell where they were falling—it wasn't back into the bay, but toward land somewhere in the distance.

Everyone was screaming, grabbing on to anything or anyone they could to prevent themselves from being flung off the ship. The twins found each other's hands in the middle of the chaos, and they held on to each other, convinced these would be their last moments alive.

With a giant thud, the *Granny* crashed to the ground. Everything was hazy from then on.... They could hear Clawdius barking.... They heard the harp yelling from below.... They heard Red and Froggy moaning.... They saw Jack and Goldilocks trying to stand....

They looked out at the land around them and saw gigantic boulders surrounding the horizon. Two figures were moving toward them—one was small and stout, the other tall and gangly. They both had large ears and ugly faces and leaned toward the twins, inspecting them.

"Well...well...well," said a gruff voice. "What do we have here?"

The twins had one horrifying realization before passing out completely: They had crashed in Troll and Goblin Territory.

CHAPTER TWENTY-TWO

TROLLBELLA, QUEEN OF THE TROBLINS

A gentle swaying stirred the twins to life. They opened their eyes and found themselves in a caged cart traveling down a long, dark tunnel, heading deeper and deeper underground. The cart was pulled by a donkey and steered by a short and fat troll with wide, bat-like ears.

"About time you two woke up!" said the harp. She rode in the same cart as the twins.

"What happened?" Conner said, rubbing his head. He and his sister were sore, bruised, and cut up a bit from the crash.

"Our ship crashed and we've been kidnapped by trolls and goblins!" the harp said. "In other words, *we're having a bad day!*"

"We've been kidnapped by trolls?!" Alex said. "No! This can't be happening again!"

"Where are the others?" Conner asked.

"They're in the cart behind us," the harp said. "No one was seriously wounded, thank the heavens. Goldilocks dislocated her shoulder but set it back in place. Red has a scratch on her cheek and has been crying about it for hours."

The twins looked in the tunnel behind them. Jack, Goldilocks, Froggy, and Red were squished together in a caged cart being steered by a goblin. Goldilocks was clutching her wrist, testing the reflexes throughout her hand. Red was sobbing into Froggy's shoulder; she had a small scrape across her cheek just below her left eye.

"It's going to take weeks to heal!" Red said. *"I'm going to look like a peasant!"*

"Where's the wand?" Alex whispered to the harp.

"The troll took everything of value and put it in *there*," the harp said and pointed to a satchel he wore around his shoulder. They could see Jack's axe, Goldilocks's sword, and the tip of the Wand poking out from the top of it.

"Are we going to be slaves now?" Conner asked in a loud and frustrated voice so the troll would hear him.

The troll let out a rumbling chuckle. "I wish," he growled. "We don't have slaves anymore. You lot are in for something much worse."

Soon the carts were passing under a stone arch the twins remembered from their last visit to the underground kingdom. The stone had two statues underneath it, one of a troll and one of a goblin, and in bold letters what used to say:

BE TROLL, BE GOBLIN, OR BE AFRAID

Now read:

WELCOME, FRIENDS!

The twins rubbed their eyes to make sure they were working properly.

"Huh?" Conner said. "Are you reading what I'm reading or do I have a concussion?"

They moved through the arch and down a long stone tunnel. The twins expected to descend into the large, noisy common room they'd visited before, but everything was completely different. Instead of being filled with hundreds of trolls and goblins being served drinks and food by human slaves, the room was completely still. All the stone tables and chairs had been removed, and trolls and goblins stood attentively in perfect lines.

"That's odd," Conner said. "It's like they're at boot camp or something."

The trolls and goblins faced an empty stone throne, all waiting for their leader's arrival. They weren't quite as ugly as the twins remembered, and the smell of their poor hygiene wasn't as strong, either. Had they finally learned to take care of themselves?

The carts turned a corner and moved down another tunnel—headed for the dungeons, if the twins remembered properly. They were shocked to discover the dungeons had changed, too. The individual cells had been removed, and now there was just one big space with furniture and torches. A dozen or so humans mingled about the room. They weren't the frail, overworked slaves the twins had seen last time, but were more a bored and restless group—yawning and twirling their thumbs.

The troll and goblin pulled the twins and other captives out of the carts and pushed them into the room with the others. They drove the carts off, taking the harp and the satchel with the Wand of Wonderment inside it with them.

"Don't let them take me away!" the harp cried. *"They're going to melt me and forge me into nose rings!"*

Unfortunately, there was nothing they could do. A large gate shut behind the carts as the troll with the magic harp drove off. Jack, Goldilocks, Red, Froggy, and the twins were trapped with the others.

"We have to get the harp and the Wand back," Jack said. He put his hands to the gate door and shook it as hard as he could, but it didn't budge.

The twins didn't look nearly as stressed as the rest of them.

"Don't worry, if we could escape this place last time, we can do it again," Conner said, once again the voice of optimism.

"Things look so much more civilized in here now," Alex said. She walked up to a woman and politely tapped her on the shoulder. "Excuse me? Hello, my name is Alex Bailey. Can you tell me what we're doing here?"

"I don't know what *you're* doing here, but *I* was kidnapped when I accidentally wandered into the Troll and Goblin Territory," she said.

"How long have you been a slave?" Conner asked.

"Slave?" Red said, and tears immediately came to her eyes—she was so distraught by the scratch on her face that the reality of the situation hadn't fully sunk in. *"Royals can't be slaves! Why is my life a reverse Cinderella story?!"*

The woman grew even more annoyed talking to them. "I'm not a slave," she said, insulted they would even think such a thing. "They just make us dance for the queen as punishment for being on their property without permission."

"They make you dance?" Alex asked. She wasn't sure she had heard her correctly.

"The Troll Queen loves watching people dance," the woman said. "So every evening after her dinner she makes her prisoners and her citizens dance with each other."

"Excuse me? Did you say *Troll Queen*?" Conner said. "What happened to the kings?"

"Don't ask me. I've only been here a week," the woman said and walked off, obviously not wanting to be bothered with questions anymore.

The twins looked around the room at the other prisoners.

"Alex? Conner?" said a voice nearby. Sitting on the ground in the back of the room was a friendly face the twins were never expecting to see in a place like this.

"Dr. Bob!" Alex gasped.

Alex and Conner were in shock and couldn't move. Bob got to his feet and ran to the twins, giving them a long, teary-eyed embrace.

"I thought I was seeing things!" Bob said. "But it's you—it's actually you!"

The twins' heads filled with so many questions they tried filtering them to the basics.

"Bob, what are you doing here?" Conner asked.

"How did you get into the fairy-tale world?" Alex said.

Bob let out a lengthy sigh. "I've had quite the adventure," he said. "I was at the house when Mother Goose and the soldiers realized you were gone. A door appeared out of thin air in the living room and your grandmother appeared. While Mother Goose was explaining what had happened, I slipped through the door and have been here ever since."

"How long have you been here?" Alex asked.

"A week or so, I think, maybe a day or two more," Bob said.

Conner's eyebrows shot to the top of his forehead. "You've been down in this dungeon for a *week*?!" he said.

"Oh no, I've been all over the fairy-tale continent," Bob said. "I've only been in Troll and Goblin Territory for a day or two."

Alex happily clasped her hands together. "So it *was* your ring the Sea Witch was wearing!" she said.

"Why were you with the Sea Witch, Bob?" Conner asked.

Bob looked back and forth between the twins, scared just at the sound of her name. "What were *you two* doing with the Sea Witch?" he asked.

"We're kind of trying to save the world. . . . It's a long story. But how did you go from the rental house to the bottom of an enchanted ocean?!"

"When I got to the fairy-tale world I started looking for you and your mother immediately," he said. "I asked every villager, every farmer, and every creature I came across. No one knew who I was talking about. I ended up getting lost in the woods—it was freezing, and there was snow on the ground."

"Sounds like the Northern Kingdom," Alex said. "Please keep going."

"Like I said, it was freezing and became dark," Bob continued. "A huge family of black bears surrounded me—I thought I was going to be eaten alive! But then the most amazing thing happened! A series of trunks and chests rained from the sky and fell on top of the bears!"

The twins side-eyed Goldilocks and Red—who shared the same stunned look on their faces.

"I don't know where they came from, but thankfully, they were full of dainty coats and scarves and jewelry," Bob said. "I wrapped myself in the clothing and was able to survive the cold night!"

"Amazing!" Red said through her teeth. Losing her belongings hadn't been such a waste after all, but she still was bitter about having had to toss them overboard.

Bob continued to animatedly recall his trip for the twins. "I searched the land for a few more days with no luck. I found myself in a village on the coast and was able to trade the jewels and the clothing to a sailor in exchange for a small boat. I hoped to have more luck traveling by water, so I traveled from port to port but still didn't find a trace of you two or your mother.

"I sailed through an enormous sea storm and was tipped over into the water. I was just about to drown when the Sea Witch's hideous anglerfish saved me—or at least I thought they were saving me. They brought me to her cave and stored me with the other animals they kept to feed the Sea Witch's sharks. I noticed the Sea Witch had a soft spot for jewelry and remembered I had your mother's ring in my pocket. I gave the ring to the Sea Witch in exchange for my freedom!

"I washed ashore and wandered around aimlessly for a couple days before the trolls found me," Bob said. "And now here I am, miraculously talking to you two!"

The twins were awestruck. They gawked at him with enormous eyes and wide-open mouths.

"That's an incredible story, Bob," Alex said in an almost-whisper.

"You went through all of that for Mom?" Conner asked.

"Of course," Bob said. "I would walk to the ends of the world if I had to—*any world*. But not just your mom, for you as well."

Alex and Conner were touched—until this moment they hadn't realized how much Bob loved them, and it was slowly dawning on them just how much they loved him in return.

"Who might this brave man be?" Froggy asked the twins.

"This is Dr. Bob," Conner said. "He's our . . . well, he's our *stepdad*."

Hearing the sound of those words made Bob smile from ear to ear—he had found his family at last.

"A doctor! Thank goodness," Red said, interrupting the sentimental moment. She showed him the scratch on her face. "On a scale of temporary to permanent, how bad is this, Doctor? Will I have to include it in my official portraits?" She braced herself for the worst.

Bob wasn't sure how to respond. "I'd say that'll be gone in a day or so," Bob said and then had a look at the four adults surrounding the twins. "Who's in your entourage, guys?"

"Oh, sorry, Bob," Alex said. "This is Jack, Goldilocks, Froggy, and Red."

"Queen Red Riding Hood of the Red Riding Hood Kingdom," Red added.

Bob gave them a friendly nod. "Pleasure," he said. "Have either of you located your mother yet?"

The twins shook their heads. "She was kidnapped by an enchantress," Alex told him regretfully. "But we still don't know where she is."

"*The* Enchantress?" Bob asked. "The one everyone is talking about?"

Conner nodded his heavy head. "Unfortunately," he said.

Bob started pacing. He looked just as worried as the twins had when they first discovered the news. "We have to find a way to save her," he said.

"Don't worry, that's what we've been doing all this time," Conner said. "We're on a quest, although it's kind of paused at the moment."

The gate screeched open and a troll carrying a whip entered the room of prisoners.

"He's not going to whip us, is he?" Red said and hid behind Froggy.

"Not if he knows what's good for him," Goldilocks said.

The troll cleared his phlegmy throat, addressing the prisoners. "The queen is almost finished with her dinner," he growled. "It's time to join us for the dancing hour."

Against their will, the prisoners in the room disgruntledly followed one another through the gate and up the tunnel to the large common room. Bob, the twins, and the others stayed as close to one another as possible. When they reached the common room, all the humans were herded to the side against the wall.

A very thin goblin with a metal belt, a cape, and a staff approached the front of the room.

"That's Rigworm," Bob whispered to the twins. "He's the queen's advisor."

"Bow down, troblins," Rigworm squealed and banged his staff on the ground. "The great imperial *Queen Trollbella* approaches!"

Alex and Conner jerked their heads toward each other.

"Queen Trollbella?!" Alex said.

"You've got to be kidding me," Conner said.

A moment later, the entire room was bowing as Queen Trollbella strolled in. She was the twins' age and looked exactly as they remembered her—short, with a round face and a cute snout nose—but Trollbella had taken the title of queen very seriously.

An enormous headdress in the shape of two horns sat on

her head with strings of teeth between them (the species of which no one could tell). A round ruffled collar Queen Elizabeth I of England would have been envious of was around her neck. She wore a long russet lacy dress, and on her large feet were golden slippers.

She made her way through the crowd of trolls and goblins, bobbling her head regally as she walked through her subjects. She took a seat on the stone throne at the front of the room. All the trolls and goblins looked genuinely afraid of her; even Rigworm appeared intimidated as he stood by her side. The twins had to admit, Trollbella was rather intimidating.

"How is a troll queen respected more than me?" Red asked herself out loud, and Goldilocks nudged her to be quiet.

"Thank you, troblins!" Trollbella called out. "I just had the most scrumptious dinner—hog-liver-and-acorn soup—and now I am ready to be entertained. *Now dance for me!*"

Rigworm hit the ground with his staff. A small band of trolls and goblins wheeled instruments into the room and began playing music. They pounded on stone pianos, blew horns made of actual horns, and played on violins and cellos made of bone and spiderwebs.

The trolls and goblins standing in the center of the common room began to dance around one another in a routine they evidently had to concentrate very hard on—they had obviously thoroughly rehearsed it beforehand. Rigworm watched them intently, counting the dancing beats to himself. The twins figured he must have choreographed it.

Trollbella smiled and nodded her head to the tempo of the

music. *"Dance, troblins, dance!"* she demanded and clapped her hands in delight.

As the dance progressed, the trolls and goblins started pulling the prisoners onto the floor, twirling and dipping them as part of their routine. Froggy was pulled in by a pair of ugly troll women—they blushed and giggled as they danced with him.

Red turned pink watching the troll women swing her beau around. A goblin tried to grab Goldilocks's hand but she shot him a nasty look that scared him off.

The troll that had captured the twins carried the magic harp into the room and set her beside the band. The twins could see he still had his satchel around his shoulder containing the wand.

"What is *this*?!" Trollbella said and excitedly kicked her feet at the throne.

"A gift for you, My Queen," the troll said and bowed to her. "We acquired it this afternoon for you."

"By acquired he means *kidnapped*!" the harp shouted.

"Someone play the shiny woman!" Trollbella ordered. "I want to hear the sounds of her strings!"

One of the goblins playing in the band tossed his violin aside and began playing the harp. The harp burst out laughing—it tickled her.

"Oooo-hoo-hoo, stop that!" the harp cried. *"That tickles! Oooo-hoo! Be gentle; it's been a while!"*

The trolls and goblins in the center of the room stopped for a moment and watched as the harp was played against her will.

Trollbella squinted at them. "Did I *say* you could stop dancing?" she yelled from her throne.

Rigworm slammed his staff on the ground and the trolls and goblins immediately picked up dancing where they had left off.

The group of prisoners to the side was getting smaller and smaller as more of them were being incorporated into the dance. Conner was hiding behind the ones who were left. He didn't want to dance but even more so didn't want Trollbella to see him.

As the dance went on, Jack, Goldilocks, Froggy, Red, Alex, and Bob were all pulled into it, one by one, and twirled around. Conner was the only one left and stood alone. Trollbella gazed around the room, pleased by all the dancing, and her eyes finally landed on Conner. The Troll Queen screamed. Her mouth opened and her eyes grew twice in size.

"Stop the music!" Trollbella ordered, and the band went mute immediately. She clutched her chest over a rapidly beating heart. *"My Butterboy has returned!"* she gasped.

Conner cringed. "Hi, Trollbella," he said and awkwardly waved at her.

Trollbella was beside herself with excitement. "I knew you would come back to me one day, Butterboy," she said softly, almost in a trance. "I have waited ever so long for this moment."

"Ah, well, *here I am*," Conner said, blinking uncomfortably slowly.

Although the music had stopped, a thousand-piece symphony

seemed to be playing in Trollbella's mind. *"Bring me my Butterboy bust!"* she ordered.

A couple trolls wheeled a very heavy cart into the center of the common room. A giant stone bust of Conner's face, sculpted to perfection, was on the back of it.

"Is that *me*?!" Conner asked, horrified to see the massive replica of himself.

Trollbella hopped off her throne and place a hand on the bust's cheek. "I made it myself. I look at it every day we're apart," she said dreamily. "But you look so different now, Butterboy. You've gotten taller, handsomer—you're my Butter*man* now!"

Trollbella walked toward the real Conner like a lioness approaching her mate. Her heart was practically fluttering out of her body. She threw her arms around him and squeezed him as tightly as she could.

Conner looked up at his sister. *"Help me!"* he mouthed at her. Alex only shrugged at him. What could she do?

"I need slow music so I can dance with my Butterboy!" Trollbella ordered. *"Now, troblins, now!"*

The band started a slow, romantic melody. Trollbella danced with Conner to the music—rather, she moved him around the room and he followed.

"Trollbella, what is a troblin?" Conner asked.

"It's what I renamed my people when I became queen," Trollbella said and rested her head on Conner's chest as they swayed. Her headdress almost poked him in the eye. "The Goblin King didn't have an heir so I inherited both thrones and combined them."

"What happened to the Troll King and Goblin King?" Conner asked.

"Rocks fell and they died," Trollbella said simply. "It was tragic, it was messy—environmental hazards when you live in an underground kingdom."

"I'm so sorry to hear that," Conner said, not sure whether Trollbella was saddened by the incident.

Trollbella shrugged happily. "But at least I'm queen now," she said. "And a great queen I have been for my troblins. We've had a bad reputation for so long. I've tried restoring honor and class by making them bathe and dance."

"You've done a nice job," Conner said.

"But I do get so lonely down here," Trollbella said and looked into his eyes. "I long to be married and start a troblin family of my own someday. Oh, Butterboy, won't you please be my *Butterking*?!"

The entire room went silent at the sudden and unexpected proposal. Alex slapped her hands over her face.

"King?" Conner exclaimed. "Me? Of the trolls and goblins?"

Trollbella silenced him with her index finger. "Shhh, Butterboy," she said calmly. "I know we've only been reunited for a mere three minutes, but I've never been so sure of anything in my life. It's a tremendous honor to be my husband, I know, but let the idea sink in and accept it. Embrace it. *Love it*."

Trollbella was so much more powerful now, Conner was terrified of what she might do to him or his friends if he turned her down.

"Trollbella, I . . . I . . . I . . ." he said with difficulty.

"I believe the word you're looking for is *yes*," Trollbella said.

Conner was saved by a bright violet flash that suddenly filled the room. A large hourglass covered in vines and thorns appeared in the center of the floor. It had purple sand that was falling quickly into its base—whatever it was timing was going to happen in a matter of seconds.

"What is that?" Conner asked.

Trollbella rolled her eyes at the hourglass. "Oh, don't worry about that, Butterboy," she said. "That's just from the Enchantress."

"The Enchantress?!" Conner yelled. "Why is the Enchantress sending you an hourglass?"

Trollbella tried waving the subject off like it wasn't important. "She visited me yesterday," she said, as if it wasn't a big deal. "She was trying to get me to surrender my kingdom to her. Apparently she's trying to take over the world or something. I wasn't listening—she was interrupting my dancing time."

"What else did she say?" Conner asked.

"She said the Elf Empire had surrendered to her already," Trollbella said. "The elves are still mad they weren't included in the very first Happily Ever After Assembly. The Enchantress figured since the trolls and goblins have *never* been included, we would want to surrender willingly, too."

"Did you surrender?" Conner asked.

"Of course not," Trollbella said. "It was dancing time! *Nobody* interrupts my dancing time."

"Did she threaten you with anything?" Conner asked her. She was a difficult troll to get information out of.

Trollbella thought about it. "Oh, she did say I had a day to think about it or she would cause horrible destruction to my kingdom," she said blankly.

"Well, aren't you worried she will?" Conner said.

"I live in a big hole with trolls and goblins," Trollbella said. "What is worse than that?"

Alex ran up to the small queen. "Trollbella! We have to get everyone out of here as quickly as possible!"

It was the first time Trollbella had realized Alex was in the room. She couldn't remember why she didn't like her—but the feeling was just as strong as ever.

"*You?*" Trollbella yelled and then gave Conner a dirty look. "You're still hanging around *her*, Butterboy?!"

"She's my *sister*!" Conner yelled. That never mattered to Trollbella; every other girl was a threat when it came to her Butterboy.

The purple sand was going fast. "We have to get out of here before the Enchantress attacks!" Alex desperately declared to the room.

"What do you think the Enchantress is going to do?!" Froggy asked.

"I'm not certain, but I have an idea," Alex said. "And I pray I'm wrong."

The final grain of the hourglass's purple sand fell into the base. *Time was up.* A thunderous rumble caused the common room to shake. Something monstrous was headed their way.

"*What's happening?*" Red yelled.

She turned toward the stone entrance tunnel and the whole room turned with her. A gigantic tidal wave was hurtling toward them. "I was right," Alex whispered to herself. "*Ezmia is flooding the kingdom!*"

The trolls, goblins, and humans screamed at the oncoming water. There was no time to waste. They had to do something fast or the water was going to crush and drown the entire kingdom.

Alex ran to the troll with the satchel over his shoulder and yanked it off him. She ran toward the rushing wave, digging in the satchel as she ran. She found the wand and brushed all the items off it into the bag until it was just an ice scepter again.

Alex pointed the scepter at the rushing water. An icy blast erupted from the tip of the scepter and shot straight into the water. The tidal wave slowed into a big icy wall yards away from where Alex stood.

The trolls and goblins cheered. "The Squishygirl has saved us all," Trollbella said quietly with wide eyes.

"You're a genius!" Conner yelled proudly to his sister. She looked back to him and they shared a smile—but it wasn't over yet.

The wall of ice began to crack and snap as more water flowed in behind it.

"*We need to get out of here!*" Alex yelled. "*The wall isn't going to hold the water back forever!*"

Rigworm slammed his staff on the ground. "Everyone follow me to the back tunnels!" he yelled and the troblins stampeded behind him out of the room.

The band abandoned their instruments, including the magic harp, and ran with the others.

"Don't leave me!" the harp said.

Jack and Froggy hoisted the harp over their shoulders and followed the others out of the common room with Red at their tail.

"My apologies, Your Majesty," Goldilocks said and scooped up Trollbella like a baby doll.

"I love you, Butterboy!" Trollbella called back to Conner as Goldilocks carried her off.

Alex and Conner stayed behind. Alex was blasting the scepter, reinforcing the icy wall as it swelled under the pressure of the water behind it.

"Alex! Conner!" Bob said. "We have to get out of here before it's too late!"

"They need time to escape!" Alex said. "I have to keep the wall up so they have a chance! Go! Save yourselves!"

Alex was holding the scepter like a flamethrower, freezing the water as it crept closer and closer. She squeezed it harder and an even stronger blast shot out of it. Conner had to grab hold of it, too, so it didn't knock her over. *Every second counted.*

Finally, the pressure was too much for the scepter to hold off, and the water rushed toward them. Bob pulled the twins in the direction the others had gone, and the three of them ran for their lives.

They ran up the tunnel the others had escaped into with the water chasing them. Luckily, the Troll and Goblin Territory was like a giant ant colony—the water had other places to go besides after them—but the underground kingdom filled quickly and the water swirled violently toward the twins. They were running as fast as their legs could carry them, but the water caught up with them and they were engulfed.

Bob and the twins shot out of the ground as if they had been stuck in a whale's blowhole. They landed hard on grassy dirt somewhere outside the territory. They were soaking wet and coughing up water they had swallowed.

The twins and Bob got to their feet and had a look around at wherever they were. They were standing in a field on the edge of a forest. The entire troll and goblin race was spread out across the field with Jack, Goldilocks, Red, Froggy, and the harp sprinkled between them. They moaned and panted and held on to the loved ones they had nearly lost.

It looked like something the twins would have seen on the news after a natural disaster had occurred.

"Where are we?" Alex asked.

"Does it matter?" Conner asked. "We're alive."

The twins and their friends gathered together in the center of the field.

"That was a very brave thing you did back there," Jack said and placed a grateful hand on Alex's shoulder.

"You saved our lives, Alex," Goldilocks said.

Trollbella strolled up to Alex. Her headdress had been knocked off and her blonde pigtails were exposed. "You saved me and my troblins, Squishygirl," she said. "We will forever be grateful."

All Alex could do was nod, overwhelmed by the gratitude

she was receiving. She dumped out the satchel and all their belongings the troll had briefly stolen from them fell on the ground. Jack took his axe and Goldilocks took her sword. Alex watched as the Wand of Wonderment reconfigured itself as the pieces of mirror, the scepter, the stepmother's ring, and the Sea Witch's pearls were reunited.

"A whole kingdom has been ruined but it looks like something can be salvaged," Alex said. She picked up her mother's silver engagement ring off the ground and handed it to Bob.

It gave them hope that everything hadn't been lost.

Jack led a group of troll and goblin men into the woods and returned with firewood. They set up a series of campfires for the night. Bob walked around and inspected anyone that had been injured in the escape, although he was a little confused by troll and goblin anatomy—some four-toed feet weren't actually missing any toes.

Everyone slept on the ground that night. The next day, the *Granny*'s crash site was discovered not too far away from the trolls' and goblins' camp. The ship's damage was irreparable, so they stripped it apart and used the pieces of woven wood and stitched fabric to create tents for the campers.

While Jack was helping the trolls and goblins tear the ship apart, he found Clawdius hiding in the destruction. Jack brought him back to the camp and he was reunited with Red.

"Oh, Clawdius! There you are!" Red said happily. "I was worried sick! I was afraid you had been gobbled up by a . . . a . . . well, a relative or something!"

They configured a tent for their group of eight (nine,

including Clawdius) to sleep under. Trollbella insisted on putting her tent as close as possible to the one Conner slept in. She talked openly about their future wedding, although he had never given her an answer to her proposal.

"Trollbella, you and all the troblins just lost a kingdom," he said. "I think you have bigger things to worry about."

"You are so wise, Butterboy," Trollbella said. "And someday you will make a wonderful Butterking."

Trollbella was homeless, but still not hopeless.

Jack, Goldilocks, Red, Froggy, Bob, and the twins sat around a campfire that evening. They were feeling pretty dismal after witnessing the Enchantress's attempt to kill an entire kingdom.

"Where do we go now?" Goldilocks asked. "We've collected everything except what we need from the Enchantress."

"And no one has any clue where she is?" Bob asked.

"No," Jack said. "But as soon as we do, it'll be our next stop."

Conner grew tired of hearing the same pointless questions being asked.

"I'm going for a walk," he said. "I need to clear my head."

"I'll go with you," Alex said. "Some air will do us some good."

The twins walked into the trees beside the campground. It was nice to have time away from the others and vent to each other.

"She's such a monster," Alex said under her breath. "I

don't think I've ever hated someone as much as I hate the Enchantress."

"I never thought one person was capable of so much damage," Conner said. "When are we going to have the answers we need to get rid of this wench? I'm so sick of asking questions!"

Something began moving between the trees in the distance. The twins looked up and saw a familiar ghostly woman floating toward them.

"It's the Lady of the East!" Alex said.

The ghost hovered in front of them. Conner took an angry step toward her. He wasn't afraid of the spirit anymore but had grown very frustrated by her appearance.

"What do you want from us?" he yelled.

The ghost didn't respond. She just stared at the twins silently, as she always did.

"Habla inglés?" Conner tried with a horrible accent.

"Conner, I don't think she speaks *Spanish*," Alex reprimanded.

"WHAT. DO. YOU. WANT?" Conner shouted.

The ghost raised her hand and pointed to the east.

"Yes, we get it, you're from the East!" Conner said. "Listen, Ghost Lady, we've got a lot on our plate right now. Unless you can help us, please go haunt someone else."

The ghost looked back and forth between the twins and nodded. She turned around and floated off into the trees but stopped to look back at them. It was the most the twins had ever seen her move.

"I think she wants us to follow her," Alex said. "I think she wants to help."

The ghost nodded again and then floated off into the distance.

"Why are ghosts so passive-aggressive?" Conner asked.

"Let's follow her," Alex said with a shrug. "What do we have to lose?"

Conner eyed the ghost nervously. "You better not be taking us on a *wild ghost chase*!"

The twins followed the spirit through the trees and into the East. They had no idea where she was taking them or how long they would be gone, but the twins hoped wherever they were going, they would find the answers they needed.

It was a few hours past sunset and the magic harp had the tent all to herself. The twins had gone for a walk and the others were gathered around the campfire just outside, quietly talking among themselves.

The harp gazed through a tear in the tent at the trolls and goblins camping around her. Even though they had kidnapped her and forced her to play music, she couldn't help but feel sorry for them. No creature deserved to have its home destroyed in such a merciless manner. She wished there was a way she could help the twins stop the Enchantress—except for the obvious one.

The Wand of Wonderment was resting on a tree stump on

the ground in front of the harp. She had been keeping as much distance from the Wand as possible. Every time she saw it, a strange, alluring sensation swept through her, as if she was being magnetically drawn to it. The harp knew she was meant to be a part of the Wand—she just worried what her incorporation would cost her.

"So tragic," said an airy voice in the tent. "I gave the Troll Queen a proper warning, so she only has herself to blame."

The harp turned to see who had snuck into the tent behind her and she saw a face she hadn't seen in more than a hundred years.

"Ezmia," the harp said.

"Hello, Gloria," the Enchantress said. "It's been ages since the last time I saw you. You look wonderful—haven't aged a day! Then again, I suppose that's one of the perks of being made of gold."

The harp was neither timid nor scared. Unbeknownst to the others, the harp and the Enchantress had a history together.

"You should know," the harp said crossly. "Or has your memory spoiled as much as your soul? You're the one who transformed me into this instrument."

"Was that *me*?" Ezmia said and playfully gestured to herself.

"The Musician fell in love with me and left you. You turned me into an object and captured his soul so I would be forced to live forever and spend eternity without him."

"How cruel," Ezmia said. "Sounds like something I would do, though."

If the harp had had tear ducts, Ezmia would have caused tears to roll down her golden face. "Why are you here, Ezmia?" the harp said. "Are you tallying all the lives you've ruined?"

The Enchantress smiled malevolently. "No, I came to see that expression on your face. I've waited over a hundred years to see those eyes fill with the bleakness of seeing your whole world crumble around you," she said. "Because you were responsible for putting that same look into my eyes once."

"You still blame me for the *Musician's* mistake?" the harp said.

"Oh, please, the fault was shared," Ezmia said. "You let him pursue you even though you knew it was breaking my heart. You didn't think hurting me would have a consequence, because, like the rest of the world, you thought I was powerful in ability but weak in spirit."

"And now are you satisfied?" the harp asked. "Now that you've shown the world the evil you're capable of, have you found your peace?"

"I may not be fully satisfied yet, but I will be soon," Ezmia said. "I have big plans for this world."

The harp shook her head, almost pitying the Enchantress. "No, Ezmia, you'll never be satisfied," she said. "You think by robbing other people of their bliss you'll find your own, but it doesn't work that way. You'll be searching for happiness your entire life but will never find it because you wouldn't know what happiness was even if it scratched you in the face."

The Enchantress's eyes grew wide with anger. Her hair was rapidly flowing above her like an aggressive flame. The harp might have infuriated her, but she was delighted by the feeling. Ezmia smiled as her spirit absorbed the emotion and her body became stronger.

"Thank you," Ezmia said. "I have a big day tomorrow and needed that extra boost. But one thing before I go—if I do search for bliss forever, I'm so glad you'll be around to see it."

The Enchantress vanished from the tent without a trace. The remark was like a knife in the heart to the harp. She couldn't bear the thought of watching Ezmia's wrath evolve for all time.

She looked down at the Wand of Wonderment and reached toward it. She was ready to sacrifice whatever she had to so Ezmia didn't win.

CHAPTER TWENTY-THREE

THE EIGHTH DWARF

A horrible storm moved through the Dwarf Forests. Rain poured down in massive amounts, trees bent in the violent wind, and thunder roared across the land. It was as if Mother Nature was mourning.

The Seven Dwarfs were nestled warmly in their cottage. They played a game of cards and enjoyed some hot cocoa at their table while they waited out the storm. It was almost midnight when an unexpected knock came from their door.

The dwarfs were very curious as to who would be visiting them so late in the night during such a harsh storm. In fact, the last person to knock on their door had been Queen Snow White herself when she was just a young princess trying to hide from the Evil Queen.

The Oldest Dwarf stood from the table and opened the door. He was taken aback by who their guest turned out to be. Standing on their doorstep, soaked to the bone in a dark cloak, was the Seven Dwarfs' youngest brother.

"Hello," Rumpelstiltskin said.

"Well, I'll be an elf's mistress," the Oldest Dwarf said. It had been one hundred and twenty-seven years since the dwarfs had seen their youngest brother.

"Rumpelstiltskin, is that you?" said the Shortest Dwarf, and he stood from the table.

"It's me, brother," Rumpelstiltskin said. "May I come in?"

The Oldest hesitated at first, but because the weather was so horrid he decided it would be cruel of him not to let his brother in. Rumpelstiltskin took a step inside his old home and the Oldest shut the door behind him.

"It's a beast out there," he said with a shiver. All seven of his brothers scowled at him, not welcoming his return home. "Playing with the old deck, I see. I always loved it when we played cards through a storm."

His brothers stared at the floor or at their hand of cards, although none of them were playing anymore.

"I saw the smoke from your chimney," Rumpelstiltskin said. "It guided me here through the storm. Thank goodness it did, otherwise I would still be out there trotting through the rain."

"Why are you here?" the Largest Dwarf asked him.

Rumpelstiltskin looked at his hands while he formed the words. "I snuck away while the Enchantress was out. I'm sure you've heard, but she is taking over the world," he said.

The Oldest Dwarf hooted under his breath in disgust and had a seat at the table. Rumpelstiltskin knew it was aimed at him.

"She isn't very clear about her plans for the Dwarf Forests, as it has no ruler to conquer, but I think she is planning on obliterating them completely," he said. "I'm fairly close to her, as close as anyone could be, and was hoping with your permission I could ask her to spare you when she takes over."

"And why would you do that?" asked the Thinnest Dwarf.

Rumpelstiltskin was hurt he had to be asked. "Because we're *family*," he said.

The Oldest angrily threw his cards on the table. "We *were* family," he said. "You abandoned this family a long time ago when you decided we weren't good enough for you. And what did you leave us for? To kidnap children for evil fairies? To spend a lifetime in prison? How dare you call yourself a dwarf or say the word *family* under this roof! Mother and Father would be ashamed of you if they were still alive."

Rumpelstiltskin lowered his head. "I was so unhappy," he said. "I didn't know what I wanted; I just knew it wasn't the life of a miner."

"So, have you found it, then?" the Shortest Dwarf asked. "Is running around doing the evil Enchantress's grunt work been everything you were hoping for?"

Rumpelstiltskin closed his eyes; he was hoping the conversation wouldn't get to this.

"I'm sorry for the embarrassment I brought to this family," he said. "And believe me, not a day goes by that I don't wish to erase the past. I would love nothing more than to get rid of my affiliation with her, but I'm afraid I can't, all because of one mistake I made years ago."

The Oldest Dwarf shuffled his cards. "Well, it was *your* mistake and not ours," he said. "We'll have nothing to do with it. You can tell the Enchantress that we would rather die than live in a world ruled by her."

Rumpelstiltskin looked to his other brothers but the answer seemed to be unanimous.

"I see," he said. "Well, at least I tried."

He headed to the door and pulled it open. The strong winds from outside instantly filled the cottage. Rumpelstiltskin turned back to his brothers before he left; he had one final thing to say.

"I'm sorry I could never be the brother you wanted," Rumpelstiltskin said. "But one day I'll make things right between us. One day I'll be a brother you can be proud of."

Rumpelstiltskin stepped into the storm and shut the cottage door behind him, knowing it could very well be the last thing he ever said to them.

CHAPTER TWENTY-FOUR

THE LADY OF THE EAST

The twins followed the ghost for hours and hours across the land. They traveled through a series of forests, over streams, and across grassy hills as they voyaged farther and farther, following the spirit into the East. Occasionally the ghost would look back at the twins to make sure they were still following her and wait for them to catch up before proceeding.

Eventually, they arrived at a large river that marked the Eastern Kingdom's border. At least, the twins assumed it was the border, since everything on the opposite side was consumed in thornbushes and vines.

"She's crazy if she thinks we're going in there," Conner said.

The Lady of the East floated upstream to a large maple tree. She lingered by its roots until the twins met her there. She pointed to the ground and the twins saw a small circular door hidden in the dirt. Conner pulled it open and discovered a ladder leading down into a narrow tunnel.

"It's a secret passage!" Alex said.

"Are we supposed to go in there?" Conner asked the ghost.

The Lady of the East slowly nodded her head. She retracted into a small, ghostly orb and flew into the passage. Alex and Conner followed her, cautiously making their way down the ladder. The tunnel was dark and dingy. The orb gave off the only light, and the twins followed it like the North Star as it continued leading them east underground.

The dirt surrounding them became moist and muddy as they traveled below the river.

"She seems to know where she's going," Conner said.

"This must be a secret entrance into the Eastern Kingdom," Alex said. "Something tells me we're the only ones who have been in here for a very long time."

There were no footprints or a single insect or rodent in sight. The twins were led through the tunnel for miles and miles. Their feet grew tired and ached a little more with every step.

"Are we there yet?" Conner asked the orb, but he didn't get an answer.

Finally, the tunnel came to an end at another ladder.

Alex and Conner climbed up the ladder and peeked through another circular door above it. They pushed the door open and climbed out of the passage.

The twins found themselves in a square room with hay covering the ground and spacious wooden stalls built around the walls.

"Looks like we're in a stable," Conner said.

"Then where are all the horses?" Alex asked.

The orb expanded back into the Lady of the East. She glided across the stable and through a pair of open wooden doors. Alex and Conner followed her again, peering through the doors before walking through them. They found a stone spiral staircase that twisted high above them.

"Conner, I think we're in Sleeping Beauty's castle," Alex said.

The Lady of the East glared at them from the stairs.

"We're coming, we're coming," Conner said.

The twins followed the ghost up the stone steps, climbing higher and higher into the castle. They finally reached one of the highest floors and followed the Lady of the East down a hallway with stained-glass windows. The windows were dark, though—as if something was covering them from the other side.

They passed a window with an unobstructed view and looked out at the rest of the castle and the land surrounding it. Alex shrieked and grabbed her brother's arm.

"Oh my gosh," she said and covered her mouth.

"Whoa," Conner said under his breath.

The castle was so consumed by the Enchantress's plants it looked like it was one large plant itself. The thornbushes and vines had wrapped around the castle, leaving nothing uncovered. The twins saw soldiers and servants and villagers spread across the land with vines coiled around them like serpents covering their prey. Some were pinned to the ground, while others were suspended hundreds of feet in the air over the castle—like ornaments on a monstrous Christmas tree.

"You don't see something like that every day," Conner said softly.

The twins turned to the Lady of the East. She floated farther down the hall and phased through a door. Alex and Conner opened the door and walked into the room, but the ghost had vanished. They looked around at the room they had just entered, and a large luxurious four-poster bed pushed against the wall caught their eye—they were in the king and queen's chambers.

"Who are you?" a deep voice called out. King Chase was seated by a fireplace, keeping warm. The twins jumped when they saw him.

"So sorry to disturb you!" Alex said. "We didn't realize we were walking into your private chambers."

The king studied them curiously. "How did you get into the castle?" he asked.

"We were following someone," Alex said.

"Who?" King Chase asked.

Neither of the twins had an answer. "Well, we're not sure who she is exactly," Alex said.

"A pushy ghost, that's who," Conner said under his breath. "She led us through a secret tunnel."

The twins expected the king to look at them like they were crazy, but he did the opposite. "A ghost?" King Chase said. "Is this ghost by chance the spirit of a woman with a flower in her hair?"

"Yes!" Alex said. "Do you know who she is?"

King Chase nodded. "You must have been following the ghost of Old Queen Beauty. She's been haunting this castle for years."

"Queen Beauty?" Conner asked with a confused face. "But we just saw your wife last week—she's alive."

King Chase rested his head on the back of his chair and let out a long sigh of relief. "I am glad to hear that," he said. "I haven't seen or heard from her since she fled the castle—no one has been able to get in or out since the plants attacked."

"So there are two Queen Beautys?" Conner asked.

King Chase stood and walked to a portrait on the wall. It was of a beautiful woman—unmistakably the Lady of the East when she had been alive.

"The ghost is the spirit of my wife's grandmother, Queen Beauty the First, who she was named after," King Chase explained. "Historically speaking, my wife is Queen Beauty the Second; the world just knows her as Sleeping Beauty."

"That's why she looked so familiar," Conner said. "Sleeping Beauty looks just like her grandmother!"

"The ghost only reveals herself to people she thinks can help in a time of need," King Chase said and eyed the twins. "I should know—I would have never kissed Sleeping Beauty and broken the sleeping curse if Queen Beauty hadn't been there to guide me to this castle."

"Interesting," Alex said and studied the portrait.

Beside it was another painting of Queen Beauty standing next to a large animal of some kind. It had thick fur, large claws, and a mane like a lion's.

Wait a second—Beauty! Alex thought. "Is Old Queen Beauty *the Beauty* from the story of *Beauty and the Beast*?"

"Indeed," said a woman's voice. The twins and King Chase turned to see the ghost of Old Queen Beauty floating toward them. "I came to live in the castle when I was a very young woman. I was meant to settle my father's debt with a king cursed to live as hideous beast, but when I fell in love with him the curse was lifted and he became human again."

The twins froze. "You can talk?" Conner asked. "Might have been nice if you explained some of this the *first time* you scared the crap out of us!"

"I apologize for my methods getting you here," Beauty said. "I can only speak when I am in my old home."

Alex was fascinated by the heritage and silently thought on it, trying to make sense of it all.

"So there were two curses in this castle broken by an act of love," Alex said. "What a coincidence."

"That is not a coincidence at all, I'm afraid," Beauty said. "The curses were cast by the same person. *Ezmia*."

Both the twins shook their head in disbelief. They weren't expecting this twist in the story.

"Hold on," Conner said. "*Ezmia* is who turned your husband into the beast?"

The ghost nodded somberly. "Yes," she said. "You see, Ezmia fell in love with my husband long before I met him. When he could not reciprocate her love, she cursed him, thinking no one could ever love a beast."

"And then you broke the spell and years later she cursed your granddaughter," Alex asked.

"Guess she didn't like the name *Beauty*," Conner said with a shrug.

"The Enchantress has cursed every generation of my family," Beauty told them. "She bewitched my son into desiring a wife who could spin hay into gold. He eventually found a maiden who claimed to do so, but only because she made a deal with Rumpelstiltskin to do it for her."

"And Rumpelstiltskin was working for Ezmia at the time," Conner said, piecing everything together. "He spun the hay into gold in exchange for her firstborn child."

"Wait, there's a theme in Ezmia's attacks on your family," Alex said. "They all involve a spinning wheel. But why?"

"Before I came to live in the castle with the beast, my sisters and I spun thread in the village nearby," Beauty said. "Ezmia couldn't stand the fact that my husband chose to love a *spinner* rather than a great fairy like herself. She has forced the spinning wheel upon my family since."

"That takes a lot of effort," Conner said. "Why would she put so much energy into cursing your family because of something that happened so long ago?"

The twins could almost see a small smile appear on the ghost's face—the twins were following her story perfectly.

"Because the Enchantress, above all things, values her *pride*," Beauty said. "And my family has always been a reminder of Ezmia's greatest loss and embarrassment."

The twins felt their hearts skip a beat.

"Her *pride*!" Alex said. "That's it! That's the Enchantress's most prized possession!"

"That's why you brought us here, isn't it?" Conner asked Beauty. "You knew what we needed!"

The ghost of Old Queen Beauty nodded again. King Chase was just as caught up in her story as the twins were—still learning things about the family he married into.

"I have a question," King Chase said. "Is that why you haunt this castle still? Because you're protecting your family against the Enchantress?"

The ghost dismally lowered her head. "In her scheme to take over the world, the Enchantress imprisoned my husband's soul just as she has your grandmother," Beauty said to the twins. "I've walked the earth waiting for his soul to be free so I can be reunited with him on the other side."

"What's up with all the souls?" Conner asked. "Can't she collect stamps or antiques like a normal person?"

"I'm afraid I don't have the answer to that question," Beauty said. "But I've asked someone who will to join us."

The ghost of Old Queen Beauty gestured behind them to the fireplace. Another spirit stepped out from the smoke of the tiny flames. It was the ghost of a short woman who wore a hooded cloak and walked hunched over with a cane. Her face was so wrinkled she looked like a log. She had an incredibly small nose with an enormous mole next to it.

The twins knew who she was without any introduction. Their father had described her perfectly in the journal they followed a year ago.

"Hagatha?" Alex asked. "Is that *you*?"

"Aye," Hagatha said and slowly made her way closer to them.

"Do you know why the Enchantress is collecting souls?" Conner cautiously asked her.

"Aye," Hagatha said. "It's what she needs to create a portal into the Otherworld."

"What?!" Alex asked breathlessly. "What do you mean, 'the Otherworld'?"

"The Enchantress never wanted just *this* world, she always planned on taking over the Otherworld as well," Hagatha said. "It's her home—it's where she was born. It's where her family was killed."

The twins couldn't believe what they were hearing. As if the stakes weren't high enough already, learning that the Enchantress wanted to take over their world, too, made them sick to their stomachs. Their quest suddenly became a mission to save two worlds.

The mayhem she could cause in the Otherworld would be catastrophic compared to the havoc she had committed here.

"But our grandmother is the only person who can travel between worlds," Alex said.

Hagatha and Beauty exchanged a remorseful look. "There is another way," Hagatha said. "It's something I learned when I was a young witch. It was such an extreme spell I never thought anyone would be crazy enough to attempt it—until I met Ezmia."

"And you gave it to her?" Alex asked.

"I met her when she was still a fairy in good standing," Hagatha said in her own defense. "She had been heartbroken a number of times and asked me if I knew how to create a portal so she could go home to the Otherworld. And, not thinking much of it, I made the biggest mistake of my life—*I told her*."

"What was it?" Conner asked.

Hagatha let out a long sigh. "To travel into the Otherworld you must first master the seven deadly sins of this world and conquer its past, present, and future," she said.

It was the most intense collecting spell the twins had ever heard of. "She has to master the seven deadly sins?" Alex asked.

"And conquer this world's past, present, and future?" Conner said. "How does someone do that?"

"Ezmia has spent a long time figuring it out, and unfortunately she's very close to completing it," Hagatha said.

"What are the seven deadly sins again?" Conner asked his sister.

Alex had to think about it. "Lust, envy, pride, greed, gluttony, sloth, and wrath, I believe," she said.

Conner gulped. "Sounds like the Enchantress, all right," he said. "And you said she's close to accomplishing all of that, Hagatha?"

The ghost of the old witch nodded. "Ezmia has imprisoned the souls of her former loves to signify her *lust*. She strips others of their happiness to signify her *envy*. Having Rumpelstiltskin under her command connotes her *sloth*. And as she slowly takes over this world with *greed* and *gluttony*, the world is exposed to the Enchantress's *wrath*, satisfying her *pride*," Hagatha said.

"But how is she conquering this world's past, present, and future?" Alex asked.

"By destroying the kingdom's historical landmarks the Enchantress conquers the *past*," Hagatha explained. "By forcing the rulers to hand over their thrones willingly, Ezmia undeniably holds the power over the *present*. And by kidnapping the heir to a throne of man and the heir to a throne of magic, she encompasses the *future*."

The twins bobbed their heads up and down as they followed along. They looked to King Chase but he was having an even harder time comprehending it all. Every move Ezmia had made from the very beginning had been carefully calculated.

"Princess Hope is the heir to a throne of man," Conner said. "That's why Ezmia kidnapped her and tried kidnapping Sleeping Beauty as a baby!"

"But who is the heir to the throne of magic?" Alex asked.

"*That* is where the Enchantress has made her greatest mistake," Hagatha said, happy to tell them about one advantage they had over the Enchantress. "She has taken the wrong person."

The twins didn't understand what she was telling them at first. Conner looked to his sister as it slowly dawned on him. Alex realized everyone in the room was looking at her.

"*Me?*" Alex asked and pointed to herself. "That's why the Enchantress wanted to kidnap me? She thinks I'm some sort of heir to *magic*?"

"Technically, you are the Fairy Godmother's only heir," Conner said.

"You're her grandchild, too," Alex reminded him. "Shouldn't you qualify as much as me?"

Conner shook his head. "Come on, Alex," he said. "You know I've never wanted to be a fairy. This has always been *your* thing."

Alex shook her head and looked to the floor, not wanting to believe it. "No, there has to be some sort of mistake," she said. "I want to be a fairy as much as the next girl—but I can't be the *next Fairy Godmother.*"

"Didn't the unicorns bow to you when you came to this world?" Beauty asked.

"Well, yes, but what does that have to do with anything?" Alex asked.

"The unicorns only bow to those that magic is strong with," Hagatha said. "Ezmia knew that if anyone could stop her, it would be another woman of both worlds with magic in her blood."

"Which is why Grandma made such a big deal about protecting us," Conner said. "She knew Ezmia would be coming after you! I bet she's known you were going to fill her shoes since you activated her *Land of Stories* book."

Alex kept trying to deny it to herself, but what they were saying was making sense. It was such a huge reality to face, but an even bigger burden to bear. Had the situation been different, it would have been the most wonderful news she had ever heard in her life, but they were talking as if she was now singlehandedly responsible for defeating the Enchantress.

"You have to get back to the others," said another voice in the room. They all turned to see a third ghost appear. She was young and pretty, but shy and kept her distance. There was something about her presence and her voice that was so familiar to the twins, but they had so many things to think about, they couldn't think exactly who she reminded them of.

"This room is getting more crowded by the minute," Conner said. "Who are *you*?"

The new ghost took a moment to answer, as if she wanted to remain anonymous. "They called me Gloria when I was alive," she said, but quickly changed the subject. "You've been gone for hours and your friends have started to worry. The Enchantress is planning another attack soon—you must return to them and finish building the Wand."

"Wait, how do you know about the Wand?" Conner asked.

The ghost of Gloria went quiet. "I know you are much closer to finishing it than you think," she said softly, almost sad to say it. "Now you must hurry—Ezmia is planning to strike very soon."

"She's right," Beauty said. She floated past the twins and headed to the door. "It's time you headed back to the troll and goblin camp."

The twins nodded, not wanting to cause Bob and the others to worry any more than they had already.

"Children," King Chase said before they left his room, "if you see my wife, please tell her I love her."

"No," Conner said. "But you can tell her yourself when you see her next."

He and King Chase shared a hopeful smile.

"Best of luck to you both," the king said.

The twins followed the ghost of Old Queen Beauty out of the room. She escorted them down the spiral staircase, through the stables, and into the secret passage. The twins ran down through the tunnel as fast as they could, reaching the other ladder in half the time it took them to get there.

They quickly hurried through the trees, over the streams, and across the hills and finally reached the woods alongside the campsite as the sun began to rise. They turned back to the ghost of Old Queen Beauty.

"Thank you," Alex said. "You helped us so much."

The ghost silently nodded her head and then disappeared. They could tell she was just as grateful to them as they were to her.

The twins ran through the campsite and found Bob and Froggy sitting at the campfire outside the tent.

"That was the longest walk I've ever heard of!" Bob exclaimed when he saw them. "Where have you been?"

"We were worried sick!" Froggy said and leaped to his feet.

"We were in the Eastern Kingdom," Conner panted. "We have so much to tell you guys!"

Alex looked around. "Where is everyone, anyway?" she asked.

Froggy and Bob looked to each other with sorrowful eyes. The twins instantly knew something bad must have happened while they were gone.

"What's wrong?" Conner asked.

Froggy didn't know how to explain. "Come have a look for yourselves," he said.

He led the twins inside the tent. Inside the twins saw Jack kneeling sadly on the ground; Goldilocks was standing at his side, gently rubbing his back. Red sat next to Jack and cuddled Clawdius tightly in her arms.

"What happened?" Alex asked.

"It's the harp," Goldilocks said. "She's gone."

"What do you mean she's gone?" Conner asked.

"She's part of the Wand now," Jack said. "We came into the tent and found it like *this*."

Jack was clutching the Wand of Wonderment. It had a shiny new golden tint to it now—the exact shade of the harp.

Red used part of Goldilocks's coat as a handkerchief to blow her nose. "Poor dear," she said. "I suppose the singer has taken her final bow."

"I never thought we would lose her completely to it," Jack said, fighting back the emotion that suddenly rushed through him. "I wish we could have had more time to figure out a better way."

Alex and Conner looked to each other and knew exactly what the other was thinking.

"*Gloria,*" Conner whispered to Alex. "*The harp's name was Gloria.*"

Alex watched over her sad friends and took a step toward them, deciding now was the best time to tell them what they had learned from the spirits in Sleeping Beauty's castle.

"The harp's loss won't be in vain," she said. "We finally know what we need to defeat the Enchantress."

CHAPTER TWENTY-FIVE

ROCK, ROOT, AND RAGE

The golden arches and pillars of the Fairy Palace could barely contain the anxieties growing inside them. The seven colorful fairies of the Fairy Council paced around the main hall away from their respected podiums, desperately trying to come up with an overdue solution to the crisis at hand.

"A whole territory has been destroyed!" Xanthous said. The flames on his head and shoulders were flickering wildly. "We need to find her!"

"Every corner of every kingdom has been searched twice, and there still is no trace of her," said Emerelda.

"But what would we do if we found her?" Skylene asked. "We're no match for the Enchantress."

"Our magic is useless against hers," Rosette added. "And she grows more powerful every day."

"But we must do something—anything!" Xanthous demanded. "The world is counting on us!"

Tangerina had grown tired of his complaining; even her bees were irritated and flew around her beehive with their stingers out. "Then why don't you think of something to do?" she said. "We've all been in here for days trying to come up with a practical solution—it's not like we're keeping anything from you."

"If we can't come up with a practical solution, then I suggest we come up with an *impractical solution*," Xanthous half-heartedly suggested. "Let's fight her at her own game. Who cares about honoring our fairy values?"

The flames on Xanthous's shoulders flickered faster as he thought about it.

"The world has always looked to us to handle its troubles with peace and understanding. We cannot abandon those morals now—that's what the Enchantress *wants*," Emerelda said. "You can't extinguish a fire by adding more flame. You of all people should know that, Xanthous."

"Then if we can't use our magic to stop her, let's gather all the witches and warlocks from the Dwarf Forests and Pinocchio Prison and have *them* defeat her!" he proposed.

Emerelda massaged her forehead. "You want to set loose the witches and warlocks that *we* imprisoned?" she asked him.

Xanthous's flames diminished and he slumped. She didn't have to elaborate for him to realize how bad an idea this was.

"Any more bright ideas?" Tangerina asked him.

Xanthous turned to respond to her but had nothing to say. They were at a dead end.

"What if we can't come up with an answer?" Coral asked in a tiny voice, cuddling her pet walking fish. "Will all of us perish if we can't stop her?"

The situation had finally reached a point that forced them to consider the consequences of failing. Emerelda eyed her fellow fairies, angered by their sudden hopelessness.

"Shame on all of you," Emerelda said and walked around the room. She stared directly into each of their eyes as she passed them. "We are the *Fairy Council*—if we lose our hope, all hope for the rest of the world is as good as gone. We cannot spend a moment humoring thoughts of failure. As long as someone remains standing with a noble heart there will *always* be a way for good to triumph over evil."

The other fairies looked around at one another, inspired by Emerelda's words. Moments like these were the reason why Emerelda was the head of the Fairy Council.

A small magenta flame abruptly appeared on the floor of the main hall. It came out of thin air and didn't appear to be burning anything but the air around it. Emerelda gazed down at it and cautiously stepped away. "Brace yourselves," she said, and her green eyes grew large. "We're about to have company."

With a giant blast, the purple flame rapidly grew into a roaring magenta fire that covered the majority of the room. The fairies screamed and shielded themselves from the blaze. A split second later, the flames vanished and the Enchantress appeared.

The fairies froze with fear. Ezmia always knew how to make an entrance.

"It's good to be home!" Ezmia laughed and looked around the room at all the frightened faces of her old peers. "For people who thought I was dead, you never look happy to see me."

Emerelda was the only fairy brave enough to address her. "Why have you come here, Ezmia?"

The Enchantress ignored the question. "Oh, look," Ezmia said happily. She strutted to a forgotten golden chair that had been pushed to the side of the room. "It's my old seat from when I was on the Fairy Council. Remember those days?"

"You've certainly shown your true colors since," Emerelda said.

"You act as if you're all so faultless," Ezmia sneered. "I can see right through that pathetic façade of a perfect loving family. I know how spiteful you can be when no one is looking. I sat in this room for hours every day trying to make the world a better place just as much as the rest of you—but why did you target me with your cruelty? Why was *I* treated so poorly by the people who were supposed to be perfect?"

"Because you became vindictive," Emerelda said.

"No," Ezmia said and shook her head. "It was because I became *better*. I was more powerful, more gifted, and more liked than any of you could ever be. When the Fairy Godmother announced me as her heir, you acted as if I had done something horrible to you. She put me on a pedestal and you all isolated me there."

"As your ability grew, so did your ego," Emerelda said.

"You thought you were above us—you even renounced your title as a fairy."

"*You're* the ones who renounced me long before I ever did," Ezmia said and glared at her. "You ignored me, excluded me, and hated me from the minute I arrived. The world may be convinced you had nothing to do with my *change of career*, but I will always know the truth. You made it impossible for me to be anything but disdained."

The Enchantress ran a finger on the arm of her old chair, remembering all the painful memories of her time as a fairy.

"The cruelest thing you can do to someone is force them to *hurt* alone—and you left me hurting on my own many times," Ezmia said. "Every time I was heartbroken, I would go to the rest of you hoping to receive some compassion, but you let your jealousies get in the way of showing any sympathy. You actually enjoyed watching me suffer, relishing the fact that *something* was distressing me."

Emerelda surprised the Enchantress and the other fairies with what she said next—*she didn't deny it.*

"I admit that even we were guilty of being less than perfect at times," Emerelda said. "But as we've grown from our mistakes, your mistakes have only grown."

Ezmia snorted and slowly clapped in Emerelda's direction. "Touché," the Enchantress said. "You managed to admit you were wrong *and* scold me in one breath. You're good at this leadership thing, Em. No wonder they replaced me with you."

"I was not a replacement," Emerelda said. "You were never what this council needed."

"No, I was never what this council *wanted*," Ezmia said sharply. "They chose you, Emerelda, because you were more *beautiful*, and the world always listens to a pretty face over an average one. And even though I changed my appearance and gained beauty over time, they still chose you over me because you were easier to control. You were the Fairy Godmother's puppet I could never be."

Emerelda returned her scornful stare. "I'd rather be a toy than a tyrant, Ezmia," she said. "But I'm assuming you didn't come here to reminisce, so what brings you to our kingdom?"

A small grin appeared on the Enchantress's face. She was delighted to get a rise out of the fairy.

"The truth is, I've become rather bored waiting for you and the other rulers to gradually hand their kingdoms over to me," Ezmia said, taking a seat on her old chair. "I've decided to invite them all to the new home I'm building for myself and get it all over with. I'm anxious for this whole thing to conclude as much as you all are."

"None of us are going anywhere with you," Xanthous said, and his flames rose.

A cunning smirk grew on the Enchantress's face. "Oh yes, you are," Ezmia said. "It's not an option."

The Enchantress snapped her fingers and the ground started to rumble with the power of a dozen earthquakes. All the fairies looked to one another, petrified of what was coming their way. Clusters of vines exploded out of the floor and seized the fairies in the room.

They desperately tried to free themselves—struggling against the plants with all their might and all their magic, but it was no use. The plants were too strong to escape. Ezmia roared with laughter as she watched the vines coil around each Fairy Council member and drag them into the ground.

Emerelda sank her hands into the ground to prevent the vines from dragging her away. *"You won't win, Ezmia,"* she said.

"Oh, but I will," the Enchantress said, looking down at her with a smile in her eyes. "You see, I'm finally building my *own* pedestal. But this time, rather than admiration, I'm building it from rock, root, and *rage*."

Things were gloomy as ever at the Charming Palace. All the other rulers had gone home after the Happily Ever After Assembly meeting except for Sleeping Beauty, who had no choice but to stay. She sat with Cinderella in her chambers, quietly comforting the distraught mother.

"It's been almost two weeks since that horrible woman took my daughter away from me," Cinderella said. "I never thought I could feel like this inside. I never thought I could be so miserable."

Sleeping Beauty dabbed the tears spilling from her friend's tired eyes.

"You have to stay strong, Cinderella," Sleeping Beauty said. "We have to be brave for our people."

Cinderella blew her nose into a handkerchief. "But who

is supposed to be brave for us at a time like this?" she asked. "When the rest of the world is looking to us for strength and guidance, who do we look up to for reassurance?"

Sleeping Beauty gently took Cinderella's hand in her own. "We have to inspire each other," she said.

Cinderella patted her friend's hand and placed her head on Sleeping Beauty's shoulder. There was a knock at the door.

"Come in," Cinderella said.

Sir Lampton stepped into the queen's chambers. His face was so long the queens knew he wasn't bearing good news.

"What is it, Sir Lampton?" Cinderella asked, bracing herself for whatever it was.

"More bad news, I'm afraid, Your Majesty," he said. "I just received a letter from Sir Grant in the Northern Kingdom. Apparently the Enchantress attacked the Northern Kingdom last night after attacking Troll and Goblin Territory. They woke up this morning to discover all their crops have been poisoned."

"Dear God," Sleeping Beauty said and placed a hand on her chest. "Does the Enchantress have no soul?"

"Queen Snow White has asked that we send what we can," Lampton added.

"Yes, of course," Cinderella said. "Gather as much food as the kingdom can spare—"

The ground under the palace began to shake. Cinderella's chambers rattled as something moved through the palace toward her chambers.

"What on earth?" Lampton said, staring down at the floor

as it began to crack under his feet. He retrieved his sword, although it was useless against what was coming.

Vines burst through the floor and slithered up to Queen Cinderella and Queen Sleeping Beauty. They wrapped around them and dragged them back from where they had come from. Sir Lampton tried rescuing the queens but it had all happened too quickly to prevent.

He looked through the cracks in the floor; he could see the vines dragging the screaming queens several floors through the palace and into the ground where they disappeared out of sight.

The ground began to rumble again, this time not from something directly below the palace but from something much farther in the distance. Lampton ran over the cracks to a window to see what was causing all the commotion.

Miles away, in the northern part of the Charming Kingdom, a gargantuan pillar made of rock, roots, and dirt emerged from the ground and rocketed into the air. The land cracked and elevated unevenly for miles and miles around it. The pillar grew higher and higher, only stopping once it had reached the clouds.

A massive coliseum was on the top of the pillar, constructed of enormous jagged stones shaped like arrowheads. Vines and thornbushes grew up the sides of the pillar, taking with them all the rulers they had seized from around the world.

The Enchantress sat in the center of the coliseum on her old Fairy Council chair like it was a throne. The plants arrived with her guests and pinned them around to the walls at various heights and angles around her. The abducted kings, queens, and fairies were now prisoners in Ezmia's vengeful, earthy web.

True to her word, the Enchantress had built herself a pedestal made of the deepest parts of the earth, powered by the deepest anger of her soul.

Chapter Twenty-Six

THE ENCHANTRESS'S MOST PRIZED POSSESSION

The ground began to tremble and quake under the campsite.

"What's happening?!" Conner yelled.

"It's the Enchantress!" Alex screamed. "She's starting her final attack!"

As if tiny explosions were being set off around the camp, bouquets of devilish vines burst through the ground and slithered through the site. They knocked over tents and people as they moved—as if they were *searching* for something.

Jack and Goldilocks immediately drew their weapons and began slicing the demonic plants, but there were too many of them to fight off.

"Help!" The twins heard a high-pitched scream behind them. They turned around and saw the vines tangle around Red and attempt to drag her back into the ground with them. *"Someone help me!"*

Jack and Froggy both ran to her, throwing themselves on the ground and reaching a hand toward her. Red was almost all the way underground.... Only one of her hands was free. She looked to Jack and then to Froggy. If these were the last moments of her life, she had to decide right then and there who she wanted to spend them with....

Red grabbed hold of Froggy's hand. He was shocked to see her hand land in his.

"You chose *me*..." Froggy said, looking into her eyes. Both of them recognized the significance of this moment.

"Yes, I *choose* you," Red said, and a small smile appeared on her face. She pulled him a little closer and kissed his slimy green lips, not repulsed by his appearance or texture whatsoever.

The vines climbed over Red and began wrapping around Froggy, too. Jack grabbed hold of one of his legs and Goldilocks grabbed the other. The vines were too strong for them to pull Froggy and Red free, but Jack and Goldilocks weren't giving up. The vines moved past Froggy and began growing around the whole group, pulling all four of them toward the ground.

Alex and Conner were on their way to help when they heard another cry.

"Butterboy!" Trollbella yelled from across the camp. The vines had wrapped around her and were dragging her into the ground, too.

Conner grunted and looked around. "Can someone else save Trollbella?" he called out, but all the other trolls and goblins were too afraid of the vines to go near her.

"Save me, Butterboy!" Trollbella cried.

"Okay, fine! I'm coming!" Conner yelled. He and Alex changed their course and ran for the young Troll Queen instead.

Conner grabbed Trollbella's hands and Alex grabbed Conner's feet. They tried to pull her free but the vines were too strong.

"This would be so romantic if it weren't for the possessed plants pulling us apart, Butterboy," Trollbella whispered dreamily into Conner's ear.

The vines began to creep past Trollbella and onto Conner, pulling him with her.

"Alex, you have to let go of me!" Conner yelled behind himself. "You can't let the vines get you."

"I'm not letting you go, Conner!" Alex yelled back.

"You have to save the fairy-tale world, Alex!" Conner said. "You have to save the Otherworld and Mom, too!"

Alex's grip around her brother's feet tightened. "I can't save anything without you," she said.

"Yes, you can," he said. "It was always meant to be you!

You're the one who got us here and you're the one who is going to get us out! You heard the ghosts—you're the heir of magic! You've got to defeat the Enchantress so this world can go on!"

The vines had wrapped almost completely around Conner. Alex was shaking her head profusely.

"I can't do it alone!" she said, terrified to lose him.

"Yes, you can," Conner said. "I'm really sorry about this!"

Conner kicked Alex off of him and the vines consumed him entirely. They dragged him and Trollbella down into the ground and disappeared.

"Conner!" Alex yelled after him, but it was no use. He was gone.

Alex looked across the camp just in time to see the vines pull Red, Froggy, Jack, and Goldilocks into the ground with one final heave. As soon as Trollbella, Red, and the others clinging on to them had been taken, all the vines in the campsite disappeared into the ground. *They had come for the queens.*

Alex got to her feet and looked around in shock. In a matter of minutes, all of her friends and her brother had been taken from her. She had no choice but to finish their quest alone—*it was all up to her now.*

Bob ran up to Alex. "Where have they been taken?"

Alex was wondering the same thing. She looked down at the large cracks the vines had left in the ground. They weren't just in the campsite, but stretched off into the distance, as if the vines had left marks on their way to and from their destination.

"I have to go," Alex said. She ran to their tent and retrieved the Wand of Wonderment. She placed it in the troll's satchel and threw it over her shoulder. Alex ran off into the distance, following the cracks in the ground as if they were a trail.

"Where are you going?" Bob asked as he ran after her, but she didn't respond. *"Alex?!"* He tried chasing after her, but she was a third his age and ran three times as fast as him.

Alex never stopped running. Her feet hit the ground in rhythm with her racing heartbeat. She was fueled by adrenaline but mostly by fear. She could have sworn she heard Red's screams and Conner's shouts as they were dragged under the ground below her.

She prayed she would get to the Enchantress before she could harm her brother or the others, and wished with all her might that once she got there she would have a plan to take Ezmia's most prized possession away from her.

Alex had to think of a way to steal Ezmia's pride, not only for a moment, but for the rest of her life. What could she say or do to her that the Enchantress would take to heart and not brush off? How could Alex emotionally scar Ezmia so deeply that her pride would never return completely?

Could an evil enchantress take to heart anything that was done or said by a thirteen-year-old girl? Ezmia had spent a century imprisoning the souls of kings, soldiers, and fairies in jars—was someone like Alex capable of leaving a mark on someone like that?

Then, like a flash of lightning, Alex realized something for the first time—what she thought of as a disadvantage was actually in her favor. It was *because* she was a thirteen-year-old that she had a greater chance of bruising the Enchantress's ego. If *Alex* could muster up enough courage to say something to the Enchantress that a king or fairy never had the bravery to before, perhaps it would have an even greater effect on her.

Alex had to choose her words wisely, though. She had to get straight to the point and straight to the punch; the Enchantress wouldn't be listening for very long.

It had to work, because Alex had run out of ideas and out of time. After following the cracks in the ground for hours, Alex found herself staring up in horror at the Enchantress's new home in the Charming Kingdom.

The vines dragged Queen Red and Queen Trollbella and the people who clutched on to them for miles and miles underground. They reached the Charming Kingdom and were pulled up the sides of a massive pillar of earth and into the menacing coliseum on top of it. The vines instantly pinned the newcomers to the walls.

Froggy was hung upside down next to Red. Jack and Goldilocks were pinned together, each with their weapon hand behind them. Conner scanned the coliseum and was sad to see they weren't alone.

Hung across the wall from top to bottom were Queen Snow White and King Chandler, Queen Cinderella and King Chance, Queen Sleeping Beauty and King Chase, Queen Rapunzel, and the members of the Fairy Council. And now, with the inclusion of Red and Trollbella, the entire Happily Ever After Assembly was at the Enchantress's mercy.

"Oh good, we're all here," Ezmia said upon Red and Troll-bella's arrival.

The Enchantress sat imperially on her golden throne. Her hair and cape flowed around her more aggressively than ever. Rumpelstiltskin peeked out from behind the throne, looking regretfully at all the confined monarchs around the room.

A large crater was indented in the floor, with a small magenta fire burning a pile of skulls like firewood in the center of it. Six glass turquoise jars were placed in a line in front of the Enchantress—Conner knew his grandmother was trapped inside one of them. And to Conner's horror, as he looked around the room, his grandmother wasn't the only member of his family being held prisoner in the coliseum.

Pinned to the wall across from him in a giant birdcage was Conner's mother. She cradled Princess Hope in her arms; the child's cries echoed through the coliseum. The toddler princess could see her mother tangled in the vines beside her and reached through the bars of the cage toward her.

"Mama!" Princess Hope cried.

"It's all going to be all right, darling," Cinderella said, hoping it wasn't a lie.

Charlotte's jaw dropped and the little color in her face drained away as soon as she saw her son.

"Conner?" she mouthed, so thrilled yet so terrified to see him in such a horrible place.

"Mom!" he silently mouthed back.

"Where's your sister?" she asked.

Conner wasn't sure what the best answer was to give her. "Safe," he decided to say.

Ezmia stood at her throne. "Let's begin, shall we?" she said. The Enchantress gazed around the coliseum with her index finger pressed tightly to her lips, as if she was a little girl in a candy shop.

"Let's start with the Charming Kingdom," Ezmia said.

The vines began to rustle. The plants hoisted Cinderella and King Chance off of the walls and forced them both into a kneeling position on the ground in front of the crater.

"You soulless monster!" Cinderella yelled up at her.

"Let our daughter go!" King Chance demanded.

"If you want your daughter back, then renounce your throne and hand your kingdom over to me," Ezmia said to him, as if it were a simple decision.

"You will never have my kingdom!" King Chance yelled.

The Enchantress glared at him through her long lashes. "Fine," she said. Ezmia snapped her fingers and her vines reached through the cage and pulled Princess Hope out of Charlotte's arms. The child was screaming; tears and snot ran down her terrified face. The vines dangled the princess over the flames of the fire.

"No!" Cinderella screamed. *"Do it, Chance, just do it!"* she begged her husband.

King Chance looked to all the other kings and queens around the room, but no one pleaded with him otherwise. The world they had tried to protect with honor and integrity was long gone.

"Very well," King Chance said. "I renounce my throne and my kingdom to you, Ezmia."

As he spoke these words, the Enchantress threw back her

head and her victorious laugh filled the coliseum. The flames in the crater grew higher and a trail of thick black smoke began to fill the sky.

"Now, was that so hard?" Ezmia asked with a large grin. She snapped her fingers again and the vines dropped Princess Hope into her mother's arms. The family was only reunited for a moment before the vines jerked them back against the wall.

"Let's move on to the Fairy Kingdom," Ezmia said with a bright smile.

The vines brought the seven fairies off the wall and to the edge of the crater.

"You know what to say, Emerelda," Ezmia said and leisurely inspected her nails. "Make it quick so we can finish this at a decent hour—or do you need further persuasion as well?"

The vines wrapped around the jar containing the Fairy Godmother's soul and held it over the fire. All the fairies shouted for it to be released.

"If it makes your cruel wrath come to an end any sooner, *fine*. I hand over the Fairy Kingdom to you," Emerelda said, against her will.

The flame in the crater grew even higher and the black smoke thickened. Ezmia closed her eyes and soaked up the moment for all it was worth. Her whole body tingled with triumph. She had waited centuries for this, and it was all finally happening.

One by one, the Enchantress called the monarchs before her and forced them to give up their kingdoms. Snow White, Sleeping Beauty, Rapunzel, and Trollbella all renounced their thrones with teary eyes and heavy hearts. And with each surrender, the magenta flames rose higher and higher and the smoke condensed.

"I just have one thing to say before you put me back on the wall," Trollbella said, begrudgingly staring at Ezmia with intense eyes. "You stopped my dancing, and you will *never* be forgiven."

The Enchantress, along with every other person in the coliseum, stared oddly at the small Troll Queen, not knowing what to make of her statement. Finally, there was only one ruler left to relinquish her throne.

"Last but certainly not least, I call Queen Red Riding Hood of the Red Riding Hood Kingdom to the floor."

Red gave a small squeal at the sound of her name. The vines lifted her to the front of the crater. Froggy fought desperately against the vines hanging him as she was moved.

"Queen Red, do you willingly surrender your kingdom to me?" the Enchantress asked, as if she already counted on Red's submission.

Red looked up at Froggy and at Jack and Goldilocks for strength. She knew that with her renunciation the Enchantress would have successfully conquered the world.

"Well," Red peeped, "I'm not sure I'm in a position to do that."

All trace of accomplishment vanished from Ezmia's face. As if it weren't already impossibly high, the tension in the coliseum grew.

"Excuse me?" Ezmia asked with a terrifying scowl.

Red went pale.

"It's easy to explain," Red said. Her hands trembled as she spoke. "Unlike everyone else here, I'm an *elected* queen. My kingdom doesn't necessarily belong to me; it belongs to all the Hoodians."

Conner, Jack, Froggy, and Goldilocks were beaming proudly at her. Even if Red had only bought them a minute, it was a minute not owned by the Enchantress.

Ezmia continued to gaze frighteningly at Red and contemplate her next move. "Very well," she said. "I'll just have every last person in your kingdom killed until you're the only one left."

"No!" Red yelled. *"I lied! I'm the only one with the true authority! It's called the Red Riding Hood Kingdom, not the Hoodian Republic!"*

The evil smirk came back to the Enchantress's face. "Then I suggest you proceed," she demanded.

Red's eyes filled with tears; she'd never thought she would be robbed of her own most prized possession on the journey— her *kingdom*.

"I, Queen Red . . ." Red started, but her voice trailed off.

"Yes, get on with it," Ezmia ordered.

"I . . . I . . . I . . ." Red continued with difficulty. "I willingly hand over my kingdom to—"

"HEY, EZMIA!" said a voice behind Red. Everyone looked up to see Alex at the front of the coliseum. She was panting and sweaty; she had just *climbed* up the pillar.

"Alex!" Charlotte gasped.

The Enchantress was infuriated to be interrupted when Red was so close to finishing. "Who is *this*?!" she asked Rumpelstiltskin.

"I don't know," Rumpelstiltskin said. "I've never seen her before."

Alex made her way farther into the coliseum. She was out of breath and so tired from the climb she could barely stand.

"Little girl, if I were you I would turn back around and throw myself to the ground," Ezmia yelled. "Trust me, it'll be much less painful than what I'm about to do to—"

"I'M NOT AFRAID OF YOU!" Alex yelled.

The coliseum went dead silent; even the fire seemed to burn quieter.

"What did you say?" the Enchantress said blankly.

Alex knew the time had come to leave her mark, and she didn't have much time to leave it in. "I said I'm not afraid of you," she repeated. "I've dealt with girls like you my entire life—you want *everything* because *nothing* will make you happy! You're not an all-powerful and terrifying *enchantress*, Ezmia—you're just a *brat*! And no matter who you kill or what you conquer, people will always pity and laugh at you because of it!"

The entire coliseum held its breath. Ezmia maintained her stoic expression but everyone knew she was outraged beyond belief, because her hair flickered violently above her head and small flames burned straight out of her eyes.

The Enchantress left her throne and slowly strolled over to Alex. Alex reached into her satchel—she could feel the Wand of Wonderment activate itself in her hand. She had succeeded in taking Ezmia's pride.

"Well, I hope that little display was worth it," Ezmia said. "Because it's the last thing you'll ever do." The Enchantress pointed her finger at her, and with a bright violet flash, Alex was blasted out of the coliseum and into the sky.

"ALLLEEEXXX!" Conner screamed from on the wall.

It happened so fast Alex wasn't sure what had happened. The last thing she heard was her brother's scream; the last thing she saw was a bright flash and then the coliseum suddenly becoming smaller and smaller as she soared farther and farther into the air.

Everything around her—her sight, her sound, and all her other senses—went black. It was as if Alex had fallen into a very, very deep sleep....

CHAPTER TWENTY-SEVEN

———◆◆◆———

THE DREAM

Alex slowly opened her eyes one at a time. She was lying on the ground facing a dark ceiling. She didn't know where she was and didn't remember how she had gotten there, but got to her feet to look around.

Alex was standing in a dark cave. A lantern was on the ground beside her. She picked it up and journeyed deeper into the cave. There was something about this place that Alex found very comforting. Despite its darkness and mystery, for whatever reason she knew she was safe.

Up ahead she saw a light. She continued toward the light

and two large boulders came into view. Two little girls were standing on top of the boulders and two were standing beside them. As she got closer, she was able to make out what they were wearing.

The first little girl wore a sweater, a skirt, and a headband, just like Alex. The second little girl wore a long nightgown and no shoes. The third little girl wore a puffy dress with an apron over it. The fourth little girl had braided pigtails and wore silver shoes.

All four of the girls stared blankly at Alex, as if they were waiting for her to say something.

"Who are you?" Alex asked the girls with a smile.

"You know who we are," the little girl in the nightgown said.

Alex raised the lantern higher and took a second look at them. "I do?" she asked. "How do we know each other?"

"You know us, but we don't know you," said the girl in the silver shoes. She spoke with an adorable twang in her voice.

"I'm afraid I don't," Alex said.

"You'll figure it out if you think about it long enough," said the girl in the sweater in a charming British accent.

"You all look very familiar," Alex admitted. "It's as if I've met you before or seen you in a movie or read about you..." Alex gasped. "Wait a second—*are you who I think you are*?"

The girls shared the same amused smile.

"Hello, I'm Lucy Pevensie," said the girl in the sweater and curtsied.

"I'm Alice," said the girl in the apron.

"I'm Dorothy Gale," said the girl with braids.

"And I'm Wendy Darling, darling," the one in the night-gown said.

Alex couldn't believe what she was seeing. "But you're the girls I grew up reading about," she said. "I used to pretend I was you when I was little. All I ever wanted was to be one of you and escape into my own magical world...."

"Sounds like you got what you wanted," Alice said.

Alex lowered her head and looked at the floor. Alice was right, but it was impossible for Alex to be happy about it anymore.

"What's the matter, dear?" Wendy asked.

Alex sighed. "I used to think of the Land of Stories as a paradise; it was my own personal safe haven," she told them. "But now an evil enchantress has taken over all the kingdoms."

"Oh my," said Lucy. "Sounds like the White Witch!"

"Worse," Alex said, and put it into terms they could understand. "She's got the White Witch's greed, the Wicked Witch of the West's anger, the Queen of Hearts' temper, and Captain Hook's vengeance."

All the girls shook their heads and showed their sympathy.

"That's horrible," Wendy said.

"Greed, and anger, and temper, oh my!" Dorothy said. "Can you melt her?"

"I wish," Alex said with a laugh.

"Can Aslan prance on her?" Lucy asked.

"No, unfortunately," Alex said.

"Can you feed her to a crocodile?" Wendy asked.

"I don't think so," Alex said.

"But then how are you going to defeat her?" Alice asked.

"My friends and I are building a powerful wand," Alex said. She excitedly reached for the satchel to show them, but it wasn't around her shoulder. "Oh no, where's my wand? I just had it a second ago."

She moved the lantern around, scanning the ground of the cave looking for a place she may have dropped it. The other girls giggled at her attempts. Alex looked up at them and slowly realized why they found her efforts so amusing.

"Is this a dream or am I dead?" she asked.

"Of course it's a dream," Lucy said.

"Why else do you think we're here?" Alice asked.

"I hope a big cave isn't what you think heaven looks like," Dorothy said.

Alex was happy to hear it. "The last thing I remember was being blasted into the sky," she said. "But how did I survive the fall?"

"Did your wand save you?" Lucy asked.

"Of course!" Alex exclaimed. "The Wand makes whoever is holding it invincible! It was in my hand the entire time! The Enchantress didn't kill me after all!"

The girls cheered, but then Dorothy went silent.

"Are you going to *kill* the Enchantress with the Wand now?" Dorothy asked.

Alex hadn't really thought about that. She had been so concerned with getting the Wand finished, she had never thought about what she would do *after* the Wand was made. How was she going to go about defeating the Enchantress with the Wand? Was she going to have to kill her with it? Was Alex even capable of killing someone? She always figured Jack or Goldilocks would do it if that was what was needed.

"I suppose I don't have a choice," Alex said.

"I'd recommend finding another way if there is one," Dorothy said with a sad look on her face. "Even though melting the witch was an accident, I've felt awful about it ever since."

What Dorothy said resonated with Alex more than she was letting on. She didn't want to hurt anyone—but how could she stop Ezmia without killing her? Would Ezmia just find another way to cheat death like she had after Evly poisoned her?

"I don't have to necessarily *kill* Ezmia," Alex said, thinking out loud. "I just have to take away her *powers*... and her powers come from a place of *hate* and *anger*... so if I took away the reasons that validated her right to be *angry*... she would be *powerless*!"

Alex excitedly jumped up and down, pleased to have come up with an alternative way. The girls clapped for her.

"Violence is never the answer," Wendy said. "I always try to tell John and Michael that when they play in the nursery, but they never listen to me."

"When you figure out how to take away her hate and anger, would you let me know?" Alice asked. "I'd like to know in case I run into the Queen of Hearts again."

Alex went silent as the wheels in her head were turning. "I think I know how to do it," she said and her eyes darted back and forth from one side to the other. "And I may not even need the Wand to do it after all..."

"So you just finished a huge journey only to find out what you needed was with you all along?" Dorothy asked. *"Been there."*

Alex thought about it. The Wand might not have been the *solution*, but it was still useful; it still had saved her life. It had also given them *hope*, and without that they would have been lost for sure.

She looked up at the girls and around the cave. "Now I understand the meaning of this dream," she said. "Deep down I knew I could never kill the Enchantress, so I was searching for another way. The cave represents my questioning and you represent the answer—because ever since I was a little girl I've always thought about you when I had a problem."

"Why is that?" Alice asked her.

"I suppose I've learned so much from you," Alex said. "I always wanted to be as loving as Wendy, or as curious as Alice, or as brave as Lucy, or as adventurous as Dorothy—I always saw a little bit of myself when I read about each of you."

All the girls smiled at her. "We're happy we could help," Lucy said.

"And we'll always be here if you need us," Wendy said.

Alex nodded thankfully to them.

"Is there anything else on your mind we could help you with?" Dorothy asked. "Since we happen to be lingering in your subconscious?"

"Actually, now that you mention it, there is something I've always wanted to ask you if I ever got the chance," Alex said. She didn't know what had caused her to believe she would ever have the chance to ask literary characters a question, but she asked them nonetheless. "After seeing amazing magical places like Neverland, Oz, Narnia, and Wonderland, why did you ever want to leave?"

The girls looked to one another; they had never been asked the question before, at least in Alex's mind.

"Because no matter where you go or what you see, you'll always want to be where you belong," Lucy said.

"Your home is where you feel most comfortable and loved," Wendy said.

"It's a part of you," Alice added. "It's where your family is."

"There's no place like home," Dorothy said, as if it was the first time she'd ever said those words.

Alex appreciated what they had to say, but wasn't sure if she entirely agreed. "I wonder, though, if *home* sometimes isn't where you're *from*," she said.

The girls looked at her as if she had already answered her own question. Alex wondered if *that* had been the real question lingering in her mind all along.

"Alex? Alex?" said a familiar voice. Alex looked all around the cave but couldn't tell where it was coming from.

"What's happening?" Alex asked the girls, but they had disappeared.

"Alex! Are you hurt? Please wake up!" the voice pleaded, and the more it did, the more the cave around her disappeared.

Alex awoke on the ground; this time she was outside. She saw the sky and the tops of trees above her, as well as the face of a concerned and balding man looking down at her.

"Bob?" Alex asked and sat up.

"*You're alive!*" Bob said with teary eyes and hugged her. "*It's a miracle! I just saw you fall from the sky!* You might be in shock—let me check your heart!"

Bob grabbed hold of Alex's wrist and checked her pulse. "I wonder if there's an intensive care unit somewhere in this kingdom," he said.

"Bob, I'm fine—*look*," Alex said. Her hand was still clutching the Wand. "It's the Wand of Wonderment! I was holding on to it and it saved me!"

Bob looked at her like she was speaking a different language. "Is it wrong that I'm still surprised by all of this?"

Alex jumped to her feet. She could see the Enchantress's pillar in the distance. The sky above it was filling more and more with the black smoke from the fire.

"I've got to get back there," Alex said.

"*Back* there?" Bob asked in amazement. "Wait—are you telling me that's where you fell from?"

"Yes, and now I have to get back," Alex said. "I just don't have time to go by foot."

"Then how are you supposed to get there?" Bob said.

Alex looked down at the Wand and then back to him. "I think I have an idea," she said, and a sly smile appeared on her face.

Bob backed away from her. "I don't like the turn this conversation has suddenly taken," he said.

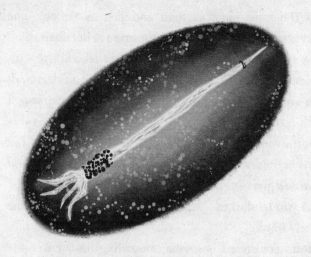

CHAPTER TWENTY-EIGHT

◆◈◆

THE GREATEST MAGIC OF ALL

The Enchantress frantically paced back and forth in front of her throne. Her hair anxiously swayed above her. *"Say it again!"* she demanded.

"But I've already said it ten times," Red said, still kneeling before the fire.

"You will say it *one hundred times* if that's what I ask of you!" Ezmia yelled.

Red did what she was told. "I, Queen Red of the Red Riding Hood Kingdom, give my kingdom to you," she said.

Ezmia looked at the fire and waited for a change, but it

remained the same—just as high and just as strong. The Enchantress slammed her hands on the arms of her chair.

"What's wrong, Ezmia?" Rumpelstiltskin asked.

"It's not working!" she screamed. "I don't understand. I've been working on this for centuries! I had *everything* I needed."

Charlotte was sobbing hysterically in the birdcage. *"You horrible…horrible…horrible creature,"* she cried. *"How could you do that to a girl?"*

"I told you to shut up, woman!" Ezmia yelled at her. She could barely think.

Charlotte continued her sobs, mourning louder in spite of Ezmia's screaming. As far as Charlotte knew, her daughter was dead and she was never coming back. Conner had been in shock since it had happened. But as he watched the Enchantress struggle, his spirits started to rise.

Ezmia needed all seven of the deadly sins and the heir of magic to activate the portal. Maybe his sister had successfully taken her pride—maybe she had finished the Wand and was alive!

"That dreadful witch Hagatha must have lied to me!" Ezmia yelled. "The fire should have grown into a portal into the Otherworld as soon as I conquered the past, present, and future, and mastered the seven deadly sins—lust, envy, sloth, greed, gluttony, wrath…and *pride.*"

A strange look came to the Enchantress's face as she thought on the spell's ingredients. She looked to the spot where Alex had been standing when she was blasted into the sky. To everyone's surprise, a giant smile suddenly appeared on Conner's face.

"What's the matter, Ezmia?" Conner said. "Did a little girl take away your *pride*?"

The Enchantress jerked her head toward him like a hawk finding its prey. "What did you just say?" Ezmia said sharply.

"Conner, what are you doing?" Froggy whispered to him.

"Don't make her angrier!" Jack said.

Conner ignored them. "I said, a *little girl* took away *Ezmia the Enchantress's* pride!" he called out so everyone in the coliseum could hear him. "That's why you can't complete your spell!"

A whispered murmur spread through the coliseum between the kings and queens. Was Conner just taunting her or was there truth to what he said?

"Silence!" Ezmia ordered them. "If you think my pride could be taken from me you're all insulting your own intelligence! Bring the boy to me!"

The vines lifted Red back against the wall and placed Conner in front of the fire.

"No!" Charlotte yelled. *"Don't you dare hurt him!"*

"Butterboy!" Trollbella yelled.

Conner wasn't afraid. "Are you going to kill me, too?" he asked.

"As a matter of fact, I am," the Enchantress said.

"Oh, good one!" Conner said spitefully. "Way to make yourself feel better, Ezmia! Killing another innocent child really shows how *prideful* you are! What are you going to do next—club a couple baby seals?"

The Enchantress had had enough of him. "Any *final* words?" she said.

Conner had to think about it, wanting to make whatever he said count. "You're ugly and you smell bad," he said. "And where I come from, everyone thinks you're green with horns!"

Ezmia raised her hand in his direction. Conner braced himself.

"Ezmia! Look!" Rumpelstiltskin yelled and pointed to the sky.

Flying toward the coliseum was a large white horse with massive wings. As it flew closer everyone in the coliseum gasped when they saw who was steering it.

"Alex!" Conner screamed.

"You're alive!" Charlotte screamed from the cage.

The horse landed in the center of the coliseum and Alex jumped off its back. She commandingly raised the Wand of Wonderment and pointed it at the Enchantress.

"Miss me?" Alex said.

The Enchantress couldn't believe what she was seeing—as if her day could get any worse. She waved her hands and the vines dragged Conner back against the wall.

"Alex, don't waste any time!" Conner yelled as he was dragged off. *"Just zap her! Strike her dead—"* Ezmia waved her hand again and the vines covered Conner's mouth.

The Enchantress glanced sideways at Charlotte in the cage

and it all suddenly dawned on her—she wasn't the Fairy God-mother's granddaughter after all. Ezmia slowly strode over to Alex, looking her up and down like she was an interesting piece of art.

"So, you're the Fairy Godmother's real granddaughter, I take it?" Ezmia said, and began circling her. Alex never lowered the Wand; she was ready to strike if Ezmia showed any sign of doing the same.

"It's interesting that we have so much in common," Ezmia said. "We're both from the same place, we both have magic in our blood, and we both possess extraordinary ability. . . ."

"We're nothing alike," Alex snapped. "I could never do all the horrible things you've done."

A smile appeared on Ezmia's face. "That's where you're wrong," she said. "You see, I came into this world just like I'm assuming you did—full of excitement and promise. I wanted to do so much good work, help so many people, and give as much as I could to those who needed me. But then I learned a very harsh lesson—*the world doesn't always give back*.

"I am not a tragic case of the world; I *am* the world—cruel, unfair, and *not a fairy tale*. People are not born heroes or villains; they're created by the people around them. And one day when your bright-eyed and bushy-tailed view of life gets its first taste of reality, when bitterness and anger first run through your veins, you'll discover that you are *just like me*—and it'll scare you to death."

Alex shook her head and gripped the Wand even tighter. "No, Ezmia, I'll never be like you," she said. "Because I would rather have nothing and a big heart than everything and no heart at all."

Everything went quiet in the coliseum. Ezmia's hair was flowing above her, out of control.

"Oh, snap!" Conner yelled. *"You need some ointment for that burn, Ezmia?"*

Ezmia waved her hand and the vines covered Conner's mouth again.

"You're brave with that Wand in your hand," Ezmia said to Alex. "But I'd like to see you cross me with it out of reach."

Alex knew this was her moment—if she wanted to defeat the Enchantress for good, this might be her only chance.

"Fine," Alex said, and tossed the Wand to the ground. "I don't need it."

The entire coliseum gasped.

"Alex, are you crazy?!" Conner yelled through the vines covering his mouth. *"Pick it back up! Pick it back up!"*

The Enchantress roared with laughter at Alex's carelessness. "You stupid girl!" she said. "You must have a death wish!"

"I don't need a wand to defeat you, Ezmia," Alex said. "Whether I have magic in my blood or not, I'll always have the most powerful magic of all inside me—*compassion*. And I have enough inside of me even for you."

"What?" the Enchantress said, amused by her foolishness.

Alex took a deep breath, praying what she was about to say would strip Ezmia of her powers forever.

"Ezmia, on behalf of everyone in this room, I *apologize* for what the world put you through, and I *forgive* you for all the havoc you caused trying to heal," Alex said. "I'm sorry your family was killed when you were a little girl. I'm sorry no one was there to comfort you when you had your heart broken over and over again. I'm sorry the fairies never showed you the kindness they showed everyone else. And I'm sorry you felt *revenge* was the only way you could piece yourself together again."

Everyone was looking back and forth between Alex and Ezmia like they were at a tennis match. Conner covered his eyes, afraid he was about to watch his sister be killed for real this time.

The Enchantress was taken aback by what Alex had to say—it had been the last thing she expected to come out of the girl's mouth. Ezmia didn't know what to do but laugh. She threw her head back a number of times and let a malicious laugh erupt and grow from inside of her.

"Apology not accepted," Ezmia said. She pointed her finger at Alex to blast her into the heavens again—but nothing happened. She pointed her finger again—still, nothing was happening. Ezmia tried with her other hand but only got the same result.

Ezmia's hair gradually lost its magenta color and faded to gray, falling in her face one strand at a time. The fire in the crater diminished more and more by the second, until there was nothing left but skulls. The vines around the coliseum squirmed like dying snakes, loosening their grip and releasing the people they held against the wall.

"*No!*" Ezmia screamed. "*No—this is impossible!*"

The room watched in astonishment as magic slowly left the Enchantress's body and Ezmia faded into an elderly and decrepit woman, too weak to stand on her own feet. *The Enchantress had lost her power.*

Alex closed her eyes and, possibly for the first time all day, exhaled. She turned back to her brother as he brushed the limp vines off his body. He, along with everyone else in the coliseum, stared at her with enough pride to knock off the ceiling had there been one. A thirteen-year-old girl in a headband had been able to do what none of the crowned monarchs could.

As Ezmia withered away, she fell to the floor and crawled on her hands and knees. A small cackle came from her as she grabbed hold of the Wand of Wonderment left on the floor.

"Alex, behind you!" Conner screamed.

Alex turned to see Ezmia pointing the Wand directly at her. As she held the Wand, her body and her magic were restored. Her hair flowed above her head, the fire in the crater ignited again, and the vines began to vibrate with life and started dragging people back onto the walls.

Without time to think, Conner grabbed hold of Goldilocks's sword and ran toward his sister, slicing the vines as they tried seizing him.

Ezmia glared at Alex with an evil smile on her face and in her eyes. "Maybe I was wrong," the Enchantress said. "Maybe I will have my own happily-ever-after, after all!"

Alex froze where she stood, petrified to her core. She couldn't believe how quickly the situation had changed—in a matter of seconds she had gone from victory to defeat. A bright blast shot out of the Wand and toward her. Alex closed her eyes, knowing it was the end—*this was how she was going to die.*

"*Nooo!*" Rumpelstiltskin yelled. He came out of nowhere and jumped in front of Alex. The blast hit him in the chest and he fell to the ground.

Ezmia watched in shock as the fatal blast meant for Alex had hit the only person she had ever considered a friend. Conner arrived at the Enchantress's side and sliced the Wand of Wonderment in half. The Wand was destroyed; the magic drained from Ezmia's body and the enchantments around the coliseum faded once again.

Alex went to the floor and held Rumpelstiltskin's head up in her lap. Conner dropped down next to her, but there was nothing either of them could do.

"*You saved my life!*" Alex said to the little man in her arms. "*Why would you do that for me?*"

Rumpelstiltskin was gasping and his eyes grew heavier by the second. "I just wanted my brothers to have something to be proud of," he grunted weakly. He smiled up at the twins, closed his eyes for the last time, and died in Alex's arms.

"Oh no," Conner said. "Poor little guy."

A heavy wheezing came from nearby. The twins looked across the floor to see Ezmia crawling toward them. Her body was decaying and wilting at a speedy rate.

"*Looks like you've won,*" Ezmia wheezed with difficulty.

Alex and Conner looked at each other, disgusted. Even as they held the body of her only acquaintance, all Ezmia cared about was her legacy. They looked down at her with the most pitying eyes she had ever been viewed with.

"No, Ezmia," Alex said. "No one wins when there is loss."

Ezmia rolled onto her back and stared up at the smoky sky. With one last rattling breath, her body rotted away until there was nothing left of her but the memory of what she had been. With nothing to validate the anger that powered her livelihood, the Enchantress's body and soul disappeared—a casualty to compassion.

The kings and queens and fairies brushed the vines off their bodies again and happily embraced one another. The nightmare was over and their kingdoms were safe once again.

King Chance and Cinderella held Princess Hope, and Cinderella wiped away tears of joy from her exhausted eyes. Sleeping Beauty wouldn't let go of King Chase; it was the first time in weeks that they had seen each other. Snow White and King Chandler helped Rapunzel brush all the leaves out of her hair, which was a several-person effort.

Red kissed Froggy repeatedly all over his big frog head. Jack tried dipping Goldilocks for a romantic kiss, but her fugitive reflexes caused her to flip him over her shoulder by accident.

Trollbella walked over to Conner.

"Hey, listen, Trollbella, I'm very flattered but I'm not really interested in—" he started, but the Troll Queen silenced him again with an index finger pressed to his mouth.

"No, Butterboy, let me do all the talking," she said. "I understand this day has been hard on you—watching the Squishygirl almost die and then narrowly escaping death yourself. I just wanted to let you know I'm in no rush for our wedding; whether it's in two days or two weeks, I'll be waiting for you."

"Thanks?" Conner said. Trollbella winked at him and walked away, leaving him even more confused than before.

The Fairy Council went to the glass jars in front of the golden chair and one by one opened the lids and released the souls trapped inside. The twins watched as the souls of the Baker, the Locksmith, and the Soldier happily flew from the jars and disappeared into the sky above—free at last. The spirits of the King and the Musician hovered in the air behind the others, though, waiting to join the other spirits.

The ghosts of Old Queen Beauty and Gloria floated into the coliseum and up to their long-lost loves. They flew around, over, under, and through each other, finally reunited after centuries.

Gloria and the Musician looked to the twins and bowed thankfully to them before disappearing into the sky with the other spirits. The ghost of the King and Old Queen Beauty looked lovingly down and waved at Sleeping Beauty and King Chase before disappearing as well.

"Who was that?" Sleeping Beauty asked her husband.

King Chase looked up to the sky and smiled. "Well, I suppose they're our guardian angels now."

Jack chopped through the lock on Charlotte's cage and she ran to her children, throwing her arms around them.

"Mom!" the twins said in unison.

"I have never been so proud of you in my life," she tearfully exclaimed.

"That makes two of us," said a voice behind them.

The twins turned to see their grandmother. She had just been released from the jar and was back to being her old solid self. The twins got to their feet and gave their grandmother an enormous hug, feeling so grateful they finally could.

Grandma leaned over and looked proudly into Alex's and Conner's eyes. "You two amaze me more and more as you get older," she said lovingly to them. "Your father would be so proud of you."

Alex and Conner smiled at each other, knowing that, wherever he was, he was smiling down at them, too.

The winged horse neighed loudly from the side of the coliseum.

"Hey, Alex, where did you find a flying horse?" Conner asked.

Alex's happy grin suddenly faded. "Oh no, I forgot about Bob!" she yelled. "Grandma, can you change him back for me?"

The Fairy Godmother laughed. She retrieved her crystal wand from inside her robes and waved it in the horse's direction. A bright beam of light traveled from the tip of her wand and spun around the horse until he was regular Dr. Bob again.

He shook his head and found his balance, dizzy from the transformation.

"Bob, is that you?" Charlotte gasped. "What are you doing here?"

"I couldn't let you have *all* the fun, could I?" He laughed.

Charlotte ran to his side and kissed him—the twins had to look away.

"You won't believe what he went through," Conner told his mom. "He was almost eaten by bears and sharks and he was captured by the Sea Witch and—"

"*And* we'll let *him* tell you all about it," Alex said while dragging her brother away. She figured it was best to give them some privacy.

The twins and their grandmother walked to the edge of the coliseum and looked out over the Charming Kingdom. The sun began to set, painting the sky a beautiful rosy shade.

"I'm sorry we ran away from the house, Grandma," Alex said, trying to sound genuine but also trying to hide a smile at the same time.

"Yeah," Conner laughed. "I feel *so bad* about that." He didn't even try to be sincere.

Their grandmother shook her head and looked to the sky, fighting a smile of her own. "What am I going to do with you two?" she said. "Magic lessons, I think, would do you some good; that way you won't sink any more houses."

"I totally forgot about that!" Conner said. "Sorry we sank your cottage, Grandma!"

"Magic lessons?! Really?" Alex asked with large eyes as she hopped up and down.

"I think you've earned it," their grandmother said. "As long as your mother is fine with it."

"After all this I don't think she'll ever be able to tell us no again," Conner said.

"What was that, Conner?" Charlotte asked as she and Bob joined them at the edge of the coliseum.

"Oh, um…" Conner said and turned bright red. "I was just saying you may have difficulty telling us no from now on because we saved your life."

Charlotte squinted at him. "I *gave* you life," she said. "You're never going to top that."

Conner tried laughing it off. "I was just kidding," he said, although there was obviously an element of truth to it.

The reunited family of five looked out over the land around them. As the sun set in the East, it also set on the reign of the Enchantress, and the twins could feel the Land of Stories sigh with relief. It was a paradise once more.

Chapter Twenty-Nine

FOR BETTER, OR FOR WORSE

All the kings and queens left the Charming Kingdom the following day to celebrate the news of the Enchantress's defeat with their people. Red was the only one who stayed behind, because at the end of the week she, Froggy, Goldilocks, Jack, Bob, Charlotte, and the twins all attended Rumpelstiltskin's funeral.

Hearing the news of his final act and what his last words had been was hard for the Seven Dwarfs to swallow, so they wanted to make sure the ceremony was everything Rumpelstiltskin would have wanted.

It was a small ceremony in the Dwarf Forests on the front

lawn of the Seven Dwarfs' cottage. The dwarfs had made their brother a casket of glass and jewels from their mines, just as they had for Snow White. He was buried in a daisy-covered field not too far from the cottage. The dwarfs said Rumpelstiltskin had spent a lot of time there when he was younger and they knew he would have been happy to make it his final place of rest. His tombstone even read:

HERE LIES RUMPELSTILTSKIN

THE EIGHTH BROTHER

OF A PROUD DWARF FAMILY

That night, when they arrived back at the Charming Kingdom, King Chance and Queen Cinderella hosted a dinner to honor the twins and the others who had sailed on the *Granny*. Conner was seated at the table in the dining hall when a man sat next to him and started up a conversation.

"I'm looking forward to this," the man said. "I miss being a part of the famous Charming dinner parties."

"Do I know you?" Conner asked him and gave the man the side-eye.

"Conner, it's me," the man said. "It's *Froggy*."

Conner shook his head and looked at the man again. He always forgot Froggy was actually human, but no matter what physical form he took, he always had the same kind eyes.

"Your grandmother changed me back as soon as we returned from the funeral," Froggy said. "The funny thing is, I had grown so accustomed to being a frog, I had forgotten she still had to change me back."

"Do you miss anything about being a frog?" Conner asked him.

"I do miss reaching the books on the top shelf without a ladder," he said. "One doesn't realize how useful frog legs can be until they lose them." A twinkle came to Froggy's eye. "Speaking of reading, I have something for you."

He reached into his lapel and pulled out a rolled-up stack of parchments.

"When we were setting up the camps for the trolls, I found these in the *Granny*'s wreckage," Froggy said and handed the parchments over to Conner.

"My stories!" Conner said. "I thought these were lost forever!"

"I must admit, I enjoyed them quite a bit," Froggy said. "You've got a real knack for storytelling. Although, I do have a few words of advice for you."

"What's that?" Conner asked.

"Never let Red read these," Froggy said. "I thought it was very clever, writing everyone as trolls, but she would have you executed if she read your interpretation of her."

Conner chuckled and playfully punched Froggy's shoulder.

"No, I'm serious," Froggy said. Conner gulped.

The others finally arrived and took seats around the table. Jack and Goldilocks looked down timidly at all the silverware, not knowing what to start with. Red entered the room and almost blinded everyone with the amount of jewelry she was wearing. Even for a formal dinner in the Charming Palace, Red was overdressed.

Bob sat down across from Conner, looking unusually tense.

"What's wrong, Bob?" Conner said. "You look like you're about to operate on the president."

Alex cleared her throat to get Conner's attention.

"He's going to propose to Mom tonight," Alex mouthed when her mother wasn't looking.

"Oh," Conner mouthed back excitedly to Bob and his sister. He gave Bob an unsubtle wink and a thumbs-up.

"Is everything all right, Conner?" Charlotte asked.

"Um . . . *yes*," Conner said. "I'm just really looking forward to the appetizers."

Alex rolled her eyes at him. Charlotte studied her son suspiciously, afraid he was coming down with a cold.

A footman presented a tray to Goldilocks with an envelope addressed to her on it.

"A letter has come for you, madam," the footman said.

"For *me*?" Goldilocks said. "I wonder what it could be." She opened the envelope and read the note inside. An amused but shocked grin came to her face—she wasn't sure how to feel about the news she received.

"What is it?" Jack asked her.

"It's a note from the Red Riding Hood Castle stables," Goldilocks said. "Porridge is *pregnant*."

Jack and the twins couldn't contain themselves. Each one laughed harder than the next. *"Buckle!"* the twins said together.

"I knew there was something going on between them!" Conner said.

The dinner began and the room was served course after course of the best food the twins had ever eaten. Just before the desserts were brought out, Bob tapped the side of his glass with a spoon and got the room's attention. Alex and Conner shot excited looks at each other—*this was it.*

"I just wanted to thank you all so much for having me tonight," Bob said. "I'm fairly new to the Bailey clan, so learning about all of you and coming into this world has been, well, the adventure of my life. And seeing that I happened to be in a room filled with people who make up the greatest love stories ever told, I would like to take this moment for all it's worth."

Charlotte looked back and forth between the twins, seeing if they knew what Bob was up to. They purposefully avoided her eyes, wanting Bob to surprise her fully. He got down on one knee and presented the ring to her.

"Charlotte, will you make me the happiest man in the world—*both worlds*—and be my wife?" Bob said.

Tears instantly filled Charlotte's surprised eyes. "I…I… I…" she said. Everyone in the dining hall was on the edge of their seat. *"Yes, I would love nothing more!"*

Bob put the ring on Charlotte's finger and hugged her. Alex began to cry, which made Conner's eyes start to water, which ultimately caused everyone else in the room to well up, too. It was a picturesque moment, even by fairy-tale standards.

"You should get married in the palace," Cinderella said from the end of the table.

"What?" Charlotte asked, not believing her ears.

"Please, we insist," Cinderella said and took King Chance's hand in hers. "We've been trying to think of a way to thank you for taking care of Hope when you were being held by the Enchantress. It would be our pleasure."

Charlotte didn't know what to say. She was stunned by the offer. "That is so kind, but I'm not sure I could ever—"

"Mom," Alex interrupted her. "Speaking on behalf of every woman who has ever lived in the Otherworld, you *cannot* turn down the offer to have an actual fairy-tale wedding!"

"I have to agree, it would be pretty cool," Conner said.

Charlotte shrugged; the decision was basically made for her. "Well, all right, then. I would be honored, thank you!" she said. "We have to get back to our jobs in the Otherworld, but I suppose we can have a quick wedding with our friends here and then another one for our friends back home."

Everyone raised their glasses to toast Charlotte and Bob.

"May you live Happily Ever After," the Fairy Godmother said.

Red tapped her glass and stood at her seat. No one could look directly at her because of the light reflecting off her diamonds.

"I would like to add to the celebration with some wonderful news of my own," she said. "After speaking with the fairies and all the other queens and kings, I would like to announce that the Happily Ever After Assembly has decided to pardon Jack and Goldilocks for all their crimes and waive all warrants for their arrest as a thank-you for their daring and valiant efforts in defeating the Enchantress."

The room burst into applause and congratulations for the couple. However, Jack and Goldilocks looked the least excited out of all of them.

"Wonderful," Goldilocks said through a pained smile.

"Cheers," Jack said, reluctantly raising his glass to the others toasting them.

"You can move back into your old house, Jack," Red said. "Which is going to be really convenient, because I've decided to build my country home right beside it!"

Jack and Goldilocks did their best to look as if this was good news and it excited them. Red went on and on about all the wonderful double dates they could have with her and Froggy and all the activities they could do now that they were going to be neighbors.

Goldilocks leaned toward Jack. "Well, at least I won't have to feel guilty about making you live the life of an outlaw anymore," she said.

"No more running from soldiers, or close encounters with ogres, or sneaking into shops to steal food, or sleeping under the stars in dangerous forests," Jack said.

"It's . . . *tempting* to live a quieter life," Goldilocks said halfheartedly. "Just imagine us living the rest of our days in your manor, watching the grass grow with Red and Charlie."

Jack and Goldilocks smirked at each other, both thinking the same thing. They couldn't imagine a *worse* fate.

Goldilocks whispered something into Jack's ear, and a big grin appeared on his face. The twins looked to each other, knowing something was up. Goldilocks stood from the table and walked over to Red. She endearingly wrapped her arms around her old nemesis and gave her a big hug.

"What's all this about?" Red asked.

"I just want to thank you," Goldilocks said. "What you've done for us is so generous; we'll never be able to repay you."

Red looked like she was about to cry. "You're so welcome," Red said. "And even though we've both tried to kill each other—I tricked you into going in a house with three furious bears; you tried to throw me into a bottomless pit—I would like it very much if we put the past aside and let our friendship bloom even more."

Goldilocks smiled at her. "I think that's a wonderful idea, Red," she said. "Now, if you'll just excuse me, I'm going to step out for a moment."

Goldilocks gave Red another hug and excused herself from the dining room. The dessert was finally served, and Conner looked up and down the table to make sure his piece of cake wasn't any smaller than the rest of theirs.

"Hey, that's not fair, Red got two pieces of—" Conner stopped himself mid-complaint. Something was different; he was looking at Red without squinting. "Hey, Red, where's your necklace?"

"My necklace?" Red asked. She reached up to her neck and screamed when she discovered her diamond necklace was missing. "That doesn't make any sense! How could it have possibly vanished—*GOLDILOCKS!*"

Both the twins turned to Jack. He wiped his mouth with his napkin, trying to hide a giant grin underneath it.

Sir Lampton suddenly rushed into the dining room. He had built a reputation of constantly bringing such awful news in the last few days, the entire room went silent to hear what he had to say.

"Yes, Sir Lampton?" King Chance asked.

"Pardon my intrusion, Your Majesty," Lampton said. "With all due respect, did you give Goldilocks permission to take one of the horses from the stable, or has one just been stolen?"

Everyone's eyes immediately darted to Jack. "Well, that's my cue," he said and stood up from the table. "Alex and Conner, it was wonderful to see you again and I'd like to thank everyone else for a lovely evening and a wonderful dinner. *Good night.*"

With that said, Jack ran down the dining hall and jumped out of the closest window. Red leaped up from the table and ran over to the window. Froggy and the twins followed her and peered through it.

They arrived just in time to see Jack sliding down the slanted roof and landing perfectly on the back of a horse that Goldilocks held the reins of on the ground. They both waved up at Red, Froggy, and the twins—Red's necklace sparkled in the moonlight on Goldilocks's neck.

"That's my necklace!" Red yelled. *"Bring that back to me at once!"*

Goldilocks yanked on the reins and she and Jack rode off into the night—happy outlaws once again.

Red slammed her hands on the windowsill. "I cannot believe I wasted an ounce of generosity on *that woman*!" she yelled. "Sir Lampton, I want you to put a team of your finest men together and go after her at once!"

"But I don't work for you," Lampton said.

"No excuses, Lampton! Find them!" Red demanded.

Lampton looked to King Chance and Cinderella—they both shrugged. "Right away, Queen Red," Lampton said with a sigh and left the room.

Alex, Conner, and Froggy couldn't help but laugh as they watched their friends ride off into the night. Much as it distressed Red, they were happy to see Jack and Goldilocks return to their own habitat.

Charlotte and Bob's wedding was just two days later. The entire palace was decorated in flowers and giant banners. Bells rang through the entire kingdom. In Charming tradition, the twins' grandmother transformed their mother's nursing scrubs into a beautiful white gown and veil.

Alex and Conner had never seen her look so beautiful, and both grew a little misty-eyed because of it. They were so happy to see their mom get the wedding she deserved.

The ceremony was held in the ballroom, and it was so crowded the twins thought the entire Charming Kingdom might have shown up. The Fairy Godmother conducted the ceremony herself. Princess Hope was led down the aisle by her mother and acted as a flower girl. Conner was Bob's best man and Alex was her mother's maid of honor.

"Do you, Charlotte, take this man to be your husband?" the Fairy Godmother asked.

"I do," Charlotte said.

"And do you, Robert, take this woman to be your wife?"

"I do," Bob said.

The vows were only interrupted once as Red loudly blew her nose from the seats—overcome by the ceremony and still upset at losing her favorite necklace.

"By the power invested in me by the Happily Ever After Assembly, I now pronounce you husband and wife," the Fairy Godmother happily called out. "You may now kiss the bride."

The twins both turned their heads the other way and the crowd cheered. Bob, Charlotte, and the twins then got into a carriage in the shape of a pumpkin and rode through the Charming Kingdom streets, waving to all the well-wishers who had gathered there.

"I think this family is off to a good start," Conner said.

That evening, as soon as all the festivities were over, the Fairy Council met the Fairy Godmother at the Charming Palace. They were there on official council business and called together a meeting so exclusive no one but the fairies was allowed to be a part of it. The Fairy Godmother waved her wand and made a door appear that led into the Otherworld, and she and the other fairies waited for Mother Goose to arrive so the meeting could start.

Mother Goose eventually emerged through the door, dragging her basket of a suitcase and a very defiant and reluctant Lester with her.

"Come on, Lester," she said. "I know you love the slot machines, but we can't stay in Vegas forever."

If her appearance was any indication, Mother Goose had done a lot of traveling in the last week. She wore a large sombrero that said TIJUANA across it, a colorful Hawaiian lei around her neck, a large I LOVE NY T-shirt, and wooden Dutch shoes. A foam finger from a football game was still over her hand.

"Looks like you were busy, O.M.G.," Conner said.

"Hey, C-Dog, just because you and your sister saved the world doesn't mean you get to be sassy," Mother Goose snapped at him. "I was afraid the Enchantress was going to cross into the Otherworld, so I went to all my favorite places before she could destroy them."

Alex looked over her worldly outfit. "I see you went to Mexico, New York, Hawaii, and a football game—but where are the shoes from?" she asked.

"Amsterdam," Mother Goose said. "They love me over there."

"I didn't know nursery rhymes were popular in Amsterdam," Conner said.

"They're not," Mother Goose said. "They don't know me as Mother Goose; they have their own nickname for me when I visit."

"What's that?" Alex asked.

"Mother Mayhem," she said.

The twins just nodded, not wanting to know any details.

"All right, let's get this hen in the oven!" Mother Goose said and clapped her hands. She followed the Fairy Council into a private drawing room.

"It's about time you showed up," Tangerina said.

"Mind your beeswax, Tangy," Mother Goose said. "No, I'm serious—your bees are getting that crap all over the floor."

The fairies shut the door tightly behind them. Naturally, the twins placed their ears up to the door and tried eavesdropping as much as possible.

"The world is still in shambles," the twins heard Emerelda's voice fade in and out. "We're slowly clearing the Eastern Kingdom of all the thornbushes and vines.... The Northern Kingdom has finally rid itself of all the poisoned food.... Ezmia's pillar of rock and dirt still needs to be removed ... and there's one thing that we haven't discussed yet that involved you, Fairy Godmother."

The twins looked to each other; their curiosity consumed them whole.

"I'll be right back," Conner said. A few moments later he returned with empty glasses from the palace kitchen. He handed one to Alex and they placed them over the door and up to their ears. They could hear what the fairies were saying much more clearly now.

"You understand how difficult that will be for my family, don't you?" they heard their grandmother say.

"We're not proposing it to be cruel; we're proposing it to be preventative," Skylene said.

"If we don't do something, it'll only be a matter of time before someone else follows in the Enchantress's footsteps," Xanthous said.

"In the end, it's your decision," Emerelda said. "It's *your* gift—*you* were chosen to be the gatekeeper. We can only tell you what we think is best for both worlds."

Alex and Conner looked at each other.

"I understand," their grandmother said. "And if it's what the rest of you think is the right thing to do, I cannot ignore that. I just don't know how I'm going to break the news to my grandchildren."

"You can take as much time as you need," Emerelda said.

The twins heard them start to come toward the door and ran down the hall so they wouldn't be caught listening.

Their curiosity ate them alive for the rest of the day. What was the news their grandmother was going to have difficulty telling them? Why did it affect them and her ability to move between the worlds? The twins' imaginations didn't do them any favors as they thought on what the possibilities could be.

Luckily, they weren't forced to suffer too long. That night after dinner the Fairy Council called everyone into the ball-room to fill them in on what they had discussed.

"It's going to take some time before the world can fully

recover from the damage the Enchantress caused," Emerelda said. "Ezmia may be gone, but the fact is, what she tried to accomplish still remains a possibility as long as the two worlds are joined."

"So what are you saying?" Conner said.

The Fairy Godmother closed her eyes, not wanting to see her grandchildren's faces when they heard it.

"For the greater good of both worlds, we have decided to close the gateway between them," Emerelda said.

Alex felt like she was being told her father was dead or her mother had been kidnapped all over again. Her stomach tightened and her heart beat at a rapid pace. She felt her palms go clammy and the rest of her body go numb.

"What?" she asked breathlessly.

"How is that even possible?" Conner asked. He also was having an incredibly hard time processing the news.

"It's possible if we use our magic together," their grandmother regretfully told them.

"So what does that mean?" Conner asked. "Does that mean we'll never be able to see you again?"

Their grandmother shook her head, happy to report one small consolation. "I was able to convince the other fairies to supply us with a way to see each other," she said. She waved her wand, and two long, square mirrors with golden frames appeared. "We'll be able to see each other using these mirrors whenever we want; we just won't be able to—"

"Travel between worlds?" Conner asked.

Their grandmother closed her eyes and nodded her head.

It was clearly almost as painful for her to tell them as it was for them to hear it. Alex was shaking her head profusely and tears began running down her face.

"No, Grandma," Alex pleaded. *"Tell me it isn't true."*

"I'm afraid so, honey," Grandma said.

Alex lost it completely and buried her head in her mother's side. She cried so hard she was practically silent except for her deep gasps for air. Charlotte tried to remain strong for her kids but she was having a hard time keeping it together herself—she knew what the news meant for them.

"And you're okay with this?" Conner yelled. Tears spilled down from his own eyes.

"I hate it as much as you do," their grandma said. "But to secure the safety of both worlds we don't have another option."

Conner could only get one word of his next question out. *"When?"* he said, and his voice cracked as he fought back emotion.

"Tomorrow at dusk," his grandmother said, waging her own emotional battle inside.

Alex couldn't stand to hear any more of it. She ran from the ballroom and headed up the stairs to her chambers, her hands covering her face as she went.

"Alex?" Charlotte called out, but it was no use.

Alex shut the door to her chambers behind her and collapsed on the floor. She cried and cried for hours and hours. She had lived through the fear of losing the fairy-tale world so many times, and now it was real; it was actually being taken away from her.

And of all times, her greatest fear had been realized right after she'd learned how much potential she had to offer this world. Right after she'd discovered she had a chance at being the future Fairy Godmother someday. Right after her uncertain future had nearly been set—it was all being taken from her.

It felt like the Land of Stories had always been dangled in front of her and her brother like a taunting cat toy. Every time they thought they had finally grabbed hold of it, it slipped out of their grip. She cried until her tear ducts dried up and she couldn't cry anymore. She lay on the bed and prayed there would be some way around this nightmare.

A soft knock came at the door. "Alex, can I come in?" Charlotte asked from the other side.

"Sure," Alex said.

Charlotte walked into the room and took a seat on the bed next to her devastated daughter.

"It's so unfair, Mom," Alex said. "After everything we've been through...after everything we've seen...why does this have to be taken from us, too?"

Charlotte rubbed her hand gently on Alex's knee. Alex sat up and looked at her mom; she was crying almost more than Alex had been.

"Why are you crying so much, Mom?" Alex asked. "You're not losing anything."

Charlotte smiled. "Oh, but I am, honey," she said. "A year ago when you and your brother first came back from this place, I knew then I had lost my little girl forever. I watched her grow sadder and sadder the more time she spent away from this place, and I knew there was nothing I could ever do to help her—because her heart belonged somewhere else."

"Mom, what are you talking about?" Alex asked.

Charlotte put a hand on Alex's face and looked at her daughter through the tears in her eyes. "I'm saying I'm not going to let you leave the place where you belong," she said.

CHAPTER THIRTY

THE GOOD-BYE

onner woke up the next morning with a mission. Before anyone else had woken, he ran down to the stables and arranged for a carriage to take him into the countryside. He kept his activities a complete secret from anyone else, fearing someone would stop him if he made his plans known. He didn't return until that evening just before dusk— and he didn't return alone. The carriage door swung open, and three additional passengers emerged from it.

Conner had brought Lady Iris, Petunia, and Rosemary back with him. After they'd spent nearly a decade suffering through constant public persecution, Conner had offered them the only chance at refuge they had ever received—and after hearing hours of Conner's descriptions, the sequestered family of women finally jumped at the chance.

They were carrying as many of their belongings as they could. Lady Iris held on to the painting of her late husband; Rosemary held her favorite cooking bowl; and Petunia grasped a stack of rolled-up animal portraits under her arm.

"There's this thing called culinary school that you're going to love, Rosemary," Conner was saying, further listing the perks of his dimension. "And just wait until I introduce you to *Animal Planet*, Petunia."

Sir Lampton emerged down the front steps of the palace toward the carriage. "What's going on here?" he asked Conner.

Conner pulled him aside so the women couldn't hear him. "I'm taking them back to the Otherworld with us," he said.

"*You're what?!*" Lampton said.

"I explained everything to them; it took them a while to understand, but they want to leave," Conner said. "Lampton, they're miserable here—they don't gain anything by staying. If they come with us they'll at least have a *chance* at starting a better life."

"Why would you help *them*?" Lampton asked.

Conner sighed and looked to the ground. "Because I'll never be able to help my sister," he said. "Alex isn't like me—she's going to be miserable the rest of her life without this place.

At least if I bring Lady Iris with us there'll be something worth looking forward to."

Lampton had his reservations but admired the boy's generosity nonetheless. "You're a good man, Conner Bailey," he said. "Everyone is gathering in the gardens for the final good-bye. Please escort your *guests* down there."

Conner nodded and led the women around the side of the castle to the beautiful gardens. The Charming garden was home to an exquisite display of yellow roses, pear trees, and a hedge labyrinth. It was a beautiful place to say a distressing good-bye.

Froggy, Red, King Chance, Cinderella, and Mother Goose had already gathered in the gardens. Cinderella had to do a double take as Conner approached—she hadn't been expecting to see her stepmother and stepsisters walking behind him.

"Stepmother?" Cinderella called out. "Rosemary? Petunia?"

Even though they knew they were headed to the palace, Lady Iris and her daughters had almost hoped they wouldn't run into her.

"Hello, Cinderella," Lady Iris said.

"What are you doing here?" Cinderella asked. She looked over all the belongings they carried and answered her own question.

Lady Iris thought for a moment about what to tell her. "We've decided it would be best to leave the Charming Kingdom," she said.

"I see," Cinderella said. She didn't argue with her stepmother, knowing her reasons better than anyone. "Where are you headed?"

Lady Iris hesitated to say. "The *Otherworld*, as fate would have it," she said. "I think a fresh start would do the girls and me some good. We'll be able to live in a place where people won't judge us as harshly, or throw rocks at the house, or boo us when we leave it."

All Cinderella could do was nod. She might have built a gate around their property, but she could never take away all the oppression they faced on a daily basis.

"What are you going to do there?" Cinderella asked.

"The boy was telling me of a place called *Florida* that I might be interested in," Lady Iris said.

"I'm going to be a chef," Rosemary said.

"I'm going to do something with animals," Petunia said. "They have so many more animals in the Otherworld than we have. There's apparently this creature called the *honey badger* that I hear is fascinating."

Cinderella was pleased for them, but couldn't deny she was sorry to be losing the only family she had outside the king and princess.

"I'm so happy for you," she said, although they knew better.

"We're doing this for you, too, Cinderella," Lady Iris said. "You won't have any black sheep to worry about lingering around now. You can raise Princess Hope without ever having to tell her about us, if you'd like."

Cinderella nodded. "But I plan on telling Hope everything about you," she said. "Especially the part about her grandmother helping a small band of courageous sailors defeat the evil enchantress who took her from us."

Lady Iris hadn't expected them to remember her request. "Did they tell you I assisted?" she asked.

"No, they didn't have to," Cinderella said. She pulled a ring off her finger she wore next to her wedding ring—it was her *stepmother's* wedding ring. "The Wand it was a part of was destroyed, but I recognized the ring—any girl would recognize her own mother's wedding ring. I figured you would want it back."

Lady Iris stared down at the ring. "I don't know what to say," she said, touched by the gesture. The girl she had been so cruel to was still showing her kindness even now. "Thank you, Cinderella. You continue to grow into a much better woman than I could ever be."

Cinderella smiled. She hugged her stepmother and her stepsisters for the first and final time. Red and Froggy took their lead to start their own good-byes.

"I'm going to miss you, old chap," Froggy said to Conner and gave him a giant hug.

"I'm going to miss you, too," Conner said. "And just to let you know, whenever I think about you, I'm always going to remember a giant frog."

Froggy chuckled. "I wouldn't have it any other way," he said.

Red kissed Conner on the cheek. "You are the sweetest boy I know," she said. "Then again, I rarely socialize with anyone of a lower age or social class."

"Hey, kid," Mother Goose said and pulled Conner aside. She slipped a blue poker chip into his hand. "If you're ever in Monte Carlo, go to the roulette table in the northwest corner of the Lumière des Etoiles casino and bet this on black." She winked at him and patted him firmly on the back.

"Thanks?" Conner said.

The Fairy Council arrived promptly a few moments later. They took their positions in a big half-circle around the gardens to begin sealing the gateway between the worlds.

"We're just waiting for the Fairy Godmother and the others," Emerelda said. "If those of you leaving this world would please just take a step forward."

Conner, Lady Iris, Rosemary, and Petunia all edged forward on the grass, stepping into the center of the crescent shape the council formed.

"Here they come now," Skylene said.

Conner turned to see his grandmother, Charlotte, Bob, and his sister walking down from the palace. Bob was carrying one of the golden mirrors his grandmother had convinced the Fairy Council of approving securely under his arm. Conner avoided looking at his sister, knowing whatever devastated expression was on her face would make him more heartbroken than he already was.

As soon as his grandmother reached the gardens, she threw her arms around Conner and said a tearful good-bye.

"You take good care of yourself, do you understand?" she said to him.

"I love you, Grandma," Conner said.

"And I love you, my darling boy," she said and wiped the tears off of her face. "I'm going to talk to you every Sunday evening through the mirror—I don't care how busy you are, there is no excuse to miss it!" She playfully pointed her finger at him.

"I'll be there." He laughed.

The sun began to set and the sky darkened. All the fairies in the half-circle nodded to one another.

"It's time," Emerelda said. "Fairy Godmother, if you will please create a portal for our travelers—for the last time."

The Fairy Godmother reluctantly nodded. She stood in front of the council and they joined hands behind her. The wind began to pick up and circled around them as their spell began, blowing the petals of the pear blossoms around like a blizzard.

The Fairy Godmother waved her crystal wand and cracked it like a whip. A large tear appeared in the air, as if the worlds had been ripped at the seam. Everyone stared at it in awe. Conner could see the living room of their rental house on the other side of it.

"It's done," the Fairy Godmother said and turned back to the other fairies. "As soon as the portal closes, the gateway will be closed forever."

The top and the bottom of the portal began retracting inward, and the seam between the worlds started closing for good. Charlotte and Bob joined Conner and the women in the center, but Alex stayed behind by the fairies.

"Alex, come on, let's go," Conner called to his sister.

Alex didn't move. For the first time Conner noticed she wasn't wearing her normal clothes. Instead, she wore a bright blue robe that sparkled like a night sky—just like their grandmother's. A headband made of the same white flowers their grandmother wore was in Alex's hair and she held a long crystal wand—also just like their grandmother's.

"Alex, why are you dressed like that?" Conner asked.

Alex's eyes welled up instantly. She looked from her mother to her grandmother for support and took a deep breath before breaking the news to him. "Because I'm staying," Alex said.

Conner felt like he had been kicked in the stomach. "You're *what*?!!" he said.

Alex had known this would be one of the most difficult moments of her life, but she never could have imagined it was going to be *this* hard.

"I'm staying here with Grandma," Alex said. "I was going to tell you this morning, but you were gone by the time I woke up."

Conner couldn't believe what he was hearing—he didn't want to believe it. He turned to his mother, hoping she would talk sense into his sister.

"Mom, tell Alex she's crazy if she thinks she's staying here," he said. But his mother didn't immediately reprimand her like he had expected; she just gazed at Alex with large watery eyes.

"She's telling the truth, Conner," Charlotte said.

Conner looked back and forth between them, shaking his head. "No, this can't be real," he said to himself. "Why would you let her do something like that?"

Charlotte placed a hand on her son's shoulder. "One day when you have kids, Conner, you'll discover that your biggest fear is not always making good decisions for your children— and while I know I'll always regret the decision to let her stay, I'll always know it was the right decision," she said. "You know as much as I do that your sister belongs here."

Conner felt like he had been ambushed. He looked to his grandmother, but there was no sign of an alternative answer in her eyes.

"Alex, what about school?" Conner said. "What about graduation? What about college? What about starting families of our own someday? Are you just going to throw all of those things away?"

Alex wiped the tears from her face, even though they were quickly replaced with fresh streams.

"There's nothing you're going to say now or in a year that I wouldn't have thought about a hundred times," Alex said. "This isn't easy for me, Conner, but I know it's what I have to do."

"You mean you've been planning this?" Conner said. He was so angry she had even considered something so drastic without telling him.

"I've thought about it every day since we got back the first time," Alex said. "I never thought the conditions would be so severe—but it was even in the Snow Queen's prophecy; we just didn't recognize it. *'Of the four travelers, one will not return'*— she was talking about you, me, Mom, and Bob. *We* were the four travelers, not the ones aboard the *Granny.*"

"You're going to regret this," Conner said. "One day you're going to look back and wish you hadn't left me and Mom—"

"No, I won't," Alex said. "Because I couldn't live without this world now that I know how much it offers me."

Conner felt like he was in a nightmare.

"Alex, I've never been anywhere without you in my entire life," Conner said. "We can't live worlds apart!"

"Don't you get it, Conner?" Alex said. "We were always meant to live worlds apart. Magic chose us to be the bridge between the two worlds—it's the reason there are two of us. I was always meant to stay here and succeed Grandma in magic, and you were meant to go to the Otherworld and continue her storytelling. Do you think it's just a coincidence that you turned out to be such a good writer?"

Every fiber of his being wanted to argue with her; every inch of him wanted to reject what she was telling him—but something about seeing his sister among the fairies made him feel like everything was right in the world, even though his was crashing around him.

Alex stepped toward him and gave him the biggest hug she had ever given him. "We'll always be together, Conner," Alex said. "In our hearts and in your stories—every time you pen another story about our adventures in the Land of Stories, I'll be right there with you. And when that isn't enough, we can always see each other in the mirrors."

Emerelda was the only one eyeing the portal. "The gateway is closing," she said. "You have to leave soon before you're *all* trapped in this world."

For every tear that rolled down Conner's face there were a dozen he fought back. He knew there was no going back now— Alex had made up her mind. There were so many things to say and not enough time to say it. Conner made sure to make his final moments with his sister count and said the only thing that mattered.

"I love you, Alex," he said and hugged her.

"I love you, too, Conner," she said and hugged him back. They could both feel each other's tears on the back of their necks.

One by one, Lady Iris, Rosemary, Petunia, and Bob stepped through the seam between worlds and disappeared. Charlotte gave Alex one last hug before stepping through it, and Conner followed her. He watched his sister through the seam as it slowly closed and the fairy-tale world vanished before his eyes—they were now dimensions apart, yet both the twins were finally *home*.

Alex was right—Conner could still feel her in his heart. However, underneath the pain of saying good-bye was a lingering certainty that their good-bye wouldn't last forever. Despite what the fairies told him, Conner knew in his heart that his and Alex's story was far from over.

ACKNOWLEDGMENTS

I'd like to thank Rob Weisbach, Glenn Rigberg, Alla Plotkin, Erica Tarin, Meredith Fine, Lorrie Bartlett, Derek Kroeger, Liz Uhl, Tom Robb, and Heather Manzutto for their contributions to the CC Army. Thanks to Alvina Ling, Melanie Chang, Bethany Strout, Megan Tingley, Andrew Smith, and everyone at Little, Brown.

I'd like to give a special thank-you to all my friends and family who sometimes get neglected in the juggling act I call a life: my parents, my grandmother, Will Sherrod, Ashley Fink, Pam Jackson, Jamie Greenberg, Megan Doyle, Barbara Brown, Roberto Aguirre, and my enormous and growing extended family.

Seeing as this is my third novel published in just one month shy of a calendar year, I would like to thank the people who taught me how to read and write, as it was not an easy task: my elementary school teachers, Mrs. Shehorn, Mrs. Keller, Mrs. Karl, Mrs. Lubisich, Mr. Schultz, Ms. Smith, Mrs. Denton, and Mrs. Ulrich.

Since he sat on my lap while I wrote the majority of this novel and acted as inspiration, I would like to thank my cat, Brian, who couldn't care less about this recognition. Also Polly Bergen, for being the real Mother Goose.